Loyalty

The Chaplain's Legacy Book 5

Mary Kingswood

Sutors Publishing

Published by Sutors Publishing

Copyright © 2025 Mary Kingswood

ISBN: 978-1-912167-60-9 (paperback)

V1

Cover design by: Shayne Rutherford of Darkmoon Graphics

Author's note:

this book is written using historic British terminology, so *saloon* instead of *salon*, *chaperon* instead of *chaperone* and so on. I follow Jane Austen's example and refer to a group of sisters as the Miss Wintertons.

About this book

One man with a secret. A family torn apart by the consequences.

Mr Kent Atherton isn't too worried about the sudden discovery that his parents' marriage was invalid and he is illegitimate — he loves machinery of all types, so what would be more perfect than a career as an engineer? The industrial future is so much more interesting than the traditions of the past. But the son of an earl isn't supposed to work in trade, and besides, he's loyalty-bound to support his brother's little enterprise. Will he ever escape his family's hold on him?

Miss Katherine Parish has been orphaned and left penniless. Happily, her aunt has given her a home, but she moves in much higher circles than Katherine is used to. How can the daughter of a mill owner mingle with the Earl of Rennington and his family? But the perpetually cheerful Kent Atherton lifts her out of her gloom, and even gives her hope of a happy future together, until she discovers a shocking secret about him...

This is a complete story with a happy ever after. A traditional Regency romance, drawing room rather than bedroom. Book 5 of a 6 book series.

Isn't that what's-his-name? Occasionally characters from an earlier series pop up, or are mentioned. Mr Ridwell and Mr Moreton, mill owners from Branton, appeared in *Woodside*. Note that this book is set four years earlier, so Mr Ridwell's beautiful daughter Ellen is not yet out.

About the series*:*

Book 0: The Chaplain: a man adrift, dreaming of a home *(a novella, free to mailing list subscribers)*.

Book 1: Disinheritance: a man freed, looking for a new purpose in life

Book 2: Determination: a man pursued, forced to outwit his adversary

Book 3: Anger: a woman alone, trying to choose a different path in life

Book 4: Secrecy: a woman neglected, scheming to secure her own happiness

Book 5: Loyalty: a man of dreams, torn between the past and the future

Book 6: Ambition: a woman thwarted, unswervingly set on making a brilliant debut in society

Want to be the first to hear about new releases? Sign up for my mailing list at https://marykingswood.co.uk.

Contents

Principal Characters   1

Prologue   4

1: Murder In The Night   18

2: Prayer And Uncertainty   29

3: An Evening At Highwood Place   41

4: A Friend   52

5: A Visitor From Branton   65

6: Horses And Engines   76

7: Marriage In Mind   86

8: Ladies And Gentlemen   100

9: An Invitation   111

10: An Evening At Corland Castle   122

11: An Unexpected Move   134

12: Conversation   146

13: Of Wives   157

14: Another Unexpected Move   168

15: Celebrations   181

16: The Tower   191

17: Tonkins Farm   204

18: An Upright Citizen   216

19: A Letter Is Received   228

20: Mule Droppings   239

21: Transgressions   252

22: Unexpected Visitors   265

23: Branton   277

24: Deception   291

25: Certainty   305

26: Good News And Bad News   318

27: A Grand Ball   332

Thanks for reading!   342

About the author   344

Acknowledgements   345

Sneak preview: Book 6 of The Chaplain's Legacy: Ambition   346

Principal Characters

A partial list; for the full list, see my website at https://marykingswo od.co.uk. under Extras.

The Atherton family of Corland Castle, North Riding of York-shire:

Charles, 11th Earl of Rennington (55)

Caroline, Countess of Rennington (50)

Their children:

Walter, the former Viscount Birtwell (29)

Mr Eustace Atherton (27), living on his own estate nearby, Wel-wood-on-the-Hill

Josie (Josephine), Lady Woodridge (26), married to Viscount Woodridge; they have two sons

Izzy (Isabel), Lady Farramont (24); married to Ian, Viscount Farra-mont (35); they have two daughters

Mr Kent Atherton (22)

Lady Olivia Atherton (18)

The earl's blind sister: Lady Alice Nicholson (48)

Her husband, the earl's chaplain: Mr Arthur Nicholson (55, deceased)

Their daughter, Miss Tess (Teresa) Nicholson (20)

The George Atherton family of Westwick Heights, North Riding of Yorkshire:

The earl's younger brother: Mr George Atherton (50)

Mrs Atherton (Jane, 45)

Their children:

Mr Bertram Atherton (25)

Mr Lucas Atherton (23)

Miss Julia Atherton (20)

Miss Emily Atherton (18)

Miss Penelope Atherton (16)

Master Philip Atherton (6)

The Franklyn Family of Highwood Place, North Riding of Yorkshire:

Mr Charles Franklyn (46)

Lady Esther Franklyn (33), daughter of the Duke of Camberley

His daughter from his first marriage:

Miss Beatrice Franklyn (21)

Their children:

Master Henry Franklyn (7)

Master Charles Franklyn (3)

The Cathcart Family of Cathcart House, Birchall

Mr Alan Cathcart (46)

Mrs Alan Cathcart (Anne, 44)

Their children:

James, (20)

Aveline, (19)

Alex, (18)

Neil, (18)

Susan, (15)

Lucinda, (13)

Their niece:

Miss Katherine Parish, (20), the orphaned daughter of a Lancashire mill owner

The Murder Investigators:

Captain Michael Edgerton (37), formerly of the East India Company Army

Mrs Edgerton (Luce, née Willerton-Forbes, 30)

Mr Pettigrew Willerton-Forbes (38), a lawyer

Mr James Neate, a lawyer masquerading as a footman

Mr Alexander Grant Saxby (Sandy, 25), now known as Mr Alexander

Miss Peach, a former governess

Prologue

BRANTON, LANCASHIRE: MARCH

Miss Katherine Parish waited in the hall, bonnet and pelisse on, her gloves and reticule beside her. At her feet were the two boxes of personal effects she was permitted to keep. She sat on the elderly wooden settle since it was fixed to the wall, and might therefore escape the attentions of the bailiffs. Nothing else escaped their notice. The silver was the first to go, and the paintings from the drawing room and dining room. Then the good furniture — the escritoire, Papa's desk, the pretty lacquered console table. She had closed her eyes when her pianoforte had been carried past. In the last hour or so, it had been boxes of books, the contents of the linen closet and the big copper pans from the kitchen. Soon their attention would be drawn to the smaller items, like the plain wooden chairs from the servants' rooms and the rows of preserves in the larder.

The afternoon wore on, and even the bailiffs began to slow down. But then, on the road outside, were the sounds of a carriage arriving, slowing, then stopping. Her uncle, at last.

He strode into the hall, the skirts of his greatcoat flying, another younger man behind him. Katherine jumped to her feet.

"Katherine! My dear girl, what are you doing here, watching all this? And alone — is there no one who could have sat with you? Where is your maid?"

"She had another position arranged, so I let her go first thing this morning."

"But have you no friends who could have borne you company?"

"Some offered, but I did not wish it," she said quietly. "No one else should witness our disgrace."

"My dear girl!" he said again, wrapping her in an embrace so tight that her nose was pressed against the damp wool of his greatcoat, her bonnet sent askew. "My poor niece! How dreadful for you! Oh... you remember James, of course. He has grown a little since you last saw him."

"I should hope I have, Father! I could not have been more than four or five when last Cousin Kate saw me."

Katherine straightened her bonnet and dipped a curtsy. "Cousin James."

She had a vague memory of a scruffy and nondescript little boy, bigger than her despite their similar age, who had pushed her about unmercifully. He had grown into a well-looking man, only a little taller than she was, and not at all scruffy. Like his father, he looked like a country gentleman, a well-dressed one with a good tailor and an efficient valet.

A footman in livery came in, and he and James manhandled the boxes out through the front door. Katherine donned her gloves and picked up her reticule.

"Are you ready to leave?" Uncle Cathcart said gently. "Is there anything you need to do? Any farewells to make?"

"I have made all my farewells. I am ready, uncle."

"Then let us go. I shall be glad to leave this smoky town behind. So many great, tall chimneys! You will be astonished how much cleaner you will find the air at your new home, my dear."

He offered her his arm and she rested one hand on it. There were times when the support of a man's arm was no more than a courtesy, but today her knees trembled so much that she was glad of it. Head lowered, she walked slowly beside her uncle, out through the door of the home she had lived in all her life.

A great crowd had gathered on the street. Some, no doubt, were drawn to the spectacle of the bailiffs' wagons filling up, but many women held handkerchiefs to their eyes, and the men were grim-faced. She recognised them from the mill, men who had lost their livelihoods now, but bore no resentment. They knew her father had been doing his best for them, and it was not his fault he had died when he had just borrowed a great deal of money to install the huge beam engine.

"God bless you, Miss!" someone called out, and many others took up the refrain. Several women rushed out from the crowd, sobbing, to hug her fiercely. Clusters of children looked on, wide-eyed and silent, taking it all in. Her Sunday school children, she realised. Who would teach them their letters now?

A little way down the street, beyond the bailiffs' wagons, sat the Cathcarts' carriage, a fine equipage drawn by two pairs of post horses, the postilions waiting patiently. The door was held open by the footman, and her uncle handed Katherine in, then went to supervise the arrangements for her luggage to be strapped on. Outside, the crowd on the street moved to surround the carriage, waving handkerchiefs at her. Hesitantly, she waved back, and someone shouted out, "Three cheers for Miss Parish!" and the whole crowd set to whooping and cheering. Katherine blushed and blushed again, hanging her head low in embarrassment, but they seemed disinclined to stop.

Her uncle appeared at the door. "Other seat, my dear. Ladies always ride forwards. James, do you sit opposite. There now, I think we are ready."

He climbed in to sit beside Katherine, the footman closed the door and set the carriage swaying as he climbed up behind. Then the postilions called to the horses, the crowd cheered again and the carriage lurched into motion, moving slowly off down the street. Katherine did not look back. What was the point? She would never forget the house as long as she lived, and she did not want to have a single memory of it as it was today, with everything dear and familiar loaded onto the bailiffs' wagons. Better to remember it as it had been... when Papa was alive, or better still, when Mama was alive, too, and her brother Harold, and they had been just another mill owner's family, slowly rising to prosperity.

Debt and disgrace were best forgotten.

***

They travelled only two stages that day, as far as Skipton, where rooms were already reserved for them at the Black Horse, and Mr Cathcart's very grand valet waited. Katherine had never stayed at an inn before, but her uncle made everything easy for her, and paid for a maid to help her dress and undress, and to sleep in her room at night.

"Just in case," he said.

"In case of what?" she said.

"Well... should anything occur during the night," he said vaguely.

Nothing did occur, except that coaches came and went at all hours, seemingly, with great noise and bustle and confusion in the yard below. In the quiet spells, the walls and roof and even under the floorboards were alive with scratchings and patterings and odd little muffled squeaks.

The second day was longer, four stages, and a lengthy delay at Boroughbridge, where there were not horses enough. At first, they waited for some to arrive, but after some discussion with the ostlers, they went on with only a pair. At Thirsk, they were able to get two pairs again, and got on a little better.

Having not slept the night before, Katherine dozed on this early part of the journey, although every lurch of the carriage or the rumble of a passing farmer's wagon or remark by her uncle or cousin brought her jerking awake again. After Thirsk, the scenery became more interesting as they came into the hills of the North Riding. She had never been so far afield before, so she peered out of the window with great interest, but neither the hills nor the small villages they passed through were wildly different from Lancashire.

At Helmsley they made their last stop, collecting Uncle Cathcart's own horses and coachman for the final climb to her new home. Cathcart House. Katherine had no idea what she would find there. Uncle Cathcart was a gentleman, so it would be a gentleman's house, but what would that mean? The largest houses she had seen were on the hill at Branton, and the largest of those was the Ridwells' fine house, but Mr Ridwell was only a mill owner like Papa. He was not a gentleman. There were proper gentlemen's houses on the outskirts of Branton, but they were all hidden behind high walls or hedges, and she had never seen them, let alone been inside one.

The horses strained up a long hill, turning this way and that, before the road levelled off somewhat. There was not much to see. They passed gateposts or smaller roads, but with no sign of any habitation. Trees closed in beside the road, then became fields, then more trees. Once or twice a vista opened up to one side, as if they were overlooking a deep valley, but the trees pressed close again before Katherine could examine the view. She supposed she would have many opportunities to travel this road in future, for the family went often to Helmsley for the shops, James told her.

"Here we are," Uncle Cathcart said, as they turned in through two neat brick gateposts.

The horses put on a little burst of speed, aware that they were almost home. The drive was short, and in a moment they were turning, the carriage slowing and then stopping. The footman on the back of the carriage hopped down and opened the door, and they all descended.

Katherine looked up at the house — her new home. It was rather plain, apart from a small portico at the front door and a tiny amount of decoration above the windows. But no statuary anywhere, nothing ornate or overwhelmingly grand, and it was not even as large as the Ridwells' house, although longer than it was tall, with three storeys only in the middle section.

But there was no time to take it all in, for the front door opened and people poured out. So many! Her aunt, sister to Mama and just a little like her, beaming and rushing down the steps, arms wide to embrace her. Two young men, Alex and Neil, at eighteen well grown and handsome, not quite identical but very alike. And the three daughters, Aveline, nineteen, Susan and Lucinda still in the schoolroom. Aveline she recalled only slightly as a rather stout child. Now she was an elegant young lady, eyeing Katherine up expressionlessly. At only a year younger than Katherine, they would be expected to be friends, no doubt. A friend! Something like a sister, perhaps. How odd that would be.

Wrapped in her aunt's soft embrace, with many kind voices expressing their welcome, Katherine felt the strangeness of it all. Having been herself an only daughter, and for many years now an only child, she was unaccustomed to being part of a large family. Six children not yet fully grown, and so many servants to look after them! Footmen and maids poured out to help with luggage, and a butler and housekeeper stood on the steps overseeing the activity.

Now the younger girls took an arm each and towed Katherine up the steps and into the house, while their mother remonstrated ineffectually with them.

"Girls! Girls! Do give Katherine a little room to breathe. Think how tired she must be after her long journey! Susan, Lucinda, do not tug her arms quite out of their sockets. There now, my dear, let me look at you. Ah, you look so pale, but that is your mourning clothes, of course. Such a *draining* colour, black, I always say. But it is some time since your dear papa passed away, so perhaps we shall persuade you into half mourning soon."

"It is only three months, aunt."

"Well, true, but that is long enough for so young a girl, and you will be going into a very different society now, my dear."

Katherine felt the now familiar spasm of terror at these words. When her aunt had written to her, just after Papa's death, and offered her a home, she had mentioned society and balls and finding a husband. Katherine had existed quite happily without such things for all of her twenty years. She had plenty to do at home, or at the mill, or amongst their workers' families, and then there was church to keep her busy. There were occasional evening engagements with their friends, and sometimes a riotous assembly at one of the inns, but a ball! What would she find to do at a ball? She had never participated in a formal dance in her life.

Susan and Lucinda towed her on, up the stairs and then up again, into a pleasant bedroom, plainly but expensively furnished, everything solid wood and polished to a high shine. There were windows on two sides, with a view over tidy flowerbeds from one, and trees and shrubs from the other. She was relieved to discover that she was not to share a room with Aveline. Her aunt chased her daughters out of the room and helped Katherine remove her bonnet and pelisse.

"Well, these are very suitable for travelling," she said, holding them up to examine them more closely. "Excellent stitchwork! You must have had a talented seamstress in Branton."

"I make all my clothes myself, aunt."

Her aunt stared at her. "Goodness me! Well, you will not need to do so any more. Ah, here are your boxes. Just the two? And here is Jenny, who will look after you... acting as your lady's maid... taking care of your clothes and so forth. I suppose you have never had a proper lady's maid before."

"Well, I—"

"Jenny looks after Susan and Lucinda, but she can easily accommodate you as well. Now, which box holds your evening gowns? This one? Unpack this first, Jenny. I need to see if you have anything suitable for Tuesday."

"Tuesday, aunt?"

"We are to dine at the Castle. Corland Castle, with the Earl of Rennington and his family, so you will need something... well, not so plain as your travelling gown."

The Earl of Rennington! Katherine's horror must have shown on her face, for her aunt laughed, and said, "Now, now, child, you have nothing to fear from the Athertons. They are very grand, of course, and live in a style we can only dream of, but you will find them not at all high in the instep. We dine with them half a dozen times a year, and sometimes they condescend to dine with us, and we always enjoy a very pleasant evening."

"Must I go? I do not know them, so—"

"Naturally you must go. You are included in the invitation. Lady Rennington is always most particular about such things. She wrote that if you had arrived by Tuesday, then she would be delighted to welcome you to Corland Castle. So you have nothing to worry about. Well, you have not many dresses, have you? We shall have to increase your wardrobe quite substantially. Ah, lay the blue one on the bed, Jenny. Now, let me see... Hmm, it is excessively plain for an evening gown."

"Aunt, I cannot wear colours! I have a black evening gown if I must go, but I should much sooner not. Indeed, I never expected to be treated like my cousins. It would be inappropriate for me to set myself up as a lady of fashion, like them. Plain gowns are very suitable for my station, and I shall be happy to make myself useful to you, in the kitchen or still room, perhaps, running errands, helping the governess... That is my place, surely. It is what I am used to."

Aunt Cathcart sat down on the bed, drew Katherine down beside her and took her in her arms for a long hug. "My dear Katherine, you are my niece, and my sister's only surviving child. The very idea that we would treat you as some kind of unpaid servant! Whatever you may have been obliged to do at Branton no longer applies. Your father may have left you in poverty, but your uncle is to settle a little money on you — No, no, do not protest, for he is quite resolved upon it, and we are agreed that we will treat you exactly the same as our own daughters. You will have your own pin money, and naturally you must wear suitable clothes. You would not wish to shame us by appearing less well dressed than your cousins, surely? What would our friends say if we appear to neglect you in that way? You need not be a lady of fashion if you dislike the idea, but you must be a lady of *quality*, Katherine. Above all else, you must be a lady, and there is no need to mention your father's mill. No need at all."

"There is no mill to mention, not any more," Katherine said sadly. "But what shall I do with myself all day if I may not help with the domestic duties? What does Cousin Aveline do?"

"Why, I hardly know, but she manages to fill her days. Embroidery... every lady must have a piece of embroidery in progress. She paints, too. Her watercolours are greatly admired. We make and receive calls, of course. She rides, sometimes, and... well, she finds plenty to do. If you like, you may sit with Susan and Lucinda and listen to Miss Harkness. She teaches French and Italian, as well as music, drawing and the usual things. That will help to fill in any gaps in your education, you know, for if you have been busy making clothes and mixing pastry, I am sure you have not been keeping up with your lessons."

"You have a pianoforte? May I practise?"

"Certainly, my dear. That is a very ladylike accomplishment. Most suitable. Yes, you may practise on the pianoforte as much as you like."

Well, that was something to be grateful for. There had never been enough time for music at Branton, but now she could play as much as she wished.

***

13

T he next morning, Katherine rose at her usual time. She had been warned that the family would not emerge from their bedrooms until breakfast at ten o'clock, so she recited the morning prayers, as she continued to do even without Papa, and then wrote letters to several friends in Branton who would be anxiously awaiting news of her safe arrival. She filled the rest of the time by reading soothing passages from the Bible.

Breakfast was like dinner the previous evening, the table groaning with food, of which only a small amount was eaten. The waste shocked Katherine, but she supposed a gentleman had to live in a higher style than a mill owner. No one at Branton would think to offer such an excess of food. She was even more shocked that no one said grace, either before or after the meal. What sort of Christian family would not give thanks for their meal, especially with such abundance placed before them? It was not her place to criticise, however, so she made a small prayer in her head before she began to eat.

"Mama, may we take Katherine to Birchall this morning?" Susan asked. "She will want to see all the shops."

"What an excellent idea," Aunt Cathcart said. "When you return, Katherine, I shall have an embroidery project for you to begin work on. I have a spare hoop somewhere."

Katherine had no great desire for shopping, or embroidery either, and would much rather have spent the morning at the instrument, but she did not like to be unsociable. Shortly after eleven, therefore, she awaited Aveline, Susan and Lucinda at the foot of the stairs. The first person to appear was a thin-faced woman of around thirty, as plainly dressed as Katherine was.

"Good morning, madam," she said, dipping a curtsy. "I am Miss Harkness. The governess."

"Yes," Katherine whispered. Never having had a governess, she was not at all sure how to address one. "How do you do? I am Katherine Parish."

The governess gave a little smile. "I know who you are, Miss Parish. I hope you will be very happy at Cathcart House, despite the sad reasons for your move here. Ah, here are the girls now. Come, ladies, let us be off before the day is half gone."

Birchall village was only a mile away, by way of the gardens and some pretty woodland, the bluebells just showing through but not yet in flower. The village was just like a thousand other villages, being no more than one main street with a few short side roads lined with cottages and a scattering of more substantial houses. A few people walking about stared openly at them, making Katherine feel very uncomfortable.

The Cathcart girls instantly ran off to a haberdashery, which seemed to be a focus for several other young ladies, but Katherine looked longingly at the church.

"Would you mind if I were to sit in the church for a while?" she said to Miss Harkness.

"By all means, Miss Parish. There are some fine memorials in St Timothy's, and the rood screen is much admired."

The chilly air inside the church made Katherine shiver, but it was still preferable to being stared at, or jostled in the busy haberdashery. Above all, she wanted quietude, and the church brought her a welcome sense of peace, with its familiar smells of damp wool, dust and candle smoke, and the echo from its high roof as her booted feet tap-tapped up the aisle. She found the Cathcart pew, one of the better ones, and sat there letting her thoughts wander. She was grateful to her uncle and aunt, naturally, and they were very kind, but oh, how she missed Branton and the familiarity of home. Everything here was strange. She would make friends in time, she knew that, but just at that moment, she felt quite alone.

Behind her, the door creaked open, and someone entered quietly, staying near the door. A few moments later, someone else came in and she heard low voices murmuring. Little of it was audible, but she caught *'thirty barrels'* and *'is that all?'* and something about storms at sea. Then, a sudden exclamation, and she heard footsteps approaching.

A man peered over the pew wall at her, a man not much older than she was herself, slender and with a smiling face surrounded by gentle curls.

"Good morning to you, madam, and an excellent morning it is, too."

His eyes twinkled with such good humour that she could not be afraid of him. "Is it?"

"Why, indeed it is, for it is not raining, which is sufficient in itself to qualify as an excellent morning. Also, my brother has been shooting, and I am promised duck for dinner. I am excessively fond of duck."

That made her smile.

"Ah. And I have brought a smile to your face, which makes the morning even better. How do you do, madam? Kent Atherton at your service."

Kent Atherton! One of the Earl of Rennington's family. She need not fear the evening at Corland Castle so much if this cheerful and friendly man was there.

"Katherine Parish. Miss... Parish."

"I am delighted to meet you, Miss Parish, quite delighted! I hope we shall meet again very often, so that I may have more opportunities to make you smile. You looked so sad when I first saw you, and since you wear black, you have reason to be sad, but is there not still so much in this world to be enjoyed? Every day brings us some new delight to beguile the eye or the ear, or even the tongue. You see, I am thinking of my duck again. May you find some small ray of hope every day to enchant you and relieve your sadness for a while. And one day, I very much hope that you will not be sad at all."

"Thank you, sir."

"And now, I must not disturb your contemplation any longer. Good day to you, Miss Parish."

"Good day, sir. Enjoy your duck."

He grinned. "I shall! I most certainly shall."

And then he was gone, leaving her smiling and cheerful. What a charming man! She felt a delightful warmth inside, which stayed with her until she heard Aveline's voice behind her.

"There you are, cousin! What are you doing hiding away in here? Come on, there are new bonnets at Miss Prinkley's."

Katherine rose obediently and followed her from the church.

1: Murder In The Night

CORLAND CASTLE, NORTH RIDING: JUNE

Murder!

It was hard to believe. Such a thing had never happened in this remote part of Yorkshire, and to have such an occurrence here, in Corland Castle, in the very home of the Earl of Rennington, was too much to take in. The Honourable Kent Atherton, third and youngest son of the earl, was the most optimistic of men, always with a light-hearted quip and a smile on his lips, but even he was reduced to silence today.

Only the earl murmured incessantly. "Nicholson was an inoffensive man, would you not say? A chaplain, for heaven's sake! Who would kill a chaplain, and in so brutal a fashion? An axe! Why an axe? Why would anyone come here with an axe and slaughter a man in his bed? Never anything wrong with Nicholson that would cause anyone to want him dead, one would have thought. Always very kind to my poor sister. Oh, dear God — Alice! Poor, poor Alice, to discover her husband like that. For once, I believe it to be a blessing that she is blind and did not see the worst of it, as we did. My poor sister!"

Kent listened in silence. They were in the earl's study, one of the corner tower rooms of the castle, the three of them, Kent, his eldest brother, Walter, and the earl, gathered around a small table where the brandy decanter sat. Only the earl was drinking. Walter had abandoned his glass after a couple of sips, and Kent's lay untouched. The matter was too serious even for brandy.

The afternoon drifted on, and even the earl had lapsed into silence when Eustace, the middle brother, walked in.

"Eustace? Were we expecting you?" the earl said, looking puzzled. Eustace had a modest estate of his own some twelve miles from Corland and rarely turned up without warning.

"No... no, I was just passing. The servants are all of a twitter... has something happened?"

"The most damnable thing," the earl said. "Nicholson has been murdered in his bed."

"Nicholson?"

"It is unaccountable, is it not?" Walter said. "Who under the sun would want to murder Nicholson?"

Walter poured Eustace a brandy and gave him all the details of the case. Eustace sat in silence, as stunned by the news as they had been early that morning when Aunt Alice's screams had woken the household.

"But what is being done? Who is out looking for the murderer?" Eustace said, when Walter's tale wound to its close.

"Strong and his brother are here, and the coroner fellow — I forget his name," the earl said, rubbing his forehead tiredly.

"Ashbridge," Walter said. "A Helmsley man. We have turned it over to Strong, as the magistrate, but he thinks we should bring in outsiders to investigate."

"Bow Street Runners?" Eustace said with a bark of laughter. "Some ruffian from London?"

"Not Runners. Strong knows some people — clever but discreet," the earl said. "From Hartlepool."

"Well, ruffians from Hartlepool, then. It is all the same. The murderer will be long gone by the time they get here, and there will be nothing to investigate."

"There is the weapon... the axe," Kent said. "And someone might have heard something, or seen a stranger loitering in the village or staying at the White Horse. There might be traces of blood... there was a lot of blood, brother."

"A pity I was not here," Eustace said. "I am a light sleeper, so I might have heard something."

"So is Kent a light sleeper, and Mother and Olivia," Walter said sharply, "yet they heard nothing. Besides, if you had been here and heard something and gone to investigate, it would have been you lying in your own blood, brother."

"That is the one bright spot in this whole dreadful affair," the earl said. "Nicholson... losing Nicholson is a tragedy, of course, especially for your poor aunt, but it could have been a great deal worse. It could have been one of you, or one of the girls... or several of you, if this fellow had gone on a rampage. We could *all* have been slaughtered in our beds last night, so let us be grateful for that small mercy."

No one had anything to say to that hideous thought. The earl reached for the brandy decanter, and the four remained wreathed in gloom, neither moving nor speaking until the dressing bell sounded.

***

The last notes of the sonata died away. Katherine rested her hands in her lap, savouring the moment. There was always a satisfaction in completing a piece of such length, knowing that she had played it a little better than the previous time. For a few precious seconds, she could almost imagine herself home again, on one of those rare days when there were no immediate tasks requiring her attention and she could sit down to play for a while.

Almost as soon as the thought crossed her mind, she remembered the truth — that Papa was dead, the mill and her home were lost, and she lived now with her Aunt and Uncle Cathcart. She was not unhappy there, she reminded herself sternly, and she had a great deal to be thankful for, but even after three months there were still many days when she found herself in low spirits. On bad days, she could not bring herself to be cheerful at all, and might start or end the day with a few tears for dear Papa and her beloved Branton. On good days, there were no tears and perhaps an hour of solitude in the garden to cheer her.

The very best days, Katherine acknowledged in her heart, were those when she saw Mr Kent Atherton. He never said much to her and had distinguished her with no unusual attention, but his wide smile, mischievous eyes and perpetual good-humour endeared him to her as no one else had ever done. She had no hopes or aspirations there, for as the son of an earl he was far above her in rank, but merely to be in the same room as him was enough to lift her spirits to the point where she would almost call herself happy.

She had no expectation of seeing him that day, for it was usually when they dined out or entertained at Cathcart House, and he was one of those invited. Only twice had she seen him by chance during the day, once when he was riding and did not see her at all, and once as he bowled past in a curricle driven by his brother, when he touched his hand to his hat in acknowledgement of her. By the time she had risen from her curtsy, the vehicle was far down the road, barely visible in the cloud of dust it raised.

Even so, this was a good day, for Aunt Cathcart had taken her three daughters to Helmsley for some serious shopping. Katherine had escaped this fate by pleading that she would like to practise the Salieri, which she would be better able to do in an empty house. She was not fond of the piece, but she was working her way steadily through the small collection she found in the music room, and Salieri's turn had arrived. Eventually, she would have played them all, and then she would have to dip into her modest allowance to buy more.

If only she could have brought her own collection, but the printed sheets were too valuable to escape the bailiffs' notice. All she had kept was her own little notebook of Scottish and Irish airs, and very few of those. She wished now she had taken the trouble to transcribe more pieces from her friends' collections, but there had never been enough time, or so it seemed. Now she had endless time, and only the rather haphazard collection at Cathcart House to sustain her.

Having completed the sonata to her own satisfaction, she donned one of her old pelisses, and a slightly misshapen bonnet, which showed the devastating effect of heavy rain on chip straw. She was not going anywhere which required the new, fashionable clothes Aunt Cathcart had insisted on, so it hardly mattered.

Davis opened the front door for her. "I am going to the rectory," she said, pulling on her gloves. "I expect to be back by four."

"Very good, madam," the butler said, adding, as he always did, "Do you wish John to accompany you?"

"Heavens, no! Not for a ten-minute walk."

Katherine knew she would be admonished by her aunt for walking alone, but these brief glimpses of freedom were precious to her. Sometimes, in a house that seemed to be constantly full of people and noise and bustle, she felt as if she were suffocating. It was glorious to walk through the gardens and woods, just coming into their summer finery, and enjoy the peace with no chatter from Susan and Lucinda, or Aveline's slightly supercilious air, or even Miss Harkness's well-meant remarks.

Katherine was perfectly aware of her status as the poor relation, and did not need to be reminded of it, but Miss Harkness seemed to think she was uneducated, too, and took every opportunity to inform her of the names of plants or insects, or aspects of society of which she might be unaware. It was useless to point out that she had been able to read at the age of four, and had had the run of her father's extensive library. If she wanted to know of the world around her, she had had all the London newspapers and journals to choose from. How did Miss Harkness think she had spent her evenings? One could not always be darning stockings, after all.

With Aveline, it was money. There had been a tricky moment not long after Katherine's arrival, when Uncle Cathcart had sat down at the breakfast table and informed them all that he intended to make the same provision for a dowry for her as for his own daughters. Since he was not quite flush enough in the pocket to find another five thousand, his own dear girls would, he was sure, be happy to have a little less. They would all have four thousand a year, he declared, and an allowance commensurate with that.

"That will be a sum of sixteen thousand set aside for you girls instead of fifteen, but I can afford the extra thousand easily. There now, is that not excellent news?"

There was a positive volley of voices disagreeing with him, Aveline's the loudest. It was quite infamous, she declared, that his own daughters should suffer such an abominable slight in favour of a girl who had no claim on him.

"My own niece, have no claim on me? What are you thinking, Aveline?" he said, his brows ominously lowered. "Of course she has a claim on me when your own mother was sister to Katherine's mother. Would you have her starve?"

"No, but nor would I have her take *my* dowry from me when her own father was so improvident as to leave her penniless," she cried. "It is too bad, Papa, truly it is! You put her on the same level as your own children."

"And why should I not? It is not Katherine's fault that her father's affairs were so perilous."

"But Papa—!" she began again, but Katherine jumped to her feet in an agony of embarrassment.

"Please... you must not fall out over me," she whispered. "Uncle, you are generous, but I cannot possibly take your money. A small allowance, perhaps, so that I can buy a new ribbon for my bonnet now and then, but I want no dowry from you. Certainly you must not deprive your own daughters on my account. I could not bear it!"

In the end, after a long family discussion, it had been agreed that Aveline, Susan and Lucinda would keep their five thousand pounds apiece, and Katherine would have the extra thousand pounds and pin money of fifty pounds a year. Even so, Aveline never lost an opportunity to mention the cost of this or that, usually with the added words, "But you cannot afford such items, cousin."

Aveline had long ceased to trouble Katherine. She understood her own place in the family perfectly well. Uncle and Aunt Cathcart might cling to the pretence that she did not differ from her cousins, and buy her endless clothes and take her into society with them, but Katherine was under no such illusion. Her cousins would marry, and she would not, so in a few years she would be the spinster left at home, looking after her aunt and uncle as they descended into old age. Or perhaps she would act as an unpaid nursemaid or governess to one or other of her cousins when they married. But she herself would never marry.

The thought gave her no pain. She had met the only man she would ever want as a husband, and he was as far out of her reach as the moon. Mr Kent Atherton, for all his affable ways, was an earl's son, and a younger son, at that. He would marry another scion of the nobility — someone like Lady Esther Franklyn, with centuries of good breeding infusing her veins. He would never marry a mill owner's daughter, even if she had a substantial fortune to bestow on him, and certainly not for a mere thousand pounds. But his cheerful good humour and friendliness had become her ideal, and she cherished every precious moment in the same room as him. Even if he spoke not a word to her, it was enough to see his wide smile, to hear his light voice, always on the brink of laughter, and to breathe the same air as him. She never approached him — she would not dare! Yet every meeting was treasured and written up in detail in her diary.

Today, she hummed a little as she walked through the gardens. She stopped to admire a few early roses, the blooms heavy with droplets after rain in the night. Passing the gate into the woods, the path was overgrown with cow parsley, and peeping through the leaf litter, the last of the bluebells and primroses, with foxgloves reaching upwards, their lowest blossoms already unfurling.

She wondered who else would be at the rectory that day. Soon after her arrival at Birchall, she had approached Mrs Dewar, the rector's wife, and asked what she might do to help. At Branton, it had been the Sunday school, but Mrs Dewar and the Miss Dewars had a sewing circle of spinsters and widows, making small garments for the children of the poor families in the parish. Such a project could easily be accomplished by the participants working quietly at home, sewing in odd moments during the day, or taking advantage of the long summer evenings to hem shirts or shifts for the labourers' children after dinner, but that would be no fun at all. Instead, the ladies gathered in Mrs Dewar's parlour most afternoons and exchanged the juiciest gossip.

Katherine rather enjoyed sitting quietly in a corner, learning a great deal about the village, both the lower orders and the higher, as she stitched. She was not much interested in the convoluted doings of the labourers, who was sweet on whom, and who was no better than she should be, whatever that meant, but she was endlessly fascinated by any talk of the earl's family — his elderly mother, whose demise was daily expected, his blind sister, married to the chaplain, and his six children. Two of the daughters had married and left home, and the much-admired heir was betrothed, although there was some tut-tutting over his chosen bride, an heiress worth forty thousand pounds derived from iron foundries.

"Set her cap at him and no mistake," Miss Dewar said with a disparaging sniff.

"Determined to be a countess," Miss Bridget Dewar said.

The other ladies shook their lace-capped heads and agreed with it.

Katherine always hoped for some mention of Mr Kent Atherton, but it seemed he did little to attract the notice of the rectory sewing circle, for his name seldom arose. The ladies laughed at middle brother, Eustace, and his rumoured but unspecified misbehaviour, and sighed over the youngest daughter, Lady Olivia, her marital prospects affected by her grandmother's illness. But it was the chaplain's daughter, Miss Teresa Nicholson, who reduced the ladies to shocked whispers, for she had formed an attachment for one Tom Shapman, a woodworker in the village, and that was a misalliance that neither the nobility nor the commoners could approve.

There was no prospect of news from Corland Castle today, however, for two days ago there had been an altercation at the White Horse amongst the smith's extensive family, which had almost resulted in violence. Such an event was likely to occupy the sewing circle for many days to come. Still, one never knew what snippets of information would be let fall, and Katherine knew her aunt would be glad to hear all that was said. She might, and often did, say that she disapproved of all the gossip that went on in Mrs Dewar's rather shabby front parlour, but she invariably followed such comments with, "And so, has aught happened of interest in the village?"

The path emerged from the cool, damp air of the woods into the summer warmth of the glebe, where the rectory cattle grazed contentedly. There was a good path across the glebe, but cows were considerably larger and heavier than Katherine, and not to be meddled with when they had calves to protect, so she took the footpath which skirted the field, where yarrow, red campion and more cow parsley jostled for position, heads nodding as she brushed past them, dampening the skirts of her pelisse.

As she drew near the rectory, she saw a great crowd gathered outside the church, amongst them Mr Dewar, his wife and daughters. Mrs Dewar was weeping... several of the women were weeping. What on earth had happened?

"Oh, Miss Parish!" cried Miss Dewar, mopping her eyes with a frilly handkerchief. "Have you heard the dreadful news? The poor chaplain at the castle... poor, poor Mr Nicholson... and what he's ever done to harm anyone I can't imagine... the poor man!"

"Whatever has happened to him?" Katherine said, trying to remember the chaplain. A man of middle years, very genial... but nothing very distinctive about him.

"Murdered!" Miss Dewar cried, throwing out one arm as if she were on a stage. "Murdered in his bed in the night!"

"And him as blameless and innocent as a babe," said Miss Bridget. "Such a dreadful thing!"

Dreadful indeed, but Katherine wondered a little just how innocent and blameless Mr Nicholson might be. Nothing justified murder, naturally, for *'Thou shalt not kill'* was an inviolable law, but if someone had been riled enough to kill, then the blameless Mr Nicholson must have done *something* to provoke such an attack.

2: Prayer And Uncertainty

The murder was all anyone could talk about. In the Birchall shops, at the rectory and around the polished dining tables of the gentry, there was only one topic of conversation, and every day brought some new snippet of information. Sir Hubert Strong, the magistrate, was called in, then the coroner. The murdered man's wife, the blind Lady Alice, had discovered her husband's body and screamed loud enough to waken even the servants in the attics and basements. The gentleman had been killed with an axe! To Katherine's mind, that was the most shocking element of all. A knife or a pistol one could understand, but an axe? How abominably barbaric.

Then came the news that some people had been sent for from Hartlepool, men with expertise in investigating such horrific events.

"That is good news, at least," Aunt Cathcart said, as they lingered at the dinner table one evening. "Sir Hubert is all very well for common thievery or poaching, but a murder of this nature, and to the earl's broth-er-in-law, too! Much better to hand it over to experts."

"All it means is that it is not a straightforward case of an intruder, as we thought at first," Uncle Cathcart said. "Strong is baffled by it, seemingly. Who would want to kill the chaplain? Surely he cannot have an enemy in the world."

There was general agreement on the point, but nevertheless, they spent the rest of the evening in increasingly wild speculation.

Katherine took no part in these discussions. She did not know the chaplain well enough to have any speculation to contribute, but there was one office she could fulfil for him, and that was to pray. The Cathcarts were not diligent in their religious observances, but Katherine more than made up for their lack. Thus the deceased chaplain was added to her morning and bedtime prayers, and even the murderer received his share of her thoughts, too, in the heartfelt hope that he would repent of his wickedness. It did not seem enough, however, so whenever she left the rectory after a sewing session, she slipped into the church to add a few more prayers to the great deluge she had already sent.

She was thus engaged one day about three weeks after the murder, when she heard the great wooden door creak open and then close again, followed by the soft sounds of someone creeping on booted feet down the aisle, and trying vainly to be silent about it. She was kneeling at the Lady Chapel rail, eyes closed, and she knew no one would disturb a praying figure. Keeping immobile, she bowed her head a little more, hoping the booted feet would pass on, perhaps to the vestry or to one of the pews. To her surprise, the feet stopped, and a little jingle of metal — fobs, perhaps, or a pocket watch chain — followed by the scraping of chair legs on the tiled floor suggested that the interloper had sat down just behind her.

Startled, she turned to see who it was, and was astonished to see the familiar face that haunted her dreams. And yet, it was not so familiar today, for there was no trace of that wonderful broad smile that always made her want to smile too.

"Mr Atherton!" she said, jumping up and spinning round to face him.

Slowly, as if it were a great effort, he rose to his feet, turning his hat in his hands. "Does it work?"

"I... beg your pardon?"

"Prayer. Does it work? Does it give you what you wish for?" His voice was bleak, empty of its usual lilting optimism.

She gazed at him blankly. That was not the purpose of prayer! Yet she could not possibly say so, not to a man of his rank, not to a man who made her twittery inside whenever she saw him. Impossible to say a word!

"Does it make you feel better, then?"

"Oh yes! Such a comfort." What a strange question! To talk to God... to unburden oneself and put all one's worries in His hands... surely everyone must feel better after praying?

"Perhaps I should try it, then." The smile flickered for a moment. "Ah, now I have shocked you. Forgive me, but not everyone is as good a person as you."

"No, no," she murmured, blushing violently. How unworthy she was of such a compliment, for was not everyone a sinner, in some way, great or small?

"I wish I *could* pray," he burst out, sinking onto the chair again, "for I am in great need of comfort just now and I see none in the mortal realm. When I was a boy, and said my prayers every night, kneeling beside my bed like the well-brought-up child I was in those days, I would ask God for all the things I believed would make me happy. The ability to learn Greek. A new toy soldier for my collection. My older brothers not to tease me. My father to praise me... or even notice me. It is dispiriting to be the third son, Miss Parish, especially one who has no especial attribute to please such a man as my father. Ah, innocent times! I long since learnt that God does not dispense favours in that way, and accepted that my life is not, perhaps, as filled with sunshine as some others, but I could make it so. I could fill it with sunshine myself, by smiling on the world and playing the jester to make everyone laugh. But today... I cannot laugh now, for the most appalling thing has happened. We are destroyed, quite destroyed and I do not know what will become of us, truly I do not, and prayer will not help me one whit."

He looked so despairing that Katherine sat down beside him and reached out one hand to touch his sleeve. "At such times, I pray for the strength to endure."

Turning himself fully to face her, he took her hands in his, so that even though they both wore gloves, she imagined the heat of his touch and blushed crimson again.

"Ah, Miss Parish, you have suffered too! You understand. I shall tell you, I think, what has occurred, for I must tell someone or I shall burst. My uncle Nicholson, the chaplain who was so foully murdered earlier this month, having preached piety at us for thirty years, was never ordained as a clergyman at all. That would not have mattered a bit if all he had done was recite the Sunday offices and read us dull sermons, but his very first act as chaplain thirty years ago was to marry my parents. Thus, we now find that their marriage is invalid and all six of the children of that marriage are rendered illegitimate. English law permits no remedy for this situation, so

Walter is disinherited, and the title and all Father's estates will now fall on Uncle George, and after him, my cousin Bertram, who has his nose so deep in his ancient books that he hardly knows what century it is. The last thing he wants is the responsibility of an earldom on his shoulders. It is appalling, and I have no idea what will happen to us all."

"That is dreadful, but you will recover from this blow, I promise you. Every challenge is also an opportunity. God never burdens us with a greater load than we can bear."

"You have such certainty!" he cried, releasing her hands and slapping his hat against his thigh. "I wish I could be so... so serene, so contented with life, yet you have suffered grievously, too. Your parents both dead, your home lost... and you had no brothers or sisters."

"Brother," she said, her voice almost a squeak. Such intimate talk! "I... had a brother."

"I did not know that. Was he older than you or younger?"

"Older. Ten years older. In the navy. Lost at sea."

"I am so sorry. How did it happen?"

"In battle... Cape St Vincent." His expression was so sympathetic that she could not resist telling the rest of it. "His friends did not see him fall, and his body was never found... many prisoners were taken, so there was some hope for a while... but we have not heard a word in ten years, so we assumed... but I still pray for him, Mr Atherton, that he is safe and well somewhere, perhaps unable to return home. One never knows. Sometimes miracles do happen."

"Indeed, they do!" he said, the smile suddenly returning in full, as if the clouds had that moment parted. He jumped to his feet. "Thank you for listening to my ramblings, Miss Parish. I am sorry I burdened you with my troubles."

"No burden, sir."

"Oh, but it was very wrong of me, and I would be glad if you would forget my ill-humoured words. We shall pretend this conversation never happened."

She nodded in acquiescence, and with a smile, a quick bow and hasty steps down the aisle, he was gone, leaving her bemused and exhilarated in equal measure.

***

Kent was uncomfortable after this encounter. To be spilling all the family secrets to Miss Parish, of all people! She was such a timid soul, and so innocent, with those great eyes looking up at him as if he were the fount of all wisdom, yet today he felt his unworthiness more than ever. If only he had taken up a career, as he should have done... as he could have done, if he had only had the determination. He was not, perhaps, suited to the army or the church, but a government post might have been appropriate. Diplomacy, or something of the sort. His father might have agreed to that.

But he had always said that he liked to have the boys at home. "The girls will marry and leave me, that cannot be helped," he had said, "but you boys need never leave. I like to have male company about me, otherwise I shall be quite outnumbered by the ladies."

When Eustace had inherited his estate three years ago and was at the castle less often, the earl had been even more adamant that Kent should not leave home. And so he had drifted on, never pressing his case, telling no one what he really wanted to do.

He was not minded to meet anyone else he might be tempted to talk to, so he used the churchyard's back gate behind the church to access the path back to Corland, then went straight to the stables for his horse. A brisk ride across the moors cleared his head a little, but he still needed time to himself... time to *think*. He was not much given to introspection, but now of all times was surely the moment for it. He had never thought much further ahead than the next meal, not liking to consider the way his life might unfold in the years to come. But whatever of good or bad he might have hoped for, all of it had been ripped away from him, and he no longer knew what was in store for him.

He knew where he was going, however, for there in front of him was the tower. It had been built for a former owner of Welwood to enable him to watch the stars move across the sky. No one watched the sky from it now, but once or twice a month, Kent came here to watch for something else entirely.

The tower was built on a low rise amidst fields. Beyond the largest field was the road from Helmsley, and beyond that, Welwood-on-the-Hill, Eustace's estate. Kent's horse ambled along the narrow lane to the tower and halted obediently, knowing that he had arrived. Kent turned him into the large field where Eustace kept the retired ponies and donkeys, lifted the stone that hid the key and unlocked the tower door.

On the ground floor, a large square room was attached to provide a kitchen and larder, as well as a comfortable sitting room with a fireplace and a table big enough for a dozen men to sit around. The tower itself was smaller, a stone stair winding up past three floors to an upper room with huge windows and a narrow balcony with outer stairs leading to the roof. The summer was rarely balmy enough to make the roof enticing, so the upper room was fitted out with a brazier, several comfortable chairs and a sofa, together with a low pallet, rough mattress and blankets, providing the watchers with basic comforts.

On a stand, looking through the eastern window, was the telescope, an exquisite construction of brass that cheered Kent just by its existence. The world could not be a wholly terrible place when there were men in it who could make such wonderful devices. There was a box in the corner that the telescope had arrived in many years ago, and inside the lid was a small brass plaque with the name and address of the manufacturer. Some years ago, Kent had written to the address inscribed thereon, and after some weeks received a very courteous reply from an elderly gentleman who remembered making that very telescope. They enjoyed a wide-ranging but sporadic correspondence for two or three years before the old gentleman died, but Kent remembered him with great affection.

After running a respectful finger along the length of the telescope, he threw himself into a chair with a wooden footstool to accommodate his feet and pondered his situation.

He must change! That much was clear to him. This moment was not quite the miracle of which Miss Parish spoke, but it was perhaps a lever to tip him out of his comfortable rut and force him to take charge of his life. Eustace... he must talk to Eustace and make changes there, and then he would talk to his father.

These resolutions thus made, he returned to the ground floor and found some cheese and stale bread in the larder. He was making a modest repast of these items when the door opened and Eustace stalked in.

"I saw that slug of yours in the field, brother, so I knew you were here. Why do you not get yourself a decent mount? Father would not quibble over it."

"There is nothing wrong with the horse — except his name, of course. Whoever called him Stupendous obviously had a different mount in mind altogether. I should rename him — Adequate, maybe. Satisfactory. Tolerable. But he gets me where I want to go without complaining or tossing me into a ditch, which is all I ask of him."

Eustace was investigating several bottles sitting on the table, but they were all empty. "Is there no brandy left?"

Kent only laughed.

His brother laughed, too. "Stupid question, I suppose, but it feels like a brandy sort of day. Come back to the house — there's plenty there waiting to be drunk."

"No, I must get back and see what Father is up to. What are we going to do, Eustace? Is there anything we can do?"

"About Nicholson? Not a thing, I suspect. He cannot be ordained posthumously, and it would not help if he could be. Nothing is going to make us legitimate again."

"No, the lawyer fellow made it clear about that, but I meant Walter. He has lost everything, and—"

"We have all lost everything!" Eustace said savagely. "We are all illegitimate, our good name destroyed, and through no fault of our own."

"But Walter is worse off than we are, brother. You have your inheritance already, so it hardly matters to you, and I... I am the third son. I was always destined to make my own way in the world. Maybe now Father will listen to me. But Walter—"

"Walter, Walter, Walter! He still has Bea Franklyn and her forty thousand pounds, Father has promised him a house... his allowance... everything. That is some consolation, is it not? Whereas we have yet to find brides, and how much more difficult is that now that we are bastards?"

Kent was silent. He had not even begun to think about marriage for himself, for he was only two and twenty, but clearly Eustace, five years older, was already considering that path.

Eustace hurled himself into a chair beside Kent, one leg cast carelessly over the arm, idly reaching for a piece of cheese. "Ugh! This is dreadful stuff. How long has it been here? Almost two weeks, I suppose. I shall restock before the next arrival."

"Brother," Kent said tentatively, "do you ever feel... well, that it may be time to give up the game?"

"Give it up? Whatever for? You are not afraid, are you, little brother?"

"Of course not, but... well, it seems wrong. It *is* wrong."

"Nonsense! Who is harmed by it? And it is an adventure, is it not? You used to find it the most tremendous fun, quite apart from bringing in a little extra money for everyone. We younger sons have to be gainfully employed, after all."

"You do not — you have a tidy income from Welwood, and I could do something more useful."

Eustace only laughed. "What could be more useful than this? Every-one enjoys the benefit."

"I mean something useful to society at large, not just our own people. I am tired of it, brother. Tired of the creeping about at night, the secrecy, the pretence. Tired of being trapped here on the moors. There is an entire world out there to be explored, full of new ideas and men of energy and ambition, while I am confined to this narrow corner of Yorkshire."

His brother shifted both feet to the floor and leaned forward, elbows resting on the table. "Now, what kind of talk is that? We Athertons stick together, always. Have we not always agreed to that? The girls may marry and go away if they please, but we brothers stay close to home. This is our place and our duty, and nothing that has happened can change that. Understand?"

Kent nodded, but the restlessness inside him was not assuaged. He rode home in a thoughtful mood to find his father in a towering rage, pacing up and down his small study like a caged beast. Walter was not, it transpired, to have the consolation of Bea Franklyn and her forty thousand pounds after all.

"It is outrageous!" spluttered the earl, waving his arms so hard that he almost slopped brandy out of the glass he held. "All she ever wanted was the title, so Walter is thrown over while she sets her cap at Bertram, poor fellow! Well, she will catch cold at that. He will never look at her unless she speaks to him in Latin."

"I am so sorry, brother," Kent said at once to Walter, who nursed his own brandy. "What a dreadful thing for you, on top of everything else."

Walter gave a small shrug. "Better to find out her true nature now rather than after the wedding, eh? But what I am to do with myself now I cannot imagine."

"Yes, we shall both have to find employment," Kent said.

"Nonsense," their father said. "I can still support my own sons, I hope. You cannot imagine you would be turned out on your ear."

"Father, I ought to have a career," Kent said. "Younger sons have to earn their keep."

"Pft," the earl said, taking a long drink of brandy. "The church, the army, the law... what would you do?"

"None of those," Kent said quickly.

"Then what?" his father said. "What can you possibly be, if not a gentleman?"

"An engineer," he blurted. "I have always been fascinated by machinery, so... an engineer. That is what I should like to be."

They both laughed at him.

3: An Evening At Highwood Place

K ent waited a few days before raising the subject again. The family was in turmoil and he had no wish to add to it, but surely now, when everything had changed, was the time for him to set his feet on the path that drew him?

It was not an auspicious time. His mother had left the castle, insisting that his father should marry a younger woman who could give him legitimate heirs, Walter had gone off to London in search of employment and even Tess Nicholson had vanished. Aunt Alice still kept to her room, and Captain Edgerton and his Hartlepool crew seemed to be everywhere.

But if not now, then when? Walter had seemingly accepted the need for a career, and how much more should that apply to Kent, the third son? He had no inheritance to drop on his head, as had happened to Eustace, and he was not handsome enough or wealthy enough to attract the attention of a marriageable heiress, so a career it had to be.

He found his father in his study, his desk spread with papers, but he was standing by the window, a glass of brandy in his hand, and since it was barely noon, it was not a good sign.

"Ah, Kent, there you are," the earl said, running a hand distractedly through his greying hair. "I hardly know whether I am coming or going, with everyone taking off like this. Your mother gone... what am I to do without her, eh? And Walter off to town. Eustace is never here, and even Nicholson... not that he was a particular friend, but family, you know. Ah, but let us not speak of that. At least I still have you and Olivia. You will still bear me company, my two youngest."

Definitely a bad time to raise the subject of leaving Corland, but would there ever be a good time? He could not postpone the moment indefinitely. "Father..."

"Sit down and have a drink with me. God knows, I need company just now."

"Father, Walter is not the only one in need of a career, so—"

"No, no, do not speak of *need*. There was no call for Walter to go, but Alfred Strong persuaded him, and a trip to town will do him no harm — a distraction just now, that will do him a world of good. But as for employment, my sons may be gentlemen at my expense as long as they wish. I make you an adequate allowance, I believe?"

"Perfectly adequate, Father. You have always been more than generous, but if I am to be truthful, I should like something more productive to do than simply being a gentleman."

"Kent, you are not going to talk about being an engineer again, are you? You are a gentleman, after all."

"It is the future, Father," Kent said mildly. "One day, engines will power all the manufacturing in the country, and mill owners will not be tied to waterways to drive their machinery. If you are set against it, then I will engage not to become an engineer myself, but I should like to learn about engines... as a gentlemanly interest, if you like. There is a place in Birmingham—"

"Birmingham! Good heavens!"

"A foundry, where they make beam engines of all types. I should love to go there and see how they are made, and the principles under which they operate. Not as a career, if you truly dislike the idea, but just as... a distraction."

"But not just now, surely? You would not desert me just now, when everything is so..."

He rubbed his forehead tiredly, and Kent had not the heart to persist.

One day, surely, he would be able to leave home and follow his heart's desire. One day soon.

***

Katherine did not know what to make of her conversation with Mr Kent Atherton. There had been a glorious intimacy about it — he had reposed such confidence in her, and revealed his family's tragedy. Yet then he had told her to forget it had ever happened, as if he were ashamed of himself for saying such things to a stranger. It was hard to understand, but inside her a little flame burned, a flame of hope that perhaps things would be different between them now. Perhaps he would finally notice her, talk to her, reveal more of his inner feelings.

Yet he did not. Whenever they met afterwards, which was seldom for they moved in somewhat different circles, he treated her no differently from before. He was always friendly, always showing her that wide, beaming smile that so warmed her inside. After exchanging a few commonplaces, however, he moved on to other, more fertile pastures, to girls who could manage more than two words at a time in his presence, and not stutter over them. How she envied Aveline her easy manners in society! There was not much in Aveline that she would wish to emulate, but that ability to chatter away and always find something to say was such a help, and Katherine's shyness such a hindrance. Her aunt chided her gently for it, and even gave her tips to help her improve, but nothing seemed to work, and especially not with Mr Kent Atherton.

Katherine had left off her blacks, apart from the gloves, so her life felt more normal. Her days fell into a placid routine, with music, Bible studies and long letters to Branton friends before breakfast. The music room was quiet at that hour, being situated off the drawing room and rarely used in the mornings, so she had an hour or two of solitude before the rest of the family rose and engulfed her with chatter and bustle.

Later in the day, if her aunt had no other plans for her, she joined the sewing circle at the rectory. Lately, there had been an exciting new addition to the little circle. Miss Peach was a middle-aged spinster, but she was also the companion to Mrs Edgerton, whose husband, Captain Edgerton, was investigating the troubles at Corland Castle.

No matter how terrified Katherine was of the earl and his grand family, just now they were simply a group of very unhappy people, after a brutal murder and now the discovery that the earl's marriage had been invalid. The latter was not generally known, but the murder was of endless fascination to the ladies of Mrs Dewar's sewing circle, so the addition of Miss

Peach to their number was thrilling. Not that she revealed anything at all about Captain Edgerton's investigations. She seemed like a twittery lady of middle-age, and her conversation was inclined to meander alarmingly off the point, but there was a shrewdness in her pale eyes that made Katherine suspect that there was more going on under her grey hair and no-nonsense spinster's cap than there seemed at first glance.

Certainly, the ladies soon gave up their excited questions, as they found they received no clear answers. An enquiry about the captain's interview with the Lady Alice Nicholson, widow of the chaplain, somehow veered into a discussion of quince jelly. A remark about how odd it was that the castle dogs in the basement did not bark at the murderous intruder was deflected onto the subject of partridge raising. And somehow, almost every subject, no matter how innocuous, became a recitation of the perfections of Mrs Edgerton, to whom Miss Peach had been governess, and who was, seemingly, a paragon of virtue.

Katherine watched it appreciatively, admiring the way Miss Peach was swiftly dismissed as being of no consequence and therefore left to sit quietly in a corner with her stitchery, saying little but listening intently. Since Katherine liked to sit quietly in a corner, too, she often found herself beside the elderly governess. They said little that did not relate to their needlework, but occasionally Miss Peach would ask a perceptive question.

"How delightful for you to be a part of the most superior society in this neighbourhood," Miss Peach said to Katherine one day. "The earl's family... so gracious and condescending, so kind to my poor self, even in the midst of all their difficulties. The countess pressed me many times to join the family for dinner. Not that I do, of course! Good heavens, no! Someone in my humble position cannot mingle with the nobility, not as my dear Mrs

Edgerton so gracefully can. I eat with the servants, as is only fitting. But you, my dear... you must enjoy the experience, I am sure."

How to answer her? *Enjoy* mingling with a peer of the realm? Katherine felt herself to be in just as humble a position as Miss Peach, but she was not allowed to eat with the servants, or to stay quietly at home while the rest of the family went off to be impressed by the size of the dining room at Corland Castle, the number of footmen and the vast array of dishes laid out on the table. Instead, she had been dragged unwillingly along, stuffed into a gown that was far too revealing, her hair elaborately coiffed, and expected to play the part of a fashionable young lady, like Aveline. She made no complaint, since it was her duty to be a credit to her aunt and uncle, but she hated every minute, was terrified of making a dreadful mistake and could never find a word to say to the fine ladies and gentlemen she met there. The only comfort such evenings afforded were the glimpses of Mr Kent Atherton and his perpetually smiling countenance.

But she could put none of that into words, so she murmured, "Oh, yes," and bent industriously to her needlework.

Another time, Miss Peach said, "How lucky for you to find yourself part of such a large family! After the tragedy in your own family, and I do most sincerely feel for you, my dear, for I lost my own excellent father at a young age, and my dear Mama when I was but fifteen, but now you are surrounded by loving relations. And your cousins must be like sisters and brothers to you. You never had a sister, I understand?"

"No."

"And one brother, who joined His Majesty's splendid navy, and was tragically lost at sea, poor young man. In battle, I believe?"

"Yes. Cape St Vincent."

"Then he died a hero, which must be the greatest comfort to you, I am sure, and now he is reunited with his papa and mama in Heaven. Such a great loss to the country, these battles and wars! Why can men not stay safely at home and not grieve their womenfolk by going off to be heroes? We would much rather they were a trifle less heroic and stayed comfortably in the arms of their family, do you not agree? But now you have three sisters, and Miss Cathcart so close to you in age that you must be the best of friends, I am sure."

The best of friends? That was not how Katherine would describe it. Aveline had never been especially welcoming, but her attitude had quickly turned to open hostility after the discussion on dowries. Even though that had been settled in Aveline's favour, she had never quite forgiven Katherine.

Aveline's other cause for resentment was, Katherine felt, less justified. There was often a time in those dreadful evenings out when the ladies were called upon to play. It was a relief to hide herself behind the instrument for a few minutes, but there was a difficulty, too. Having the lowest rank, Katherine was usually the last to be called upon, but that made it worse, somehow. Having listened to the bumbling efforts of Aveline earlier, her own performance was often greeted with relief. It was of no use to tell her cousin that the difference was not due to any innate talent, but rather to hours and hours of assiduous practice on her part and a far greater interest in bonnets and ribbons on Aveline's. So she had to hear herself praised, and her aunt say, "There, Aveline! You could play just as well as your cousin, I am sure, if you put some effort into it." It was mortifying.

Katherine had long since given up hope of making a friend of Aveline, and she was too shy in company to attract the attention of any other young ladies, even if she had felt herself to be a suitable companion for the daughters of the nobility or gentry. The earl and his brother both had daughters, but Katherine could not conceive of befriending them. Sir Hubert Strong, the local magistrate, had daughters, too, and Lady Strong and her eldest daughter, in particular, had been very welcoming, but her utter lack of conversation was such a handicap. She saw others chattering away and wished with all her heart that she could talk so easily, but somehow her mind emptied and her tongue froze in such elevated company, and even the most determined talker would eventually give up the struggle to extract more than a single word from her.

That evening saw another trial, for the Cathcarts were invited to dinner at Highwood Place with the Franklyns. Mr Franklyn, she had been told, was a former attorney who had inherited vast wealth, and that should have made him more approachable to the daughter of a mill owner. Yet somehow he was even more gentlemanlike than Uncle Cathcart, always immaculately dressed and his accent with no hint of his Newcastle origins. And his wife was an even more terrifying prospect, for the Lady Esther Franklyn was the daughter of the Duke of Camberley, and although she was perfectly civil to Katherine, there was a ducal haughtiness in her bearing that made Katherine feel like a worm in her presence.

Nor was she at all sure how to address so elevated a personage, for she had got it wrong once and her cousins had all tittered. Aunt Cathcart had explained it to her, but she could not remember. Was it Lady Esther or Lady Franklyn? She would have to listen to everyone else to understand how it was done.

The drive to Highwood Place was enlivened by a monologue from Aunt Cathcart to Katherine on the correct behaviour to be expected.

"You have managed well enough at Corland, for the earl's family are relaxed about protocol, but the Franklyns are another matter. Your deepest curtsy to her ladyship... you may follow Aveline's example. Do not speak unless spoken to, especially to her ladyship, or to any of the gentlemen. No reaching across the table for food. Always wait for a gentleman to serve you. And Katherine, dear, do try your best to make conversation with whoever is sitting next to you. You will never attract a husband if you never open your mouth, you know. There are no likely prospects for you here — the Athertons are well above our touch — but it will be useful practice for when we go to York next year. You may watch Aveline's behaviour for guidance, for she has a delicate way of not quite flirting but showing a young man that she is interested in him, and that is what you must learn to do."

Katherine said nothing beyond *"Yes, aunt"* and *"No, aunt"*, but she had no intention of taking Aveline as her guide in any aspect of her behaviour. Besides, if her simpering and fluttering and fan waving was *not* flirtation, she did not know what it was.

They were the first to arrive, ushered past a long line of liveried and bewigged footmen into the Gold Saloon, one of several splendid apartments recently added to the house. The Franklyns moved amongst them, making the usual polite enquiries of newly arrived guests. Aunt Cathcart addressed their hostess as *'Lady Esther'*, but perhaps that was because they were of a similar age? If Katherine used the same term, would that be too forward? Terrified that she might be called upon to speak, she tucked herself out of sight behind the broad shoulders of James, Alex and Neil, hoping fervently to escape notice from their formidable hosts. Happily, they were soon drawn away by new arrivals to be greeted in the hall.

Gradually the room filled up, natural groupings appeared and the level of conversation rose to a point where Katherine felt tolerably safe in retreating to a seat. Lady Esther Franklyn's saloon was too well-lit to permit any shadowy corners, but there was a chair tucked away between a pillar and an ornate bureau where a terrified girl could safely hide. She could catch glimpses of the door between the moving sea of silk gowns and knee breeches, so she knew at once when Mr Kent Atherton arrived. There was something in that cheerful face that lifted her spirits instantly. How could she be afraid when Mr Atherton was so full of bonhomie?

His presence stirred her to rise to her feet and drift a little closer to the safety of her aunt, who was talking to another unthreatening guest, Lady Strong. She was a motherly person who smiled kindly at her, and hoped she would have an opportunity to hear Katherine play later. If she was Lady Strong, surely it must be correct to call their hostess Lady Franklyn, not Lady Esther? How difficult it all was! She was so distracted she could not even begin to formulate a suitable response to Lady Strong.

"Oh, but there is to be dancing," Aunt Cathcart said, happily jumping into the conversation. "Mrs Dewar is to play for us, and there will be dancing. Although my niece does not yet dance."

"No, of course not," Lady Strong said sympathetically. "So soon after your dear father's demise, you would hardly wish to do so."

Katherine opened her mouth to say... she knew not what. How could she explain that she had never learnt the formal dances that graced the gentry's ballrooms? A reel or a simple country dance she could manage, but the complicated steps and movements were beyond her. She loved to watch, but could never imagine herself moving with the graceful ease she had seen in her cousins and their neighbours.

Just as the long-case clock in the hall sonorously sounded the hour, the butler announced loudly, "Dinner is served, my lady." Naturally, meals would occur at precisely the appointed time in the well-regulated home of a duke's daughter. There was a little genteel bustle at the door furthest from the hall, as guests paired up for the procession to the dining room. All the older guests drifted in that direction, following instructions from their hostess, and Mr Bertram Atherton, eldest son of the earl's younger brother, followed them with Miss Franklyn on one arm and Lady Olivia Atherton on the other. Only a few of the younger guests were left to make their own arrangements.

Mr Kent Atherton was one of them! Sudden hope flared in Katherine's heart as his gaze swept over those left behind. Only two ladies remained... surely he would—?

"Miss Cathcart?" he murmured to Aveline, offering his arm. "Shall we?"

With a smirk of satisfaction, she laid her hand on his arm and they set off at a sedate pace after the others. Katherine could not suppress the disappointment that speared painfully through her. Now only Alex and Neil remained, and they turned away as one. Only when they reached the door to the next room did they think to turn to her.

"Come along, cousin," Alex said.

"You will not want to miss dinner, I am sure," Neil said.

They both grinned at her, those wide smiles that were so similar but not quite alike. Then they turned again and passed through the door side by side, leaving Katherine alone, to scurry after them as best she could.

4: A Friend

Katherine hastened after the twins, through another saloon, decorated in shades of pale green and white, although with as much gold paint as the previous room. A line of footmen stood to attention across the room, marking the way to the dining room, where there was a great bustle of seats pulled out and pushed in, as everyone settled in their proper places.

Katherine waited until only one seat was left, then slipped silently into it, her cheeks scarlet with shame to be the last. An unseen footman behind her pushed her chair forwards as she sat, catching the back of her legs so that she half fell into it. Then she had to shuffle the chair nearer to the table herself, the footman attempting to help and only making the whole manoeuvre more difficult. Around the table, silence fell as everyone's gaze was upon her, the last to be settled. She blushed and blushed again from mortification. When finally she was in position, Mr Franklyn said grace and the meal began.

However, Katherine found herself awkwardly placed, for she had Miss Bridget Dewar on one side of her, and Aveline on the other, and Aunt

Cathcart had given her clear instructions not to reach across the table for a dish, as she had been accustomed to do at home, but to wait for a gentleman to fetch it for her. The soup presented no difficulty, for the footmen handed round the bowls, and after that there was fish, again distributed from the head and foot of the table. But when those items were removed and the first course laid out on the table, Katherine had no idea what to do, with no gentleman to enquire what she would like to eat and to stretch across the table to the right dish.

So she sat, her plate empty, paralysed with fear of a wrong move. Once a footman leaned over her shoulder and murmured, "May I fetch something for you, madam?" but Katherine whispered, "No... no, thank you." Only when the second course was set out and she saw that many of the ladies reached for nearby dishes without hesitation did she dare to take a couple of spoonfuls from the nearest dish, but so hastily, to escape notice, that she dripped gravy on the immaculate white cloth.

It was a relief when the ladies rose to leave. She rather liked the ceremony of their departure, as all the gentlemen stood also, and bowed as the ladies filed past. Mr Kent Atherton rushed to the door to hold it open, smiling to every lady who passed him. Katherine blushed and lowered her head, lacking the courage to look at him.

She followed the straggling procession, last, of course, for she was painfully aware of her place in this august company, into another magnificent apartment, the walls lined with paintings of stern-faced men in huge wigs and a few unsmiling females in the ornate clothes of half a century ago.

"My Bucknell ancestors," their hostess was saying as a footman closed the door behind Katherine. "Copies of the portraits at Marshfields, the principal seat of my father, the Duke of Camberley."

Aunt Cathcart was standing near the door. "Ah, Katherine, come and sit beside me... over here, I think." She chose a small sofa some distance from the rest of the guests gathered about their hostess. "Now then, my dear, I did not quite like to see you draw attention to yourself at dinner."

Katherine blushed for shame at the reprimand, but could not help saying, "Me, aunt? What did I do?"

"You ate nothing, child! Such an insult to Lady Esther. She was so concerned she sent a footman to attend to you. But perhaps you are unwell?"

"No... no, but I thought... there was no gentleman. You told me... I must wait for a gentleman to offer me a dish."

Aunt Cathcart sighed. "But you were not seated beside a gentleman, were you? Not that it was your fault in the slightest. I was very cross with Alex and Neil for neglecting to look after you, but there, they are still young and thoughtless. I will have a word with them tomorrow. One of them should have stayed with you, but there are more ladies than gentlemen tonight, so there are bound to be one or two ladies left to fend for themselves. You are not expected to starve, my dear! One does not quite like to see ladies standing to stretch the full width of the table, as Miss Franklyn did tonight, but you may always ask a neighbour to pass you a dish, be it a lady or a gentleman, or you may summon a footman. There are so many footmen here tonight so it is no imposition. You will get into the way of it very soon, I am sure. Oh, I must just have a word with Kitty Strong."

Kitty Strong... but surely she was Lady Strong? Or should that be Lady Kitty Strong? It was too confusing for words.

Aunt Cathcart bustled away, leaving Katherine alone in her quiet corner. The ladies settled into groups, the younger ones around the noisy Miss Franklyn, who never seemed to stop chattering and laughing loudly, and the older ones clustered more quietly near Lady Esther — or was it Lady Franklyn? Another lady, whose name Katherine could not quite remember, was engaged in chasing everyone away from the open windows and adjuring them to keep their shawls tightly drawn about their persons.

After a while, a little train of footmen came in to roll up the carpets ready for dancing. It was clear that this was not an impromptu event, however, for the chairs had already been pushed towards the walls, and a couple of extra chairs placed beside the pianoforte, waiting for the fiddlers who now crept in. Bowing low to the ladies, they took their places and began to tune their instruments. Mrs Dewar, the rector's wife, took her place at the pianoforte.

This was more like it! Katherine could not dance or make conversation, but music, any music, lifted her spirits enormously. Soon, the gentlemen arrived from the dining room, and the dancing began. In her quiet corner, she had a fine view of the dancers, admiring once again the elegance of their movements and the precision with which they positioned arms and legs and even fingers. So graceful! And the gentlemen just as agile and precise as the ladies. It was nothing at all like the style of dancing she had seen at Branton, entered into there with more enthusiasm than grace, on the whole, but enjoyed by young and old alike, even the children joining in.

After a while, one of the young men discovered her in her secluded spot.

"Well, Miss Parish," he said, taking the seat beside her, "what do you think of the dancing so far? Are we not an energetic lot?"

"Oh, yes," she said, blushing violently. What was his name? He was one of the Athertons, a son of Mr George Atherton, the earl's brother... was it Bertram? She thought it was.

"Who do you think is the best dancer?"

"I... I cannot say."

"Very diplomatic. I would say my cousin Olivia is the most graceful of the ladies, but for the gentlemen, and it pains me to say so, the palm must go to Mr Franklyn. I never saw a man of his age dance so well. He quite outshines the rest of us." He paused, but when she said nothing, he went on, "I know you are still in black gloves for your father, but in a setting such as this, amongst friends, it would not be improper for you to dance, surely? May I have the honour?"

"Oh... no, no! Indeed, no." Then, remembering her manners, she added, "Thank you."

"Then I shall stay and enjoy your company, Miss Parish."

How kind he was! But Aveline was watching them closely from not far away. "No, no, you must not... look there, Aveline... Miss Cathcart..."

His smile never faltered. He rose, bowed, and went straight to Aveline, who bore him into the next set triumphantly. However, his partner did not seem to please him much, for after a brief exchange, they remained silent for the rest of the dance, and then separated at once. A few moments later, however, Katherine saw the same man approaching her again. Surely he would not—? But he had a young lady with him, who smiled at her shyly.

"Miss Parish, since you are not dancing this evening, would you be so good as to bear my sister company? Emily does not wish to dance, either, and it seems to me that you would both derive more pleasure in the evening by having a companion to talk to. You have chosen a wonderful vantage point, ma'am, from which you may admire whatever is admirable in the dancing and deplore whatever is deplorable, and such thoughts are best shared with a like-minded friend, are they not?"

And with a bow, he was gone.

"You do not mind?" Emily said in a soft voice that Katherine liked at once. "I am too terrified to dance, and it would be so lovely to have a friend to sit with... if... if you have no objection?"

"No, indeed," Katherine said very readily.

A friend! Yes, that would be lovely indeed. So she patted the seat beside her, Emily sat down and they smiled at each other with genuine pleasure.

***

Katherine soon found that, although Emily Atherton was only eighteen, she was exactly the friend she needed to guide her through the shoals of the society in which she now found herself. Not only did Emily know precisely how to address the daughter of a duke or the wife of a baronet, but she could explain the distinction easily.

"The daughter of a duke, marquess or earl has a title from her father, and keeps it for life, so if she marries a commoner like Mr Franklyn she becomes Lady Esther Franklyn. If she had married a lord, she would take his title over her own, like every other lady. Lady Rennington, for instance. Or a baronet, like Sir Hubert Strong — his wife is Lady Strong."

"So... I would address them as Lady Esther and Lady Strong?" Katherine said hesitantly.

"Yes! Although Mama says that if one is feeling particularly deferential, one may address Lady Esther as *'my lady'*, as a sign of respect. She is quite the grandest lady for miles around. Lady Rennington is much easier to talk to."

That was a point where Katherine could not quite agree. To her, everyone in this new world she now inhabited was difficult to talk to. Emily's problem was more modest — she could talk comfortably to ladies, or to older gentlemen, but a young man, particularly a handsome and amiable one, rendered her mute and covered in confusion. She was not one to put herself forward, however, so even with ladies, she tended to creep into corners, just as Katherine did. Now they could creep together, and it was a very comfortable thing, Katherine found, to have someone with whom to hide away.

Within a week of Lady Esther's evening party, the two had fallen into the habit of meeting almost every day. If Emily did not walk down the hill to Cathcart House, Katherine would walk up to Westwick Heights. Then there would be long walks in the garden, or visits to Birchall village, and on wet days they sat companionably indoors with a handkerchief apiece to be embroidered, and whispered together.

Like the Cathcarts, Emily was one of six, having two sisters and three brothers. Julia was Katherine's age, but seemed very grown up, for she was betrothed already, and Penelope was barely out but had all the confidence in society that Emily lacked. The two older brothers were distant creatures, seldom seen, Bertram because he spent all day in the library with his books and Lucas because he was constantly in the stables or out riding, like his father. The youngest child, Philip, was still confined to the nursery on the uppermost floor.

Emily's mother, Mrs Atherton, was a kindly soul who fretted perpetually over the health of her family. Whenever Katherine visited, this solicitude extended to her, too, and she found herself exhorted to borrow one of the many thick shawls left in every room, or draw her chair nearer to the blazing fire. At all costs she must not venture near the windows, in case of stray draughts which would invariably settle on the chest, become a putrid fever and carry the sufferer off within days. Katherine quickly learnt to swathe herself in a shawl when advised, relinquishing its suffocating embrace as soon as Mrs Atherton had left the room.

Somehow, she felt far more at home at Westwick Heights than at Cathcart House. Even though Emily's father was the younger brother of the Earl of Rennington, and now the heir to the title and estates, and even though the whole family was indubitably aristocratic, there was an ease and friendliness about them that was most agreeable to a rather lonely girl. If she had to be part of a large family, she mused to herself sometimes on the walks up or down the hill, she had far sooner be part of the relaxed Athertons than suffering the supercilious Aveline, or Aunt Cathcart's constant worries about appearances, and the possible humiliation that might result if it became known that Katherine was the daughter of a mill owner.

The Athertons were not even perturbed by her father's occupation. Mr Atherton came into the parlour one day, a folded newspaper in his hand.

"Miss Parish, I noticed this piece in one of the Manchester newspapers. It will interest you, I believe."

Surprised, she took the newspaper from him and read where he indicated. It was about Branton! At first, it merely described the opening of a new, modern mill, but then—

"Longfarley!" she cried. Her father's mill!

"You know it, then?"

"Oh, yes, for it is—" She clamped one hand over her mouth, recalling that she was not supposed to mention such things. Then, she slowly said, "I am glad to hear that it has reopened. There were many workers laid off when... when it closed."

"Last year," Mr Atherton said gently. "Just before Christmas, so the newspaper says. Is that correct?"

Wordlessly, she nodded, feeling tears pricking, and hoping she would not disgrace herself by crying openly. Not in front of the earl's brother. How embarrassing that would be!

"Do you know the new owner? This... Mr Ridwell?"

She nodded again. "He has other mills. Cragforth is his biggest, but Longfarley is bigger... it has the very latest type of— Oh, I beg your pardon, sir. This is of no interest to you."

"On the contrary, Miss Parish. I deduce this is... *was* your father's mill, which was lost after he died? Then I am very glad to hear that it has reopened and given employment to so many men. There is much in the article about the significant improvements to the manufacture of beam engines that make this particular mill of such interest to our men of industry."

She read the article avidly, and although her father's name was not mentioned anywhere, and all the praise instead went to Mr Ridwell for his forward thinking in the new mill, she knew the credit was all to her father.

When she left that day, Mr Atherton emerged from his study to push into her hand a folded paper — the article, cut from the newspaper.

But a few days later, Katherine's old and new lives clashed in a most unexpected fashion.

***

"B ut Kent, you would not have me imprisoned here, would you?" Olivia wheedled as they sat at breakfast. "I have to escape, and with Mama gone, who better to escort me than my own brother?"

"You escaped only yesterday, as I recall, and with my escort," Kent said but without heat, for when Olivia had set her mind on something, she was quite unstoppable. Besides, with Walter gone to London and Eustace busy about his own affairs, Kent was the only one left. He sipped his coffee and watched her marshal her arguments.

In truth, he felt sorry for his youngest sister. She was eighteen now, an age at which both Josie and Izzy had made their come-outs in town, but the Dowager Countess's lingering illness had sunk poor Olivia's chance of a season this year. Yet Grandmama still clung to life, and now Nicholson's deceit had ruined Olivia's future even more. With her pretty face and lively nature, not to mention a substantial dowry, she would still make a good match, but as an illegitimate daughter of an earl, her possibilities were reduced. Not for her the marriage to a peer or future peer, as both Josie and Izzy had achieved. The best she could hope for was a country gentleman of means, and that would be such a waste. So he was not unwilling to squire her about.

"Oh, pooh, yesterday was only Aunt Jane. That hardly counts."

"And the Strongs, and the Franklyns the day before. Who else would you call upon?"

"The Cathcarts."

"Really? Mama is not keen on Mrs Cathcart."

"Lord, no, she is quite *encroaching*, and the daughters are just as bad, but their cook makes the most delicious cherry cake... so moist and sticky! And she does not fuss if one has a second or third slice, the way Aunt Jane does. *'So sweet and bad for the digestion',*" she added in a passable imitation of her aunt's voice. "*'Do have a dry biscuit, dear, and wrap yourself in this horrid scratchy shawl, and at all costs keep away from the nasty draughty windows.'* Her drawing room is always so overpoweringly hot."

Kent chuckled. "Aunt Jane means well, and she has good reason, for she was very sick when she first came here, Mother said, and is still prone to illness. Naturally, she is concerned for the health of others. But by all means let us sample the Cathcarts' cherry cake, if you wish. Cathcart keeps an excellent cellar, so at least I will be offered something more interesting than tea. But I depend upon you to rescue me if Miss Cathcart sidles up to me batting her eyelashes."

Olivia giggled. "She is such a flirt! Very well, we need not stay long."

"Only three slices of cherry cake, then," he murmured.

"Hmm, shall we say four?"

He laughed and rang the bell to order the carriage.

The Cathcarts were at home, and although the ladies were sitting in the small parlour just off the hall, the drawing room was hastily opened up for the distinguished visitors from the castle. A footman was still wrestling with shutters when Mrs Cathcart led Olivia in, while the daughters clustered around Kent, smiling hopefully up at him.

Someone was playing the pianoforte in the music room next door, someone far more competent than the Cathcart daughters. Miss Parish, undoubtedly. Kent saw Mrs Cathcart glance in that direction, open her mouth to speak and then think better of it. Was she wondering whether to summon Miss Parish? Yet she did not. As she directed the ladies to chairs, he wondered if perhaps Miss Parish, so much prettier than her cousins, was seen as a threat to their prospects?

So much prettier? Where had that thought come from? Miss Cathcart and her younger sisters were generally accounted pretty girls. Not beauties, but few women could bear comparison with his own sisters. Izzy, in particular, was beyond compare, and Olivia was very like her. But Miss Cathcart... surely she was prettier than Miss Parish?

Perhaps she was, but the way she eyed him speculatively and tried her hardest to attract his attention was deplorable. The younger girls were no better. But Miss Parish, with her guileless eyes and her ready blush… yes, she was much prettier.

Even if she had been a positive antidote, he did not like to see her pushed aside in favour of her cousins, and perhaps there was a niggle of guilt at the back of his mind for pushing all his worries onto Miss Parish that day in the church. It would please him now to make amends to some degree by giving her the proper notice that her aunt seemed disinclined to ensure.

Ignoring the smiles of the Cathcart ladies, therefore, and the sofa where Miss Cathcart sat expectantly, Kent strolled through the open door into the music room. Miss Parish was seated at the instrument, facing him but entirely oblivious of her surroundings. All her focus was on her music, her hands flying over the keys. How wonderful to have that intensity, to lose oneself so completely in an activity that one noticed nothing else. The roof could fall in, and he doubted Miss Parish would notice.

The roof did not fall in, but the effect was the same, for Mrs Cathcart appeared at Kent's side.

"Katherine, dear, we have callers. Pray come and be sociable for a little while. *Katherine!*"

The music stopped abruptly, a jangle of discordant notes bereft of their fellows to make them harmonious. Miss Parish looked up with a gasp of dismay, her cheeks bright red.

"So sorry! I did not— I had not— Beg pardon, aunt."

Jumping to her feet, she scurried round the instrument and rushed past Kent into the other room.

"Mr Atherton?" Mrs Cathcart said, with that wide smile that did not quite reach her eyes. "Do have a seat."

Suppressing a sigh, Kent allowed himself to be ushered back into the drawing room, dutifully settling beside the triumphant Miss Cathcart and preparing himself to be bored. No matter how good the cherry cake, he was not sure it was adequate compensation for such tedium.

5: A Visitor From Branton

Kent's good humour was sorely tested by Miss Cathcart's efforts to engage him in a flirtation. He had no objection to it on principle, but he liked to choose the recipient, and he could not help but despise a woman who clearly saw him as a pigeon ripe for plucking. A woman should surely wait for a man to display some interest in her before launching into quite such a determined effort to ensnare him, in his view.

The hoped-for cake arrived soon afterwards, not cherry, but Olivia fell on it with glee anyway. Happily for Kent, the cake was followed almost at once by Mr Cathcart and his eldest son, and Kent took the opportunity to escape to the relative safety of male company. With a glass of Madeira in his hand and some sensible conversation about horses to sustain him, his mood improved.

From his new vantage point, he could see Miss Parish cowering on a footstool in a corner. No one made any effort to draw her forwards. She jumped up to help when the cake and tea arrived, but Mrs Cathcart waved her away and set Miss Susan Cathcart to handing around plates and cups. Several times Kent was offered a slice of cake, a biscuit or a fruit pastry, but he declared himself content with his Madeira.

On one such circuit, having a view through to the music room window, she glanced out and exclaimed, "Mama! The most peculiar coach is coming up the drive, with luggage all over it. Not from round here, that much is certain. Who are we expecting?"

"No one, dear," Mrs Cathcart said. "Passing travellers asking directions, perhaps."

Miss Susan ran through to the music room, which overlooked the turning circle in front of the house. Running back, she cried, "It is stopping, Mama. The footman is getting down. Shall I go and—?"

"By no means, Susan. Davis will deal with it."

A few moments later, Davis came in bearing a card on a silver salver. Mrs Cathcart read it, gave an exclamation, then firmly shook her head. The butler bowed and withdrew.

Susan called through from the music room. "A lady is getting down, Mama."

"It is no one we know, dear," her mother said, rather flustered.

"But her footmen are unstrapping the luggage, Mama. Should we not—?"

Mrs Cathcart reddened, then smiled at Olivia. "Do excuse me a moment, Lady Olivia. I shall be back directly. James, pray ensure that Lady Olivia has another slice of cake."

Amused, Kent wandered through to the music room. It was indeed a peculiar coach, of a large, old-fashioned style, drawn by four horses, with a liveried coachman and groom on the box. Two footmen, also in livery, were unstrapping a large wrapped item from the roof, while two outriders looked on. As Kent watched, a woman appeared from behind the coach and gave some orders to one of the outriders, who nodded and rode away down the drive.

The woman was elderly, he guessed, from all he could see of her behind her voluminous hat, which might have been fashionable fifteen years ago. She was dressed from head to toe in black, her wide skirts swaying as she moved. Yes, definitely elderly.

But not shy, that much was certain. Davis was on the drive, perhaps remonstrating with her, but she only laughed at him and the footmen continued their work on unfastening the item on the roof. Whatever was it? Not a traveller's box for luggage, since it was well wrapped against the dust and rain of the road. Now they were gently lifting it down to the ground. Furniture, perhaps? It could be a small writing desk.

Now Mrs Cathcart was out there, flapping her hands ineffectually, but the woman in black roared with laughter. She was nearer now, and her words carried even through the glass.

"I just want to see little Katy, that's all, ma'am. A small gift for her. No need to get in a pelter over it."

Little Katy? And the strong Lancashire accent told its own story. Kent laughed, and elbowed his way through the crowd that now thronged the music room, heads craning to see the arrival. Back in the drawing room, Olivia was talking composedly to Miss Cathcart and James, her plate heaped with cake. Miss Parish was still huddled in the corner, a cup of tea balanced on her knees.

"Miss Parish?" Kent said quietly. She started and blushed a fiery red. "I think the visitor is here to see you."

"Me?"

The cup of tea wobbled precariously. He lifted it from her lap, setting it safely on a side table. "Will you come and see?"

He offered his arm and, still as red as a beetroot, head down, she allowed herself to be led out into the hall and through the front door.

She gasped. "Mrs Vance? Oh, Mrs Vance!"

Tearing down the steps, she hurled herself at the black-clad figure, who scooped her to her ample bosom with cries of delight.

"Katy, dear! Well, now, let me look at you. So thin, but my, how grand you've grown, in your fine gown, although the house is not quite what I was expecting. So plain! Why, I declare, the Ridwells' house is far grander. I like a bit of ornamentation, myself, not so dull as this. But I like to see *you* dressed up a bit finer than you used to, child. Quite the lady you are now. I wonder you still want to acknowledge a disreputable character like poor Mrs Vance. Now, now, child, no more tears. This lady must be your aunt, I suppose. Do tell her I'll not be stopping long, for she won't want the likes of me cluttering up her drive. Is that fine gentleman your uncle?"

She pointed at Davis. Kent could not hear how Miss Parish replied, for her voice was not above a whisper, but the lady in black roared with laughter.

"Well now, fancy me mistaking the butler for a gentleman! Lord, how Mr Vance will laugh when I tell him. There now, child, this is all I came for, to bring you a little present. Couldn't get here before, what with my Lottie's confinement, and then Janey's boys came all over spots, and I couldn't neglect poor Mr Vance, could I? But I'm here now, aren't I?

There!" She pointed triumphantly to the package now sitting on the drive. "Where do you want it? My men will bring it in to the house."

"A gift for Katherine? How kind," Mrs Cathcart said hastily, attempting to wrest control of the situation. "Davis, see to it, will you? Thank you so much, Mrs... er, Vance." She paused, and even from his vantage point at the top of the steps, Kent could see the struggle on her face between good manners and the burning desire to rid her drive of this vulgar person. In the end, catching sight of Kent's amused face, she settled for good manners. "Will you step inside, Mrs Vance? While Katherine unwraps her... gift."

"Well, now, that's most gracious of you, ma'am. I don't mind if I do, and a glass of something wouldn't go amiss. Thirsty work, travelling in the summer. All that dust quite parches a body's throat. Well, what a narrow hall! I declare, I prefer a larger entrance myself, but there, I expect tastes differ in Yorkshire."

Mrs Cathcart ushered Mrs Vance and Miss Parish firmly into the front parlour, while Davis and a couple of footmen manoeuvred the large package in there too. Then the door was firmly closed on the little crowd of onlookers.

"Do go back to the drawing room, everyone. Mr Atherton? May I tempt you to a slice of plum cake?"

Kent followed the general drift back to the drawing room, retrieved his glass of Madeira and picked up a second glass. Olivia was still there, still eating, still talking to Miss Cathcart, whose eyes lit up at the sight of Kent. Bending over Olivia, he murmured into her ear, "When the cake runs out, the parlour might be amusing."

Then, ignoring Mrs Cathcart's urging him to stay, he set off for the parlour again, opening the door with difficulty, trying not to spill Madeira, and sidling in. Mrs Vance was seated on an overstuffed sofa, looking rather uncomfortable, but her face lit up when Kent handed her the spare glass of Madeira.

"Well now, that's just the thing to set me straight. Thank you kindly, sir."

Meanwhile, Miss Parish knelt on the floor, wrestling with the knots securing the mysterious parcel. And talking! She chattered away as if she had not talked for a month and had stored up all her words, while Mrs Vance gave brief answers to the questions that tumbled out one after the other.

"—take the waters, but I am so glad he is somewhat improved. And what of Mrs Silver? Is she better now? She was so poorly when I left. Oh, I am glad to hear it. And did Mr Tiller propose to Miss Berkeley in the end? Oh, no! Poor Miss Berkeley! And how is the new curate working out? Are his sermons less soporific than Mr Tybald's? Oh, goodness, I—"

Kent watched, mesmerised. This was a side to Miss Parish that he had never suspected. Not only was she talking more than he had ever seen before, but her face was alive with enthusiasm, her eyes sparkling and her lips... such lips! Had they always been so red, so downright enticing? He was aware of a tug of interest that was not merely pity for a lonely, shy girl, and not even the twinge of guilt that he had unburdened himself so disgracefully to a near stranger.

She became aware of him, falling silent as her cheeks took on the familiar fiery hue.

"Are the knots giving you trouble?" he said gently. "Shall I cut the string?"

"No... that would be wasteful," she murmured, eyes downcast. Then, flushing even more, "But thank you, sir."

"Then may I try to unpick them?" he said, and when she nodded, he knelt down beside her and set to work. She slid along the rug to put some distance between them, her head still lowered, hands neatly folded in her lap.

When the silence began to feel oppressive, Kent said, "Have you travelled far today, Mrs Vance?"

"Only from Thirsk, sir. I don't hold with these long days in the carriage, so I never plan more than a stage or two a day. That way, I can keep my own horses and my reliable coachman. I don't hold with post horses, not when I have my own."

"Very wise," Kent said. "And are you staying in these parts long? Miss Parish will not want you to rush away, I am sure."

"A few days, perhaps. If the inn is to my liking."

"The White Horse? It is reputed to be a very comfortable establishment. Mrs Haslet's mutton pie is the best in the North Riding. She tells me so herself, so it must be true. There!" he said triumphantly, as the first knot was teased apart. "One done, only another dozen or so waiting. Your servants wrapped this excessively well, Mrs Vance."

She chuckled, but said, "You have the advantage of me, sir. Are you one of the Cathcarts?"

Kent jumped to his feet. "I beg your pardon! How rag-mannered of me. Mr Kent Atherton at your service, ma'am." He made her a respectful bow.

"Oh, Mr *Atherton?* Mr *Kent* Atherton? The earl's youngest son, then. Oh, I've heard all about you, and how kind you were to Katy when she first arrived. *'May you find some small ray of hope every day to enchant you and relieve your sadness for a while.'* That was what you said to her. Oh, don't colour up like that, Katy dear, that letter's been read by everyone in Branton. Mrs Tybald was moved to tears by it. All Katy's letters are read out loud to all our friends, Mr Atherton, and we was all shocked to pieces to hear of the trouble that's come to your family. A murder! Such wickedness in the world, and now it turns out the clergyman was never ordained, seemingly. Is that so, sir? For Katy won't talk about that, says it's all gossip and she don't like to trade in gossip. But you live in the castle, don't you? What a fine thing! And here you are, unpicking knots, and you the son of an earl. Well, everyone will be so interested when I tell them back in Branton."

"Branton… is that where you come from, Miss Parish?"

She nodded.

"Strange. For some reason, I thought it was Lancaster." In fact, he recalled Mrs Cathcart saying so.

"Near…" she began, her voice a whisper. "Lancaster is the nearest large town."

He so much wanted to see that animated face again that he said impulsively, "Tell me about Branton, Miss Parish."

She blushed even more strongly, if such a thing were possible, then gave the tiniest shake of her head.

"A fine town, sir, very fine," Mrs Vance said robustly. "Very forward looking."

Amused, Kent's hands stilled on the current knot and looked up at her. "Forward looking? In what way?"

"Very modern," she said firmly. "Is there any more of this delicious wine?"

Laughing, he jumped to his feet and took the empty glass from her hand. "Would you like a piece of cake as well?"

"Now, that would be most agreeable, sir."

He returned to the drawing room, the hum of conversation lapsing into silence as he entered.

"Mr Atherton," Mrs Cathcart trilled. "So glad you could join us again. Would you care to—?"

"I am only here momentarily," Kent said smoothly. "I find that in all the excitement, Mrs Vance's refreshments have been overlooked."

He filled a plate with an array of cakes and pastries, refilled the glass and then, with some juggling from hand to hand, tucked the decanter under one arm and strode out of the room, trying very hard not to laugh at the shock on Mrs Cathcart's face.

Reaching the closed parlour door, he stopped, daunted. There was no servant to be seen. Instead, he found Olivia behind him. "You are wicked!" she whispered, grinning at him.

She had remembered to bring her plate with her, he noticed, still laden with cake. "Is that your third slice or fourth?"

"Third... I think. I have lost count rather. It is very good. Is she dreadfully vulgar? Mrs Cathcart looks as if she has eaten a whole lemon."

"Mrs Cathcart is unspeakably rude to a friend of Miss Parish's. Sister, are you going to stand there all day, or shall you open this door? My hands are rather full."

Giggling, she opened it and followed him into the parlour. Mrs Vance's eyes brightened at the mound of food on the plate and the nearly full decanter.

"Ah, you are a gentleman, sir. How very kind of you. Oh!" Her eye fell on Olivia. "Now let me guess... small, dark, beautifully proportioned and pretty as paint — you must be the Lady Olivia, my dear."

Olivia actually blushed.

"What a delightful compliment," Kent said, amused. "I must suppose that is from another of your letters, Miss Parish?"

But that only made Miss Parish blush even harder. While he had been gone, she had loosened several more knots, and as Olivia sat down to discuss the cake with Mrs Vance, as one connoisseur to another, Kent released the final few lengths of cord, and gently unwrapped the gift. It was a small cabinet in the delicate modern style, with two doors that concealed an array of drawers within. Miss Parish uttered a cry of delight.

"My music cabinet... and all the music still within! Oh, Mrs Vance, how came you by it? For the bailiffs took it, I saw them."

And she burst into tears.

"There was a great auction of all the household items, dearie, and Mr Vance authorised Mr Monteath to buy a few pieces that I'd set my heart on. That lovely black and gold table you had in the hall, and the two vases that always stood there — they are in my hall now, and very much admired, I can tell you. And I bought a silver coffee set that I gave your mama and papa when they married, or at least, it may not be the exact one, but very like it. Mr Monteath bought your pianoforte for Annabelle, so you know *that's* gone to a good home. Mr Moreton bought the whole dining set, and some of the pictures, too, and Mr Ridwell bought some paintings, too. Oh, and John Dyson bought the portrait of your mama with Harold as a baby. He always was sweet on her, you know, and now he's going to have her hanging in his study."

And all the time Miss Parish was weeping, and pulling out favourite pieces of music, murmuring, "Haydn... Mozart... Boccherini... Bach..."

"There now, I knew you'd be glad to have it back," Mrs Vance said with a smile of satisfaction. "My, this cake is so good. This will put me on beautifully till dinner, I declare."

"A little more Madeira, ma'am?"

"I don't mind if I do. Thirsty work, all this talking, don't you think?"

Kent agreed to it, and topped up her glass again, and wondered if Miss Parish would ever stop crying. At least she was not blushing any more, and he could admire her smooth cheeks while they were pale, for once. Yes, definitely prettier than the Cathcart girls.

6: Horses And Engines

Katherine found there was a subtle change in the house after Mrs Vance's visit. Nothing was said openly, at least not by Aunt Cathcart, and Aveline's hostility still smouldered, but there was some shift in the air. It was hard to pin down, but was definitely there.

The first tangible sign was when Aunt Cathcart took Katherine to Helmsley to be fitted for a new riding habit. She had brought two with her, but they were not fashionable enough for Aunt Cathcart.

"All this walking about is all very well, but for proper exercise you need to ride more," she told Katherine as the carriage brought them home. "There is a very docile mare in the stables that the girls no longer need, so you can have exclusive use of that."

"Thank you, aunt. I should like that very much, if you can spare me now and then."

Her aunt smiled and patted her gloved hand. "Well, now, Katherine, I believe I can. It seems to me that you are not at all comfortable with the formality of our life here — the morning calls and so forth, and perhaps

time for Katherine to scramble into her evening gown before dinner. Trivial incidents, but they rankled just the same.

The girl raised her tear-stained face, looking rather puzzled. "Well... I suppose. Just need to keep out of the way, because if I'm asked... not sure what to say. I mean, *he* told me what to say, and I did it right enough, but... well, if I'm asked again, I might not say the right thing, see?"

Katherine was not entirely sure she did see. Tentatively, she said, "So, was it a lie, what you were told to say?"

The girl nodded.

"The best way to assuage your conscience over a lie is to tell the truth," Katherine said firmly.

The girl blanched. "Ooh, miss, I couldn't do that! It would upset *him* to no end, that it would. No, all I'm s'posed to do is keep out of the way, like, in case... well, just in case. That's why I'm here but me uncle's a clerk with an attorney, so there's not much for me to do. I wish I could go home. At least I'd be busy there."

"There would be plenty of work in Birchall for you, if you want it, surely?"

"Who'd take me on, miss?" she said, giggling.

"Can you press a gown? Brush mud from a coat? Arrange hair?"

"Oooh, I love doin' hair, miss!"

"Then you can be my lady's maid... what is your name?"

"Daisy, miss. Daisy Marler."

"Well, Daisy, you can be busy at Cathcart House, and if you have a quiet moment to yourself, you can ponder the wisdom of telling lies, the damage to your immortal soul thereby and how much better you will feel if you unburden yourself by telling the truth."

Daisy looked at her doubtfully. "Um... yes, miss."

It was not to be supposed that Aunt Cathcart would accept this change in her household without protest.

"Is Jenny not giving satisfaction, Katherine?" she said frowning.

"Of course, but she has enough to do attending to Susan and Lucinda. A third person added to her duties is something of a stretch, so I have often been later than I should wish going downstairs. I know how Uncle Cathcart likes his dinner on time, and it mortifies me to be the means of delaying the meal. This way will not inconvenience anyone, and Susan and Lucinda will not have to share Jenny with me." Then, when her aunt still looked dubious, she added, "I should pay her wages myself, naturally."

"There is still her board to take into account."

"She may live out, if you prefer. She lives with her uncle at present."

"Who is her uncle?"

"Roger Bright, clerk to Mr Whistley."

"Her name?"

"Daisy Marler. Her father is a farmer at Welwood."

"I know of Marler, of course. A respectable family, by all I hear. Very well. She may live in. A lady's maid must live in, Katherine, so that she is always on hand when needed, even when you return from a ball at four in the morning."

On the whole, Katherine felt she was better off than before. She was no longer dragged along reluctantly to social events, she had her afternoons of riding, and she had her own lady's maid again. Not that Daisy was particularly competent, but she was very willing and eager to learn, and Katherine's needs were not great. So long as her gowns were clean and pressed when she needed them, she asked nothing more, being quite happy to mend tears and make adjustments herself, and her hair was always simply dressed.

But her greatest joy was riding again, despite her sluggish mount. Within a few days, Emily had learnt of her outings and her easy-going parents had agreed that she might ride with Katherine whenever she wished. The two ambled along side by side, chattering away, the two grooms trailing behind, also talking. Sometimes, Emily's brother Lucas rode with them, too, although since his horse and Emily's were much faster than Katherine's, they tended to ride ahead at speed, and then wait for her to catch them up.

The best day, however, was the one when they encountered Mr Kent Atherton also out riding, and he stopped to chat. Then, glory of glories, he wheeled about and rode with them, not riding fast with Mr Lucas and Emily, but walking his horse at Katherine's slow pace and chatting companionably to her. As if she were someone worthy of his attention. As if they were *friends!*

Katherine returned home with her head in the clouds, unable to suppress a smile of pure happiness.

***

Kent was restless. The description of Branton as a forward looking town, without further elaboration, had led him to look it up in various itineraries, which had described it as a *'thriving manufacturing town, with much production of cotton, linen and worsted. The population has grown rapidly in recent years, leading to the provision of numerous fine public buildings and a handsome new church. It has the privilege of markets on Wednesdays and Saturdays.'* All of which could describe a hundred undistinguished northern towns.

If only he could see it! He knew so little of these industrious northern towns, churning out woollens and cottons, spoons and buckets, nails and glass and who knew what else. His experience was limited to London, York and Cambridge, a few coastal or small market towns, and the country estates of his friends and relatives. Other towns were passed through as quickly as a change of horses or an overnight stop allowed. What a dull life he had led!

One evening, when he and his father were the only men lingering over the port, he mentioned again his wish to learn more of engines.

The earl had shaken his head tiredly. "A gentleman does not deal in such matters, Kent."

"I should not be *dealing* in engines, Father. I merely wish to under-stand how they work. If it is a question of money, my allowance would be enough for lodgings in Birmingham, I am sure, and—"

His father sighed heavily. "You are bored, I dare say. There is little enough for a young man to do here. You would be more settled if you had a wife. You are what, twenty-two now? I was not much older than that when I married your mother." He paused, one hand rubbing his eyes. "I wish she had not gone away," he went on querulously. "She knows I cannot manage without her. The place feels so empty now, with Nicholson gone, Alice keeping to her room, Walter gone off to do heaven knows what and Eustace never here. Thank God for you and Olivia, that is all I say. Without the two of you, I should run mad, I swear it. A wife, that is what you need, Kent. Every man needs a wife to keep him straight and give his life purpose. Find yourself a little woman to marry and bring her here to live. That would liven us all up, would it not? A woman about the place, and grandchildren to enjoy — that is what we need here."

Kent gave it up. His father was not himself at present, with Mother gone away now that their marriage was invalid, and urging the earl to marry again and have more sons to inherit. No son who cared about his father could abandon him at such a moment. The engines must perforce wait a little longer.

Perhaps he could write to the foundry at Birmingham to ask their advice about reading materials to help him learn the principles behind beam engines? Steam power had so many possibilities, but he had only picked up snippets of information from the newspapers or gossip amongst the gentlemen who invested in the new mills or in mines where engines were employed to pump out water. There was so much more to learn!

He was riding the next day, mentally composing a letter to be sent to Birmingham, when he came across a little group of other riders — his cousins Lucas and Emily, and the blushing Miss Parish, whose face lit up with a smile of such brilliance as he approached that he could not resist turning his horse about to join them. And there was another motive, too, for perhaps in the less formal setting of a ride on the hills, Miss Parish would feel sufficiently at ease to talk to him freely. He could learn something of the manufacturing town of Branton, and also something of Miss Parish, too.

So when the track opened up and Lucas and Emily raced each other to a distant tree, he settled beside Miss Parish's slower mount.

"Does she ever move beyond a walking pace?" he asked, pointing to her horse with a wry grimace.

"Only when she nears home and the prospect of oats."

"How dull that must be!"

"I do not mind. It is pleasure enough to be out on the hills."

She still blushed whenever she spoke, but she was a great deal more articulate than usual.

"Did you ride a great deal at Branton?"

"Perhaps once or twice a week."

"Where did you go to? Along the rivers, through the fields or up onto the hills? Are there hills around Branton?" he added, realising he had no idea how the town was situated.

She gave a little laugh. "There are! And that is where I mostly rode. I loved to look down on the town from above, to watch the carriages and wagons coming and going, the chimneys smoking and people scurrying about like little ants, busy on business of their own."

They were above Birchall, looking down past Westwick Heights, where Emily and Lucas lived. Cathcart House was hidden in the trees, but most of the village was visible and in the distance to the north, the roof of Corland Castle could just be perceived.

"A little different from this view, I suppose, although we have our share of smoking chimneys, too."

"Oh no," she said seriously. "Branton has proper chimneys... big ones. Very tall, belching out clouds of smoke. Sometimes, when the wind was in the wrong direction, the whole town was hidden by the smoke, like a great, dark blanket covering everything."

"Ah, steam-powered engines?" She nodded. "What are they used for? Pumping... or manufacturing?"

"Both."

"How fascinating!" he cried. "I should love to see your town, Miss Parish."

She turned astonished eyes on him. "Truly? But why? It is a very ordinary town."

"Not to me, Miss Parish. Not to me. A town full of mills? And boasting beam engines and all manner of delights? Yes, I should love to see it, to examine all those beam engines and watch them in action, for I must tell you that I have read about them, and heard them described in the minutest detail, but I cannot picture it in my mind's eye. I cannot understand how it all works — the pistons and valves and condensers and rods, the coal and water and steam. You see, I have all the terms at my fingertips, but I cannot *see* it. I need to see all the moving parts to truly understand it."

"Oh yes!" she said, smiling at him in a way that melted him inside in the most peculiar way. "To see one moving... yes, that is something indeed. But it is the *noise* that awes me most... the tremendous sound of such massive machinery, everything rising and falling, or turning, turning, great metal rods in constant motion and such sounds! The very ground shakes beneath one's feet. And the smell of smoke and the hissing of steam and— oh, such engines are magnificent, Mr Atherton, and my father's was the largest and most magnificent of all."

"Your father... he had a beam engine? A mill?"

"He did, and if he had lived for the three years he estimated it would take to pay back the loans and begin to make a profit, we should have been rich, and I should not be living in my uncle's house as the poor relation. But pray do not mention this to anyone, for Aunt Cathcart is ashamed of my father's occupation."

"But you are not?" he said gently.

"No! My father was a good man, an honest businessman. He may not have been a gentleman, but he was clever and hard-working, and he looked after his workers just as a gentleman looks after his servants and tenant farmers. He started as a manager in a small mill, and worked hard enough and invested shrewdly enough to become a mill owner himself, and I shall never be ashamed of him, *never!*"

7: Marriage In Mind

Once the shooting season started, Kent found himself inundated with invitations, or rather, his father received the invitations, and was minded to take Kent with him.

"Walter seems to spend all his time with Alfred Strong, learning about this Treasury position, and Eustace is never here," the earl said. "All my dependence is on you, Kent."

It would be a hard-hearted son indeed who would fail his own father, and besides, Kent enjoyed a day's shooting as much as any man. So he went out with his guns, and he continued with Eustace's little venture, and whenever he could, he rode with Miss Parish, the two talking endlessly about engines and mills and spinning jennies and all the little difficulties of operating a cotton mill, which he had never suspected. And more and more he wished he could go to Branton and see all these wonders for himself.

Sometimes Miss Parish drew neat little diagrams for him, but it never made things clearer.

One such ride ended early when a rain shower caught them out. Emily, Lucas and their groom turned directly back to Westwick Heights, but Kent escorted Miss Parish to Cathcart House and lifted her down from her horse.

"I am sorry our ride was cut short," he said, taking her hand to help her up the steps. "We will talk more of flying shuttles on our next outing, I hope."

"You truly are interested in this, are you not?" she said.

"I truly am, Miss Parish."

"Then you do not despise people like my father... mill-owners?"

"Heavens, no! Where would we be without men who make things? There is a virtue in the old ways, of hand-spinning and weaving, and some goods, like lace, are works of art in their own right, but using machines to speed the process and produce goods cheaper — that is a great benefit to society, is it not? It means that those with less money can still have warm clothes and blankets. No, I do not despise your father, Miss Parish. In fact, it is my ambition to be just such another as he was, if I can."

They had reached the top step, and Davis already had the front door open to receive Miss Parish, yet Kent was unwilling to relinquish her. He still held her hand, gazing at her lovely face as those clear eyes looked straight back at him. There was no deception in her, he realised, no artifice at all. She was exactly as she seemed to be, a straightforward, unassuming girl.

He raised her gloved hand to his lips. "Thank you for your company, Miss Parish."

And there for the first time that day was the blush and the lowered eyes. He collected his horse from the groom, mounted and, with a cheery wave to Miss Parish, rode off down the drive, quite delighted with her.

***

Katherine watched him go, the warm glow inside whenever she was with him making her smile. Such a lovely man, and if only— But there was no point pursuing that train of thought. She might be deeper in love with him with every meeting, but he had no such feelings for her, that she understood. Katherine had been courted with some intensity at Branton, and Mr Kent Atherton's casual friendship was nothing like that. Whole weeks might pass by when he made no effort to seek her out, and when he did, his conversation was all on the subject of machinery and manufacturing, with nothing personal about it at all.

As she turned to enter the house, she found Aunt Cathcart standing in the hall, an unreadable expression on her face.

"Aunt?" Katherine said uncertainly, wondering if she had inadvertently transgressed again.

"Were you riding alone with Mr Atherton?"

"No, aunt. Emily and Mr Lucas were with us until it came on to rain, but then Emily was anxious to get home."

"And Mr Kent very obligingly escorted you home. I see. Come, child, let us get you out of those wet clothes. Davis, send Marler up to Miss Katherine's room."

Katherine meekly followed her aunt upstairs, and allowed herself to be peeled out of her wet habit. When Daisy arrived, Aunt Cathcart thrust the habit and hat into her hands.

"Take that downstairs and see what you can do with it," Aunt Cathcart said. "I shall find a clean gown for my niece."

Daisy bobbed a curtsy and disappeared, while Aunt Cathcart rummaged through Katherine's gowns, emerging with a pretty blue muslin that was normally kept for visiting. She bustled about, fastening the buttons, and all the while keeping up a patter of seemingly innocuous questions. Did Mr Kent ride with them very often? Did he usually accompany Katherine home? Did she talk to him? What did they talk about?

Katherine hesitated over that one. She knew her aunt disliked any reference to her father's occupation, but she had to answer honestly.

"About Branton, mostly."

"Branton? What aspect of Branton?"

"The mills and manufactories," Katherine whispered.

"The *mills!* You talked to a gentleman about mills?"

"He asked me, aunt. He is interested in such things... machines of all kinds."

"Ah." She paused, a little frown on her face. "Come, sit down, child, and let me see if I can do something with this wet hair. You like Mr Kent, I think."

Katherine blushed, of course. Oh, her unruly cheeks were such a trial to her!

"Well, that is not so surprising," her aunt said. "He is very... gentlemanly. Naturally he is unfailingly courteous to you. He treats you exactly as he would treat Aveline... or any other lady."

"He is very kind," Katherine said in a low voice.

"Kind... yes, he is kind to you, out of respect for your uncle. But you must not allow your imagination to run away with the idea that his... his *kindness* means anything more than politeness."

"Oh, no, aunt! I would not... I have never... I have no expectation of... He is just being friendly."

"Precisely. After all, he is an earl's son, and just because his status has shifted somewhat of late, does not mean that he would look so low for a wife. He has not yet been formally presented at court, for he only came down from Cambridge last year and the family stayed at home this spring on account of the Dowager Countess, but next year, when Lady Olivia makes her come-out, Mr Kent will spend the full season in town. There he will meet the daughters of the nobility and that is where his wife will come from, when he chooses to marry."

"Yes, aunt. I understand."

"Ah, you are a good, sensible girl, Katherine, and you know not to set your sights on the moon. Aveline likes to flirt with him, of course, and he is good-natured enough to humour her, but he will never marry her, or any of my girls. They grew up together like brothers and sisters, and that is a high barrier to overcome. If ever he had developed a true affection for Aveline we should have seen it by now. She was wild to go riding with you sometimes for the chance of seeing him, but I would not let her. It is quite a waste of her time. Whereas you are a new face here, so there is always a possibility. That is why I throw no rub in the way of your friendship with Mr Kent, for if he *should* happen to fall in love with you... However, you must not get your hopes up, for I see no sign of it, and I dare say the earl would disapprove, so it is not to be thought of. And with only a thousand pounds to your name... you understand me, I am sure."

"Yes, aunt."

"Besides, if all he talks about is mills and such like, that does not sound very romantic. Next year, when Susan is old enough to venture into society, we shall all go to the assemblies at York... and Scarborough, too. We cannot aspire to London, but we shall find some way to show you off and find you a husband suitable to your station, you may be sure. There now, you look a little less bedraggled. I shall order some tea in the parlour. That will do you good. Come down whenever you are ready."

"Thank you, aunt."

Her aunt bustled out again, leaving Katherine in welcome solitude. The room was still filled with her aunt's strong perfume, so she opened a window to allow fresher air to penetrate. Then she returned to her dressing table, and unlocked the lowest drawer. From it, she drew forth her mother's prettily lacquered jewellery box. Inside there were three layers.

The top section contained the modestly unassuming pieces that Katherine wore regularly — simple crosses and pendants, a few pairs of ear drops, a bracelet or two. Beneath that, her mother's beautiful items that Katherine would wear for formal occasions when she married — a diamond set that dazzled in the sunlight, some garnets, a sapphire pendant, several hair ornaments. She tried them on sometimes, just for the pleasure of seeing and touching them, feeling the weight of each piece and the chill against her skin when she first put it on.

But below that was another, secret, layer. All it contained were the few coins she had managed to save over the years, no more than a hundred pounds or so, and the precious papers in Papa's hand. One contained the names and directions of the trustees of her mother's dowry, now hers, and there were letters of authority to the trustees and the bank, the records of her baptism and confirmation, and a copy of her parents' marriage settlement. These papers were all bound up together with red string, and she had never read them, but Papa had explained them to her when he had handed them over. It was two years ago, just as he was about to borrow a great deal of money to build the new mill.

"Katherine, your mother's money has always been set aside for you, but now that the bank is taking such a close interest in my financial affairs, I don't want there to be any confusion about what's yours and what's mine. Your grandfather always trusted me with your mother's money and made no conditions, but I never took so much as a penny piece from it, and now I've tied it all up in a trust fund so the bank can't get hold of it, no matter what."

"Is it a great deal of money, Papa? Am I rich?" she teased.

He laughed. "I'm sorry to disappoint you, but no. Just a modest amount and some investments, which have never brought in more than a few pounds a year, but it's yours, and I won't let anyone take it away from you. If ever you lose the papers and I am not here, you can go to Mr Monteath. He knows all about it. But don't tell anyone, sweetheart. It's our little secret, understand? I wouldn't want any fortune-hunters to think you're a worthwhile target. When you marry, make sure he wants you just for yourself."

She had counted the coins and gently lifted out the bundle of letters many times while the new mill was being built, and the beam engine and spinning machines installed. It was a comfort whenever there was a delay, or something cost more than expected, and her father's usually cheerful face wore a frown. Whatever the value of her trust fund and the jewellery itself, it would be something to help them to rebuild their life if the new mill should fail.

Now that hope was gone, but still she kept the secret and it reassured her that if ever life at Cathcart House became unbearable, she had the means to leave.

***

For Kent, kept busy by his father's need for company, by Eustace's little games and by his discussion of engines with Miss Parish, the summer quietly slipped away, but it was not without its share of surprises. If the idea of Walter, lazy, easy-going Walter who never exerted himself in the least, knuckling down to learn to be a man of numbers at the Treasury in London was astonishing enough, he managed to astonish his relations even more by betrothing himself to Winnie Strong. No one had the least objection to Winnie, a sensible good-hearted girl who had known Walter all her life, especially considering that his previous choice, the bouncy Bea Franklyn, had been the very opposite of sensible. Still, it was unexpected, that much was certain.

Then there was an even bigger shock, for quiet, bookish Cousin Bertram was betrothed to the not at all quiet or bookish Bea Franklyn. And the most curious element of all was that both these pairings turned out to be love matches, and the four of them drifted about with beatific smiles all day long.

Neither of these events managed to amaze the inhabitants of Birchall and Corland quite as much, however, as the news that a man had confessed to the murder of the earl's chaplain, Mr Arthur Nicholson.

"Do you know him, this Tom Shapman?" Kent asked Miss Parish, the next time they rode together. "He lives in Birchall. You might have bumped into a murderer any time you went into the village."

"I would not recognise him, no," she replied. "I know his little workshop, and sometimes when I passed by, the door was open and a man was in there, hard at work, but I never had any reason to go in or to speak to him. The sign on the door says that he is a woodworker and locksmith, so I suppose he was able to break into the castle. A locksmith could open any door, could he not?"

"A locked door, yes, but not one that was bolted on the inside," Kent said. "The main doors to the entrance hall had two locks and two bolts, and two butlers who swear they were all fastened, but at the basement level there are four doors, and no one is sure whether they were locked or bolted at all. There was a window with a broken latch, as well. It would not have taken the skills of a locksmith to enter the castle that night. Any random wanderer could have done it."

"But it was not a random wanderer, it was Tom Shapman, wood-worker and locksmith, and the real question, surely, is why? Why would a woodworker want to kill a chaplain?"

"Ah, now as to that, one might hazard a guess. Shapman wanted to marry Nicholson's daughter last year. Went to the castle in his best Sunday suit and asked Nicholson for permission, as bold as you please."

"I imagine the answer was somewhat brief," she said.

"And loud. Nicholson called him an insufferable puppy, as I recall, and other, less savoury, expressions. Ranted about it over the port until we were all sick of it."

"It does seem a little presumptuous."

"Well, Tess put him up to it, naturally. Cousin Tess is a wild spirit, Miss Parish, who goes her own way, regardless of the wishes of other people or even propriety, it has to be said. She will go her length one of these days, and even my father will not be able to save her."

"How old is Miss Nicholson?"

"Tess must be... let me see... twenty, I suppose."

"Then she will be of age in under a year and may marry wherever she pleases, even a woodworker and locksmith. Those few extra months of waiting are hardly worth killing for, I should have said."

"Precisely," Kent said, pleased by her quickness. "It makes no sense at all, and the funniest part is that Captain Edgerton is exceedingly cross about it."

"Cross that someone confessed? Surely he should be pleased?"

"But he is not at all pleased because he did not uncover the murderer himself. And also, I suspect, because he is not entirely convinced by this confession."

"But if the confession is false... it can only be because Mr Shapman is protecting the real murderer, and that could only be—"

"Tess," he said. "Precisely so. And although Tess is capable of almost any outrageous behaviour, even she would draw the line at murder of her own father, I suspect. But still, a confession has been made and so it must stand, and even Captain Edgerton cannot continue his investigations now. Did you ever have the misfortune to be interrogated by him?"

She laughed. "Not interrogated, no. He asked me very politely where I was on the night of the murder, and I told him that I dined at Westwick Heights that night, arrived home somewhat after one and fell, exhausted, into bed, where I stayed until eight or so the next morning. All of which he already knew, of course, since I was the last to be asked."

Kent chuckled. "Last but not least, Miss Parish."

"Oh, but I am," she said seriously. "I am very much the least in that household." But then she went on in more lively tones, "So what is to become of the good Captain now? Has he another murder to investigate?"

"Only a disappearance. Did you ever meet Miss Peach, Mrs Edgerton's companion?"

"Oh yes! She used to come to the rectory sewing afternoons sometimes. She always seemed like a rather bird-witted elderly lady, but I think she was a great deal sharper than she appeared, and was using the rectory gossip to gather information. Has she disappeared?"

"She has. Eustace was very scathing, as you may imagine. Not only has the captain failed to solve the murder, but now he has lost one of his own people — that sort of remark. Eustace can be rather cutting sometimes. But he gets around more than Father and I do, so he is going to look out for her."

"I hope nothing bad has happened to her," she said, frowning.

"So do we all," he said. "So do we all, Miss Parish."

***

O ne afternoon, Kent came in from a long day's shooting, muddied from head to toe and longing only for a bath and a good dinner, to find a note awaiting him.

'Atherton, Would you be so good as to call on me at Cathcart House when convenient. There is a matter I would discuss with you. Alan Cathcart.'

Kent was somewhat puzzled by this curious missive. Cathcart was a good sort of man, but not one with whom Kent generally had dealings, beyond the occasional social encounter. The family were included in the earl's circle of acquaintances, but as Cathcart was neither the owner of a sizeable estate nor a sporting man, there were no common interests to pull him into the orbit of the other gentlemen of the parish. It could only be to do with one of the ladies, but although Kent examined his conscience punctiliously, he could not recall any slight or insult of which he might be accused.

He would not know until he spoke to Cathcart, so he sent a brief reply that evening, to the effect that he would call at noon, if that suited him. Since he expected to be berated for something, even if he was not sure of the precise nature of the offence, he dressed with more than usual care that morning, and, since it was raining and he had no wish to appear mud-bespattered, took the carriage.

Cathcart was in his study. In fact, now that Kent thought about it, he suspected the fellow seldom left his own fireside, for he was an indolent man. It was a comfortable enough nest, several tables liberally covered with books, newspapers and journals, a desk with a row of wooden boxes for bills, letters and other papers, and a well-used leather chair beside the fire, a glass of wine resting on a table within easy reach.

"Ah, Atherton... yes, do come in. Thank you for coming so promptly. Very much obliged to you. A glass of something? Madeira or Canary? I have claret, if you prefer, or port or... or brandy? Or—?"

"Madeira, thank you. What was it you wished to discuss with me?"

"Well. An awkward business, Atherton." He stopped, throwing anxious glances at Kent. Then, taking a heavy breath as if he were about to dive into a deep lake, he said, "The thing is, Atherton, Mrs Cathcart is... a little troubled."

"Indeed?"

"Indeed. Troubled. For myself, I would not say anything about it... these things work themselves out for the best, one way or another, but... Mrs Cathcart feels that... and she is quite right, I am sure. One can never be too careful, can one?"

"I cannot say, sir, since I have not the privilege of understanding you as yet."

"Oh. Of course. It is my niece, you see."

"Miss Parish?" That got Kent's attention all of a sudden. "I hope nothing I have said or done has distressed Miss Parish. I should be sincerely sorry for it, if so."

"No, no! Far be it from me to imply any criticism. I would not dream... not the least thought of such a thing."

"She has made no complaint against me?"

"Heavens, no! Katherine is such a timid little thing, she never complains about anything. The difficulty is that she has led a very different life... a much more restricted one, and she has never met... well, anyone like you before. It is not surprising that she is a trifle dazzled by you."

"Dazzled by me? Is she?"

"Not to put too fine a point on it, she has developed a little *tendre* for you, so you see, if you were to pay her too much attention, you might be... drawn in, so to speak. Find yourself in deep waters, and if you should not wish to... erm, find yourself there... well, it might be awkward."

Kent huffed a breath. "You speak in riddles, sir. Please tell me in plain terms what it is you are trying to say, for I cannot tell whether your concern is for me or for her."

"Why, both, sir! Both. I should like to prevent my niece from disappointed dreams, and I should like to prevent you from stepping unwittingly into a marriage which you might regard as beneath you. Her father... well... difficult business, so the child has only a thousand pounds, at my discretion, and I can do no more for her. With your connections, you could do much better than that, so I would advise you to step with the greatest care around Katherine."

"So you think, do you," Kent said haughtily, "that if I occasionally ride with my cousins and Miss Parish, accompanied by two grooms, and if I should happen to have some conversation with her on these occasions, that she will insist on calling the banns? Is that it?"

"No, no! You misunderstand me, sir. Katherine herself would never... she is not a girl who would... but she might begin to have ideas, and to pin all her hopes of future happiness on you, and then you might feel obliged... you know how these things work. You could end up... and you might not wish... although of course, if you did wish, we should be delighted, naturally, although your father... Well, you understand me, I am sure." He chuckled. "Just a friendly word of warning, that is all, to tread carefully, Atherton."

Kent swallowed his ire, and smiled and bowed and thanked Cathcart with as much sincerity as he could muster. He hardly needed to be warned to take care in his dealings with Miss Parish. But was it true that she had a liking for him? How interesting! As he drove home, Kent wondered for the first time what it would be like to be married to a woman like that.

8: Ladies And Gentlemen

Cathcart's warning, well-meant as it was, had exactly the opposite effect from his intention. The suggestion that Katherine had developed a *tendre* for Kent was an intriguing one. He was used to young ladies eyeing him speculatively, and even flirting with him, but he had always suspected it was his status as the son of an earl which made him attractive to them.

Was it possible that Katherine genuinely liked him for himself... perhaps *loved* him? She blushed so dramatically in company that it was impossible to imagine that she preferred any one person above any other. But when he went riding with her... yes, she blushed, of course, and lowered her head in that sweetly shy way she had, but there were smiles, too. And such smiles! Eyes sparkling, she beamed at him so widely that he could not mistake her pleasure in his company.

For himself, he liked her, that much he would admit. Now that he had found a topic on which she was well-informed and interested, she was articulate and even blushed less readily. They had ridden together often enough that she was no longer shy with him, although he had not encountered her in formal society for some time. Perhaps at dinner engagements she would retreat into her shell again.

Was there anything beyond liking? He could not say. As for marriage, he had never thought much about it. Was love an essential prerequisite? His parents had always seemed to have the most casual affection, but now that their marriage was rendered invalid, Mother had gone away without a second thought, while Father quietly fell apart without her. His affection must be more deep-rooted than hers.

The other example at the castle, that of his Aunt Alice and the deceased Mr Nicholson, had been very different. Theirs was an abiding love which wrapped them so tightly in its embrace that they had little to spare, even for their own daughter. But then Aunt Alice had been blind since childhood, so her need for a supportive helpmeet was greater than usual.

Other married couples that came to his mind displayed little sign of any great affection beyond a friendly accommodation. Uncle George and Aunt Jane, Sir Hubert and Lady Strong and especially Lady Esther and Mr Franklyn were always polite to each other, and seemed to rub along pretty well, but was that love? Impossible to say.

Of Kent's own brothers and sisters, only Josie had had the glow of love in her eyes when she married Woodridge. Izzy's only glow had been for Farramont's title and position in society, and Walter had been downright neglectful of Bea Franklyn when he was betrothed to her. To be fair, Walter was certainly in a glow now over Winnie Strong, which was odd when they had known each other forever, and even Izzy looked more settled with Farramont after rampaging all over the country to escape him.

But these thoughts led him to one inescapable conclusion — that love was not an essential requirement before marriage might be considered.

In which case, why should he not marry Katherine Parish, if he were so minded?

So, by slow degrees, he began to wonder how his life might be improved if he had a gentle wife like Katherine, and children, in time, and a life that was not drifting away in idleness. Had his father not already proposed it?

He found his father in his study one day, standing by the window gazing unseeingly at the rain-heavy clouds, the trees tossed about with the first taste of autumn winds. The earl turned as he came in, and Kent was shocked at the bleakness in his father's face. It was beyond sorrow, verging on despair.

But as his eyes fell on Kent, his expression lightened into a smile. "Ah, Kent! Come in, come in, my boy! Pour yourself a drink, and you can top up my glass, too, if you would be so kind. Have you come about the brandy? Our stocks are somewhat depleted."

"We should have more in the next few days, and I will see that you get yours first. Father, I have been thinking about what you said to me once... that I should think about marrying."

His father's face lifted even more. "Excellent, excellent! It would be the making of you, you know, and you need not worry about money. You can bring your bride here. The guest suite could be made over to you, so she would have the tower room as a sitting room... a boudoir, as the ladies like to call it. And the nursery can soon be made ready for the little ones. How lovely that would be, to have children at the castle again." He sighed heavily, twirling his brandy glass in his hand.

"I suppose there would be no possibility of a separate establishment... Langley Villa, perhaps, since Walter will not need it now?"

The earl raised his brows. "That would be expensive, and of course that house was intended for Walter and the Franklyn girl, with her forty thousand pounds. One can employ a great many housemaids and footmen with money like that. Whereas I... I am not sure that I can afford the expense of another house. Nicholson squirrelled away a great deal of money that should properly have been mine, and now no one can find it, so... You see how it is, my boy? But plenty of room for you and your bride here. Have you settled on the lady? One of your Cambridge friends has a sister you admired when you visited, as I recall."

"I was thinking of Miss Parish."

"Miss Parish?" The earl sounded as incredulous as if he had named one of the rector's pudding-faced daughters, or Miss Prinkley, the village milliner. "Miss Parish, the girl who turns into a beetroot if anyone should happen to look at her and has not a word to say for herself? Miss Parish, who has not a penny to her name, and even the clothes on her back were paid for by her uncle? Is that the Miss Parish you mean? Not but what she is perfectly respectable, but I would have thought you might prefer someone more lively. She would be a shade too docile for my taste."

Kent only laughed. "She is shy of strangers, it is true, but she is perfectly conversable when one gets to know her."

"Is she, indeed," the earl said, sounding unconvinced. "Perfectly conversable... well, I have seen not the least sign of it, and if she expects to marry into *this* family, she will need to stop being shy of strangers pretty quickly, that is all I have to say about it. But if you have already spoken, then I suppose we must make the best of it."

"I am very far from having spoken, Father. Indeed, I have said not a word to her beyond the impersonal. The idea is in my mind, that is all, and so I mention it to you, but if you disapprove—"

"Do you like her?" the earl said, gazing intently at Kent.

An easy question to answer. "I do like her, yes."

"Do you like her enough to spend the rest of your life with her? Do you love her?"

Much more difficult questions. "That is what I should like to find out."

"Hmm. Let us have her here for dinner one night. Olivia is wild to start entertaining again, now that this Shapman fellow has confessed to the murder and your Aunt Alice has emerged from seclusion. We can have a few people to dine, and perhaps a bit of dancing afterwards, for those so minded. It will almost be like the old days, when your mother was here. I shall tell Alice and Olivia to start planning. And I shall expect to see some sign of this conversable Miss Parish, Kent, understand?"

Kent laughed. "I shall do my best, Father."

***

E ustace had word that there was to be a delivery within the next day or two, given that the moon was nearly gone and the night sky was clear. Kent's rôle on these occasions was more to support his brother than to participate directly, but he enjoyed keeping watch from the topmost room of the tower, peering eastward through the beautifully engineered telescope, admiring its elegant lines and wondering at the skill of its maker as the hours passed by.

One of the men came up shortly after midnight to bring Kent a pot of ale, cool from the cellar, and a plate of bread, cheese and ham for his supper.

"Lord, it's hot up here! Don't you find it stuffy, Mr Kent, sir?"

"It is a bit, but these windows are warped shut. Open the roof door, if you like. That will let a bit of air in."

He rattled the knob. "It's locked, sir."

"The key is in the lock."

"No, 'tisn't, sir."

"Really? Well, it should be." Ambling over to the door, his hands full of bread and cheese, Kent peered at the lock, then frowned. "How strange! I wonder who could have taken it? Maybe it is downstairs."

But no amount of searching discovered the missing key.

It was the second night before the train of pack ponies finally became visible on the horizon, winding their way across the moors from... well, Kent was not entirely sure where the barrels were first stored when they came ashore. Eustace probably had some idea, but he always said that the less everyone knew, the better.

"No one can let slip something unknown, after all," he said. "We all play a small part in the operation, with no need to know anything more than our own duties."

Kent had only asked once, and after that he simply did as Eustace bade him without comment. But it made him uneasy, all the same, and he wished once again that he could find some escape from Eustace's crazy scheme.

***

Katherine was happier than she had been since the dreadful day when Papa had died. No, that was not the worst day — that was when Mr Gray, the attorney, accompanied by both his brothers as well as Mr Humber and Mr Wentworth from the bank, had come to tell her, very gently, that all the mortgages were to be called in, and Katherine was not merely penniless, but homeless, too. That had been her lowest moment.

But now, she felt optimistic for the first time. She had gradually become accustomed to her new home, and some of the wearisome aspects that had depressed her spirits when she first arrived no longer troubled her. Her riding afternoons meant that she missed most of the dreary morning calls which Mrs Cathcart and Aveline undertook. Sometimes she was even allowed to stay at home when the rest of the family went out to evening engagements. She had her own lady's maid, and no longer had to wait for Jenny to attend to Susan and Lucinda first. Miss Harkness had realised she was not an uneducated peasant, and had stopped trying to instruct her. And to her great relief, Aveline no longer made pointed jibes at her, instead mostly ignoring her. They would probably never be great friends, but perhaps Aveline now saw that Katherine was not her rival in the quest for a husband.

Best of all, of course, she had the shivery joy of Mr Kent Atherton's company sometimes as she rode. It was not a regular occurrence, for he had many other calls on his time, but perhaps once a week he would be there waiting at Westwick Heights with Emily and Lucas, and then her heart skipped about in delight.

At first, he had only wanted to talk about beam engines and mill management and how her father had dealt with his workers, almost as if he planned to become a mill owner himself. But after a while, the conversation turned to other channels.

"Tell me about your house at Branton," he said one day. "It was very much smaller than Cathcart House, I imagine."

"It was narrower, certainly, but taller, so the number of rooms was not so different. More old-fashioned, of course. But that is not the greatest difference. At Branton, there were never more than four of us living there, and latterly only my father and me. We managed with only five servants. At Cathcart House, there are nine of us in the family, and I have no idea how many servants. It is so noisy, Mr Atherton! Sometimes I retreat to my room just to escape the tumult."

"Ah." He seemed to ponder that for a while, before saying, "Corland is not noisy like that. Perhaps it was, once, when all my brothers and sisters were at home. Six children and my parents, Aunt Alice, Uncle Nicholson and Tess — that is eleven, but it never seemed... *tumultuous*. I suppose the castle is so much bigger than even Cathcart House that it never seemed to be overpoweringly noisy, although I confess we spent a great deal of time outside, roaming the estate, and the Strongs' estate, too. But even indoors, one could always find a quiet corner to hide away, if one wanted, and now... the place feels empty."

"All those rooms for just a handful of people."

"True. More than thirty principal rooms, not counting ante-rooms, basements or attics. Would you enjoy living in such a place, do you think? If you had quiet corners to retreat to?"

She hesitated before answering. "I should not be comfortable in such a place, no. Cathcart House is not so very different from houses in Branton, and less imposing than some. The wealthiest mill owners and mercers and bankers lived in very large, ornate houses. But Corland Castle... that is a different matter. It is on an entirely different scale, as is fitting for his lordship's position in society. I do not feel entirely at ease in my uncle's house, for he is a gentleman and I am not a gentleman's daughter, but I should find your father's house overwhelming. I find the Franklyns' house overpowering, too. It is so... grandiose, I suppose, but then Lady Esther is a duke's daughter."

"It sounds to me as if what overpowers you is not the scale of these houses but the rank of the occupants. You must not be overawed by Lady Esther, or my father, either. They are mere mortals, beneath the carapace of superiority that nobility brings them."

"Oh, I know it, sir. Nevertheless, it is only fitting that I should respect their rank, and accord them due deference. For that reason, I do not like to be treated by my uncle and aunt as if I were another daughter. I should far prefer to make myself useful to them in some way — in the kitchens or the schoolroom, perhaps, but they will not hear of it. That is what overpowers me in society — that I am expected to be a *lady*, which I am not and never will be."

Mr Atherton laughed out loud. "Why, Miss Parish, you must not so denigrate yourself. You are far more of a lady than— Well, perhaps it is better not to name names, but believe me when I say that there is nothing about you that is in the slightest bit unladylike."

"Perhaps not, but one may behave in ladylike ways and still not be truly a lady, just as a man may behave in gentlemanlike ways even if he is not a gentleman."

"And there are gentlemen who behave in very ungentlemanlike ways, too," he said.

"Oh yes," she said, suddenly serious. "I have heard of some cases— But it is not a matter of behaviour, or appearance, either, for I certainly *look* like a lady, I will concede that much. My aunt has ensured that. It is a matter of birth, Mr Atherton. One cannot leave behind the circumstances of one's birth. Your father was born noble, my uncle was born a gentleman and that will never change. And I was born a mill-owner's daughter, and that can never change, either."

He halted his horse, so that Katherine was obliged to stop too. "Your logic is faulty," he said with a frown. "I was born noble, too — the Honourable Kent Atherton. Walter was Viscount Birtwell. Olivia was the Lady Olivia Atherton and is now plain Miss Atherton, although it pleases me that most people still address her by her former title. And now we are nothing... fatherless, in the eyes of the law. I am not even a gentleman any longer, if one wishes to be pedantic about it. Whereas you, Miss Parish, could marry a duke and hold higher rank than any of us."

That made Katherine laugh. "Yet I would still be a mill-owner's daughter, would I not? And everyone would know that. They might bow deeply and call me *'Your Grace'*, but they would know who I really am. Marry a duke! How absurd you are, Mr Atherton."

"And why should you not marry as high as you please?" he cried with such vehemence that his horse started into sudden motion. "You must marry *someone*, so why not a duke?"

"I doubt I shall ever marry," she said, rather breathlessly, for she had had to scramble to catch him up.

"But you would like to, one day, I am sure," he said. "Is that not what all women want, a husband?"

"Most of them need one," she said sharply. "The life of a spinster is not easy, and being a wife, particularly to a wealthy man—"

"Or a duke!"

"To a wealthy man, titled or not, is a more attractive prospect. What every woman wants, in fact, is financial security, which is what a husband provides."

"It is not all he provides, surely? What about affection? Respect? Kindness? Generosity? Like-minded companionship? A comfortable home?"

"Certainly, but mostly a good character. That is vital, to my mind. A good husband is a man who has absolute integrity. He must be both honest and trustworthy, for there should be no secrets between husband and wife, and no shady corners of his public life, either. And more than that, he must be a good Christian, and accord God His proper place."

He was silent for a moment, his face unusually serious. "Prayer... there must be prayer. That is what you mean, is it not?"

"Prayers, yes, on a daily basis, but also regular attendance at church, not merely the great festivals, and reading suitable works to improve one's understanding of the church's teachings. One should always strive to improve oneself, Mr Atherton. Do you not agree?"

"Yes. Yes, I do, Miss Parish. Heavens, Emily and Lucas are entirely out of sight. Shall we see if we can coax your mount to a little more speed?"

"We can try," she said.

9: An Invitation

This conversation powerfully affected Kent. If he were to have any chance of marrying Katherine, then he needed to be the kind of man she wanted... the kind she deserved, and honesty compelled him to admit that he fell short in several aspects. Praying... he did not pray nearly enough, or go to church very often. In fact, since Nicholson had died and his little services in the castle chapel had ceased, Kent had rarely attended church at all. In that, he was no different from many others of his class, and no one thought any the worse of him for it. Except Katherine, of course. Perhaps her religious bent was a little too zealous, but it would do him no harm to improve his own observances.

As for honesty and integrity... he thought he was as honest as most people. He did not lie or cheat, he was respectful towards women, and he treated servants and tradesmen fairly. At this point the smuggling enterprise rose unbidden in his mind, and how easy it was to justify in his own mind! Yes, it was not strictly legal, but, as Eustace tirelessly pointed out, everyone benefited by it. The gentry and local inns were supplied with good, cheap brandy, the smugglers themselves made a little money from it and only the Excise men lost out by way of collecting a little less duty than they should have done. So he reasoned with himself, and ruthlessly suppressed the twinges of conscience that assailed him now and then.

And it was fun, he had to admit that. There was little enough for an active young man to do, so remote as Corland was situated, so how could he resist the chance for a little excitement now and then, with the added amusement of putting one over on the Excise men. If he could not go to Birmingham and learn about engines, then he would just have to find entertainment nearer to home.

Besides, just now he had no inclination to leave home at all. His rides with Katherine, and the delicate business of drawing her out of her shell and wondering whether he should marry her, kept any regrets for Birmingham at bay. And since Olivia had taken up the idea of a dinner with dancing afterwards, Kent was determined to show Katherine off to advantage in front of his father.

"I shall see you on Friday night, of course," he said casually one day as they drew near to Birchall again after a ride.

"Friday night?"

"This dinner that Olivia is organising. The Cathcarts are invited... everyone for miles around is invited."

"Oh, that. I was invited, but I have declined."

"Declined? But why? There will be no one sensible to talk to if you are not there."

The colour bloomed in her cheeks but she answered composedly. "You are very kind to say so, sir, but you know I am not comfortable in such company."

"Does your aunt wish you not to go? Or your cousin? Miss Cathcart can be... capricious, sometimes."

"Oh, no, no! It is my own wish! I told my aunt when I first came here that I did not wish to move in the grand society that prevails here, and although at first she insisted, she has come to see that I was right and no longer presses me."

"Then it falls to me to press you instead. Miss Parish, you will not overcome your shyness in society if you never leave your own hearth. May I entreat you to be of the company on Friday? I shall undertake to sit beside you at table and carry the conversation single-handed if you prefer not to speak."

She smiled a little wanly. "How kind you are, but I must decline."

Kent could feel his face falling. He had not realised until that moment how much he had depended on seeing her there. "There will be no pleasure in the evening if you are not there," he said glumly.

"I believe you exaggerate, sir."

"No, indeed, for if I cannot depend on you to protect me, your cousin will attach herself to me like a limpet, and there will be no getting rid of her. Since there is to be dancing as well, I shall not even be able to escape to the safety of the card table."

Colour flared in her cheeks again, and this time there was a definite chill in her voice. "Mr Atherton, you are cruel to tease me in this way."

"Tease you? No, no, I do not mean to tease you. Pray forgive me if I have offended you, but I speak the absolute truth. Do but consider my doleful situation, Miss Parish. I am obliged by my position as a young, unmarried male to do the pretty to young, unmarried females. Normally, this makes such evenings an exercise in tedium, and listening to an endless stream of inanities on the subject of bonnets and lace and ribbons and then more bonnets. What is it about bonnets that so fascinates girls of that age? And why should they suppose that the subject is of the slightest interest to me? But with you, Miss Parish, I can spend the evening talking about beam engines and the price of wool and brown lung disease and... oh, a thousand other subjects far more interesting than bonnets."

She threw him an amused glance. "Perhaps I am interested in bonnets, too, Mr Atherton."

"Ah. Now I am appropriately chastened, for I have never asked you about bonnets, have I? Very well. If you will dine at Corland Castle on Friday, I shall pledge myself to talk about bonnets all night, if that would please you."

She burst out laughing. "No, no! That would indeed be too tedious for words. I should sooner talk about... oh, almost anything. The Duke of Portland, the French alliance with Russia, the Oystermouth Railway... you do not know about the Oystermouth Railway? Then that is what we shall talk about on Friday."

A burst of happiness ran through him. "Then you will come?"

"I will come, but no dancing, if you please. I do not dance."

"Why not, when you have all the requisite limbs and lungs for the exercise? You are out of mourning, after all."

"I do not know the steps."

"Does no one dance in Branton? Are there no balls, no assemblies, no carpets enthusiastically rolled up on a whim?"

"Of course, but it is only simple country dances and reels and the like. I have never been taught the elegant movements of your sort of dance. I love to watch, but that is all."

"But if there were to be a reel... would you dance a reel with me? Please?"

There was the blush again, and the delicately lowered eyes, but he thought she seemed pleased. "If there is a reel, and... and if you should ask me, then yes, I would."

He cheered so loudly that his horse half reared in alarm, and he was hard pressed to control it.

***

K atherine was so bubbling with happiness after this exchange that she could not wait to inform Aunt Cathcart of her change of plan. Learning from Davis that her aunt was in the still room, she went straight there.

"Aunt, I have been thinking about the invitation from Corland for Friday, and if it will not be too much trouble, I should like to go after all."

Her aunt looked up from the jar she was examining, and said expressionlessly, "It is too late for that. I have already sent my response, refusing on your behalf, and undoubtedly Lady Alice has now made alternative arrangements. There is a deal of planning goes into an occasion like this, and it would be such an inconvenience if guests were to change their minds whenever they liked."

Katherine's excitement drained away in an instant. "Oh. Of course. I beg your pardon."

Her aunt smiled at her. "There now, do not look so sorry for yourself. You cannot know, brought up in the casual way that you were, how things are done in a more superior society. There will be other invitations, I make no doubt."

Bobbing a quick curtsy, Katherine crept away to her room and sent for Daisy to help her out of her riding habit. How stupid of her to imagine that she could simply change her mind. In Branton, no one would have minded a bit — in fact they would have said how glad they were that she could come after all. But she was not in Branton any longer, and must play by different, stricter, rules now. Lady Alice had no doubt already invited someone else to fill her place.

It was a pity she had listened to Mr Kent Atherton. Had she been more circumspect, she would have said that she would ask her aunt... could not say for sure... and such like. Instead, she had as good as promised, and now she would not be there and what would he think of her then?

Could she possibly get word to him that she would not be there? She could not write to Mr Atherton herself, but a note to Lady Alice... or Lady Olivia, perhaps? But how presumptuous of her that would be, when her acquaintance was of the slightest, and they were so far above her in rank. She could have wept to have all her hopes crushed in an instant.

But Aunt Cathcart was not a person to let go of a subject, and especially not when there was a possibility of instructing Katherine in the ways of her betters. When they were all gathered at the dinner table that evening, she related the story to the entire family, not to mention the butler and footmen standing impassively in the background. Katherine was mortified to be so publicly discussed, but her aunt was impervious.

"I suppose she wants to see Mr Kent Atherton," Aveline said waspishly. "She is violently in love with him, after all."

"Enough," Uncle Cathcart said, frowning at her. "Such personal remarks ill become you, Aveline, nor is this discussion a fit topic for the dinner table."

It was not clear whether this latter comment was aimed solely at Aveline, or whether it encompassed Aunt Cathcart too, but she looked dismayed and turned to more general subjects while they ate. But when the servants had withdrawn, Uncle Cathcart resurrected the matter himself.

"I am sorry that you should not be able to accompany us on Friday, niece," he said, with a gentle smile in Katherine's direction. "It would do you good to mingle more with our neighbours, but I suppose we must not insist on overthrowing all their plans at this late stage."

Surprisingly, it was James who came to Katherine's defence. "Well, I do not see why she should not go, if she wishes it," he said stoutly. "The Athertons are not fussy about numbers — the earl likes to invite as many people as can be squeezed in, so one more is neither here nor there."

"But I have already sent Katherine's refusal," Aunt Cathcart said.

"You could write to ask if Cousin Kate can be accommodated at this late stage," James said. "With suitable apologies, naturally."

"You do not appreciate how abominably rude it is to expect others to bend to every passing whim," Aunt Cathcart said.

"It is not an expectation if one asks politely," James said robustly. "Lady Alice can say no if she wishes, but she might say yes."

"Really, James, must you argue with me on every point?" Aunt Cathcart said. "You must take my word for it that such behaviour is simply not done. Whatever would people think of us if we change our minds every time the wind blows?"

"But Cousin Kate was riding today with Emily, Lucas and Kent Atherton, and no doubt they expect to see her there, and look forward to her company, so friendly as they all are now."

"Is that so, Katherine?" Uncle Cathcart said gently.

Speech was entirely beyond her, but she was able to nod her head, for James was not so far out in his supposition.

Aunt Cathcart glowered at him, and would have rebutted his point at once, but Uncle Cathcart held up one hand.

"Even so, I believe we must accept your mother's greater experience in such matters, James," he said. "No more of this, if you please."

Katherine bowed her head and said nothing, glad when Aunt Cathcart rose to lead the ladies to the saloon and she was able to retreat into her music until the gentlemen joined them. James, Alex and Neil drew her into a game of whist after that, and kept up a light patter of amusing anecdotes until she was able to retreat to her room and the solitude that brought only anguished thoughts. Her prayers that night were impassioned, and it was many hours before she was composed enough to sleep at last.

The morning, however, brought a new perspective, for not long after noon, a carriage emblazoned with the earl's coat of arms arrived bearing the Lady Olivia Atherton.

"I am come to beg for Miss Parish to favour us with her company on Friday," she said as soon as she had sat down. "Kent tells me that there was some discussion on the subject yesterday, and Miss Parish expressed a desire to attend, but now I find that there is a refusal set against her name on Aunt Alice's list. I hope, therefore, that you will change your mind, Miss Parish, for I assure you, I am quite determined that you should come, and no answer will satisfy me but a positive one. What do you say? Will you honour us with your company?"

Katherine threw a desperate glance at Aunt Cathcart, but was astonished to find her smiling broadly.

"Of course Katherine will come! She would be delighted, will you not, dear?"

"Yes, I—"

"Some confusion arose, but it is a relief to have the matter cleared up. Yes, we shall all be there on Friday. Should you care for some tea, Lady Olivia? And perhaps a slice of cake?"

"How very kind! I might just manage a little something."

Katherine said nothing, but exhilaration bubbled up inside her. She was to go after all! How kind of Lady Olivia to visit, specifically to reissue the invitation. And yet... surely it must be Mr Kent's doing? He would have asked Lady Olivia to call, knowing that such an appeal could not be refused. Even Aunt Cathcart could not stop Katherine from attending when the earl's daughter herself insisted on it.

The first matter to be settled was what she should wear. Aveline's gown had already been settled — she was to wear pink with a spangled net over-gown and heavy trimming on bodice and hem. Katherine determined at once that she would go in a different direction. Her new gowns, chosen for her by Aunt Cathcart, were very much in the same style, but her Branton gowns, most of them still languishing in their travel box in a corner of her room, were plainer and more in keeping with her more reticent character.

She drew out two that appealed to her, a pale green silk with elegant sleeves and a delicately embroidered bodice, and a pretty cream satin with a net overskirt embroidered with tiny rosebuds in palest pink.

"What do you think, Daisy?" she said, when the maid came to dress her for dinner, holding both against her. "Which one for Corland Castle on Friday?"

"The green," the girl said at once. "It picks up something in your eyes."

"Does it? But my eyes are brown!"

"No, there's green in them, too, miss, and that gown's so clever — the way it's all folded over round the— well, at the top there."

"The bodice," Katherine said. "That part is the bodice. Very well, the green it is. You know how to press silk?"

"I'll ask Miss Rathbone. She's a bit sniffy about the likes of me pretending to be a lady's maid but she'll explain things if I ask nice. She's taught me ever so much."

"You are getting on very well, Daisy," Katherine said. "Do you like it here?"

"Ooh, yes, miss. I have me own room which I've never had before, and so much food to eat I'm sure I'll get as fat as a pig."

Katherine could not help laughing at this image. "I am sure all the running up and down stairs will keep you slim. And is your conscience troubling you less now?"

"Conscience, miss?"

"Remember when we first met? You were in great distress because of some untruth you had told."

"Oh... that. It don't bother me no more, miss."

She looked a little conscious, so Katherine forbore to ask about it any further. Apart from reminding the girl to say her prayers each day and ensuring that she went to church, she could only trust to time and the girl's own sense of morality to bring her to the point of confessing her sin.

Katherine had expected Aunt Cathcart to try to impose her own choice of gown on her, but nothing at all was said and so she descended the stairs on Friday in the green silk, quite without hindrance. She had dressed her hair with ribbons of the same material, interspersed with tiny silk flowers, and wore only her mother's silver cross at her throat, just as she had done many times at Branton but never before here. Aunt Cathcart's eyebrows rose as she looked Katherine up and down assessingly, but she made no comment. It was Aveline who giggled.

"That must be one of your Branton fashions, cousin."

"Katherine looks very well," Uncle Cathcart said repressively.

James was one of the last down. "Here we all are, ready for a night of pleasure." His eyes fell on Katherine, and his face lit up in a most unexpected way. "Well! You look delightful, Cousin Kate. What an elegant gown."

"But very plain," Aveline spat.

Happily for Katherine's blushes, the carriage drew up at the door just then, ready to take the first group of revellers to the castle, and in the bustle of donning evening cloaks and getting themselves out to the carriage door, nothing more was said. The first journey was to take Uncle and Aunt Cathcart, Aveline and Katherine, with the three young men following later. Katherine, naturally, was the last to ascend the steps, but as she did so, James materialised by her side and offered his hand to help her into the carriage.

"I shall see you again very soon," he said, and there was that glow in his eyes that she had seen before. That would never do! Katherine dropped her gaze and squeezed herself into the small space that Aveline had left for her. James folded away the steps, closed the door and called to the coachman, and in moments they were rolling away down the drive and into the blessed darkness that hid Katherine's flaming cheeks.

10 : An Evening At Corland Castle

A long string of carriages snaked up the drive to Corland Castle. The Cathcart conveyance stopped in its turn and disgorged its occupants. Katherine followed the others across the bridge and into the entrance hall, lit up as bright as day with hundreds of candles. There they were greeted by the earl, Lady Alice and Lady Olivia.

"So glad you could come after all, Miss Parish," the earl murmured.

"Thank you," Katherine whispered. "So glad to be here."

Then, with a great press of people following behind them, they moved on, the ladies to one ante-chamber to deposit their cloaks, and the gentlemen to another to leave their hats. On again to the great hall with its high glass roof, already busy with chattering groups, the ladies' gowns shimmering as they moved, jewelled bracelets sparkling in the candlelight with every gesture.

Aunt Cathcart and Aveline whisked off to greet friends at once, but Katherine took a moment to look around. At her first visit to Corland Castle not long after her arrival, she had been overwhelmed by the scale of the place, the great branching staircase, the massive chandelier suspended on a long chain from the roof and the walls covered with a multitude of fearsome weaponry. It was an appropriate home for an earl descended from a long line of earls and barons stretching back to the middle ages, men loyal to long dead kings, wielding those great swords with determination against equally ferocious opponents.

Now she could look around and see the castle as the backdrop it was, like the scenery on a stage. People did the same in Branton, like Mr Ridwell, whose vast new house proclaimed him a man of great wealth, if not much taste. Katherine's own home had been less ostentatious, but each item of furniture, every picture or clock or carpet, had been carefully chosen by her mother with her impeccable sense of style.

At Corland, there was a great sense of history. Even the staircase was adorned with a dull display of armour and weapons, although she admired the two large urns in the Chinese style that flanked them. Elsewhere, however, the furnishings were modern, both tasteful and elegant, the rooms decorated in a pleasingly restrained manner. She could see it now as a home as well as a statement of wealth and power.

There was another difference, too, between her first visit and this one. Then, she had known no one but the Cathcarts, and even they were new to her. Elsewhere there was only a sea of unknown faces. Now, she recognised many of those pouring into the great hall. Near the stairs was pleasant Sir Hubert Strong, the magistrate, and some of his family. By the door to the gallery was the imperious Lady Esther Franklyn and her fashionable husband. Near the dining room was sweet Mrs George Atherton, fussing over her daughters' shawls in case there may be the least draught. Emily waved cheerfully to Katherine. And over there was Mr Walter Atherton, and beside him—

Her heart jumped painfully, for there he was, Mr Kent Atherton, looking impossibly fine in his well fitted evening attire. He had not the muscular build of his brother, but she thought she preferred Kent's slender good looks. His shoulders were broad enough, his waist narrow enough, his calves shapely enough, without the overpowering masculinity that some men had that made her wilt like a plucked bluebell in its presence. Kent was reassuringly male, but not intimidating, even to someone as shy in company as Katherine.

He looked across the room, he saw her and his face lit up in that warm smile that instantly had her insides turning somersaults. She blushed, of course, because she always blushed, but she no longer lowered her gaze as if turning away from him. She *wanted* to look at him, to watch what he did, to glory in the fact that, after a quick word to his brother, he ploughed through the crowds straight to her side.

"Miss Parish! Now the evening is set fair, with your presence. And how delightful you look! That is a new gown, I think. I have not seen you in anything quite so becoming before."

That made her blush even more — what a charming compliment! But she thanked him very composedly. Before she could say another word, Aveline materialised at her side.

"Why, Mr Atherton! There you are! Where have you been hiding, for I could not see you at all at first?"

"Not hiding, Miss Cathcart, merely standing beside my brother Walter. No one notices me when he is in the room."

He grinned widely at her to signal the jest, but she took him seriously.

"There you are quite wrong, sir," she said archly, tapping him with her fan.

"No, no!" he protested. "He is a great handsome fellow, and casts me quite into the shade. Now, if I were a fashionable fribble, and wore shirt points high enough and sharp enough to put an eye out with an unwary move, and dazzled the room with a dozen fobs at my waist and a diamond pin in my cravat, why then I might attract attention, but for myself, I eschew all such ostentation. I prefer simplicity in all things, Miss Cathcart, that is my watchword."

"Oh, indeed, and so do I," she cried, quite oblivious to the frills and flounces and multitude of ornamentation on her dress. "Simplicity is always preferred to... to..."

"Ostentation," he said, with a twitch of his lips. "Then we are of one mind. How splendid! What a wonderful world it would be if every two people were so admirably in accord. Why, there would be no arguments, no discussions... in fact, one might dispense with conversation altogether. You brighten my life immensely, Miss Cathcart."

"Why, thank you, sir!" she trilled happily. "Oh look, the earl and his ladies are joining us. That must mean dinner will soon be served. How glad I shall be to sit down and enjoy the meal. You have a very good cook here, Mr Atherton."

She rested one hand on his arm, quite casually, as if completely unaware of it, but in effect claiming him as her dinner companion. Katherine saw it, but was helpless to intervene. How would he react? Would he feel obliged to lead her into dinner?

He looked down at the offending hand, his face puzzled. "Dear me! Are you unwell, Miss Cathcart?"

"Unwell? Why, no, never better, sir. Why should you think otherwise?"

"You grabbed my arm so suddenly I was concerned that you might be feeling faint. Miss Parish, have you any smelling salts about you? I believe they might aid Miss Cathcart at this moment."

"Yes, indeed I do," she said, reaching into her reticule. "They are very efficacious."

Angrily, Aveline withdrew her hand. "Do not concern yourself, cousin. I am perfectly well and have no need for your smelling salts."

"What a relief!" Kent said cheerfully. "Ah, there is Simpson now. It is time for dinner. Miss Parish, may I escort you into the dining room?"

Aveline glowered even more. "Why are you taking *Katherine* in? Would you not prefer to sit with someone you can talk to?"

"An interesting question, Miss Cathcart. Who did you have in mind as a more entertaining dinner companion for me?"

He tipped his head on one side enquiringly. Katherine waited to see if Aveline was brash enough to respond in the obvious way. Surely she had a modicum of restraint that would prevent her from putting herself forward?

With a giggle, she lowered her head with seeming demureness. "I am sure you can think of someone, sir."

"Indeed, I assure you I cannot."

"Well... I do not like to... but you know Katherine never talks at all in company, so it is of no consequence who she sits beside. Whereas I... I do not like to boast, but I can converse very readily."

"What a happy talent to have! And on what subject would you entertain me?" he said, still smiling.

"Oh... anything you like. What would you like to talk about?" The hand made its way onto his arm again, seeing success within sight.

"The Oystermouth Railway," he said at once.

"*What?* What on earth do you imagine I know about that?"

"Nothing, I should suppose, and nor do I, but Miss Parish does, and she has promised to tell me all about it this evening." Gently detaching Aveline's hand and ignoring her chagrin, he held out his arm to Katherine. "Shall we, Miss Parish? You had better make haste, Miss Cathcart, for most of the ladies have already gone in."

She scuttled away, scowling, while Kent murmured, "I should not tease her, I suppose. She is a good sort of girl, even if she knows nothing about the Oystermouth Railway."

Katherine quite agreed that even Aveline, trying as she was, did not deserve to be teased, and recognised that her own satisfaction in this small triumph over her cousin was equally reprehensible. Yet somehow, these thoughts did not cast her down as they might otherwise have done. Later, perhaps, she would consider the matter more fully, but for now all she could think about was that she was to dine beside the man she loved with all her heart. Two hours of his company, perhaps, and not jostled about on horseback, but sitting in comfort beside him, just as if they were true friends... or more than friends. It was a boon too overwhelming for words.

She took his arm, glowing inside to be chosen by him above Aveline... above all other ladies! It was astonishing, but she was not so foolish as to be carried away with unrealistic hopes. His interest was still on machinery, and her greater knowledge of such things. But that did not matter. She would tell him about the Oystermouth Railway, and for an hour or two she would have his undivided attention, and enough memories to warm her through many a dark hour in the future when he was not with her.

They had not taken two steps towards the dining room, and were almost the last to make their way there, when the earl emerged, a frown on his face which lifted when he saw them.

"Well done, Kent. I was just coming to find Miss Parish. Will you honour me with your company at dinner this evening, madam? You have been a part of the neighbourhood for some months now and I should like to become better acquainted with you."

Katherine hardly knew how to respond to this. One could scarcely refuse an earl, naturally, but she had so looked forward to sitting beside Kent. She threw him a desperate glance, but it was the earl who rescued her.

"Yes, yes, Kent may sit on your other side, you know, and between the two of us, we shall look after you very well, you may be sure."

Thus it was that Katherine found herself, to her own amazement and that of the watching Cathcarts, led to the far end of the table, to sit at the left hand of the earl himself, with Kent on her other side. Aveline glowered at her from her position in the middle of the table, but James, a little nearer, beamed at her and waved encouragingly.

Katherine hardly knew what she ate or drank that night. All she was aware of was Kent beside her, his arm only inches from her own, for the dining table was crowded rather, his eyes gazing into hers with an intensity that left her breathless. Always his wide smile and cheerful demeanour lifted her spirits, but this was something more, something almost ecstatic inside her, welling up like a spring, pulsing pure happiness through her veins.

Sometimes the earl drew her attention, to offer her some choice dish, or to ask her a question, but she could not say that she acquitted herself very well. With the son, the words poured out of her unstoppably, without the slightest effort, but with his father, she stuttered and hesitated and mumbled, reduced sometimes to monosyllabic answers.

It was frustrating, for her as much as for the earl, but she could find no point of contact with him. Where Kent asked her about Branton and mills and all the familiar sights of home, the earl questioned her on balls and gowns and horses, none of which subjects fired her with enthusiasm. At one point, he touched on music and she grew temporarily loquacious, but after determining that he could not distinguish Bach from Mozart, she fell back, defeated.

And if he could find no subject of interest to her, she could think of none for him. Whatever did earls think about or worry about? She dared not talk about politics, for he was bound to be of a different persuasion from her father and his friends, and she knew nothing about estate management or riding to hounds or the sports prevailing amongst the aristocracy. The only time she raised a response from him was when she asked after his mother, the ailing Dowager, and his wife, the absent Countess. Then his face melted into sorrow, and he shook his head dolefully.

"I wish either of them, or preferably both, were sitting at this table just now," he said in a low voice. "I miss their wisdom. We men... we cannot do without our women to guide us, Miss Parish. It is a great grief to me that I have not the two most important women in my life beside me now, when we are in such trouble."

Katherine murmured something, although she hardly knew what, for her heart was filled with grief for her father all over again. The earl might miss his mother and his wife, but Katherine desperately missed her father, with his easy-going approach to life. In some ways, he was very like Kent, in that nothing daunted him. He had planned his businesses with the utmost care, and left no detail unconsidered, but he accepted the vagaries of life without complaint. When one of his earliest mills had burnt to the ground, putting their financial affairs in great peril, he had merely shrugged and said it was only bricks and wood and cotton, and at least there had been no loss of life.

Two courses came and went, the cloths were cleared and dessert laid out and yet Katherine noticed none of it. It was only when chairs were pushed back and everyone started to rise that she realised that the ladies were departing for the drawing room. The gentlemen all stood and bowed as they left, and abruptly Katherine was cut adrift from the pleasure of Kent's company, finding herself in a sea of soft feminine voices, and the swish of silk skirts and ivory fans.

She found a corner near the instrument to hide herself away, and was relieved that no one came near her until Lady Alice asked for the instrument to be opened. Then, Aveline's clear voice rose above the murmur of conversation.

"Katherine will play. She would rather play than talk."

Lady Alice spoke quietly to Mrs George Atherton, who sat beside her, and that lady rose and came towards Katherine.

"Miss Parish, Lady Alice has charged me to enquire if you would oblige us with a little music while we await the tea things. She was delighted with your performance the last time you were here."

Katherine readily agreed to it. For once, Aveline was doing her a favour, for she would indeed rather play than talk, at least while Kent Atherton was not there to talk to. She settled at the pianoforte and began a gentle piece that would not overwhelm the many quiet conversations around the room. After a second piece she paused, sure that someone else would want to take over, but when no one volunteered she began a third piece. It was pure pleasure for her, for the instrument was an excellent one, superior to the one at Cathcart House, and she had no desire to surrender it yet awhile.

Eventually the gentlemen began to drift in, and at once Lady Olivia called for the carpets to be rolled up and dancing to begin. Those wishing to play cards were directed to the library, and the parlour adjoining the drawing room was available for quiet conversation, but the drawing room was to be given over to the dancers.

Katherine rose from the instrument and retreated to her corner, but after a few minutes, Lady Olivia found her there.

"Miss Parish, would it be very presumptuous of me to ask you to return to the instrument? I had arranged for Mrs Dewar to play for the dancers, but she has not yet arrived and it would be such a shame to delay our enjoyment for a moment longer than necessary. But you have played so splendidly for us already, so if your fingers are quite worn out, I shall beg your pardon and leave you in peace. I can always play myself, if need be."

"No, indeed, I should be delighted to provide the dance music," Katherine said. "There is nothing I enjoy more than playing, and I can continue all night if need be. If Mrs Dewar arrives, she may dance herself, if she chooses. But what would you have me play first?"

"The music is all set out in order over here," she said, gathering a pile of papers from a side table and carrying them to the instrument. "I am sure there is nothing in there that will give you the least trouble."

"Ah, yes, I know all these," Katherine said, swiftly leafing through them. "Just give the word when you are ready to begin. Enjoy your dancing, my lady."

She gave a brilliant smile. "I shall! Oh, I certainly shall!"

Katherine was accustomed to being ignored as she played for those dancing. For musical performances, a performer might be listened to attentively, or joined at the instrument by someone wanting to sing, but when the company is caught up in the enchantment of the dance, the musician is treated as if she is not even there.

Not tonight, however. Her cousin James danced once with Lady Olivia and once with Miss Strong, but the rest of the time he sat near Katherine, watching her play, complimenting her performance and jumping up to help her find the next piece between dances. Fortunately, he did not attempt to turn the pages for her, which would have been nothing but a distraction, when she knew every piece by heart already, but she wondered greatly what he meant by such attentions.

At first, there were only three couples dancing, but gradually more joined in. Kent, one of the last of the gentlemen to return, danced first with Emily's older sister, Julia, and then her younger sister, Penelope. Then it was Miss Franklyn, followed by Miss Strong. After that, since the Dewars had now arrived, he danced with one of the Dewar sisters. Katherine watched it all surreptitiously, noting Aveline's increasing annoyance at being repeatedly overlooked, and Kent's cheerful manner of completely ignoring her. It was not that she lacked partners, for she stood up for every dance, but the one she wanted eluded her.

After that, as Katherine was reaching for the next piece of music, Lady Olivia approached her again.

"A little change, Miss Parish. I am to play the next, and you are to dance."

"Oh no, I do not dance."

"I am assured that you do indeed dance if it is a reel, and lo, the next is indeed a reel, you see." Triumphantly she waved the music at Katherine. "Look, your partner awaits you."

And there was Kent, holding out his hand to her and smiling, smiling... and behind him, Lucas and Emily, urging her to make up a set with them.

"I cannot wait to see you dance, my dear friend!" Emily cried.

Katherine was scarlet with embarrassment, but how could she resist the combined entreaties of all of them, and especially that warm smile? She ceded the instrument to Lady Olivia, and allowed herself to be led onto the floor and take up the proper position as the opening was played. And then she danced, and the happy faces of her companions brought reward enough for her bravery.

A reel was not the most challenging of dances, for the steps and movements were simple, and many despised it for that reason. Only one other group joined them in the dance. From the side of the room, Aveline glared angrily at her, but Katherine did not care. She could not remember a time, even in Branton, when she had been happier, and she could not suppress her own joyful smile as she wove in and out, spun and turned, savouring every second of the experience.

Whatever happened after, this moment was one she would never, ever forget.

11: An Unexpected Move

It was not to be supposed that Katherine's dance would be allowed to pass without comment, and Aveline began as soon as they were seated in the carriage.

"Mama, I hope you will give Katherine a little hint that a reel is not a ladylike dance. I trust I should never make such a spectacle of myself."

"What is this?" Uncle Cathcart said, rousing from a half-dozing state. "Katherine dancing? I am sorry now that I was tucked away in the library, for I should dearly have liked to see such a thing."

"It was a *reel*, Papa," Aveline said. "Mama always tells us that we should never participate in such an uncouth dance."

"If it is danced at Corland Castle, there cannot be anything wrong with it. Was your partner agreeable, Katherine?"

"Oh yes, sir. Most agreeable."

"And who was he?"

"Mr Kent Atherton, sir." And then, because she did not wish to make too much of Kent's participation, she added, "We danced with Miss Emily Atherton and Mr Lucas Atherton, and Lady Olivia played the music."

"There you are then, Aveline," Uncle Cathcart said. "If the Athertons approve the reel, who are we to imagine we know better? Is that not so, my dear? For you always tell me that the earl and his family are the epitome of good breeding in this neighbourhood, at least."

"But surely Lady Esther Franklyn is better bred than any of the Athertons," Aveline said robustly, "and *she* did not approve of the reel, I am sure, nor Lady Alice. They are both so correct, and Mama was sitting between them while Katherine was making a spectacle of herself."

"We shall speak more of this in the morning," Aunt Cathcart said, sounding tired. "It is late, and we are all ready for our beds. At least I am, and my head has been aching this past hour or more."

"Why did you not mention it sooner, my dear," Uncle Cathcart said gently. "We could have left earlier if I had known."

"It is of no consequence, but perhaps we may refrain from talking any more?"

"Of course, my dear."

They drove the rest of the way in silence.

***

K ent found his father still in the library, sitting at one of the abandoned card tables, a glass of brandy in his hand.

"Father? Are you quite well?"

135

"Hmm? Oh, Kent... yes, yes, I am well enough. Did you enjoy the dancing?"

"Very much. I finally persuaded Miss Parish to stand up with me." A hesitation, but now was as good a time as ever. "What did you think of her, now that you have had a chance to get to know her better? Is she not perfectly conversable?"

His father gave a wan smile. "With you, perhaps. She grew quite animated at times. But I still could not get more than two words together from her."

"You will when you get to know her better, I am certain of it."

"Perhaps. Are you quite set on this? She is a meek little creature... is that truly what you want? You will always have the mastery of her, but for myself I should prefer a girl with more spirit."

"I am not sure what I want, to be honest," Kent said. "All I know is that I like her and enjoy her company. Beyond that... I cannot yet say, but I would not pursue the matter if you were to disapprove."

"Kent, it is for you to decide what sort of woman would suit you best," the earl said tiredly. "I know of nothing against Miss Parish. She is not of our class, and she has no dowry to speak of, but that is of no consequence if she is the woman who can make you happy. I should be delighted to see you settled and the nursery put to its proper use, but do not rush into anything unless you are quite sure. You are young yet, and have not yet spent a full season in town, and you may find that Miss Parish shows to less advantage when you move more widely in society. I recommend you to take a little time to get to know her better before you take an irrevocable step, but I shall support you whatever you decide to do."

"Thank you, Father."

It was not quite the ringing endorsement he had hoped for, and his father's support did not extend to allowing him to take up a career, but it was approval of a sort. All that remained was for Kent to decide whether Miss Parish was indeed the woman who could make him happy, not just in casual rides on the moor or during an energetic reel, but for the rest of his life. It was a heavy decision indeed, and he had no idea how he would reach a conclusion.

***

To Katherine's surprise, but also relief, nothing further was said about reels or uncouth dances or agreeable partners. By the time everyone gathered the next morning for a late breakfast, all was serene and there was not the slightest hint of a disagreement. Aunt Cathcart exuded goodwill, and even Aveline bade Katherine a cheerful, *'Good morning, cousin'*, as if she had not spent the evening glowering at her.

The usual round of rides with Emily and her brother Lucas resumed, and although nothing was seen of Mr Kent Atherton, that was not un-usual. The more days that passed without a glimpse of him, the happier Katherine would be when he finally appeared. One day she would enter the drawing room, or leave the rectory, or take one of her walks through the woods and there he would be, his smile lighting up her day and warming her right down to her toes.

She could not be under any illusions, however. However attentive he had been that evening at the castle, however intently he gazed at her or widely he smiled, he was not in love with her. How could he be, when he made no effort to see her again? If he felt any affection for her beyond friendship, he would have sought her out within a day or two of the dinner.

The fact that he did not was a salutary lesson in her importance to him. However much he filled her thoughts, it was clearly not the same for him, and she clung to that raft of reason when all her turbulent emotions threatened to sweep her into imprudent hope. Perhaps he would break her heart in the end, but he had never given her any reason to expect more from him than brotherly affection.

About a week after the dinner, Aunt Cathcart called Katherine into her sitting room. It was a gloomy room, and chilly, for the fire was seldom lit, being used only when she needed quietness to work on her accounts or to write difficult letters. It was also the place she summoned her daughters to 'have a little chat', as she put it, after some transgression or other, so Katherine was filled with foreboding.

"Sit down, child. I have something I want to say to you."

Dutifully, Katherine took the seat indicated, racking her brain to recall any action of hers that might have provoked a lecture. The reel, perhaps? But that seemed to have passed now. She tried to discern from her aunt's expression whether she was cross or disappointed or simply resigned about some perceived misdemeanour, but if anything Aunt Cathcart seemed pleased about something. Katherine folded her hands in her lap and waited to hear her fate.

"You are aware of our hopes for you, Katherine," her aunt began. "When we offered you a home here, it was with the fixed intent of treating you exactly like our own daughters, and, in time, finding you a husband, and that is still our dearest wish, for you to be well settled. However, we are not well placed here to offer you the wide society that is necessary for you to make a sensible choice. Birchall is such a small village, our neighbours are far above us in rank and you are not quite comfortable in such society. You appreciate the problem, I am sure?"

Katherine nodded, although she was not sure that it was such a problem as her aunt implied. After all, if one had no expectation of ever marrying, the lack of potential husbands was hardly an issue. But her aunt would say whatever she had decided to say, and there was no point trying to deflect her from that course.

"But now an opportunity has arisen... and it seems to me that it might answer very well. An old friend of mine, a widow, a very wealthy woman... she lives in Helmsley, and she is in need of a companion, a young lady, she says, who will be full of energy and cheer her up. Now, I know you are very settled here, my dear, and we are delighted for you to stay here for as long as you wish, naturally, but it does seem to me that this is a situation that would suit you perfectly. You have long wished you could be of more use than at present, but we have servants enough for household tasks and there is little else for you to do here. But this is a chance for you to be of the utmost use to a lady who needs your services far more than we do."

Katherine listened in increasing horror. Helmsley? A companion? She was so confused she hardly knew what to think. She understood only that she was being sent away from Birchall — from her friend, Emily, from the church where she had begun to feel useful, and most of all, from the man she loved. "Have I displeased you in some way, aunt?"

"No, no! Nothing could be further from the truth! We will miss you abominably, you may be certain of that, but just think, Katherine — you will be living in a town, just as you used to do, and Mrs Ryker will take you about, you know, and introduce you to everyone. She has a great many friends, and you will meet lots of young people, and who knows what may come of it? You will be very well situated in Helmsley, and you will be the greatest comfort and help to Mrs Ryker."

When Katherine said nothing, she went on, "It will not be forever, for Mrs Ryker's nephew, who is her heir — the heir to a great fortune, in fact — is looking about him for a wife, and when he marries, his aunt will not need a companion and you may come back to us then. Do you see, my dear?"

Katherine saw very well. It was a way of removing her from Aveline's sphere, and also from her growing friendships with Kent and Emily. The daughter of a mill owner was no fitting companion for the family of an earl. In that regard, Katherine and her aunt were in full accord. But after so recent an upheaval in her life, to be uprooted again and sent away to a new home amongst strangers who were not even relations was not a happy prospect. She could not help feeling that this was a punishment of some sort, and that therefore she must have transgressed.

"May I take Daisy with me?"

"But of course. We would not send you off without your maid. We will travel to Helmsley tomorrow—"

"So soon!"

"There is no point in delay, is there? So you have the rest of today to pack all your things. There! I am glad that is all settled, and you will be very happy there, I am sure."

Dazed, Katherine went to her room and sent for Daisy. The rest of the day was spent in a whirlwind of packing. Jenny came to help, her face long.

"We'll all miss you so much, miss," she said glumly. "You was never any trouble at all, not like some I could name. And there'll be no music in the house no more. We all used to like to hear you playin' and playin' all day long. House won't be the same without you, and that's a fact. Everyone says so."

"Thank you, Jenny. I am very sorry to go, too, but... but my aunt believes it to be for the best."

"Best for who, though?" Jenny said darkly.

But Katherine could not allow that sort of speculation. "My aunt and uncle are thinking only of my interests, Jenny."

"Of course, miss," Jenny said at once, but she looked unconvinced.

Katherine was unconvinced, too. She was being got out of the way, that much was certain. Her aunt had never interfered in her friendship with Kent before, apart from warning her not to get her hopes up, but perhaps after the evening at the castle, she felt it was time to step in. Perhaps it was just as well. The more she saw of Kent, the deeper in love she fell, and the more pain she would suffer later when he married someone of his own class. Yes, it really was all for the best.

It was late in the afternoon before Katherine remembered that she had planned to ride with Emily the next day. She dashed off a note and sent it off to Westwick Heights, and then prepared for her last dinner at Cathcart House.

Emily and Lucas arrived before breakfast the next morning, their faces anxious, and were shown up to Katherine's room where she was finishing her packing.

"You cannot go away! Not when we are such good friends," Emily wailed. "Who shall I ride with now? Have you told Kent? He will be so upset!"

Katherine's cheeks flamed, but she answered quietly, "I cannot write to him as I did to you, so I depend upon you to tell him. Pray thank him for all his kindness to me."

"His kindness!" Emily cried, and would have said more, but Lucas frowned at her.

"We will tell him," he said. "And you will not be so far away. Helmsley is hardly the other end of the country, after all. It is barely ten miles from here, an easy ride."

"Oh, yes! We could come and call upon you!" Emily said happily. "It will not be the same as seeing you almost every day, but it is not so bad. And perhaps... I should not say this, but perhaps you will be valued there as you are not here."

"I have no complaint to make of my aunt and uncle," Katherine said sharply. "I should not wish you to think there is any point of contention between us."

"Then why send you away?" Emily said, and the question was unanswerable.

***

The journey to Helmsley was accomplished without difficulty. Aunt Cathcart chattered away, telling Katherine about the duties expected of a companion, most of which she forgot as soon as she heard it. Her spirits were very low, as she racked her brain to recall the misstep which was so dire that she needed to be sent away. It must have been dancing the reel, she decided, for she could think of nothing else. It was fortunate that her aunt needed no response, beyond an occasional 'Yes, aunt' or 'No, aunt'.

On the backward facing seat, Daisy practically bounced with excitement. It was the first time she had ever been to Helmsley, the first time she had ever left behind her family altogether, and the first time she would be acting as a lady's maid without the support of the knowledgeable Miss Rathbone.

Helmsley was as busy as any other town, the streets choked with carriages and wagons and riders and carts, not to mention a man herding a small flock of sheep, and walkers weaving in and out of the traffic as they went about their business. Katherine had not taken much notice of the town before, on the few occasions when she had been there to visit the shops or the seamstress. Now she looked about her with new interest, for this was to be her home for the foreseeable future.

It was a pretty little place, the houses almost all built in the same pale stone, which gave a pleasing uniformity. Most were one or two storeys, but there were some larger houses, too, and the carriage drew up outside one such house, the windows indicating three principal storeys. To Katherine's pleasure, it sat directly opposite the church, and just round the corner from the market square. What could be more convenient!

Almost before the carriage came to a complete halt, the front door opened, and a well-rounded woman of Aunt Cathcart's age rushed down the steps, her face wreathed in smiles.

"Annie! My dear friend!" She threw her arms around Aunt Cathcart the instant she set foot on the pavement, and it was some moments before she could disentangle herself.

"Well! Audrey! It is not as if we have not met for years, after all," Aunt Cathcart said, rather flustered, as she straightened her bonnet. "And this is—"

"Miss Parish, or may I call you Katherine? Oh, so pretty! You didn't mention *that*, Annie. Come in, come in! Your coachman must bring in the luggage for I have no manservant just now, only a boy to help in the kitchen. Ah, there you are, Ned, Ellen. Show them where to put the luggage, will you? Come on in, Annie. I've ordered tea to be brought up the moment you arrive. How were the roads? Tolerable, I trust? You made good time. I hardly thought to look for you for another half hour, at least, and here you are already, sooner than I dared to hope. Come upstairs, Katherine. This way, ladies."

Katherine wondered if she ever stopped to draw breath. At least there would be no difficulty if she herself could find nothing to say, for clearly Mrs Ryker could talk enough for both of them. Her accent was not strong, but she was not quite from the top level of society, just like Katherine.

The drawing room was a prettily appointed apartment overlooking the street and the church opposite, where two maids brought tea and an array of pastries and cakes. Katherine and her aunt sipped and nibbled, while Mrs Ryker tucked in with gusto, while still managing to talk nonstop.

"You're musical, I hear, Katherine," she said at one point, waving a half-eaten strawberry tartlet to emphasise the point. "I have an instrument here, you see. I've noticed you eyeing it longingly, and indeed, I hope you'll play whenever you wish. My two girls played when they were at home, but they've been married these two years past and it's scarcely been touched since. But I've had it tuned, and it awaits you whenever you wish to play.

"Thank you, ma'am, I shall—"

"I adore music, myself. I played a little when I was young, although nothing like this. These modern instruments are quite different. I learnt on a spinet, a charming little instrument, but nothing would do for my girls but a proper pianoforte, and I have to say it makes a most effective sound, although—" She paused to pop the remains of the tartlet into her mouth, swallowing it almost instantly. "—personally, I prefer the more delicate sound of the spinet. But there, one must change with the times, I suppose. Another of these little pastries, Annie? Katherine? No? Well, I might have one more myself, then. So do you leave any heartbroken young men behind you, Katherine? I am sure you do... oh, look how she blushes! There's someone, I swear it."

"Katherine blushes a great deal, Audrey, without the need to invoke young men."

"Oh, shy, is she? Well, my dear, you'll find my friends very easy to get along with. We won't be rubbing shoulders with any earls or duke's daughters here, just pleasant, friendly people. Goodness me, those little pastries are all gone. What a pity. Do you want to get off, Annie? I'm sure you want to get back home before it gets too late, and it's all uphill from here."

The carriage was sent for from the inn where the horses had been baited, and Katherine bade her aunt farewell. If she shed a few tears as her aunt embraced her, it was as much from fear of the future as sorrow to be parting. She was fond of her aunt, in a dutiful sort of way, but she could not quite understand why she had been invited into the family and welcomed almost as another daughter, and now was to be exiled to live amongst strangers. After six months, when she had just begun to feel settled, she had been uprooted again. And here, there was no possibility of meeting Kent.

How would she bear it?

12: Conversation

The note from Cousin Emily was brief.

'Kent, Katherine Parish has been sent to Helmsley to live as companion to Mrs Ryker, a friend of Mrs Cathcart. Emily.'

Kent was on the doorstep at Westwick Heights within the hour, only to find that Emily had gone out with Aunt Jane and her sisters. He found Lucas at the stable, however.

"What is all this about Miss Parish going away, cousin?" he said without preamble.

"Oh... Kent. Yes, I thought you might be upset about that."

Upset? He did not want Lucas drawing conclusions from his manner, so he said more temperately, "I am surprised, that is all. She was going to explain about the new sort of valves, and now I find her gone, and with no warning."

Lucas eyed him oddly. "Valves, eh? Yes, it was a bit sudden. Even Katherine herself had no notion it was in the wind, just told one day and off the next."

"Who is this Mrs Ryker?"

"A wealthy widow, apparently. Lives alone, needs a companion. More than that I cannot say. Emily has the direction, if you want to go down there."

For an instant, Kent's spirits lifted, but he realised at once that if he called upon Katherine at Helmsley, that would be as good as a declaration, and he was not at all sure he wanted to take that step yet. He liked her very well, that was true, but marriage was a big step, and once he was committed, there would be no possibility of a career for him. He would be dependent on his father's largesse forever.

So he went home and pondered his future. Surely there would be a change in his fortunes soon? Something would turn up, he was sure of it.

***

K atherine found it easier than expected to settle into her new home. Mrs Ryker was a kindly soul, who spared neither expense nor effort to provide her with everything necessary for her comfort. The demands on Katherine's time were few, so she was free to play the instrument, read or write letters, as she preferred, no one insisted she attempt to embroider and no objection was made if she ventured down to the kitchen to make a cake or a pie, or talk to Sukey, the cook, about meals. All Saints Church was directly across the road, and its cool, echoing interior made an acceptable replacement for St Timothy's. An array of shops was located within easy walking distance, and she found a reason to go there almost every day.

Saturday was the day for the market, and Mrs Ryker happily walked about on Katherine's arm talking to the sheep farmers and wool merchants. Her late husband had been in the wool trade, having interests right the way through the process from the sheep, through carding and spinning, and finally weaving, and many a weather-worn farmer's visage broke into a broad smile at the sight of her.

The house was comfortably appointed, rather than elegant. It was not as large as Katherine was used to, having only a book room, dining room and small parlour on the ground floor, the drawing room and Mrs Ryker's bedroom on the first floor, and two more bedrooms above that. Katherine's room was at the back of the house overlooking a long, narrow strip of garden, with a view of Helmsley castle beyond. The room was pleasantly appointed, the bed was comfortable, and with a small table and chair in the window, and a larger chair beside the fire, she could retreat there for solitude if she was not needed elsewhere.

In some ways, she was reminded of life in Branton. The house was different, in fact, the whole town was different, with its pretty little thatched cottages and houses in pale stone, whereas Branton felt darker, the tall houses, mills and warehouses looming over the people scurrying about below. And then there were the many mill chimneys belching out their clouds of dark smoke, to add to the smoke from kitchens and fireplaces in the houses.

Still, the Helmsley house held only the two of them above stairs and five servants, including Daisy. There was no butler and, with no man in the house, nor carriage in the coach house, not a single male servant, apart from the kitchen boy. The food was plain fare, such as she preferred, and not so excessively abundant as at Cathcart House. Life in Mrs Ryker's house was, Katherine decided, very pleasant. It was not quiet, for Mrs Ryker was never silent for more than two minutes together, but there was not the crowded feeling Katherine had experienced at Cathcart House, surrounded as she was by so many other people.

Her Branton friends continued to write to her regularly, expressing surprise at the sudden move, but avid for news of her new home, and sharing all the little doings from home, and she wrote often to satisfy their curiosity. When she had first moved to Cathcart House, such letters had reduced her to tears of longing for the familiar faces and streets. Now, she delighted to hear their news, naturally, but somehow it was as if she looked back on Branton through a fog, for some of her memories were hazy. She had to struggle to bring some faces to mind, or recall which of the Mason brothers had just got married and which had the child with croup. Then she would panic a little at the thought that perhaps Kent's face would fade away, too.

Emily wrote to her sometimes, but she was not a regular correspondent, and she did not describe things in sufficient detail, so the page might be crammed with outings and dinners and new gowns, but Katherine could not get a clear picture of any of it. But sometimes she mentioned Kent, which was a little thrill, the words read and reread to brighten the hours when Katherine had retired to her room.

Mrs Ryker's social engagements were numerous but they were very consistent. A dinner out once a week, a dinner hosted once a month, and every other night but Sunday spent playing whist with a group of friends after dinner, one group for Mondays, one for Tuesdays, and so on. On Thursdays the friends came to Mrs Ryker's house to play. This would have been dull for Katherine if she had wanted to play cards herself, for the whist players were precisely four, with no room for an extra, but she was quite happy to sit at the instrument and play soothing pieces, or else read or sew.

On Fridays a larger group gathered, with a number of young people, and then she was drawn into a noisy round game. On Sundays, she could attend three services if she were so minded.

There were things she missed, of course. Her friendship with Emily. Her rides on the moors. The beautiful instruments that the Athertons and Franklyns had at their disposal, that she had been privileged to play on. Her music cabinet, which Aunt Cathcart said was too bulky to take with her. The walk through the woods to Birchall village. The gossipy sewing circle at the rectory. Most of all, her long conversations with Kent Atherton. But all things considered, she was not dissatisfied with her present life, and was not even sure she would want to return to Birchall if the opportunity were offered.

About a week after she had moved, a familiar carriage drew up outside the house. Looking down from the drawing room, Katherine squeaked in delight. Emily! There was Emily stepping from the carriage with a beaming smile on her face, and Lucas handing her down. By the time Katherine had raced downstairs and hauled open the front door even before the doorbell could be rung, there was another smiling face gazing at her, a face so familiar in her dreams that she almost could not believe she was actually awake. Had she nodded off over her hemming, and was imagining this?

"Miss Parish," he said, the smile widening even further. "How delightful to see you again."

If there were one sight guaranteed to brighten her day, it was Kent Atherton bowing over her hand with all his customary grace, rendering her speechless with joy.

"Are you surprised?" Emily cried, throwing her arms around Katherine. "I hope you are... and that it is a pleasant surprise... but if you are otherwise engaged... or it is not convenient..."

Mrs Ryker arrived just then and swept the visitors into the house, Katherine scurrying in her wake mumbling introductions, while the kitchen boy directed the coachman and groom to the inn.

Kent bore a large package, and as soon as Mrs Ryker's tongue allowed, he passed it to Katherine while Emily explained.

"Mrs Cathcart would not agree to us bringing your music cabinet with us, for she says it is far too fragile to be transported—"

"Even though it came all the way from Lancashire unscathed," Kent added.

"Exactly so," Emily said. "I think it is such a pretty piece that she wants to keep it in her drawing room. But she could not prevent us from bringing some of your music, for it is yours, after all."

"Goodness, what a great number of sheets," Mrs Ryker said, as Kent cut the strings on the parcel for Katherine to unwrap.

"Oh, Katherine knows hundreds of pieces," Emily said. "She was quite the best performer for miles around at home, and I am sure there will be few to equal her in Helmsley."

"Oh, no, I didn't mean... I'm very well aware of her talent, Miss Atherton. I meant only that printed music like this is very expensive. To have such a fine collection must have cost your father a pretty penny, Katherine, dear."

Emily's eyes widened. "And this is no more than a quarter of it. But I thought you were poor!" She blushed scarlet. "I beg your pardon, that was abominably rude of me."

"No, no," Katherine said. "It is a natural supposition, but we were not poor when Papa was alive, no. His income latterly was above three thousand pounds a year, but of course he had borrowed money for the new mill and when he died it was all lost. I am very poor indeed now."

Emily wriggled uncomfortably. "I beg your pardon, Katherine. It must be intolerably painful for you to talk about, and I would not for the world distress you."

"It does not distress me, not any more," Katherine said, feeling no little surprise to find that it was so. "When I left Branton, with the bailiffs still in the house, that was very dreadful. But all our friends and neighbours gathered on the street to bid me farewell, even the mill workers who had lost their employment and the little children from my Sunday classes, and many friends still write to me and remember me kindly, so I am not downhearted. And I have new friends and a new home. Mrs Ryker could not have been kinder to me, and if I have very little money, I also have little need of it."

Emily hugged her, and Mrs Ryker wiped a tear from her eye, murmuring, "Such bravery!"

Fortunately, Etta came in just then with tea and cakes, and there was a scramble to find suitable wine for the men, not to mention glasses of sufficient quality to touch the lips of the son and nephew of an earl, so nothing more was said of money. It was only later, when Mrs Ryker had shooed them outside for a while — "Do go and show your friends the garden, Katherine dear. I am sure they will be pleased with my hazelnut tree, and the arbour beneath it." — that Emily raised the subject again.

"May I ask... if it does not distress you... your father's income... I mean, one should not talk about such things but—"

"But everyone does," Lucas put in. "What she means to say, Miss Parish, is that your father's income once exceeded Mr Cathcart's. I wonder whether he is aware of that."

"I do not think he suspects," Katherine said with a little smile. "My aunt and uncle know very little about me, or my father. They are ashamed of what he did, and so they never speak of it."

"That is why Aunt Alice knew nothing of it until that evening when we all danced the reel, do you remember?" Kent said. As if she could forget! "Lady Esther Franklyn asked Mrs Cathcart about you, and about your father, so she was obliged to confess that he was a mill owner and not a gentleman. Poor Aunt Alice was rather shocked, and saw fit to warn me against keeping such low company. I put her straight on the matter, you may be sure, for whatever your father was, you are a lady through and through, Miss Parish."

She blushed deeply at the compliment, and when she dared to look at him again, he was gazing at her with the intimate smile that she loved. Oh, if only it were just for her! But he was the same friendly man with everyone, she knew that.

Still, his closeness was unnerving, rendering her unable to do more than shake her head.

The garden being small and its secrets soon exhausted, they made their way to the ruins of Helmsley Castle, and strolled about, Emily and Lucas racing ahead, just as they did on horseback, while Katherine was left to walk beside Kent.

At first, he talked about the castle, for he knew more of its history than she did, but after a while he said in a low voice, "And are you truly content in your new home, Miss Parish? For I know well that you are not one to complain about inconveniences or slights, but I cannot be easy in my mind until I know the truth. Your departure was so abrupt that I was sure there must have been some breach with the Cathcarts, and coming, as it did so soon after the evening at Corland, I should be very sorry indeed if anything that happened that night had caused trouble between you."

He meant the reel, of course, but she thought it was not that at all. Now that she knew that Aunt Cathcart had been forced to disclose

Katherine's origins, and that Lady Alice had been shocked to discover it, she understood it very well. She remembered now that Aunt Cathcart had seemed out of sorts on the way home that evening. No doubt Lady Alice had impressed upon her that a match between Kent and Katherine would be highly unsuitable, and Aunt Cathcart had taken steps to see them separated. As if Katherine had ever had any hopes in that direction! She had as soon wish for the moon. But she could not say that to Kent.

"Oh, no, nothing like that," Katherine cried, quite horrified that he should seek to take some blame for her situation. "I do not think it was anything that was done, only that Mrs Ryker wrote to Aunt Cathcart of her need for a companion, and my aunt thought it would suit me very well. Which it does."

"Truly?" he said, looking at her with a quizzical expression. "She is not the social equal of the Cathcarts."

"But nor am I!" Katherine said, with a low chuckle. "Mrs Ryker is not quite as vulgar as Mrs Vance, but she is cut from the same cloth. Her husband was a wool merchant, and I assure you, I feel far more at ease in her company than ever I did with my aunt and uncle, kind though they always were to me."

"You would have grown accustomed in time to their different ways," he said, and he frowned, as if he disapproved of her answer. "Miss Parish, I would not have you under the illusion that you cannot mingle with those of higher rank, just because your father was a mill owner."

"Yet it is true," she said sadly. "I do not mean that I am forbidden from doing so, for that is obvious nonsense. There is no rule of law that prohibits the mixing of high and low ranks, so long as the initiation comes from the higher rank. I mean only to say that I myself find it difficult. It is not that I cannot speak at all or hold a conversation, for I can do so well enough if

I have a subject within my sphere of experience upon which to talk. But if I do not know my companion very well, when everyone is a stranger, and especially when the disparity of rank is large, then there are no common points on which to converse. When I sat beside your father, for instance, I had not the least idea what to say to him, or how to find a topic of interest to him, and he had the same difficulty with me. We contrived, after a fashion, but it was not easy. Whereas with you, sir, you talk about matters on which I can speak with some authority. There is never any difficulty talking to *you*."

"No, indeed, I was astonished to discover the depth of your knowledge on certain subjects. But you are a woman of great good sense and intelligence, and if you can learn to play that piece from Handel that you performed at Corland, I have no doubt that you can learn other skills, to aid you in society. I believe if you applied yourself to the problem, you could easily discover topics of interest to my father."

"The countess... he grew animated when I enquired after the countess, and the Dowager Countess, too."

"Yes, his family is always in his heart. He can talk endlessly on that subject."

"But what about Lady Esther Franklyn? What on earth might I say to her?"

"Oh, that is easy, and the answer is the same — ask her about her family. She might tell you about her two sons, but I suspect it will be her father, the Duke of Camberley, or her brother, the Marquess of Ramsey, and the endless array of Bucknells who infest the duke's principal seat at Marshfields. She will tell you about Marshfields itself, too, with very little prodding."

"So all I have to do is find one subject of compelling interest. With you, that is easy — mills and beam engines and such like. What about your brothers?"

"Walter is typical of many gentlemen, so you may ask about his horses, his guns and his various sporting endeavours, although just now I suspect he would prefer to talk about his future wife, Winnie Strong. Eustace..." He frowned. "Ancient weaponry and armour, I suppose. He has a great collection at Welwood, and knows all about the Corland collection, but do not ask unless you wish to be bored for some considerable time."

"And your sister?"

"Olivia? Cake! That is what interests her most. And gowns, of course. Always a reliable subject with a young lady. But do not mention balls or Almack's or the Queen's drawing rooms or anything to do with the season, for she will begin to rant and probably end by weeping on your shoulder, having missed her first season this year. You see, it is quite easy really, Miss Parish."

"Oh yes. What a pity it is that I shall not be able to try out these stratagems in earnest, for I shall not see any of these people again, I expect. But I shall try to apply the same principles to my new friends in Helmsley, and see if I get on better. I believe we have been walking for long enough, sir. Mrs Ryker may need me, and I must not neglect my employer for my own pleasure."

"Then let us return to the house," he said quietly.

13: Of Wives

K ent was unutterably depressed after this visit. He had been so pleased with himself, discovering that the music cabinet was still in place at Cathcart House, and proposing to Emily and Lucas that perhaps Miss Parish would like to have her music with her, and even though they had not been permitted to take the cabinet itself, he had been excited to see Katherine's face when she received some of her music. Excited to see *her*, he admitted to himself. And now he was thrown into gloom.

All the way home in the carriage, as Emily and Lucas chatted easily, he was silent, mulling over Katherine's words. All this time, ever since he had first come to know her better, he had looked forward to raising her up a little in society, so that she was less terrified to mingle with the nobility, or even the lower levels of the gentry, like the Cathcarts. And now he found that she had happily sunk down to her previous merchant class, relieved that she was back where she felt she belonged. If only she could see that she was just as good as anyone else — better than many, in fact. Why should she not meet on equal terms with the earl, or even Lady Esther, who for all her haughtiness and her ducal relations, was married to a former attorney? Why should the daughter of a mill owner not marry the son of an earl, if she chose to?

And why should not the son of an earl marry a mill owner's daughter? And he could, for his father was complacent about it. As long as they were to live at Corland Castle, they would be financed indefinitely. Not only would they be fed and clothed and provided with every comfort, but their children would be educated and raised to be ladies and gentlemen, like their Atherton relations.

And I shall never be able to leave, he thought despondently. Never be an engineer, never go to the foundry in Birmingham, never see a real beam engine in majestic action — or hear it, or even *feel* it, as Katherine had so vividly described. He would never defy his father so far as to take up a career as an engineer, but he badly wanted to know more of those wonderful machines and what they could do. Even better, he wanted to know what they might do in the future, with clever men developing them and finding new ways to use them. For now, they might be pumping water from mines and driving spinning machines, but who knew what they might be capable of in the years to come?

Instead, he would stay in Yorkshire, on the land his family had owned for centuries, watching farmers pursuing the traditional methods as if nothing had changed since the middle ages.

He was still in the deepest gloom when they arrived at Westwick Heights, but Lucas having a mind to see the new hunters recently acquired at Corland, Emily alone was deposited at her home, while the carriage rumbled on with Lucas and Kent. Lucas took advantage of the increased space to stretch out his legs and lean back against the squabs.

"So, cousin, are you going to marry her?" he said with a sly grin.

Kent did not pretend to misunderstand. "I cannot say. It is... difficult."

"It always is, for younger sons. Neither of you has two shillings to rub together, not of your own, and you cannot expect Uncle Charles to fund you. Looks like the army for you, then. Or no, the church! She is a pious soul, always praying, so a little country parsonage would suit her very well. She will not mind waiting until you can be ordained, I am sure."

"Actually, my father has offered to house us at Corland Castle."

Lucas shot upright. "No! Then you have already discussed it with him."

"In a hypothetical way," Kent said. "Not in an *'I plan to do this'* sort of way, more a case of *'If it should happen to come about, what would you think?'* sort of way. He was very positive about it, but only if we live at Corland. He does not want me to leave home."

"Well, there you go, then. You can propose as soon as you like, you lucky dog. You will have a wife of your own. Everyone is getting married, except me."

"Do you want to? Are you thinking about it?"

"Of course I am thinking about it!" Luke said, with a laugh. "I think about it every single night when I retire, alone, to my cold and empty bed. I have been thinking about it since I was... well, for a number of years, let us say."

Kent laughed, and shook his head. "There is more to marriage than that! And you need not even marry if all you want is a woman in your bed. Ask Eustace if you want advice."

"I would never dare take a mistress. Lord, all that fuss over Walter's little woman, and Mother was as distraught as if it had been one of us. I thought she was going to have an apoplexy over it. No, it is not worth it, but I should like to marry, and sooner rather than later."

"Have you anyone in mind?"

"No, because I plan to follow Father's example and marry an heiress, and there are none around here that I could stomach."

"Not even Bea Franklyn?" Kent said, amused.

"Especially not Bea Franklyn. The woman is a leech, and just because my brother thinks the sun shines out of her does not improve my opinion of her in the slightest. Scheming hussy! No, I shall go to town next spring and look about me. Izzy will take me around and introduce me to a few people. If nothing comes of that, Mother has a list of possible girls. She is a great one for match-making, as your father is finding out. I sincerely hope he marries again and sires a string of legitimate sons to cut Bertram out of the succession, because if Bea Franklyn becomes Countess of Rennington after all her devious scheming, it will be a travesty of justice."

The carriage arrived at the castle just then, and the two cousins went off to the stables to talk about horses for a pleasant hour or so, and Kent was able to push his dilemma to the back of his mind again for a while. It was not until late that evening, when he retired *'alone, to his cold and lonely bed'* as Lucas had it, that he thought about Katherine again and wondered what it would be like to find her waiting for him there, smiling up at him in that glowing way she had that made him feel like a king.

Then he wondered just what it was that attracted him to her so strongly. Was it simply because, of all his acquaintances, she was the only one who would talk to him about beam engines? Or was it Katherine herself, with her quiet ways and her modestly downturned eyes and her soft voice?

He could not honestly say.

***

K atherine had little opportunity to try out Kent's advice on making conversation, for Mrs Ryker and her friends were all themselves great talkers and left no openings for her to tentatively ask a question or two. But when she had been in Helmsley for three weeks, an opportunity arose, for Mrs Ryker's nephew came to stay.

Since the drawing room window seat had become her favourite vantage point, with its views across to the church and a little way into the endlessly fascinating market square, she was the first to see the post chaise draw up outside the house.

"Are you expecting a visitor, ma'am? For a gentleman has just arrived in a post chaise, with luggage."

Mrs Ryker rushed to the window. "Goodness, 'tis William! And not a bit of beef in the house today. But there, he does like to surprise me, so he must take his pot luck for today, at least. Well, how glad I am that you will meet him so soon, for I'd thought he might be busy until Christmas, so popular as he is. Come now, my dear, come and meet my nephew."

Mr William Ryker was twenty-eight years of age, and a fine, handsome young man, as he was very well aware. He made his aunt a florid bow, and then turned his gaze on Katherine as they were introduced with the sort of practised eye which bordered on rudeness, surveying her swiftly from head to toe before sweeping her hand to his full lips. She was relieved that he restrained himself from pressing those lips upon her flesh, and withdrew her hand as soon as she was able, but Mrs Ryker chuckled.

"Well, you've made quite an impression, my dear, that I can see. But come inside, William, do. Let's not be standing around in this damp air."

They left the kitchen boy and Mr Ryker's valet to deal with the luggage, Mrs Ryker sweeping them all back into the house and up the stairs to the drawing room. With Mrs Ryker in the first flush of excited chattering over her nephew, he was not required to say very much apart from *'Yes, ma'am'* and *'No, ma'am'* and occasionally *'That is so, ma'am'*. He had written quite recently, so there was little in the way of news to impart, but Mrs Ryker rattled on anyway.

Katherine had nothing to do except sip the tea which shortly appeared, and decide what she thought of Mr Ryker. He was certainly fashionably dressed in the town manner of pantaloons and hessians, rather than a country gentleman's usual breeches and top boots. His coat and waistcoat were expensive, his neckcloth snowy white, his shirt points jauntily high and the fobs at his waist gleaming silver. He had dispensed with the smart beaver hat, gloves and cane with which he had arrived, but he was very much the gentleman, in appearance at any event.

His attire reminded her a little of some of the young men at Branton, those with a large allowance and not much sense of style. She could not help comparing Mr Ryker with the gentlemen of her recent acquaintance, and it was here that he was found to be lacking. The Atherton men dressed with a certain casual disregard for their appearance, as if they had simply pulled something from the wardrobe without much thought. And yet they were always elegant in a way that Mr Ryker could not match.

It was the details, she decided. Mr Ryker's coat was in the height of fashion, but it did not mould itself to his form in the way that Mr Kent Atherton's did. The neckcloth was intricately tied, but it was still slightly awry. And the waistcoat... it was too brash, she decided. A true gentleman, one brought up to the state from birth, exhibited an effortless style that undoubtedly arose from a combination of patronising the very best tailors and boot makers, and employing a highly skilled valet.

She even knew what it was, for she had heard Aveline and Aunt Cathcart discussing it once — town bronze, it was called, that combination of innate style and perfect manners that the upper classes had. Whereas Mr Ryker was a provincial man aping the aristocracy. Now that she thought about it, the Cathcart men were a little the same — the coats that did not quite fit as snugly as they should, the waistcoats that were slightly the wrong shade for the coat, and the styles that called attention to deficiencies of the body instead of enhancing advantages.

There was another difference, too, which she only gradually began to appreciate. Mr Ryker said very little to his aunt, and nothing at all to Katherine, but his eyes turned to her very often. Not for long, merely flicking his gaze momentarily in her direction, and then back to his aunt, but it gave Katherine a strange unsettled feeling. That was something she had never once felt with Kent or any of the Athertons, or with the Cathcart sons. She had encountered it sometimes at Branton, for not everyone she had met there was a gentlemen, or had the manners of one, and of course one experienced it all the time on the street, and public places like the post office, or the inns she had passed through on the journey to Birchall. A man — for it was always a man — would look at a woman in a certain way, not quite insolent, but verging on it, and that was just how Mr Ryker looked at her now. Assessing her, perhaps, in a way she did not want to be assessed.

Now she was uncomfortably aware that the boxes bumping up the stairs were to be deposited in the only free bedroom, the one next to hers on the second floor, and she was not at all sure she wanted Mr William Ryker, with his assessing eyes, so close to her.

When she went to her room to dress for dinner, there were male voices rumbling in the room next door. Whispering in case she might be overheard, she said to Daisy, "What is being said of Mr Ryker below stairs?"

Daisy was behind her, unbuttoning her gown, but her hands stilled momentarily. "Not much, miss."

"He makes me uncomfortable."

"Oh yes, miss! That's what Etta said, that he makes her uncomfortable, but Sukey just told her not to be silly, it was just being in a house with no men and not being used to it, that's all."

"But I *am* used to being in a house with men, and none of the Cathcart men ever made me uncomfortable the way Mr Ryker does. Is there a lock on the bedroom door, Daisy?"

"A lock but no key, miss, I've looked and Etta's looked and we can't find one."

"In that case, I should like you to sleep in here at night, Daisy. You can share with me, for the bed is plenty big enough. I am probably making something of nothing, but your company will help me sleep soundly."

Dinner gave Katherine an opportunity to practise her conversational skills, for Mrs Ryker's tongue was fully engaged by the meal, at least until she had eaten her fill. Katherine knew little of Mr Ryker except that he was Mrs Ryker's heir and lived at York, but, mindful of Kent's advice to ask about families, she began there.

"Do you have brothers and sisters, Mr Ryker?"

"None at all," he said cheerfully. "Nor mother or father, either. Aunt Audrey is my only surviving relation in the whole word."

"Oh dear. How sad for you," Katherine said, not quite sure how to progress without a single family member to enquire upon. "And... and are you married?"

He raised his eyebrows in surprise. "No, certainly not! Whatever gave you that idea?"

That set Katherine blushing furiously. "No, indeed... I had no... not the least... I beg your pardon, sir."

He chuckled then. "Ah, you are teasing me, I suppose. I am sure my aunt has told you that I am in the very process of planning to marry."

"Then you are betrothed! My felicitations, sir."

He laughed more heartily. "Very witty! No, I am not betrothed, Miss Parish, as you are aware. But my plans for matrimony are well advanced. I already have a pleasant house in my eye in York. At present, I only have lodgings, but I shall want my bride to have her own establishment, naturally. A very pretty little house, not over large, but well positioned on one of the best streets, and within easy reach of all the amenities of the city. On the ground floor..."

Katherine let him talk on, puzzled by his assumption that she must know he was not betrothed. Perhaps he thought that Mrs Ryker had told her all about him, but on the contrary, she had barely mentioned him. After dinner, Mrs Ryker resumed her command of the conversation, Katherine retreated thankfully to the instrument and was able to retire to bed at an early hour, where she discovered sleep to be elusive despite Daisy's presence. Katherine was so unused to another person in her room that even Daisy's gentle snores were enough to keep her awake.

For some days, Mrs Ryker arranged daily entertainments and unusually good dinners for her nephew, so that Katherine scarcely had a moment to herself and was rarely in bed before midnight. It was not until Sunday that there was finally a quiet day to catch up with her letter-writing, read a sermon or two and retire to bed early enough to ensure a reasonable night's sleep.

Once again, however, Daisy's soft snores kept sleep at bay. Thus Katherine found herself awake when she heard a door opening on the landing, together with a sound rather like the clink of glass on glass. Mr Ryker fetching himself a late-night brandy, perhaps?

But to her horror, the next sound was her own door opening, and through the gap in the bed curtains she saw flickering candle-light making the shadows dance and jump. The door closed again, but the light remained. Katherine held her breath, for surely this was a mistake? Mr Ryker had gone downstairs, perhaps, and on his return had opened the wrong door. In which case he would soon realise his error and creep out again.

There was the chink of glass again nearby. The little table, perhaps. Whatever he carried had been set down there. Silence. Surely now he must be looking around and seeing that this was not his own room.

The curtain was wrenched back and Mr Ryker's face loomed over her, not six inches from her own.

Katherine screamed.

"Hush, hush!" he said, flapping his hands at her. "No noise, or you will wake everyone."

"What are you doing here? Go away!"

"Now, that is not very friendly. I only want to talk to you. Look, I have brought wine." And he smiled at her, as easy as if they were sitting in the drawing room, even though he appeared to be wearing nothing but a nightshirt — not even a nightcap, she thought distractedly, and there she was in her night gown, which covered her from neck to toe yet she still felt as if she were naked.

He stretched out an arm towards her, as if to touch her shoulder or perhaps her face, and she screamed again, and slithered out of the bed and under his arm to escape, ending up on the floor.

"Hoy, what are you doin' in a lady's bedroom?" That was Daisy, thoroughly awake and lurching upright. "Get out of here, you *lecher*, you!"

He uttered a most ungentlemanly curse, and began to back away. "I only came to talk to— Ow! Stop that!"

Daisy had grabbed the bolster and was laying into him with some force. Katherine scrabbled across to the fireplace on hands and knees, and took hold of the poker.

"Get out, Mr Ryker. If you want to talk to me, you can do it in daylight, properly dressed and with your aunt as chaperon. Now go away!"

"All right, all right! Ooof! Stop hitting me, you foolish girl."

He ran for the door, wrenched it open and slammed it shut with some force. His own door banged, and then blessed silence fell, apart from the two women's heavy breathing, which gradually stilled.

After a while, when it seemed likely there would be no repetition, Katherine deemed it safe to blow out the candle he had forgotten in his haste to take with him, and climb back into bed. Daisy slowly fell back into slumber, but Katherine lay curled up on her side, her pillow damp with tears, and wondered what she had done to deserve such an insult.

14: Another Unexpected Move

As soon as it was light, Katherine slipped out of bed and curled up in a chair beside the cold fire. On the small table, the wine bottle and two glasses still sat. After a while, Ellen crept in to relay the fire.

"Ooh, you're up already, miss. Anything you want?"

"No, thank you."

After a moment's hesitation, the maid said, "You all right, miss? Heard the screams last night."

"You did not think to investigate?"

"Orders, miss. From the mistress. We're to keep well out of the way when *he's* here and not interfere. He's never done anything... well, you know, anything really bad, but if you ask me, she should stop him wandering at night. You're the fourth companion she's had since the young ladies married and went away, miss, and it's no wonder, is it?"

Katherine could hardly believe it. So this was not merely an isolated incident, but a habit of Mr Ryker's. When Daisy woke, Katherine dressed and then waited until she heard the sounds of Mrs Ryker leaving her own room on the floor below. Then she went downstairs to the little parlour where Mrs Ryker filled the time until breakfast.

He was there. She had half expected that, having heard his valet arrive and then the sound of both of them going downstairs, but she hoped Mr Ryker had gone out for his morning walk and she would not have to face him at all. He was sprawled at his ease in a chair by the fire with a newspaper, while Mrs Ryker was seated at the table, letters, pens, wafers and ink pots spread over its surface. As Katherine entered, the two of them were laughing together — laughing! As if nothing untoward had happened at all.

"Ah, Katherine, there you are," Mrs Ryker said. "You have had something of an adventure in the night, I understand." And they both laughed again.

An adventure! Was that how she saw it? What on earth had Mr Ryker told her of the night's events?

"You must not mind William, you know," she went on. "He means you no harm, quite the reverse. In fact, he has plans for you, don't you? If things work out, that is, but he'll need to get to know you a little better first. But you'll get used to his ways soon enough, I'm sure."

"I doubt I shall ever get used to a man entering my bedchamber uninvited at midnight," Katherine said.

They both roared with laughter at that. "Uninvited!" Mr Ryker said. "Why, you have been encouraging me in that direction from the moment I arrived, Katherine."

"I have done no such thing! And I have not given you permission to address me by my Christian name, sir. Mrs Ryker, I cannot accept a man wandering in and out of my room whenever he pleases. Either I must have a new lock fitted to my door, or Mr Ryker must leave at once."

"Now, Katherine, dear, you mustn't be so melodramatic. We're just like family here, aren't we, so my nephew may come and go as he pleases. He likes to talk over a glass of wine late at night, that's all, and as my companion, I don't expect you to make all this fuss. It would be well worth your while, I assure you, and you can keep your maid with you to maintain the proprieties until you're married."

"I see."

Katherine spun on her heel, ran upstairs to her room and rang for Daisy, while donning her bonnet and pelisse.

"You wanted me, miss?"

"Yes, Daisy. Please pack all our things. We are leaving."

"Now, miss? Today?"

"As soon as I have obtained a post chaise. Just throw everything into the boxes, and we can sort out the mess later, for I cannot stay another moment in this house of wickedness."

***

The leaves surrounding the house had all turned, that was Katherine's first, irrelevant thought. In the month she had been gone, the trees had been transformed from a green only lightly tinged with brown to full-blown gold and red and orange, some branches already almost bare. But otherwise, Cathcart House was unchanged, its familiar façade bringing tears to her eyes. Here at least she would be safe!

The family was still at breakfast, so they were all there, pouring out of the house with bewildered expressions to greet her.

"Katherine, dear! Whatever has happened?" Aunt Cathcart cried, as James strode forward to hand her down from the chaise before the footman could reach it.

"I could not stay any longer," Katherine said. Then, seeing the concern on their faces, she added, "Do not be alarmed, I am quite well. Everyone is well."

Divesting herself of her bonnet and pelisse, she allowed her aunt to shepherd her into the breakfast parlour, the rest of the family crowding in behind them.

"Now, dear, tell us all about it," her aunt said, in such gentle, sympathetic tones that Katherine burst into tears, and it was some minutes before she could compose herself sufficiently to speak.

"Mr William Ryker was staying with his aunt. I believe I said as much in my last letter. He seemed... he seemed... but last night... he offered me insult. And... and Mrs Ryker saw nothing wrong in it and would not send him away, and I could not stay so I came home." Then, seeing consternation in her aunt's face, she added, "But if you do not wish me to stay, I can go to Branton... I have friends who—"

"We are very glad to have you back with us," Uncle Cathcart said firmly.

"Of course," Aunt Cathcart said quickly. "But we thought you were settled. It seemed to be working out well, and I cannot believe that Mrs Ryker would permit you to be... *insulted* under her roof. Is it possible that you may have misunderstood?"

Katherine lifted her chin. "I do not know what there is to misunderstand about a man entering my bedroom in a state of undress at midnight," she snapped.

"Did he touch you?" James said sharply. "Did he hurt you in any way?"

"No. Thank you, but I am unharmed. I had Daisy with me, and she set about him with the bolster and I took up the poker, and between us we drove him out of the room. But there was no key for the lock on my door, and I could not obtain an assurance that the event would not be repeated, and Mrs Ryker would not ask her nephew to leave — she said I should not make a fuss! As if I could possibly agree to such a thing, so I hired a post chaise from the inn and came away. But if it is inconvenient—"

"Katherine, dear," Uncle Cathcart said, "you have a home with us whenever and for as long as you need one. We are delighted to have you back."

"We have missed your playing at the instrument," James said. "The house is so quiet without you."

"Oh! My music!" Katherine said fretfully. "In my haste to leave, I have left my music behind, that the Athertons were at such pains to bring to me. How vexing! But at least I still have most of my collection. Aunt, may I go to my room now? If I still have a room, that is."

"Of course, dear. What a trying time you have had of it. Come, now, I will see that everything is in order for you, and then perhaps a tray in your room with some breakfast, and a little sleep? You look exhausted."

Upstairs, Aunt Cathcart chased out the maids hastily making up the bed, and the footmen with the travel boxes, and sat Katherine down on the chaise longue by the window.

"Now, my dear, tell me the truth — did he touch you at all?"

"No."

"Not even briefly?" She shook her head. "That is something, then. And when you say he was in a state of undress... shirtsleeves? Neckcloth unfastened?"

"In his nightshirt, aunt."

Her aunt's intake of breath was audible. "No robe?"

"Just a nightshirt, bare feet, bare head. He brought a bottle of wine and two glasses, just as if— Well, I do not know what he was thinking. He said he wanted to talk to me, but that is ridiculous. At midnight!"

"That is quite disgraceful! I hope you know that I would never, ever have sent you there had I not supposed... I thought he might make a good husband for you, to be honest. Audrey told me he was keen, and looking for a suitable girl, someone quiet and well-mannered. Well, it seemed ideal, for Audrey has a hundred thousand and he will have the lot, in time. And such an agreeable situation for you, or so I thought. Audrey seemed such a pleasant, sensible person."

"Oh, she is... was... in every other way. Aunt, I understand what you were trying to do for me, putting me in a situation where I could feel comfortable... with someone who is from the same sort of background as I am, and it was lovely at first. I missed you all, of course, but Mrs Ryker was so easy to be with, and let me help in the kitchen, and even the meals... she ordered good, plain dinners, just what I was used to in Branton. I truly thought it would suit me very well. Until *he* arrived."

"But you had Daisy with you, I think you said, so you must have had some inkling that he was not a gentleman."

"It was the way he looked at me, making me feel... oh, I cannot explain it. I did not like it at all. It made my skin crawl, and then his bedroom was right next to mine."

"Oh! And here you are next door to Alex and Neil... perhaps I should not have done that, and left you alone on this floor with the boys."

"No, no, I have never had a moment's concern about either of them," Katherine said. "They have never looked at me that way."

"What about James?" she said sharply.

Katherine shook her head. James had certainly shown admiration on occasion, but not that unpleasant leering look that had so unsettled her.

"Ah. Good. You have had a most unpleasant experience, but you have survived it very well." She chuckled suddenly. "Daisy hitting him with the bolster — that I should like to have seen! And you would not tamely submit... even got yourself home. You are a sensible girl, and I can only hope my own girls would be so stalwart in a crisis. It is a pity that they know the whole story, for there will be no keeping it secret now, but we can simply say that Mr Ryker's entering your room was a mistake, and you were too shocked to stay. And you had Daisy with you to protect your reputation. We must be sure to mention that — and the bolster! She defended you admirably, and Mr Cathcart will be sure to see that she has a little reward for her loyalty. Now then, dear, I shall have Mrs Travis put up a tray for you, and then you can go to bed for the rest of the day, for I doubt you got much sleep last night." She kissed her, and murmured, "Welcome home, my dear."

Katherine slept much of the day away, and the sky was already darkening when she finally descended the stairs and sought her usual refuge, the pianoforte. Her aunt came in, smiling, but sat quietly until she had finished her first short piece.

"Ah, how lovely to have you back at the instrument, where you belong," Aunt Cathcart said, kissing Katherine. "Are you feeling better now? You looked so pale when you arrived."

"Thank you, I am much better."

Just then, the sound of horses arriving at some speed, followed by her cousins' voices calling loudly for grooms, echoed through the house, followed almost at once by the same voices in the hall, and many booted feet stamping about. Aunt Cathcart winced at the noise.

The door opened, and James, Alex and Neil jostled their way into the room, grinning widely.

"Boys, please!" Aunt Cathcart said sharply. "No mud on my rugs, if you please, and do not come barrelling in here like ruffians on market day! Katherine deserves peace and quiet after her ordeal."

"But we have something to cheer her up," James said, waving a package at her from the doorway.

"She will want it straight away," Alex said, and Neil nodded.

Smiling a little, for they were so pleased with themselves, Katherine crossed the room to take the package. It was not very well wrapped, so as soon as she tugged at the strings, they unravelled, scattering papers all over the floor.

"My music!" she cried, bending to gather it all up. "You went to Helmsley to ask for it! How kind you are."

"We demanded it," Alex cried.

"We have had some fun. Are you pleased, Cousin Kate?"

"I am, very pleased. But James, what happened to your face? That is a nasty bruise."

"Oh, I walked into a door," he said airily, but the other two laughed so much that Katherine was struck by a hideous thought.

"Did you... see *him*? You did not call him out, did you?"

They all laughed. "Nothing like that," James said, "but we wanted him to know that he cannot get away with such behaviour. He is a dreadful coward, did you know that? He hid behind his aunt, and Alex and Neil had to drag him out so that I could get a clean shot at him, for I did not want to draw Mrs Ryker's cork by mistake. And then he just fell down at the first little tap, so they had to pick him up again before he put his fists up to defend himself. I let him get one pop at me before I hit him properly, but it was too easy. No challenge at all. Nasty little man."

"Really, boys!" Aunt Cathcart said. "Brawling in the street like the veriest urchins!"

"We were not in the street," Alex said. "He would not come outside, so we had to have a go at him in the drawing room."

"Not much got broken," Neil said cheerfully.

"Except his nose!" Alex cried, and the twins fell about laughing.

"Great heavens, whatever were you thinking!" Aunt Cathcart said distressfully. "We shall never live it down. Whatever will people say?"

She was trembling from head to foot, but Katherine laid a hand gently on her arm. "People will say that I am fortunate to have such chivalrous cousins to defend my honour. Thank you, James, all of you, and thank you for my music, too. You have made me very happy."

***

Kent heard of Katherine's return in the same way he had heard of her departure — by a letter from Emily.

'Kent, Katherine is back! We are to call upon her tomorrow. Be here at noon if you wish to join us. Emily.'

It was rather a large group gathered in the hall at Westwick Heights when Kent arrived the next day, for the whole of Uncle George's family were agog to know why Miss Parish had returned so abruptly, in a hired post chaise and with no warning, or so the servants had whispered. Apart from Uncle George and Aunt Jane, all six of his cousins were there, including six-year-old Philip, and also Bertram's betrothed, Bea Franklyn, who happened to be visiting.

They walked in a straggling train down the hill and through the woods to Cathcart House, although Aunt Jane fussed the whole way about the dampness of the air, adjuring everyone to keep well wrapped up and walk briskly, to keep the chill at bay, but not too briskly, for fear of overheating. As usual, no one took very much notice of her. Having been ill for much of her early life, she had the greatest terror that one of her children would succumb to the same weakness and could never be reassured that they were in the rudest of health.

They were received with bright smiles by Mrs Cathcart, and by blushes and downturned eyes by Katherine, as they all crowded into the drawing room. She looked well, Kent thought, and when he managed to catch her eye she smiled at him so warmly that he could not doubt her pleasure at seeing him. Such a sweet girl, and so guileless that her affection shone as bright as a star. The contrast with Miss Cathcart was striking, the one all innocence and demureness, the other brash in her attempts to attract his notice. He had never been deceived by such flirtatious behaviour, but now that he had Katherine's shining honesty before him, he was repelled by Aveline's duplicity.

The Strongs were already ensconced in the drawing room, and in possession of Katherine's person, Lady Strong sitting on one side of her, and Winnie on the other. No doubt they were also driven by curiosity, and since Lady Strong was holding Katherine's hand in a motherly fashion, and Winnie had one arm round her shoulders, perhaps there was more to this sudden return than mere whim.

Kent could not have imagined the truth, however, for when Mrs Cathcart recited the whole of it, he was appalled that his Katherine should have been subjected to such ungentlemanly behaviour. The ladies gasped when hearing that Mr Ryker had entered Katherine's bedroom, wearing only a nightshirt! Then they laughed at the maid hitting him with the bolster. They gasped again to hear that Mrs Ryker thought nothing of it, and clapped and cheered at Katherine refusing to give way, and hiring a post chaise on her own.

James Cathcart rather smugly described his own and his brothers' part in events, and although Kent was relieved that Katherine had male relatives to step forward when she was ill-treated in such a despicable fashion, he wished with all his heart that it could have been his duty to defend her honour. And yet... surely that meant he wished he were her husband, did it not? Was that truly what he wanted?

When the Strongs rose to leave, Kent swiftly took the vacated seat beside Katherine, while Emily sat down on her other side.

"I am so sorry you had to endure such a horrible occurrence," Kent said, "but I know I speak for all the Athertons when I say we are very happy to have you back amongst us."

"Oh, yes!" Emily said. "Such a shocking thing... I should have been terrified! One never imagines a *gentleman* would behave in such a way."

"I think we may safely say that this Ryker was no gentleman," Kent said. "But how fortunate that you had a maid with you. Was that one of Mrs Ryker's maids?"

"No, no," Emily said. "Katherine has her own maid now, Daisy Marler."

"Marler?" Kent said. "Related to Dan Marler, the farmer over at Welwood?"

Katherine nodded.

"She left there to stay with her uncle in the village here, and Katherine met her... somewhere, I forget where."

"In church," Katherine said, in a low voice.

"*Daisy* Marler? In church?" Kent said. "That would be a novelty, by all accounts."

"Oh, no, she was praying at the Lady Chapel, in great distress at some transgression... her conscience was troubling her."

"Praying? Well, perhaps she has changed..." He frowned. "Or perhaps I am confusing her with someone else, for the Marlers are generally regarded as a respectable family."

"I am sure they are," Katherine said. "Farmers are such hard workers, are they not? Out in all weathers to tend their animals and crops, and always threatened by an unseasonal snowstorm or floods or pestilence."

"Like the Bible," Emily said.

"Although perhaps there are not so many plagues of locusts in Yorkshire," Kent said, and was pleased to see that his modest jest raised an answering smile from Katherine. When she talked, she forgot to be self-conscious and the blushes died away, revealing the creamiest skin he had ever seen. Lord, she was pretty when she smiled at him in that artless way! How was he supposed to decide what to do when she was so... so *enticing*.

Mrs Cathcart came bustling over, with that over-bright smile on her face. She was excited to have her drawing room filled with well-wishers, no doubt, but then she always seemed a trifle excited to him.

"Miss Atherton, Mr Atherton, we are planning to hold a small celebration dinner in honour of Katherine's safe return to us after her ordeal. It will just be a few of her friends, young people like yourselves. I hope I can depend on you to honour us with your presence?"

"That would be lovely," Emily said at once. "We are engaged at Birchall House on Wednesday, but we have no other engagement, that I know of."

"Next Tuesday, perhaps?" Mrs Cathcart said. "Mr Atherton, would that suit you? And perhaps the Lady Olivia would like to come, too?"

He agreed to the date, and thought that very likely Olivia would be agreeable too, for she never missed an evening out if she could possibly help it. Like her older sister Izzy, she was a sociable creature, who came glowingly alive in company. Katherine was the very opposite of those two. Kent had decided many years ago that he would never marry a woman like Izzy, for it would be too exhausting for words, whereas Katherine's quiet ways and gentle demeanour were just the thing to make him feel like royalty. To her, he was not merely the youngest son, a man of no account and with no prospect of advancement.

And here he was making comparisons again, and daring to wonder what it would be like to marry her. He really must make a decision soon.

15: Celebrations

K ent stood before the altar of St Timothy's church beside Walter, watching Winnie Strong walking towards them on her father's arm, her face filled with radiance. Alongside him, Walter, too, was glowing with happiness.

Was this how it would be for Kent if he married Katherine? He could picture her on her uncle's arm, but she would be blushing, her head lowered, the very image of demure maidenhood. When she reached his side, she would look up at him and smile, that look that made him feel like a giant walking the earth.

Would he, too, be joyful? Would he smile back at her adoringly as Walter now gazed at Winnie? Would he speak the responses in a clear, confident voice, in the certainty of a happy future?

It was all so difficult! Should he or should he not? Marriage was such a risky venture, their whole lives at stake. Katherine liked him well enough now, but if once she became accustomed to the wider world of London, would she find him dull? He was not a fine, handsome fellow like Walter, nor a man who took what he wanted from life, like Eustace. He was a nonentity, if he were being honest with himself, a nobody, the unwanted third son with no redeeming features. He had always drifted through life, asking very little from it, but now he had to decide, and he could not bring himself to settle one way or the other.

The service over, the locals meandered away to drink the newly married pair's health in the White Horse, while carriages conveyed the earl's guests back to Corland, for much the same purpose, although in champagne instead of ale. Everyone gathered in the great hall, the autumn sunshine filtering down from the glass roof far above.

There was another cause for celebration, too. Mr Nicholson, the seemingly benign chaplain murdered in the summer, had not only not been ordained and thereby rendered all the earl's children illegitimate, but he had been quietly lining his pockets for years at the expense of the estate. But now his accumulated wealth had been tracked down and a sizeable proportion of it returned to the earl — no less than forty and perhaps as much as fifty thousand pounds.

For about five minutes, Kent had been excited — surely now his father would allow him to establish himself in a profession? But not so. He was still happy to finance Kent if he married, but he would not hear of him leaving the family home.

"Walter is insisting on going away to London to make a name for himself, and Eustace is hardly ever here. You will not deprive me of my only remaining son, surely?" he said plaintively.

"Indeed, I would not wish to leave you, Father, you know that, but nor do I wish to live on your charity forever. I should like to make my own way in the world, as third sons have done since time immemorial. It is only right, and especially so now that I am not even a legitimate son. Yes, yes,

I know it makes no difference to you, but to the world, it does. Father, I should like to be respected for myself, not simply because I am your son. If Walter has the chance to do that, why not me?"

"I could not stop him," the earl said glumly, "and in all honesty, I had not the heart to do so. Walter has had by far the worst of this business. For almost thirty years, he has been the heir to the title and estate, he was Viscount Birtwell, a person of some importance in society. Now, he has nothing, and if playing around at the Treasury with Alfred Strong gives him a little pleasure, who am I to deny him that? He will get bored soon enough, I dare say, and Langley Villa will still be there waiting for him and Winnie."

"And I have no quarrel with that, but..." Kent hesitated, but if he did not ask directly, he would never know. "What about this fortune of Nicholson's that has found its way back to you? A very little of that would set me up perfectly."

"To run off and play about with engines? An *Atherton*, fooling about with such devices, and getting his hands dirty? I should think not! Besides, I shall need a good bit of that money to set up Olivia with a suitable dowry. She has ambitions, that girl, and I should like to see her well married. As for a career, my boy, what is wrong with the church? Dewar is still young, but old Hammond over at Welwood is not likely to see out many more winters, and think how convenient that would be, to have you so close! I cannot bear to think of you leaving us altogether, you know. You keep us all cheerful with that ready smile of yours, my boy. What would we do without you, eh?"

It was a compliment of sorts, and Kent had not the heart to insist. So he sipped his champagne and ambled about, finding himself eventually beside his cousin Bertram.

"Your turn next," he said cheerfully.

"I expect so," Bertram said, his face lighting up just as Walter's had done. "Bea has settled on a date, so Dewar will read the banns for the first time next Sunday. Of course, there is still the possibility that Uncle Charles will get there before us. Mother has a new candidate for him." He indicated with a little tilt of the head a woman in green velvet, standing beside Mrs George Atherton. "Miss Marjorie Quick. Quick by name and quick by nature, apparently, for she is reputed to be a bruising rider. Has a huge string of hunters, I am told."

Miss Quick laughed just then, a great honking laugh. Kent thought she sounded like nothing so much as a goose.

"A keen rider should please Father," Kent said. "Better than some of the others Aunt Jane has put forward as the next Countess of Rennington, anyway."

"Oh yes!" Bertram pulled a face. "The terribly pious one — that would never have done."

"Or the bluestocking."

"Heavens, yes! What was Mother thinking? But she will leave no stone unturned to get him married off and avoid the dreadful possibility of our branch of the family inheriting, and none of us have any quarrel with that." He shuddered. "The last thing I want is to be the Earl of Rennington, so the sooner Uncle Charles marries again and cuts me out the better. But what of you, cousin? Now that Walter is wed, since Eustace seems to like his freedom, it must be your turn and you have someone in your eye, if Emily is to be believed."

"I cannot say," Kent said. "I have not yet settled in my mind what I want to do. How did you decide? You were determined not to succumb to

Miss Franklyn when she first announced her determination to marry you, and yet... here you are, banns about to be called."

"I kissed her," Bertram said, with a quick laugh. "Or at least, she kissed me... no, I definitely kissed her... There was kissing, anyway, and then... everything was different. I am not much help, am I? But even if you were to kiss Miss Parish, there is no getting past the lack of dowry, although perhaps that does not matter so much, now that Nicholson's ill-gotten gains have been recovered. Your father will put up some of that tidy sum to settle on your bride, I am sure."

"He would do so, but the price for that is that we live here, and then I shall never escape, cousin. I shall never see the foundry in Birmingham where those marvellous beam engines are constructed. I shall never see one in action, never hear the noise or feel the power as it works."

"You could always take a wedding tour to Birmingham, if your bride were agreeable. Most women prefer a more scenic location, but I am sure she would be happy to oblige you. Or there are engines here in the north... Leeds, I have heard. Many of these mill towns have engines."

"Branton," Kent murmured. "Katherine's home, Branton, is a mill town."

"What could be better? Take her to see all her friends, then, and while she chats over the teacups, you can look at these engines."

All Kent could see was that at the end of it, they would have to come back to Corland Castle and live there for the rest of their lives. "I need something more, cousin, something new and exciting and fascinating, and most of all, I need a profession so that I may live an independent life and not be forever beholden to my father for every last farthing.

"Perhaps you are right, cousin," Bertram said ruefully. "Far be it from me to give you advice, but you will never get yourself a profession and an independent life if you sit under your father's wings all the time. You are a grown man, so why not simply pack up and go? To Birmingham, if that is where your interest lies. You must have money enough for it, for your allowance is larger than mine and you cannot spend even the half of it. Presumably you have made something from Eustace's little enterprise, too."

Kent laughed. "You make it sound so easy — just pack up and go!"

"It *is* easy. You know, Kent, you are far too good-natured for this world. Your father wants you to stay, so you stay. Eustace wants your help, so you help. Miss Parish likes to ride, so you go riding with her. Olivia wants you to squire her about, and you do it. No doubt if Miss Parish decides she would like a husband, you will oblige her in that, too, whether you want it or not. But giving way to everyone else is not necessarily going to make you happy. Do something for yourself for a change."

"But do I have any right to be happy?" he murmured.

"Ah, you are minded to be philosophical," Bertram said, with a quick laugh. "I shall need far more champagne before I can tackle a question like that."

All through the rest of that day, Kent pondered Bertram's words. *Why not simply pack up and go? You must have money enough for it.* It was a good point.

That night, Kent unlocked the bottom drawer of the small desk in his room where he kept his money. From the day he left for Harrow, his father had given him an allowance suitable for his position in life. He had returned from his first term with a sum still unspent, and the purse had been tossed into this drawer. Every quarter day since, another purse had joined it, the amounts within increasing as he grew to adulthood. Then there had been his winnings from cards to add to the collection, and a few IOUs which he had never bothered to redeem. He had dipped into the drawer whenever he found himself in need of funds, but he had never bothered to count up the total to see what his accumulated worth might be.

Now, he took the drawer out of the desk, and tipped the contents onto the bed. He was astonished at what he saw. How had he managed to build such a hoard? His father had always been generous, he supposed, and he himself had never had expensive tastes. His wardrobe was modest, he rode whatever he could find in his father's stable, and he had never gambled to excess or kept a mistress. Whenever he travelled, his father always gave him extra money to pay for post horses and rooms at inns. His tailor's bills and his valet's salary were his only regular expenses.

Three thousand two hundred and forty seven pounds, that was how much he was worth. There were IOUs worth another four hundred pounds from Eustace and Walter, but he was hardly likely to dun his own brothers, so they went in the fire. Several more long-forgotten IOUs from his Cambridge days, but they went on the fire, too. Two rings that Izzy had pledged once instead of an IOU. He would have to return them to her, of course.

Right at the back of the drawer he found two bundles of letters. One bundle was from the man who had made the wonderful telescope at the tower. Those he would keep. The other was from a young lady he had met briefly in town, who had fancied herself to be violently in love, and had written him increasingly impassioned letters declaring her undying affection. Since she was no more than thirteen at the time, and he barely fourteen, the affair had speedily reached its inevitable conclusion, but those letters had warmed him for a long time. He had kept them to prove to himself that whatever happened to him, whether he ever married or not, he would always have the knowledge that one person in the world had loved him passionately. He supposed she was happily married now and had long since forgotten him, as he had forgotten her until that moment. She would certainly not thank him for keeping her most improper letters, so they, too, were consigned to the fire.

Three thousand pounds! Enough to pay his way to Birmingham or wherever he wanted to go. He could stay there for a while, find lodgings, eat at chop houses or cheap inns. Or with so much money at his disposal, he could buy a share in a mill, and be at least a partial owner of one of those wonderful machines. It would be an investment, and his father could not object to that.

***

K atherine found herself receiving an unexpected degree of attention from Aunt Cathcart before the proposed dinner to celebrate her return. Her aunt's own lady's maid was to dress her hair, and there had been a lengthy discussion on her choice of gown, although in the end, Katherine's wishes had prevailed.

When Rathbone had been dismissed, Aunt Cathcart sat down beside Katherine and took her hand.

"You think me a fussy old woman, I suppose, for becoming a little excited about this evening, but I truly believe you have a wonderful opportunity before you."

"If you mean Mr Kent Atherton, ma'am, then—"

"I know, you have no expectations, he is just being kind to you, I fully appreciate that. I thought so myself, and Lady Alice certainly tried her best to hint me away from any thought of it... Well, I supposed nothing would ever come of it. But you see, Katherine, his kindness is... somewhat extensive. All that riding you do together, and you cannot be talking about mills and such like the whole time, not to mention his determination to see you dance. And then... well, I will tell you something that I have not divulged to a single soul, but there was an additional reason why I wanted to send you to Helmsley for a while. I wondered, you see, if a man who had fallen into a habit of companionship with you might find, when you were not there, that he missed you more than he thought, and that therefore... well, I hoped he might go down to Helmsley to see you, and he *did*, Katherine, he did! And no sooner are you returned to us than there he is on the doorstep again, the very picture of an anxious friend."

"Aunt, I do not think—"

"I know, dear," she said, patting Katherine's hand gently. "You do not want to get your hopes up. But still, this evening is an opportunity to... well, to see how the land lies, so to speak. You need do nothing special, and indeed, I do not think you have any tricks in your arsenal, so innocent as you are. You need only be yourself, my dear, and we shall see what happens tonight, and of course, his rank is so much higher than yours, despite the recent turn in events, that perhaps it is a little ambitious still. But you would be so well suited, with his interest in mills and other subjects that most gentlemen would not at all wish to speak of. Indeed, most gentlemen would be repelled by your background, I make no bones in saying to you. But not Mr Kent Atherton, and if you could secure him, it would be such a triumph, would it not? The son of an earl! It is more than I aspire to for my own girls, as you know. So I want to give him every opportunity to become closer to you, and then we shall see, shall we not?"

This conversation terrified Katherine. She had so looked forward to the evening, and now she discovered that her aunt was expecting her to *'secure'* Kent — somehow, for she had no *'tricks in her arsenal'*, as she put it. She could not flirt, still less could she dissemble. She had grown comfortable enough with Kent that she no longer blushed furiously when he was nearby, but if she thought there was the slightest possibility that he could return her regard, even in the smallest degree, she would be reduced to incoherent stammering again. She wished her aunt had said nothing at all.

But in the event, the evening passed off without the least discomfort. She was the focus of everyone's attention, naturally, since the purpose of the dinner was to celebrate her return from Helmsley, but after everyone had congratulated her formally as they arrived, there was no undue attention. She was not quite allowed to melt into the background, as she might have wished, for there was always someone at her side. Yet she did not feel awkward at all, for these were all her friends, and apart from her aunt and uncle, all her own age. They teased her gently about bolsters and pretended they were now terrified to get on the wrong side of her, and she found she did not mind a bit.

At dinner, through some fairly transparent manoeuvring by her aunt, she found Kent sitting beside her, to guarantee her pleasure in the meal. Afterwards, all the young people played a boisterous round game of cards, Kent keeping everyone in a ripple of laughter. He was so much fun! Always teasing and joking, and in the kindest way, raising everyone's spirits. No one could be downhearted when he was in the room. He smiled at everyone, but was it just her imagination that saw some additional warmth in his eyes when he looked at her? She was almost sure of it, and for the first time she allowed herself just a sliver of hope.

It was altogether the happiest occasion she could remember since Papa had died. For the first time since she had left Branton, she felt as if she belonged.

16: The Tower

The riding excursions resumed, and by some artful arrangement of Aunt Cathcart's, Katherine was permitted to ride a more spirited steed, borrowed from Emily's family. No longer was she restricted to just the environs of Corland, but whenever Kent or Lucas were of the party, the group might venture as far as they pleased.

"I trust the two gentlemen to look after you and Emily," Aunt Cathcart said. "They will not lead you astray, but you must take the groom with you too."

"Is that necessary, aunt? If we have two gentlemen with us, we are surely prepared for any eventuality."

"A groom may tend the horses if you dismount and walk for a while, as you may wish to do on a longer ride."

Katherine could not object to so pleasing a proposal. It was wonderful, she found, to have the freedom of the moors for her rides. The Athertons, having grown up there, knew every inch of the land, and took her to places she would never have found on her own.

One place she had already seen on a carriage ride with her aunt in the summer, for it was visible from the road north of Corland. On one of their riding expeditions, they came over a low rise and there it was, away in the distance.

"What is that tower over there?" Katherine asked. "I have often wondered."

"It was built by the man who first built Welwood-on-the-Hill, my brother Eustace's house," Kent said. "Sinclair was a bookbinder by trade, but when he sold his business and retired, he bought a parcel of land here from the 9th Earl of Rennington."

"Your grandfather?"

"Great-grandfather. My father is the 11th Earl. Sinclair was interested in the heavens and the movements of the stars, and finding the smoke from the house too often obscured his view, he built the tower. His telescope is still there. Would you like to see it?"

"Very much."

"Then let us ride that way. Shall we—"

"Oh! Look how fast she rides!" Katherine cried, pointing with her whip. On the horizon, galloping as if she were in a race, was a woman in a green riding habit, the feathers of her hat flattened against her back by her speed.

Kent gave a short laugh. "That, Miss Parish, is Miss Marjorie Quick, a friend of Aunt Jane, who thinks to marry her off to my father."

"She will not survive long enough to get him to the altar if she rides so recklessly on this uneven ground," she said. "It is madness."

"Indeed. Oh but look, there is my father in hot pursuit... he is more circumspect, I think. He knows how an unexpected rabbit hole can catch the unwary."

There indeed was the earl, riding somewhat more slowly. He saw them watching and waved cheerily, but with no pause in his pace, and before long both riders had vanished over the brow of the hill.

"Did you see that?" Lucas, who had been riding ahead with Emily, cantered back to where Kent and Katherine were. "Miss Quick was described as a bruising rider, and I can see why. She brought four of her own horses with her, did you know that? Would not risk mounting one of our hacks. Father was somewhat offended. One thing he does know is horseflesh, and Bertram's horse is the equal of anything Miss Quick brought with her."

"It was indeed a fine animal she was riding," Katherine said. "Perhaps she simply prefers to ride a familiar mount."

"Having seen how she rides, I am very glad the poor creatures are hers and not ours," Lucas said. "Inevitably one of them will break its neck before too long. Where to now, Miss Parish? This is all new to you, so you may decide."

"Miss Parish has expressed a wish to see the tower," Kent said.

"Then by all means let us go there," Lucas said equably. "You must show Miss Parish the view from the top floor, cousin."

When they arrived at the tower, Kent lifted Katherine down from her horse, which set off all her blushes, but his manner was so practical, not lingering over the business a second longer than necessary, that she soon regained her composure. The grooms took the horses to graze a little distance away, and Lucas and Emily wandered off along the lane between the fields, looking for blackberries, while Kent lifted a stone to find the key to the tower's weathered wooden door.

After a moment's bemused fumbling, he lifted the latch of the door and pushed it open. "Hmm. It must have been left unlocked last time someone was here. Come inside. This is the main room, with a kitchen and various store rooms through there, but you will want to see upstairs, I am sure."

"What is that door over there?"

"Oh... that leads to the cellars."

"I wonder why such a place needs cellars. Does anyone live here?" she said, looking about at the table with numerous chairs set round it and several well-worn sofas, as if for a large family.

"No one has ever lived here, no, but it is a useful resting place for men working out here. There are occasional parties to dig ditches, trim the hedges or mend the roads, that sort of thing."

"It looks very clean... well-tended. Someone takes good care of it."

He looked a little uncomfortable. "It belongs to Eustace, so that would be his responsibility. Shall we go upstairs? It is clear enough today that we will see for miles from the top."

The stairs wound round the tower, the narrow windows giving changing views of the surrounding land. Katherine counted three floors, each circular room empty of all furniture or draperies. At the top was a room with large windows on all sides, provided with a brazier, a rather moth-eaten rug, several sagging chairs and sofas, and a low pallet with blankets disarranged, as if someone had just that minute risen from it. A table beside one of the windows bore a candlestick, a plate speckled with crumbs and a half eaten cake, and a tankard, as well as a key.

"Ah, there it is," Kent murmured. "I wish people would remember to lock up when they leave."

"If they leave," Katherine said, pointing to the abandoned cake and tankard. "Are you sure no one lives here?"

Kent laughed. "Quite sure. The men who use this place are not the tidiest of creatures. Look, this is Sinclair's telescope. Is it not the most beautiful object?"

"Oh, it is lovely," she said, running one finger appreciatively over its gleaming brass. "Your brother must be assiduous with the polish to keep it in such wonderful condition."

"Ah, that is my doing," he said, grinning at her.

"It is a credit to you. What is that house over there?"

"My brother Eustace's estate, Welwood-on-the-Hill."

"Of course. But why is the telescope pointing towards it? Do the men who come here like to spy on your brother?"

He frowned. "I cannot say. It is odd, for normally the telescope is set up at the eastern window looking out over the moors, but usually I am the only one who touches it. Perhaps Eustace has been here and moved it. Do you want to step out onto the balcony? There is a stair up to the roof if you want the best possible view."

"Is it safe?"

"Quite safe. There is a wall all around, so you cannot slip and fall."

She agreed to it, but when he turned to the door that led outside, he found it already unlocked. "I think you are right, Miss Parish. Someone has definitely been here, and left the place in disarray, and now that I think about it, last time I was here, this door was locked and the key was missing. The key is still missing, yet now the door is unlocked. I will talk to Eustace about it. Well, shall we venture outside?"

The balcony did indeed have a wall all round it, but it was low, and the balcony was narrow. A gust of wind buffeted Katherine, and she gave a gasp of alarm, flattening herself against the outer wall of the tower.

Kent immediately stood in front of her as if to protect her from the unruly wind that threatened to hurl her over the precipice to the ground. His smile was gentle. "Hush, sweetheart. I will protect you, Katherine."

"Thank you," she whispered, wondering that her voice could operate at all when he stood so close to her, so distractingly close, his face only inches from hers.

"I will look after you," he murmured, his voice so low she could barely hear it above the wind.

Then he leaned forward and kissed her, and Katherine melted into his arms. Oh, how long had she wanted to do this! Yet she had never dared to hope. Now, suddenly, he had made himself clear. It was a declaration of sorts, and she gloried in it, giving herself up to all the delirious joy of his lips, his arms around her, his hands firm against her back. Happiness radiated through her whole body, and she wondered that her legs could even hold her up.

All too soon, he pulled away a little, still holding her with one hand while the other brushed a stray curl from her face.

"Sweet Katherine," he whispered. "You need never be afraid. I will always take care of you."

She hardly knew how she got back inside, she was so exhilarated. All she had dreamed of for so long... no, all that she had tried very hard *not* to dream of was suddenly hers. He loved her! Surely he loved her... or felt *something* for her that was more than friendship, more than simple kindness to a neighbour. *I will always take care of you...* that was almost a proposal of marriage, was it not? Almost... very close to one.

Yet as soon as they were back inside, he became practical again, moving the telescope back to its usual position. "This is where it should be," he muttered, peering through the eyepiece and adjusting this and that until it was just as he wanted it.

Katherine was not composed enough to be still while he worked, so she walked round and round the small room, into the corners and out again, restlessly circling the furniture, until her foot caught something hard and she almost tripped. Her exclamation of surprise drew Kent's attention.

"What is it?"

"Something tucked away behind this sofa... a bag of some sort." It was a green leather portmanteau, rather worn, and firmly locked. "You definitely have a visitor."

Kent picked it up and turned it over, then shrugged. "Someone has been staying here, that is true enough. If we ride down to Welwood, I can leave a note for Eustace to look into it, but it will be one of his men, I imagine."

Katherine was too shivery and light-headed to quibble, so as soon as Kent was satisfied with the position of the telescope, they descended to the ground floor. Here Kent paused, his face unusually serious.

"You asked why a tower needs cellars. Katherine, I would have no secrets between us, so I will show you what goes on in the cellars."

He disappeared into the one of the store rooms, emerging with a lantern and a key. In moments the lantern was lit, he unlocked the door and led the way into the darkness.

"The stairs are in good condition, but hold tight to the rope... or you can hold my hand if you prefer."

She did prefer, so they slowly made their way down into the dank gloom of the cellar. It did not totally surprise her that there were a number of barrels stored there, for that, after all, was one of the purposes of a cellar. It was more surprising that the marks on them were in French.

"These are smuggled!" she said.

"They originated in France, yes. They arrive somewhere along the coast, I know not where, and eventually they end up here. We transfer the contents into local barrels, and then distribute them, and the French barrels are burned."

"*We?* You are involved in this?"

He shuffled his feet. "Well, yes. My part in the operation is to man the telescope when deliveries arrive, and take orders. Katherine, it goes on all over the country, you know. No one is harmed by it, after all."

"But it is illegal!" she cried. "You are depriving the government of rightful duties."

"No, because French wines and brandy would not reach these shores at all, if not for the smugglers. We are providing a service for those who can get their preferred drink no other way, and also offering work for local men."

"Dishonest work, Mr Atherton. *Illegal* work, and it is immoral for you as a gentlemen to encourage working men into law-breaking. You should be setting an example. Would you be so tolerant if they were poaching from your father's land?"

"Of course not, for that would be stealing! Nothing is stolen here, merely sold secretly."

She could see that he was not about to acknowledge the wrongness of his actions, and she fell silent.

"Let us not fall out over this, Katherine," he said quietly. "I did not wish to keep this a secret from you, but I can see that the idea is strange to you. Perhaps when you have thought a little about it—"

"You will never convince me that it is right."

"Then let us say no more about it."

They returned to the ground floor and thence outside. Kent punctiliously locked the door and replaced the key under its stone. They rode on to Welwood, left the note for Eustace who was away from home, and then rode back to Birchall in near silence. Kent made a few attempts to initiate conversation, but Katherine was too dazed to respond.

When she reached Cathcart House, he lifted her down from her horse, and this time his hands rested on her waist a little longer than necessary.

"I should be very sorry if this has damaged your good opinion of me," he said quietly.

"It would not do so if you were to give it up," she said.

He sighed. "I wish I could but it is a question of loyalty to... to those involved. The men depend on the income to feed their families. I cannot expect them to take the risk of being caught if I take no risk myself."

"I understand you," she said. "Goodbye, Mr Atherton."

"Goodbye, Katherine. I hope we shall ride again very soon."

She turned and walked slowly into the house, and straight up the stairs to her room. There were no tears. The matter was too serious for weeping.

It was the best day of her life, the day that Kent Atherton had kissed her and as good as told her he loved her.

It was the worst day of her life, for she knew beyond the slightest shadow of a doubt that she could never marry him.

For many days, and nights too, she fretted anxiously over her new knowledge. It was only after a particularly prolonged session of prayers at the rail of the Lady Chapel that she rose from her knees, her mind clear at last.

She knew what she must do.

***

K ent's spirits were low. How could he have been so foolish as to reveal the smuggling operation to Katherine? The day had been so wonderful up to that point, and that moment on the balcony was one that would linger in his memory for ever. She was so trusting, so sweet, so innocent that he had been quite unable to resist her, entirely comfortable with the idea that he would marry her, in time.

But then he had remembered her insistence that there should be no secrets between husband and wife, and this was such a big secret that it could not be concealed indefinitely. Once they were married, he could not disappear for whole nights without raising suspicions in her mind, so she had to know... yet now she despised him, and he had no idea how to rectify the situation.

For some days, rain prevented any riding for pleasure, and he did not see Katherine at all. Eustace returned from wherever he had been — no one ever knew where Eustace went to, for he was always dashing about here and there, without a word to anyone.

'Brother, I received your note about the tower, and have examined it carefully, but can find no trace now of anyone staying there. There is no bag to be found, and the blankets on the pallet are all neatly folded, with no plates or other items out of place. I can only conclude that some itinerant broke in, stayed for a few nights living on the meagre supplies in the store room, and when those were exhausted, moved on. There is no cause for alarm, therefore, although we might want to think of a less obvious place to hide the key. E.'

As the days slid past, Kent began to feel that he had made too much of Katherine's reaction to the smuggling. She was a very upright person herself, so naturally it was a shock to her. Once she grew accustomed to the idea, she would think no more of it than anyone else. So when the rain continued, he called at Cathcart House but was unlucky enough to find her not at home. He sent a posy of flowers from the Corland hothouses, and a little note expressing the hope that he would see her again soon. There was nothing more he could do.

But then he received a terse note from Sir Hubert Strong asking him to call at Birchall House. Sir Hubert was the local magistrate and a genial sort of fellow, so Kent was unprepared for his worried face.

"A damnable business, Atherton," Sir Hubert said, pressing a glass of something into his hand. "Quite damnable. Sit, will you, and I shall explain as succinctly as I can."

"Whatever is it, sir?" Kent said, now thoroughly alarmed.

"I hardly know how to say this." Sir Hubert rubbed his face tiredly. "The nub of the matter is this — someone has laid a charge against you."

"A charge? Against me? What sort of charge?"

"Smuggling," he said. "I have been told that you are operating a smuggling business from the tower at Welwood. You may guess whence this information emanates, I imagine."

Kent set down his glass abruptly, for the wine tasted of ashes in his mouth. "Katherine Parish."

"Indeed. Atherton, I am not cognisant of all that goes on in this parish, and my wife tells me I must be the world's least observant magistrate, but even I was aware that... well, not to put too fine a point on it, that there was an understanding between the two of you. And now this! It is unfathomable to me."

"And to me," Kent said, jumping up and pacing across the room, too restless to be still. "I thought... it was better for her to know, and she disapproved, she made that very plain, but I did not expect *this*."

"Disapproved! Aye, she disapproves all right. Asked me to use my powers as magistrate to warn you off — persuade you to give it up, as she put it. Talked a great deal about sin, and quoted the Bible at me. I had a very uncomfortable half hour, I can tell you."

"What will you do?"

He sighed. "Miss Parish was very anxious to ensure that you would not hang. As if I would drag you off to the Assizes — the son of an earl, and a man of good unblemished character heretofore! Not that I could explain the way these things work, not to a young lady. But she has officially informed me of the matter, and therefore I must investigate, of course. Impossible to ignore so serious a charge. However, I believe..." He chewed his lip, looking speculatively at Kent. "I believe it will take me some days to gather together the necessary men for such an investigation. Wednesday, perhaps? At noon?"

Kent nodded. "Wednesday. Very well."

Sir Hubert nodded, satisfied. "Good, good. I can leave that with you, then."

Kent rode at once to Welwood. Eustace was away again, having stopped only one night, but Wallace, the head groom, was one of the regulars at the tower, and undertook to ensure that no trace of illegal activity would remain by Wednesday.

And then there was nothing for Kent to do but seethe with rage, and wonder that he could ever have been so foolish as to want to marry a woman like Katherine Parish.

That Sunday, he made a point of attending the service at St Timothy's, knowing that she would be there. After the service, he made straight for her, where she stood in a cluster of Cathcarts.

"Miss Parish. A word, if you please."

The colour flared in her cheeks, and for an instant he feared she would refuse, but she nodded and stepped a little aside with him to a quiet spot beside a yew tree.

"How dared you!" he hissed, as soon as they were far enough away from listening ears. "I trusted you with my secret, and you go running to the magistrate with the tale. What did you think you would achieve? Do you not understand that *all* the gentry for miles around benefit from our little scheme? Just as well, for otherwise we could all be hauled before a judge for it."

"Which is precisely why you should not be doing such a terrible thing."

"It is harmless."

"It is *illegal!* A hanging offence!"

"Do you want me to hang, is that it? Do you hate me so much that you would see me swing from a gibbet?"

The colour flared again, and this time it was anger, not embarrassment. "You know I do not hate you, but I cannot stand aside and watch you walk into darkness. What is your life compared to your immortal soul? If you repent of your sins, you may yet be saved."

"I thought we understood each other. I even dared to imagine a future with you, but how can I trust you after such a betrayal? Where is your loyalty to me?"

"My loyalty is to a higher power - the laws of man and of God."

"What an insufferably sanctimonious woman you are. Thank heavens I found out your true nature before it was too late. Goodbye, Miss Parish."

17: Tonkins Farm

Katherine had known from the day at the tower that her hopes of marrying Kent were entirely gone, but it was not until she saw the raw anger in his face and heard his words of contempt that she understood just what she had lost. When he spoke of betrayal and lack of trust, she saw it for the first time from his point of view. He hated her! He had kissed her so tenderly, and now he hated and despised her, and she was not sure that she did not despise herself.

Grief rose up inside her until she felt as if she were drowning. Weeping bitter tears, she walked home as fast as she could, heedless of the rest of the family. Behind her, she heard Aveline's shrill voice asking what had happened, followed by her aunt's low murmur, and after that they followed her in silence.

She went straight to her room, and threw herself onto the bed in despair, her tears an unstoppable flood. Her aunt came into the room a little while later, persuading her out of bonnet and pelisse, and closing the curtains.

"I have brought some wine, dear," she said, her voice so soft, so sympathetic. "You will feel better if you have a little sip now and then."

There was no wine on earth that could make her feel better, but obediently she sat up and took a mouthful, as her aunt held the glass for her.

"There now, that will do you good, I am persuaded. Dearest, do you want to talk about it?"

Katherine shook her head.

"Very well. I will not press you, for I can see that something serious has occurred. I must ask one thing, however. Has Mr Atherton behaved at all improperly towards you?"

"No. No, aunt."

"He has not asked you to do anything which would make you uncomfortable?"

"No." She sniffed, accepted a handkerchief proffered by her aunt and blew her nose. How could she explain it? "We had... a difference of opinion... a fundamental difference."

"Do you think in time, perhaps, that there might be second thoughts? A reconciliation?"

Katherine shook her head vehemently. "Impossible!"

"Your uncle and I would be happy to intervene if—"

"No!" Katherine said with some force. "All friendship between us is at an end, and that is all there is to it."

"Very well. I believe you will not need to see him a great deal, for he will not call here again or ride with you, and once people know of your... difference of opinion, no one will invite both of you to the same event. If he comes to church again... well, if he does, he will ignore you, I expect. Poor Katherine! And everything seemed to be in such a promising way. I thought for certain there would be a spring wedding. But there, one never can tell. I shall leave you to sleep for a while now, but Daisy will sit outside your door, so if there is anything you need, you have only to call. Drink your wine, my dear. You will feel better by and by."

Katherine was quite certain she would never be better again.

***

In Pickering, Captain Michael Edgerton was at his wit's end. His investigation into the murder of the earl's chaplain, Mr Nicholson, had run into the ground. For four months he and his team and followed up every possible lead, and a few that had even seemed to verge on the impossible, but they were no nearer to finding the solution to the case. Even when a man had confessed to the murder, it had turned out to be false, serving only to hinder them.

And now he had another problem, for one of his own investigators was missing. Miss Peach was a lady in her middle years, a former governess now retired and finding a new lease of life searching for murder clues. She had taken off on her own, insisting that it was the best way to uncover nuggets of information, but she had not been seen or heard from now in almost two months, and Michael was beginning to fear the worst. He had returned to Pickering in desperation, one final push to ensure that every possible clue had been thoroughly probed.

He kept returning to the last place she had been seen, the chandlery shop where she had lodgings. He had interviewed all the residents individually, so now he planned to gather them all together to go over every detail one last time.

"And if nothing new comes from this, then I am afraid we must abandon poor Peachy," he said to his wife.

"Anyone but you would have abandoned her long since, Michael," Luce said sadly. "It is so long now since anyone last saw her that we must accept, I fear, that she has met with an accident somewhere."

There were five people gathered in the modestly proportioned parlour above the chandlery shop. The chandler's wife, Mrs Stroud, presided over the teacups, while Mr Stroud himself handed round thick slabs of rich fruit cake. Mr Cartwright, a portly gentleman rather reticent about his profession, nursed a glass of sherry. The widowed Mrs Tasker sat primly upright, as far from Mr Cartwright as possible. The final lady was Mrs Clegg, whom Michael knew to be the former mistress of the present earl's father.

He had brought Luce with him, and at first she led the conversation, since Miss Peach had been her governess when she was a girl. When Michael had brought Luce to Corland Castle at the start of the investigation, Miss Peach had come in the guise of Luce's companion. Michael had hoped that Miss Peach would sit quietly with her needlework in a corner of the castle drawing room, listening in to all the gossip. Instead, she had gone off on her own to pursue her own enquiries.

The five went over everything that they could remember of Miss Peach, although there was nothing that Michael had not heard already.

"I must confess," Mrs Clegg said, "I was somewhat concerned about the poor lady. It was hard to tell whether she genuinely knew something significant, or was simply muddled in her head."

"She were very excitable," Mrs Stroud said. "If you ask me, she just wanted to feel important. She'd had a dull time of it, by the sound of it...

no offence, Mrs Edgerton, but being a governess ain't much of a life, and then she lived with her sister in Harrogate."

"Oh, I know," Luce said easily. "She was so happy to feel that she was useful, and she was convinced that if she were on her own, she would become just another harmless elderly lady and could glean all manner of helpful information, but I am afraid she became rather carried away. After I left her here in Pickering, her letters became increasingly garbled."

"What was the last letter she wrote to you?" Mrs Clegg said. "Perhaps it might jog our memories a little."

"Of course." Luce handed over the now rather bedraggled paper, and they passed it from hand to hand. Michael had pored over it so many times that he knew it off by heart.

'My very dear Mrs Edgerton, So much new to tell you, but I cannot speak too openly, for fear of our communications being intercepted. I shall be brief, therefore. I have seen a Person of the Greatest Interest here, which has sent me in a new direction. I have been experimenting with a Substance of Interest, but with little success so far. I have received aid from an Unexpected Quarter, which will be of the greatest benefit. More details when I see you next. My regards to your charming husband, and all your friends. Yours most respectfully, Philomena Peach (Miss).'

Mrs Clegg laughed as she read. "Oh dear! It is not very informative, is it?"

"Does any of it suggest anything to you?" Michael said eagerly. "The person of interest, perhaps?"

Mrs Clegg shook her head. "She never mentioned a specific person to me. Mrs Stroud? You talked to her more than any of us."

"No. It's all nonsense, ain't it? Poor lady, she hardly knew what she was doing, I'll wager."

"The substance… that might be laudanum," Mrs Clegg said thoughtfully. "She told me she was having trouble sleeping, and wondered how much laudanum would help her obtain a full night's sleep. Perhaps she was experimenting with that?"

"But why would she tell me of that?" Luce said. "It is hardly relevant to the investigation."

"Perhaps she thought it was," Michael said. "Mrs Stroud, Miss Peach talked to you of laudanum and mule droppings, did she not? Can you remember what was said? The exact words, if you can recall."

"Ooh, it were a long time ago, Captain. Months, now. All I can remember is what I told Mrs Edgerton when she came here asking after Miss Peach. She mentioned laudanum and mule droppings together… something about laudanum being the key, and then… then… oh, I forget. She made the mule droppings sound like one of those puzzles… charades, maybe."

"So she was puzzling over it?" Michael said.

"No… no. She were right pleased with herself. She'd worked it out… that's it, she said she'd *solved* it… the mule droppings, that is. And then she clamped a hand over her mouth, as if she'd said too much, and laughed. One of those silly little laughs, like a girl. I thought then she weren't right in the head, and I still think it, if you want to know the truth. Laudanum and mule droppings indeed! How ridiculous!"

And that was as much as Michael could get from them. It was not much, not much at all. If only Miss Peach had been less secretive! If she had confided in anyone, he would have discovered where she had gone and could have gone after her, and then whatever accident had befallen her could perhaps have been prevented. It was frustrating, but then everything about the chaplain's murder was frustrating. None of it made any sense to him. It was like a wooden puzzle which was meant to slot together, but some of the pieces were missing so nothing fitted.

They walked back to the inn in silence, both aware that this was the end of the search for Miss Peach. They had met a solid wall and could proceed no further.

The innkeeper met them at the door as they arrived. "Beg pardon, sir, madam, but there's a gen'leman awaitin' for you in the parlour."

"I will see him," Michael said.

"No, sir, he said it were the lady he wan'ed to see. Asked for Mrs Edger'on by name."

"Very well. Send up some wine, will you, and whatever else you have."

"Already done, sir."

"Thank you. How very mysterious!" Michael said as they climbed the stairs to their private parlour, rather amused. "I will come with you, though, unless this is an assignation with a lover, in which case I shall tactfully disappear."

"Oh, surely not! I should expect you to challenge him to a duel, at the very least. Pistols at dawn, my dear. Nothing less will do."

"No, no! *Rapiers* at dawn. Much more the thing. Pistols are so unreliable."

They were both laughing as Michael opened the door and ushered Luce inside.

Mr Eustace Atherton turned towards them and they knew at once from his face that he brought bad news.

"Oh, no!" Luce cried. "Not Peachy!"

"I cannot be certain, for I did not know her well enough to be sure, but... I believe so. There is... a body. In a field some two miles or so from here. It matches the description of your companion. Mrs Edgerton, I am so very, very sorry."

Luce gave a little sob, one hand covering her mouth. "What happened? Did she suffer, do you think? Was it some kind of accident?"

Atherton's expression hardened. "I cannot be sure... Captain Edgerton will confirm it, but I suspect she was murdered... strangled. Her throat is badly bruised."

"Oh, poor Peachy!" Luce said. "Do you want me to come and identify her? Oh... was it some time ago? Is she... is she...?"

"No, no! It was quite recent, I believe. The body is not... disfigured. Even so, I believe your husband is the best person to look at her remains."

"How did you come to find her?" Michael said. "In a field, you said?"

"Yes. I have been on the lookout for some sign of her for some weeks now, ever since you mentioned that she was missing. Not constantly, but whenever I had a few hours free. I know a great many people, so I thought to ask around in case anyone had seen her. An elderly lady on her own... one would imagine someone would have seen her, but no one had. So then I thought to examine some of the remote barns or sheds, places where someone who does not wish to be found might hide." He pulled a folded paper from a pocket and unfolded it onto the table to reveal a map, with several points circled. "These are the likely places I identified, all within walking distance of Pickering, for I discovered early that she had not been seen on any of the public coaches."

"You have been impressively thorough," Michael said with genuine admiration. "I have covered some of this ground, but mostly I just asked at inns and the like. I never thought to check the barns."

"She must have been sleeping somewhere," Atherton said, "and since it was clear she wanted to remain out of sight, it seemed sensible to look in such places where she might have taken shelter. But I had no luck until today. This barn here... I discovered blankets, supplies of food, a bag of clothing. No sign of the lady, so I started looking in the nearby fields, and caught sight of what looked at first like a bundle of clothing under a hedge. It is quite near Tonkins Farm, so I have left a couple of Tonkins' sons to guard the spot. They will not touch anything. I know you will want to examine the body and its surroundings carefully."

"You have done an excellent job, sir," Michael said. "If ever you want to take up a career, I should be delighted to take you in as a fellow investigator. Luce, will you mind if I leave you here for a while? You might start composing a letter to Miss Peach's sister in Harrogate."

Tears trickling unheeded down her cheeks, Luce shook her head. "No. I shall come with you. I want to see... where she met her end."

They found the place to be just as Atherton had described it, the body in its old-fashioned round gown and ancient wool cloak half concealed by the hedge, with two sturdy farmers standing a respectful distance away, and a little cluster of children watching from the gate nearest to the farm. The smoke from the farmhouse chimneys could be clearly seen above a small clump of trees. The barn was visible on the far side of the field.

It took Michael only a moment to confirm that it was indeed Miss Peach, and that she had been strangled.

"Why would anyone kill her?" Luce said sadly. "Such a harmless lady, one would think."

"A robbery, perhaps?" Atherton said. "She carries no reticule. Did she wear any jewellery?"

"No jewellery, and she was old-fashioned in her ways, so she still had pockets under her skirts," Luce said.

"May I look for them?" Michael asked. "She might have written all her findings in a notebook, so if the pockets are still there..."

"Should you like me to look?" Luce said.

"If you feel able to do so, that would be helpful. I do not like to rummage under the skirts of a lady I knew so well."

Luce moved the cloak aside and quickly found the slit in the skirt that concealed one pocket. It contained a few coins, a handkerchief, a small box of lozenges and an apple.

She hesitated. "Will you... roll her over a little? So that I can get to the other pocket?"

He obliged, but it contained only a prayer book and several keys on a ring. "No notebook."

"Do you need to... examine the body?" Luce said in a low voice.

"The coroner will do that," Michael said hastily. "He will tell me if there are any other injuries, or marks of interest. I should like to see the barn where you found signs of habitation, if you will, Atherton."

The barn was full of hay. Just inside the door, where the hay was more spread out, Michael saw a pile of blankets arranged in the form of a rough bed, a paper bag containing a half-eaten loaf of bread and some cheese, a flask and a rather dilapidated portmanteau made of thick, woven wool, containing a few items of clothing.

"So this was how she was living," Luce murmured. "Poor Peachy! And she was so fastidious about her person, as a rule. She was thrilled to be at Corland Castle where there was always hot water for washing."

"I wonder why there is no notebook?" Michael said distractedly.

"There is not much here to go on, is there?" Atherton said sympathetically.

Michael could only agree. Atherton left, having other business to attend to, while Michael spent some time talking to Mr Tonkins and his family, but no one had noticed anything amiss or seen any sign of Miss Peach. After that, he allowed the farmers to carry Miss Peach gently into the farmhouse until she could be conveyed to Pickering. He gathered up all the belongings from the barn, and he and Luce rode slowly back to Pickering.

"I do not think she could have suffered," Luce said after a while.

"No, I should imagine not. It would have been very quick, for a slight creature like that would have no defence against a man bent on mischief."

"But why, Michael? Why would anyone want to murder poor Peachy? Even her few coins were not stolen."

Michael pulled his horse up sharply. "Yes, why? And that is what has always bothered me about Mr Nicholson's murder, too. Why would anyone do such a thing? It makes no sense, and Miss Peach's murder makes no sense, either. Did you notice anything odd about her clothes, Luce?"

"They were very old, but that is hardly unexpected."

"There was no straw on them. She was living in a hay barn, yet there was not a scrap of straw on her."

"She was lying out in the open. Any stray wisps would have blown away."

"No, for look at us. You have straw in your hair, I have it on my coat, and we were only in the barn for a few minutes, and not even lying down in the hay. She would have been coated in the stuff. When you pulled open her cloak, bits of it would have flown out."

"What are you saying, Michael — that she was never in the hay barn at all?"

"I am not sure," he said, frowning. "All I know is that there is something odd about all this. However, we have keys to identify, and her bag to examine thoroughly. Let us go back to her room at the chandlery and see what we can find out."

18: An Upright Citizen

Kent's anger sustained him all the way from the church back to the castle, and then, as abruptly as the popping of a soap bubble, it was gone. How could he have spoken so, and to Katherine, his sweet Katherine, of all people? Such intemperate language! He could not think without horror of his words to her, and she so gentle and innocent, to be harangued in such terms. *What an insufferably sanctimonious woman you are!* He could hardly bear to remember it, when she had only been trying to rescue him from his evil ways.

And yet, what could he do about it? She deserved an apology, but if he went to see her, he could not be sure that his rage would not flare up again. She had been angry, too. No, that would not do. For a while he toyed with the idea of writing to her. It was improper, but under the circumstances... and he could address the letter to Mrs Cathcart in the first instance. He even attempted to pen a few lines. But the difficulty of finding the right words discouraged him.

It was hopeless.

For the rest of Sunday, he gave himself up entirely to grief-stricken misery. Katherine was lost to him, that was all he knew, just when he had never been more certain that she was the one woman in the world who could make him happy. If she had died, he could not have been more overwhelmed with sorrow. In his mind, he stood on the balcony at the tower and kissed her again and again, remembering that moment of supreme joy and pretending that the madness just minutes later had never happened. If only he had not taken her into the cellar! If only... if only...

The next morning, after a sleepless night, he rose as soon as the first streaks of light appeared on the horizon, with just one thought in his head — no more agonising over what was done and could not be undone. He needed something to occupy his hands if not his mind, so he took his tools to the sunken garden, where there was a broken fountain to be worked on, and set about scrubbing and poking and delving. Then there were leaks and blockages to be looked for, and, eventually, repairs to be effected. Early in the afternoon, he had the satisfaction of seeing water playing over the nymphs who cavorted around the centre of the fountain.

And the instant it was done, as he sat watching the drops shimmering in the weak autumn light, all his grief came roaring back. Having something worthwhile to do could help him forget for a while, but it could not last forever.

Eustace arrived while he was still mired in misery. "Here you are, brother! I have been looking everywhere for you."

"Oh? Is it about the tower?"

"The tower?"

"Wallace has everything in hand. It will be clear by Wednesday."

217

"Oh, that," Eustace said with a quick laugh. "Yes, I am sure everything will be fine. Wallace is a good man. You will not need me, I take it? Or anyone else?"

"No. Mine was the only name mentioned, I believe. I will be there to show Sir Hubert round the empty cellars, and he will not notice if there is a strong smell of brandy in the air."

Eustace laughed. "Strong is an ally. He will not betray us. Not like— Well, never mind that. No, I wanted to talk to you about another matter entirely. Do you remember that old biddy that the Edgertons had trailing round with them for a while — the one who went missing?"

"You mean Mrs Edgerton's former governess, Miss Peach?"

"The very same. A body has been found, over at Tonkins Farm. Seems to be her. She had been living in the hay barn there. I have been checking all the remote barns and sheds, and happened across the body this morning."

"I am very sorry to hear it," Kent said. "What happened to her?"

"Strangled."

"What! Another murder? Does Captain Edgerton know?"

"Of course," Eustace said testily. "Naturally I went to him straight away. But it can hardly be connected to Nicholson's death, so perhaps now he and his odd bunch of cronies will take themselves back to Hartlepool and leave us in peace. They have done nothing except cause disruption for months now."

"They found Father's missing money," Kent said. "That is hardly nothing. But what was Miss Peach doing at Tonkins Farm?"

"Who knows? Her mind was not sound, so there need not be a rational reason for it."

"Why did you check there? You said you were checking remote barns, but that one is hard by the farmhouse, and there would have been people in and out of it when the hay was being got in. Miss Peach could hardly have been living there then."

Eustace huffed in annoyance. "What is this, brother? You are getting as bad as Edgerton for asking questions. Perhaps she moved about, who knows. The point is, she has been found at last, so Edgerton will have no cause to poke around in our affairs."

"Did you think he would?"

"He pokes into everything! The man is incorrigibly nosy, and imagines that everything is his business. Strong is sound, but if Edgerton got wind of our little enterprise, he could cause us a world of trouble. Do not let him, that is all I ask. Keep him well away from the tower, or any mention of it."

Kent chewed his lip thoughtfully. "You do not think, then, that perhaps our mysterious visitor there might have been Miss Peach?"

"What? What crazy nonsense is that? The tower is above twenty miles from Pickering, and how do you suppose she got there? She never took the public stage coach, and I hardly think she walked all that way, do you?"

Kent frowned. It was possible, surely. It was almost two weeks since he and Katherine — ah, that day! Pain lanced through at the memory. He must try not to think about it. Almost two weeks since... since *he* had seen signs of occupation at the tower. Time enough even for an elderly lady to make her way to Tonkins Farm. Walk five miles, stay in a disused barn or shepherd's hut for a day or two. Then another five miles. Yes, it could be done.

"If she was wandering about from barn to barn, say..." he said slowly.

"Kent, she was last seen in Pickering, and her body turned up only a couple of miles away. I doubt she was ever more than two or three miles from the town."

That was a good point. Just because a thing was possible did not mean it had happened that way, and what would Miss Peach be doing at the tower, anyway? She believed herself to be investigating Nicholson's death, so she would focus her attention on Corland or Pickering, surely? The tower had no connection to Nicholson at all. No, it was foolish to imagine she had ever been there. He resolved to put the idea out of his head.

"Do not start putting ideas into Edgerton's head, I beg of you," Eustace went on, "or he will be crawling all over the place looking for who knows what, and if he finds so much as a drop of candle wax in the wrong place we shall never be rid of him. Remember your loyalty to me and to the enterprise, and keep him away from the tower at all costs."

Kent laughed, although uneasily. "Very well, brother. Let us at all costs keep the nosy Captain Edgerton away from our affairs."

But he wished with all his heart that the enterprise was not his affair. When Eustace had first drawn him into it, making it sound so harmless, he had seen nothing wrong with it, and it was thrilling to his younger self to scurry about at night. But lately he had grown uneasy with it, appeasing his conscience with the thought that others depended on him. And now that Katherine had made him see the wrong in it—

Instantly, his thoughts were filled with Katherine again. His lovely Katherine, with whom he had hoped to spend the rest of his life. Was there anything he could do to recover his position with her? He tried to recall their happier exchanges, where she had told him what she expected from a husband. No secrecy... he remembered that one, and look how much trouble it had brought him!

What else? A good character... integrity, honesty, trustworthiness. All of those came into it. Ah, that was more difficult. He regarded himself as being of good character, but was he? Or would the world view him as

Katherine did, as a smuggler, a law-breaker, who encouraged working men to break the law with him?

There was something else, too. She had said that a man must be a good Christian, and he could find no fault with that. He must learn to pray, as she did, in faith and utter confidence in the goodness of the Almighty. She was so certain, and at that moment, when he felt the foundations of his life crumbling, he wanted just a little of that certainty.

She had been entirely certain that smuggling was wrong. No matter that no one seemed to be harmed by it. No matter that wealthy men wanted their brandy and wine, and poor men wanted the extra coins to feed their children. It was wrong, and that was the end of it, and he would be better off to be hanged for his wickedness if that might save his immortal soul.

In his heart of hearts he could not disagree with her. It *was* wrong, it was illegal and if Sir Hubert Strong's cellar had not contained several barrels of excellent French brandy, Kent would have been in very deep trouble now, and Eustace with him, and the family plunged into even more trouble than Nicholson had brought them. It was all very well to talk about loyalty to the family, but one of the sacred duties of any son is to do nothing to dishonour his family. If he were to be hauled before a judge for smuggling, then even if his father's influence could ameliorate his sentence, there would still be disgrace and scandal.

Yet what could he do?

That night, he spent an hour on his knees at his bedside, trying to pray. His prayers were impassioned, it was true, but how could he be sure that they were heard? And what good could come of it? He remembered meeting Katherine in church when she was praying at the Lady Chapel rail. In despair at the disaster that Nicholson had inflicted on his family, he had asked if her prayers worked, and although she had not answered him, she had agreed that they made her feel better.

Kent did not feel better. It did not help that he had a meeting on Tuesday in the very church where he had seen her praying... where he had first met her, in fact, when she had looked so sorrowful in her blacks that he had wanted desperately to cheer her up, just a little. Even then he had been drawn to her, wanting to make her smile... to make her happy. And he had, for a while, until he had told her the truth about the smuggling. They had both been happy, for a while. Now he wondered whether he would ever be happy again.

Richards was in the church early, sitting in their usual pew and wearing a cheerful grin. "A good haul this time. Sixty-two barrels, mostly brandy, and some claret as well, but the winter storms will be upon us soon, so who knows when the next delivery will be? Won't affect me, though. I'm getting out."

"Getting out? Is that allowed?" Kent said, with a wry grin.

"Not as a rule, but I'm getting wed next week and we'll be living with her family out on the farm. They're honest, God-fearing folk, and if I start creeping about at night — well, you can guess how that would look. So I'm about to become an honest, God-fearing man myself."

"You, an upright citizen?" Kent said, laughing.

"I know, I know, who'd have thought it, eh? But we can all change, when there's a woman involved."

"Can we?"

"Well, I hope so, cos she's a real peach and I'd hate to make her cry. Tommy'll let you know the exact dates for the delivery. Look after yourself, sir."

"You, too. Oh, and my felicitations to you and Mrs Richards."

With a wave and a wide smile, Richards disappeared, but Kent sat on in the empty church long after the heavy wooden door had thumped shut and deep silence had descended.

Get out? Was it truly possible? *We can all change, when there's a woman involved.* Perhaps Kent could change, too. After all, Katherine was a peach, was she not? She was worth changing for, and even if she would never take him back, he would be a better man for it.

Slowly, he walked down the aisle and turned aside at the Lady Chapel. This was where he had seen her praying, kneeling at the rail, head bowed and eyes closed. At the exact spot where she had knelt, he lowered himself to his knees, bent his head and began to pray. He prayed for the strength to do the right thing, whatever that was. He prayed to become a better man — an honest, God-fearing man, if that were possible. He prayed for forgiveness for all his foolishness. And most fervently of all, he prayed for Katherine to be well and happy and perhaps find a man who deserved her.

It was the oddest thing, but he felt better. Calmer, perhaps. Less mired in grief and uncertainty. The clouds that seemed to have hovered around him had drawn back a little. He could not honestly say that the sun was shining on him, not yet, but the sky was less grey.

He rose, rather bemused, and began to walk back down the aisle. He had almost reached the door when it creaked open and a familiar form stepped around it. She gasped when she saw him, flushing scarlet, and would have turned at once and left again.

"No, do not go," he cried out. "I am just leaving... there is no one else here... you will have solitude for your prayers."

She turned again, hesitating, uncertain. He drank in the sight of her, becoming aware that she did not look at all well. Below the flushed complexion, he thought she was tired, her eyes not sparkling as they usually did.

"You are ill, Miss Parish?" he said quickly.

"No, no. I am... quite well. Thank you. And... and you?"

"I am well, also." No, he was not well, not when he had behaved so abominably towards her. He might never be truly well again. But he could not say that, could not say any of the things that were in his heart. He knew he should apologise to her, but he had no idea where to begin. Instead, for what reason he could not guess, he said, "I have been praying."

"Oh." A glimmer of a smile. "Does it help?"

He smiled back at her, remembering, as she clearly did, their previous conversation on the subject. "Yes. Yes, it does. I bid you good day, Miss Parish."

She curtsied, he bowed and stood aside for her to enter the church. Then he pulled the door quietly shut behind him and walked home to Corland Castle, knowing now what he had to do.

He knew something was amiss the instant he came within sight of the bridge to the front door. Corland Castle was a modern building but the architect, in a fanciful moment, had designed it with a dry moat all round, housing not water, but access to the basement level of the castle, and the underground stables and stores. Thus the entrance was reached by way of a bridge, and the distinctive figure of the butler could be seen standing at the near end of it, wringing his hands.

"Oh, Mr Kent! Your father will be so pleased to see you. You will be able to keep him quiet until the surgeon gets here."

"Surgeon! Whatever has happened, Simpson?"

"A fall from his horse, sir. Nothing serious, we don't think, just his shoulder again, but you know what he's like when he's in pain."

"Where is he? In his room?"

"Yes, sir."

Kent tore through the house, scattering clusters of distressed servants at every corner, and raced up the stairs and into his father's room, where a scene worthy of Bedlam greeted him. A young woman in a riding habit was shouting at Turner, the earl's valet, Olivia was crying noisily, while three footmen were engaged in holding the earl down on his bed while he bellowed in pain.

"Olivia! Out" Kent said.

"But—"

"No buts. If all you are going to do is cry, you can do it somewhere else. You, madam!"

Now that he could see her closely, he realised it was Miss Quick, the bruising rider whose reckless pace had no doubt caused the earl to fall.

"Miss Quick, out, if you please."

"I am trying to tell this dunderhead that he must bring ice at once, but he insists on laying hands on Charles, and I will not have it, do you hear?"

"Turner knows precisely how best to help his lordship, madam, and you are hindering him."

"Yes, but—"

"*Out*, or I shall carry you out myself."

"But—"

With a muttered curse, Kent picked her up and threw her over his shoulder, ignoring her screams. "Away you go, Turner."

"Thank you, sir."

Kent marched out of the room and deposited Miss Quick unceremoniously on the floor, under the wide-eyed gaze of Olivia.

"Stay away from the earl until he requests your presence, madam, although if it were left up to me, I would have sent you packing long since. Break your own neck if you want to, but leave my father alone."

He went back into his father's room, and firmly shut the door on the women. Turner was kneeling on the bed, and as Kent watched, he took hold of the injured arm and pulled sharply. The earl screamed once, then sank back onto the pillows in relief.

"Thank you, Turner. Whatever would I do without you? Kent! There you are, my boy! Did they tell you what happened? Thunderer caught his hoof in something and we both ended up on the ground. Happily he was unscathed, unlike me."

"Dislocated your shoulder again, eh?"

"I really should teach Turner to ride so that he can be on hand for the next time. Would save me a lot of grief, for he knows just how to pop things back into place."

"Or maybe you could ride a little more cautiously, Father?"

The earl laughed and rubbed his nose ruefully. "No fool like an old fool, eh? Poor Marjorie! Such a spirited rider, but I should never have tried to keep up with her. I am fifty-five years old, Kent, and I should not be attempting to compete with a slip of a girl almost thirty years my junior. Where did she go?"

"Mr Kent conveyed her out of the room, my lord," Turner said, handing the earl a glass of brandy. "Drink that, my lord. It will dull the remaining pain."

"Conveyed her out of the room? What precisely does that mean?"

"I carried her out," Kent said. "She was... unhappy about it."

The earl gave a bark of laughter. "Obnoxious woman! Did you ever have the misfortune to hear her laugh? She barks like a dog."

"I thought it was a goose myself," Kent said.

The earl chuckled. "Lord, yes! Poor Jane! She is trying so hard to get me married off, and I am trying to find another wife, truly I am, but they are all very poor substitutes for my dear Caroline. Your mother is a wonderful woman, Kent, and is proving very hard to replace."

"Then why not marry her again, instead of one of these improbable women?"

The earl sighed. "It is what she wants. She thinks I should have more sons... legitimate sons, which she cannot give me, and I always do whatever she wants, because I love her dearly. But I do miss her. I miss her dreadfully."

"We all miss her," Kent said sadly.

19: A Letter Is Received

Michael watched his wife pack with her usual efficiency.

"You will take the greatest care? If the weather should turn—"

"Stop worrying. It is only fifty miles to Harrogate."

"Remember to stop at the Three Tuns in Thirsk."

"I know."

"And after that—"

"Stop it, Michael. Sandy will look after me, and we shall be back tomorrow, all being well, and if not, then certainly the day after. Miss Elspeth Peach will not wish to delay her sister's funeral, I am sure."

"Poor lady! What sad news you will be bringing her! You will be sure to ask for any letters."

"I will remember. There! I am ready. Oh Michael, do not look so anxious. Just because Peachy fell afoul of a ruffian on her travels does not mean that I will. On the turnpike roads, with two postilions, not to mention Sandy and his pistols, I shall be quite safe. It is far more likely someone will take a shot at you, you know."

His face lightened. "And I shall be ready for it, if it should happen. But you—"

"Michael, hush." She stopped him talking in the simplest way possible. When they surfaced a little while later, she sighed and said, "I live with worrying about you every moment that you are not by my side, and sometimes even then. It is time you had a little taste of what that feels like."

"Yet you have never asked me to give it all up. I would do it, Luce. I would give up all this scrambling around after murderers if you wished it. If it would make you happy."

"I know you would, but I cannot imagine how irascible you would be if you were confined to live the life of a country gentleman. You would drive me to Bedlam within weeks. It is in your nature to take risks and sniff out villains, so that is what you must do. All I ask is to be allowed to share your life until you fall off a roof or are run through with a sword. Now, husband, are you going to carry my bag for me, or must I do it myself? My carriage is waiting."

Chuckling, Michael hefted the bag onto one shoulder, then stopped, frowning. "That bag in the barn... it seemed far too dilapidated for someone as good with a needle as Miss Peach. It was torn in several places. Surely she would have mended it?"

"I expect she wanted people to think she was a very ramshackle person. It was part of her disguise, no doubt. Carriage, Michael."

He laughed. "I beg your pardon. It is so hard to stop thinking about these little details."

"I know, but think about them after I am gone, if you please. I want to reach Harrogate tonight, not next week."

They made their way down to the inn yard, and he saw the bag, his wife and the blond Scotsman, Sandy, safely into the carriage and away down the road. He was about to turn back up the stairs when he heard his name spoken.

"Aye, 'tis the captain over there." One of the ostlers was speaking to a woman of middle years and drab appearance. She nodded and set purposefully across the yard towards Michael.

"You wished to speak to me, madam?"

"Aye, I do, if you're the man who found that poor woman's body yesterday."

"I did not find her myself. That was Mr Eustace Atherton, but he alerted me because she was an associate of mine and I had been looking for her."

She nodded. "Aye, I remember Mr Eustace. Came askin' after the lady, he did. Askin' everyone he was. But he ain't here, so I'll say what I've come to say to you, if it's all the same to you. What I'd like to know is this — where's my mule?"

"Your mule, madam?"

"Aye. Went off with it, she did, a few weeks back, and that were fine, cos she paid on the nose for him for a full month, and then come back and paid for a second month. But if she's dead, she'll not need him no more, so I'll have him back, if you don't mind."

"A mule!" Michael said, appalled. "Then she need not have stayed near Pickering. She could have been anywhere!"

"Aye." She chuckled throatily. "Wanted to get about a bit without folks knowin', she said, although she never let on what she were about. Some mischief, I make no doubt. But I'd be glad to have the beast back, all the same."

"I am sure you would, madam, but I regret to inform you that I have no knowledge of any mule. Do come inside, and tell me all about it. Have you come far? You must be thirsty... and hungry, I dare say."

"Oh... well, I wouldn't say no to a bite to eat and a drop of somethin'."

She did not say no to anything, as it turned out, eating her way stolidly through everything that Michael put in front of her, and scooping up what few scraps remained into a kerchief *'for the bairns'*, as she put it. Mrs Markley was from a farm to the west of Pickering, where she raised donkeys, mules and pack ponies *'for the trade'*. Michael took that to mean smuggling, for most legal goods went by wagon on the roads or by canal.

"She come out to see me quite a while back," she said, through a mouthful of pork pie, "cos she liked the mules, like. Had one as a girl, seemin'ly. Kept comin' back to see them. Then asked if she could borrow one. Not comfortable ridin' a horse, but a mule she felt she could manage. We come to terms and off she went."

"Who knew you had rented your mule to Miss Peach?"

"No one, I dare say. No one at t'farm would care, and she made me swear to secrecy. Couple of folk came askin' after her — Mr Eustace Atherton, he came, and a fine lookin' man, very polite despite bein' Scotch. He came a couple of times."

"And what did you tell them?"

"Nothin' at all!" she said, in surprised tones. "If a person swears me to secrecy, not a word drops from my lips. Not a word."

Michael sighed in frustration. "It is a pity we knew nothing of this, and especially about the mule. We have been confining our searches to places she could have walked to, without realising she could have got considerably further afield."

It was only as Mrs Markley was about to depart that Michael thought of something else. "I do not suppose Miss Peach ever talked to you about... mule droppings, did she?"

She laughed throatily. "Aye, obsessed with them, she were. They'd give her away, or some such nonsense. Away with the fairies, she was, but her money was good so who am I to question it? But when she came to pay for her second month, she said she'd fixed it. The droppings, that's to say. No idea what she meant by it, though."

Which left Michael not much the wiser. But he had a surgeon arriving to examine the body, so he pushed the matter to the back of his mind for the moment. None of it would bring Miss Peach back from the dead, so there was no urgency.

***

K atherine was at breakfast with the Cathcarts one morning when Davis came in bearing a silver salver.

"A groom from Corland Castle has just brought this letter for you, madam."

"Oh! For me? Oh!" With a little trill of excitement, Aunt Cathcart took the letter. Any missive from Corland was note-worthy, but one so early in the day surely heralded something important. "I do not recognise the hand," she went on, a little uncertainly. "It is not Lady Olivia's. Perhaps Lady Alice has a new secretary."

"Do open it, Mama!" Aveline cried. "Perhaps there is to be a ball."

"They have only just held an evening party," Aunt Cathcart said. "Well, I had better see what it says."

Her face changed as she read, first to surprise, and then, oddly, with a glance at Katherine, to thoughtfulness. Silently, she passed it to Uncle Cathcart, who registered the same expressions, and he too looked at Katherine.

It was about her, that much was clear. Her toast turned to ashes in her mouth. Something had happened... she was to be sent away again... she was not sure she could bear it if— No, of course, she would endure whatever must be endured. That was her duty.

"Well?" Aveline said. "What is it? An invitation?"

"It does not concern you," Aunt Cathcart said briskly, folding the letter and tucking it into her reticule. "Aveline, I wish you could learn to restrain this unbecoming curiosity. See how composed Katherine is! There are no questions on *her* lips, even though she must be just as interested as you are."

"Oh, Katherine is perfect, of course!" Aveline spat.

"No one is perfect, dear, but Katherine is a well-mannered and demure young lady, who is a credit to her uncle and to me, and will undoubtedly make a good match in time because of it. Gentlemen prize such qualities when they look for a wife."

"I shall make a good match, too!" Aveline cried. "There are other qualities men look for."

"No one likes a pert hoyden," her mother said sharply, "especially one who has so little respect for her own mother that she thinks to venture her own opinion in preference."

Aveline flushed angrily, eyes flashing. Throwing down the morning roll that was in her hand she flounced from the room.

No one spoke. The boys exchanged glances, seeming amused, but Uncle Cathcart returned to his mutton chop, and Aunt Cathcart calmly drank her tea. As soon as Uncle Cathcart left the room, however, she whisked after him.

"That letter was about you, Cousin Kate, or I am a Chinaman," James said, grinning at her. "Do not look so apprehensive. If it had been bad news, it would have been you getting a scolding instead of Aveline, you may be sure."

Katherine could not agree with him. Any letter from Corland about her was bound to be bad news, as far as she could see. What was there of good news to be had? Kent was no longer her friend, and nothing else mattered to her at that moment.

When she left the breakfast parlour, Davis was waiting for her. "The mistress would like you to attend her in her sitting room, madam."

The sitting room! The place of reprimand and, most recently, of banishment to Helmsley. As she entered the room, terror filled her heart — she was to be sent away again, she was certain of it now, and she could not—

"I have received a letter from Mr Kent Atherton," her aunt said brightly.

Kent! A letter! That was not what she had expected at all, and it could not be about anything terrible, for her aunt was smiling. Her astonishment must have shown on her face, for her aunt laughed.

"Yes, I was surprised, too, but it is very proper of him. He could not write to you directly, so he wrote to me instead, and a very good letter it is, too. I do not entirely understand it, for it concerns matters of secrecy, so I shall not press you on the point. I am sure if the Athertons have secrets, they must have good reason for them, so there is no need for me to know anything about it. I would never ask you to break a confidence. Your uncle and I are agreed that you should have the letter, for it is intended for you, my dear, and there is nothing in it to put you to the blush. Well... any more than usual, that is. I never saw such a girl for blushing! But you will grow out of it in time, I dare say. There, my dear. Read it, and if you want to talk about it later, I am happy to do so."

Pressing the letter into Katherine's hands, she rose and left the room, leaving Katherine in a state of utter turmoil. But there was only one way to settle her mind, and that was to read what Kent had written.

'Mrs Alan Cathcart, Cathcart House, Birchall. Madam, Pray forgive me for approaching you in this unusual way, but I am at a loss to know how else to proceed. A situation has arisen regarding Miss Parish which my conscience absolutely requires me to address at the earliest opportunity, yet I cannot write to her directly, nor do I feel that I can speak to her. Not only must the subject be a painful one for her, but I feel it important to measure my words with the utmost care lest I make a difficult situation worse. I must throw myself on your mercy, therefore, and trust to your excellent judgement as to how much of this to convey to Miss Parish.

'You will, I am sure, be aware that a breach has occurred between Miss Parish and me. I do not know how much she has disclosed to you, but for my part I cannot speak of it, since it is a matter of secrecy involving others which I cannot honourably expose. You may therefore have to take my word for it that the cause is a serious matter of principle. Miss Parish then acted according to her own high principles. At the time, this made me angry, and to my shame I spoke to her in terms which no gentlemen should ever use against a lady. This occurred on the Sabbath, too, and within the shadow of the church itself, which only makes my disgrace the greater. I am deeply ashamed of my behaviour,

and beseech you to convey to Miss Parish my profound apologies for the insult I offered her. I do not ask for her forgiveness, for I know it to be impossible that she should ever think well of me again.

'As to the other matter which stands between us, I cannot yet resolve the argument in my mind, or make a clear separation of right and wrong, for there are good and proper considerations on both sides. Accordingly, I do not know whether we can move forward from this, and if so, how it may be done. I can only say that my discussions with Miss Parish have led me to consider my own principles more seriously than I have ever done before, and for that I am deeply grateful to her.

'I shall shortly be going away for a while to reflect upon recent events more carefully without the distractions of familiar surroundings, where it would be too tempting to fall back into my previous ill-considered ways. I hope to emerge from this process improved in character, at least in a small way, so that I may look to my own future with greater confidence.

'If it please you, madam, may you convey to Miss Parish my very good wishes and assure her that I shall always hold her in the greatest esteem. I am respectfully yours, Kent Atherton.'

Katherine hardly knew what to make of it. He held her in esteem! That was something, surely? It was not a complete rejection, and he talked of reflecting on his own principles and his previous ill-considered ways. That sounded almost like a repudiation of his wickedness, and yet he said he could not determine what was right or wrong. That was very bad — surely he could see the evil in his actions? And yet... on the whole, she thought it was encouraging.

But oh, how she would miss him when he was away! However awkward it might be to meet him occasionally, or even if she never saw him at all, the knowledge that he was still there, somewhere in the neighbourhood, was a comfort. Merely knowing that at any moment — at church, perhaps, or in the village, or on one of her rides — she might look up and there he would be was something to brighten every day. Now there was only the sorrow that infused her heart and seeped throughout her body whenever she was alone, and especially in the dark, lonely hours of the night. Only in her music could she find any solace.

***

K ent arrived early at the tower to check that all was in order. Wallace was there, and together they walked through the now empty cellars.

"It all looks suspiciously clean for an abandoned tower," Kent said.

Wallace gave a grunt that might have been laughter. "Sir Hubert won't say owt, Mr Kent. Don't worry. I've brought some decent wine, beer for the men and summat to eat, so if owt goes amiss, at least you can get tha'sen foxed."

Kent chuckled. "You think of everything. Thank you! Now get yourself off. I am the only one needed today."

After that, there was nothing to do but lay out food and drink on the big table in the main room and await the arrival of the magistrate.

He came in state, with half a dozen hefty fellows, although two of them Kent recognised as part of the smuggling operation, and all of them were local men who greeted him deferentially. Sir Hubert patted him cheerfully on the back with a reassuring smile. At least he knew that Sir Hubert was on his side, and quite happy to turn a blind eye to the smuggling, so long as his supply of brandy was unchecked.

But there was one additional man in the party, and it was the one that Kent dreaded.

"I have invited Captain Edgerton along as a pair of independent eyes," Sir Hubert said. "Make sure we do everything in the proper form, you know. You have no objection, I am sure?"

And Kent was forced to smile and bow to the captain, and say that no, he had not the least objection in the world.

The captain smiled, baring gleaming teeth, and made him a florid bow. At his side hung his habitual sword, and his greatcoat pockets were weighed down with what Kent was sure were pistols.

The day had just become immeasurably more dangerous.

20: Mule Droppings

Kent lost no time in showing the visitors into the tower's cellars, where they walked all around, ostentatiously looking behind the two empty wine racks, tapping the walls and scuffing the floor for signs of a trapdoor. Kent had to admire the convincing way they set about their work, even though it was obvious nothing could possibly be concealed in so empty a place.

Captain Edgerton ambled about behind the others, looking very much amused, as if he saw through the pretence. Would he comment on the noticeable smell of brandy pervading the air? He would not. He said not a word, merely nodding when Sir Hubert asked if he were satisfied, and then brought up the rear as everyone trooped back up the stairs.

Tankards of beer were passed round to the men, who stuffed their pockets with pastries and wandered outside. Sir Hubert Strong and Captain Edgerton sat down and sipped wine, chatting about nothing in particular, as if this were merely an ordinary morning call.

Eventually, Sir Hubert rose. "Well, I shall write up my report, Atherton, but unless the captain has any concerns, I think we may safely say this matter is now closed."

"I have no concerns," Edgerton said. "If Mr Atherton will indulge me, however, I should very much like to see the view from the top of the tower. I have passed this place so many times yet never before had an opportunity to look inside."

"With pleasure," Kent said through gritted teeth. Edgerton was far too observant a man for comfort, and there was still the possibility that he would detect some trace of the smuggling operation, and put everyone in grave danger.

Strong left thereafter, but Edgerton, with his customary wolfish smile, picked up his glass and the wine bottle. "Lead on, sir."

Carrying his own glass, for he had a suspicion he was going to need something more to fortify him than the half a glass he had already consumed, Kent led the way up the stairs. Edgerton peered interestedly into every room they passed, but since they were all empty, Kent was untroubled by it. In the top room, he saw at once that the telescope had been moved again, and was pointing towards Welwood once more. He said nothing, however, for he had no wish to draw Edgerton's attention to it, instead beginning a recital of the history of the tower.

Edgerton listened gravely, while walking slowly round the room, gazing intently through every window, as if memorising the view. Even when Kent's tale wound to its conclusion and he fell silent, Edgerton continued to prowl. Eventually, he stopped, refilled his glass and looked at Kent thoughtfully.

"Your brother inherited the house and tower, I understand. The bookbinder who owned the estate died some three years ago, and left it to Mr Eustace Atherton."

"Mr Sinclair had no children of his own, never married, in fact, his only sister had died and he was fond of Eustace, so he left him everything in his will. The estate of Welwood-on-the-Hill and an income of fourteen hundred pounds a year."

"And whatever he can make from... other interests," Edgerton said blandly.

Kent's glass was halfway to his lips, but he lowered it, feeling panic rising in his breast. He knew! Edgerton knew about the smuggling!

Edgerton chuckled. "No need to look so stricken, Mr Atherton. Even had Sir Hubert not told me all about it, I would have guessed that something of the sort was going on here. An isolated tower, well away from most habitations, yet easy to reach over the moors by pack pony — I would have been astonished if it were *not* being used as a base for smuggling, and naturally your brother is aware of it, and turns a blind eye. Perhaps he himself suggested the idea."

He did not know, then, that Eustace was the leader of the scheme. Well, he would not find it out from Kent.

"So... what are you going to do?"

"About the smuggling? Absolutely nothing. I have dined at all the respectable houses of the neighbourhood, and a few of the inns, too, and drunk excellent wine and brandy at all of them. I have no quarrel with such supplies, however they might be obtained. Besides, I am engaged by Lord Rennington to investigate the murder of Mr Nicholson, and I have seen nothing so far that would connect him to smuggling. He has businesses in Pickering, both legal and less so, but he does not strike me as a man who would involve himself in anything as risky as smuggling. He must have known of it, for he was a great brandy drinker himself, but did he ever interest himself in where it came from?"

"Never, that I heard," Kent said.

"He was not, for instance, threatening to betray the scheme to the Revenue men?"

"No!" Kent cried, shocked. "Heavens, no! Why, do you think one of us murdered him to stop him exposing us? There is only one person I have ever come across who disapproved of the arrangement so strongly as to try to do something about it, and that was far short of murder."

The pain as he spoke the words coursed through him just as powerfully now as when he had first heard of Katherine's betrayal.

Edgerton must have seen his grief, for he said gently, "I beg your pardon, Atherton. It was not my intention to reopen that wound. Sir Hubert told me something of the matter, so let us speak no more of it. Tell me, if you will, how the smuggling came about. Your brother must have seen the possibility when he moved into Welwood."

Kent took a deep breath. He must put all thought of Katherine out of his mind, at least while Edgerton was here. He might seem sympathetic, but there was no knowing what he might see or do, and he must keep Eustace out of it if he could.

"It was some years before that. Let me see... perhaps thirteen or fourteen years ago at least that Eustace became friendly with the Sinclairs at Welwood. At first, it was just a casual friendship, but when Miss Sinclair died, he took to spending more time with Sinclair — staying for several days at a time. The old man was lonely, I think, and enjoyed Eustace's company. Eustace persuaded him to allow the tower to be used as a transition point for the barrels of brandy and wine. Sinclair was a grateful recipient himself, so he made no objection."

"And then he died and left everything to Mr Eustace. What a fortunate young man!" He began to prowl again, stopping beside the telescope and putting his eye to it. "This is the telescope that Mr Sinclair installed for his star observations, I presume. And now it has a fine view of Welwood. To spy on your brother?"

"No! That would be dull work indeed, for he is hardly ever at home. Usually the telescope faces east, to watch for the train of goods arriving from the coast. I have no idea why it has been moved."

"Who has access to the tower?"

"Anyone! The key is left under a stone outside the front door, and all the locals know that. There is a usable bed over there, and usually food and drink left downstairs, so a man may well bring a companion here for an evening."

Edgerton nodded. "A groom from Welwood, for instance, might bring a housemaid here for a private assignation, and they might well turn the telescope round to spy on their employer."

Kent said nothing, but although Edgerton nodded as if satisfied and began prowling again, he had a sinking feeling that the captain saw more than he acknowledged. Kent could not help remembering his visit with Katherine, and the signs that someone had been living at the tower. The disordered bed, the remains of a meal — that could have been a groom and housemaid, or perhaps someone from Welwood village, no more than half a mile further down the road. But the green leather bag? That was not a local loitering for a few hours. Yet it had nothing to do with Nicholson's murder, and Eustace had charged him with keeping Edgerton away from the tower if possible, so he determined he would not mention that.

"Is the roof accessible?" Edgerton said.

"It should be," Kent said, but when he tried the door to the balcony, it was locked. "Well, that is annoying. Someone has locked the door and taken away the key."

And if it had been the man with the green leather bag, there would be no possibility of getting it back.

"No matter," Edgerton said easily. "I have already detained you for too long. I should get back to Pickering, now that I have a second murder to deal with."

In all his own troubles, Kent had forgotten that. "Eustace told me that your friend Miss Peach came to a sad end. I am very sorry. Pray convey my condolences to Mrs Edgerton and all your colleagues. I do not remember her well, for she was a very self-effacing lady, as I recall, but she seemed an inoffensive person."

"She was. Thank you for your condolences, sir. My wife is very upset. Miss Peach was her governess for a number of years and they have remained close."

"It is hard to imagine why anyone thought to kill such a meek old lady," Kent said. "At Tonkins Farm, too, which is hardly a place where ruffians congregate. What was she doing there?"

"I have no idea," Edgerton said sombrely. "She believed she was investigating Nicholson's murder, and was so secretive about the business that she told no one what she was up to or where she was."

"Did Tonkins or his family know why she was there?"

"They never saw her."

"But if she was living in their hay barn…" Kent stopped, perplexed. "How is that possible?"

"It is not, of course," Edgerton said tersely. "Have you ever slept in hay, Mr Atherton? Or played about in it, as a boy, perhaps? How much hay did you acquire when you did so?"

Kent laughed. "A great deal!"

"Exactly! Bits of hay and straw work themselves into every nook and cranny. The Tonkins' hay barn had blankets arranged as a bed, and Miss Peach's bag was there, and bags of food, but on her body was not a single speck of straw. I asked the physician who examined the body yesterday to look for that in particular, and he found no trace. Nothing lodged in her hair or in her clothes."

"So... are you saying that she was never in the barn?" Kent said. "Then... someone put the blankets there."

"Exactly. The scene was staged, just like a play, to make us believe that she had been living there, but in fact, she could have been anywhere, anywhere at all. But unless we know where she truly was, there is no possibility of finding her killer."

Kent was very struck by this revelation. Was it possible that the mysterious visitor with the green leather bag was Miss Peach? Surely not! There was nothing about the tower connected to the murder of Nicholson, which was her principal focus.

"Surely she could not have been *anywhere*," Kent said cautiously. Edgerton looked at him enquiringly. "What I mean to say is that she must have been somewhere associated with Nicholson, surely?"

"That is logical, yes. Unfortunately, there is no certainty that Miss Peach's mind was... entirely rational, shall we say. Unless I can find some clue to her train of thought — a notebook, say — I cannot be certain that she had not veered onto some other trail altogether. But I must get back to Pickering. Thank you for showing me the tower, sir. I am very glad to have seen inside it at last, and you may be sure that whatever goes on here is of no interest to me."

They made their way downstairs again, where Edgerton efficiently pumped water to clean the used tankards and glasses, while Kent tidied away the remains of the food and wine.

"Little wonder that you get the occasional unauthorised visitor when the place is so well supplied," Edgerton said, grinning. "A fine starry night, with a bottle of decent wine and something for a light supper — an appealing prospect, is it not?"

Kent laughed. "I suspect all this will have disappeared in a day or two."

Outside, he locked the door and placed the key under its stone again. "I know, I know," he said, in answer to Edgerton's quizzical glance. "We should find a more secure arrangement."

Edgerton only laughed, and began strapping his sword onto his horse. "Where is your mount, Atherton? Do you have a better place to keep him than right outside the door, with the reins draped over a bush like this?"

"I have turned him into the field. It minimises the amount of droppings to be cleaned up here."

"Droppings," Edgerton murmured. "I wonder..."

Kent retrieved Stupendous from the field, to find Edgerton leaning on the gate with a frown on his face, gazing out at the animals pastured there.

"Whose are these beasts?"

"I suppose Eustace owns them. They are retired mounts, too old for riding, seeing out their final days at leisure."

"Most of them are not riding horses, though," Edgerton said. "Ponies, mostly, and a few donkeys. Or are they mules?"

"There might be mules amongst them. I cannot say I have ever looked at them closely enough to be sure."

"Hmm. It is possible. It is just possible, and no hay, a comfortable bed and fresh water supplied. Even food, perhaps."

Kent said nothing, not fully understanding the interest in mules.

"I beg your pardon," Edgerton said, opening the gate for Kent to lead his horse out. "You must think me insane, I suppose, but I have recently discovered that Miss Peach had a mule to ride, so she could have ventured a great deal further than we originally supposed. Even here, perhaps."

"Why would she come here?" Kent said uneasily.

"No reason in the world, that I can see," Edgerton said easily. "It was just the mention of droppings that set a hare running in my mind. Miss Peach had talked about mule droppings — it was a problem, but she had solved it, somehow. It occurred to me that droppings would betray that she and her mule had been at a certain place, but if she could put the animal into a field like this one, neither the mule nor the droppings would be noticed, and the tower would supply her with a safe hiding place. But there can be no reason why she would be here, so put it out of your mind. Shall we ride down to the road together or are you going over the moors?"

For the first mile or so, they were heading in the same direction. Edgerton was humming, a low, melodious tune, clearly satisfied with his morning. Kent was less satisfied. In one sense, it had been a successful meeting, for Strong had seen nothing untoward, and Edgerton had professed himself uninterested in the smuggling operation. Kent had not managed to keep the captain away from the tower, as Eustace had wanted, but no damage had been done.

Yet the question of Miss Peach occupied his mind. Was it possible she had reached the tower on her mule? She could have left the mule in the field, and stayed inside the tower, and no one any the wiser... unless someone arrived unexpectedly and saw her bag there. But it was so unlikely! There was no need to tell Edgerton, surely? If he knew of it, he would be crawling all over the tower looking for clues, and any hope of reviving the smuggling would be gone for weeks, perhaps, and Eustace would be furious.

But Miss Peach had been murdered, and Kent knew beyond all doubt that he ought to tell Edgerton that she might have been at the tower. It was the right thing to do. He understood suddenly just why Katherine had felt obliged to report him to the magistrate — that, too, was the right thing to do.

By the time they came to the point of separation, when Edgerton was to head east to Pickering, Kent had made his decision.

"Edgerton, it is just possible that your Miss Peach was at the tower two weeks ago."

The captain's eyes lit up. "Tell me more."

"I was out riding with... with Miss Parish and my cousins Lucas and Emily, and I brought Miss Parish into the tower to show her the view. In the room at the top of the tower, we saw that the bed had been used, and there were signs of a meal being taken, and a candlestick. And a bag, a green leather bag, hidden behind the sofa. The telescope had been moved round to face Welwood, just as it is today. I moved it back, yet someone has moved it again. And... if she rode a mule, it could have been put in the field to graze. I thought you ought to know."

"Thank you, Mr Atherton. That is most interesting," Edgerton said. "So you did not see Miss Peach yourself?"

"No. There was no one there, just the bag and things to show someone had been there."

"What was in the bag?"

"It was locked, so I cannot tell you."

"And what did you do about it?"

"Nothing myself. The tower is Eustace's responsibility, so I left a note at Welwood to let him know about the intruder. He was away at the time, and by the time he checked, there was no sign of anyone. The bag had gone and the place was tidy. You may ask Miss Parish if you wish to verify all this."

Edgerton smiled, showing his teeth. "Oh, I have no doubt that she will corroborate everything you have told me. But I wonder, Mr Atherton... I very much wonder whether you did, in fact, return to the tower and find Miss Peach there. I wonder whether she told you unpalatable facts that she had discovered, and whether you then strangled her in a fit of rage. Then, no doubt, you conveyed her body to Tonkins Farm to throw us completely off the scent, and arranged the hay barn in a way that was almost convincing. Did you, Mr Atherton?"

It was said so calmly, so conversationally that Kent was almost too taken aback to speak. It was so preposterous he actually laughed. "No! You are insane if you think any such thing, Captain. Why on earth would I murder Miss Peach?"

"Because she had discovered that you murdered Mr Nicholson."

Kent laughed again, shaking his head. "You forget that I saw the murderer descending the main stairs as I raced towards Aunt Alice."

"Perhaps you lied."

"And again I ask — what reason could I possibly have for murdering Nicholson?"

Edgerton heaved a sigh. "Yes, that is where all my clever explanations founder. What reason indeed? I can make a case for anyone murdering Nicholson — you, your brother Walter, your father, Tess Nicholson, the Lady Alice, the butler. All of you were in the castle that night. I can even see the parson doing it — Mr Dewar is not a young man, but he is spry enough.

I see him striding about the village, full of energy. I can even explain how your brother Eustace might have done it."

"He was at home at Welwood."

"So he was, with an entire houseful of servants to swear that he was tucked up in bed with Daisy Marler at the time. But perhaps he waited until she was fast asleep, crept out of bed, dressed, saddled a horse, rode across the moors at night, broke into the house, picked up the axe that he himself had brought there, and slaughtered the chaplain as he slept. He then slipped away, rode home, and got back into bed beside the sleeping Daisy with no one any the wiser."

"That is preposterous!"

"No, no. I can call upon an excellent barrister who will make a very credible tale out of it. Credible enough to convince a jury, in any event. And do you know what stops me from doing any of this? I cannot find a single reason why anyone would have wanted Nicholson dead. No one bore a grudge, no one resented him enough to risk the hangman's noose, no one was desperate enough to kill him. And until I can find the reason for it, I cannot know who it was who killed him. For myself, I think the answer lies at Pickering, so that is where I focus my efforts now."

"Well, I am glad you are not seriously accusing me," Kent said. "I should have regretted telling you about the visitor at the tower, if I had thought that would be the consequence."

"I do not seriously accuse Mr Eustace, either. His grooms swear no horse left the stable that night, nor was any saddle taken, and Daisy Marler swears he was in bed all night."

"Daisy Marler?" Kent frowned. "Do you know she is now acting as lady's maid to Miss Parish?"

"Is she? I cannot imagine where Miss Parish might have met a girl like that."

"In church!" Kent said, laughing. "Miss Parish is always in church. Oh! But I have remembered how it came about. Daisy was weeping and praying because she had done something wrong."

"Indeed she has, and it is time she repented of hopping into bed with everyone who offers her money," Edgerton said. "This is all very interesting, and I thank you for telling me, but I cannot think that Daisy Marler's conscience bears on my present concerns. In return, I shall tell you something about your intruder at the tower. It was not Miss Peach. Her bag was made of stiffened cloth, a very shabby affair, not green leather, and it had no lock."

"Then Eustace was right, it was just a casual wanderer."

"So it would appear. What an interesting conversation this has been."

21: Transgressions

It was a gloomy group that gathered in the parlour at the Black Swan at Pickering after Miss Peach's funeral. Her sister from Harrogate had retired to her room, but Luce, Pettigrew, Sandy and James Neate sat around the table with Michael, sipping wine and nibbling unenthusiastically at the last remains of an extensive repast.

"What next?" Sandy said brightly. "Are we going to look at this tower over at Welwood?"

"What is the point?" Michael said morosely. "Miss Peach was never there."

"Ye cannae be sure of that," Sandy said.

"Wrong bag."

"Ye've only Mr Kent Atherton's word for that," Sandy said. "Maybe he lied."

Michael heaved a sigh. "Of course, but unless we can catch him out, what is the use? We have no specific suspect — anyone might have murdered Nicholson or Miss Peach, and, more to the point, we have no reason for murder. We have been in Yorkshire for more than four months, and we have discovered *nothing*. This has been my year of utter failure. I failed to protect the viscount in Westmorland, and I have failed to find the chaplain's murderer. It is time to admit defeat and return to London, and maybe time for me to give up pretending to investigate murders altogether. I am clearly useless at it."

The others all protested, but Michael shook his head. He had never felt so inept in his life.

"Michael Edgerton, I'm ashamed of ye!" Sandy cried. "What kind of cowardice is that? Giving up? When have you ever given up? To start with, ye can check if the man's lying by asking Miss Parish."

"Who is in love with him, so she is bound to support his version of events."

"She's also the lassie who reported his smuggling to the magistrate. She's a fine Christian lady who'll not lie to ye, but if ye'll not go yerself, maybe I will. Aye, and I'll ask her about Daisy Marler, too, and find out what's troubling her conscience. She swore she was with Eustace Atherton the night of the murder, but maybe she lied about that. And someone needs to look properly at this tower place, to see if there's any trace of Miss Peach there."

"I admire your enthusiasm," Michael said, "but I cannot see what good it will do. All our efforts so far have just been so much flailing about. We have nothing at all to show for it."

"Nonsense, Michael," Pettigrew said. "Your efforts have uncovered all the nasty little schemes set up by the supposedly virtuous chaplain, and you have recovered a great deal of the earl's lost income *and* found Miss Nicholson's fortune, too."

"But look at the damage caused by going through Nicholson's papers. We learnt that he had never been ordained, and thus threw the earl's entire family into the most distressing situation. That was an appalling shock for them all, and they need never have known."

"It would have come out when the earl died, and his son attempted to claim the title," Pettigrew said sombrely. "Better to know the truth now rather than later. Michael, if you want to slink away to London, then go, but I for one am not ready to give up yet. You have said many times that we are missing something crucial, and I agree, but if we stop looking we will never find it. We must keep going. Give it until the end of the year — six months after Nicholson's death. If we still have nothing, then I think we will all be ready to concede defeat, but while we still have new tracks to follow, we owe it to the earl and his family, and to Miss Peach, to pursue them."

Michael sighed. "Very well. Miss Parish, Daisy Marler and the tower."

"And the mule," Sandy said. "There is a missing mule to be found, too, and I for one would like to know if there are any mules in that field beside the tower. Oh, and two keys on Miss Peach's keyring that wouldnae fit anything we could find."

Michael laughed. "What a very persistent Scotsman you are, Sandy Saxby."

Sandy grinned. "Aye, ye've taught me well, my friend."

***

Michael went alone to see Miss Parish. Sandy was wild to go with him, having been the one to persuade Michael of the necessity, but Michael wanted to see Miss Parish alone, and Sandy was far too young and personable to pass muster with the lady's cautious aunt and uncle.

He went first to Mr Cathcart in his study, and put the case to him. As he had expected, Mrs Cathcart was then summoned for her approval.

"Alone? Is that necessary, Captain? She was not alone when you spoke to her before."

"On that occasion, ma'am, I only required Miss Parish to confirm what everyone else had already told me. This time, I need her to describe everything she can recall about the interior of the tower, and in such cases, the presence of another person can be a great distraction."

"Oh, but I could sit quietly in the corner with my embroidery, you know. I should not say a word."

"Even so, ma'am, Miss Parish will be able to concentrate her thoughts more fully if she is alone. She will speak more freely without an audience, even one so benign as your good self, and that is what I hope for, you see — those little drops of information that arise unbidden when one has nothing to distract one. It may be that Miss Parish, if her mind is left to roam freely, will light upon the one vital clue that resolves this case once and for all."

It was tosh, of course, and Mrs Cathcart would have pressed the point, but her husband said quietly, "We must allow Captain Edgerton to know his own business best, my dear. Katherine is a sensible girl, and the captain is a respectable man of some standing in the community. His wife is cousin to the Earl of Morpeth, remember, and he has been a guest of Lord Rennington these many months."

"Oh yes! I never meant to suggest otherwise," she said, flustered.

"Katherine cannot get into the slightest difficulties in here with the captain with Davis in the hall outside. Or you might wait out there yourself, in case Katherine should call for you."

"Of course," she said, rather pink. "I beg your pardon, Captain, if you thought... I intended no offence."

"And none was taken, I assure you, ma'am," Michael said, rising to bow to her. "Your concern for Miss Parish's welfare is commendable."

And finally, after only three more apologies, she left and Michael awaited Miss Parish. She had rather high colour when she arrived, but he knew that was her habitual state, so he took no notice. One could not be ascribing every young lady's blush to guilt or the gaols would be overflowing.

"You wished to talk to me, Captain?"

"I do, ma'am. I understand that you were recently inside the tower over at Welwood, and I should like you to tell me everything you can remember of the interior."

Her colour came and went, and for a moment he was afraid she was going to burst into tears. But he busied himself with pulling out his notebook and pencil while she composed herself, and by the time he looked at her again, she had straightened her spine and lifted her chin.

Sitting on the nearest chair to the door, she said, "The interior? All of it?"

"I am particularly interested in the top floor."

And so she told him essentially the same tale as Mr Kent Atherton, of the disordered bed, the candlestick, the food remains and the bag. Every detail was the same, even the green leather bag. There was only one new piece of information, that the brazier was cold.

"You checked it?" Michael said, looking up from his notebook in surprise.

"I was curious about whoever was staying there, for the tower was chilly even in the daytime, but at this time of year it would be very cold overnight. But the brazier was stone cold. I do not think it had been lit for some time."

"Hmm. Interesting. And the bag was definitely locked?"

"Yes."

"And no sign of a key?"

"No. Oh, that reminds me. The key for the door to the balcony and roof was missing, too. The door was unlocked, though, yet Mr Atherton said it had been locked on his previous visit, and the key was missing then, too."

"Now, that is very curious," Michael said thoughtfully, for when he had visited the tower, the door had again been locked. Who was locking and unlocking it, yet keeping hold of the key?

When he had exhausted every aspect of the tower, he said, "I understand that you have engaged Daisy Marler as your lady's maid. Could you tell me how that came about... how you met her?"

"Daisy? Oh... let me see... we met in church... not at a service, though. I had never seen her at a service. I had gone in one day to pray, and there she was, weeping at the altar rail. She told me her conscience was troubling her, I advised her that she would feel better if she corrected her transgression, although she did not seem to want to. She told me she had too little to do, and as I was sharing a maid with two of my cousins, I saw a way to improve all our lives a little. She has never been a lady's maid before, but she is proving to be a quick learner."

"She has not caused any trouble in the household?"

"Daisy?" she said, sounding surprised. "No, not at all. She is a willing worker, and gets along with everyone."

Michael chewed his lip thoughtfully. It was not for him to warn Miss Parish against talking too intimately with Daisy, a girl who had made a useful additional income by being obliging to Eustace Atherton, and no doubt plenty of other men. And perhaps Daisy had repented of her former ways, and only hoped for a fresh start in a more respectable occupation.

Still, he had to ask the obvious question. "Did she tell you anything of her... transgressions?"

"Not in detail, and I did not like to pry, naturally."

"In general terms?"

"She said that she had told a lie."

Michael sigh of relief was almost audible. "Oh, a lie! That is... interesting." But his next thought was that perhaps Sandy was right again, and she had lied about being with Eustace Atherton on the night of the murder. That would be a far worse transgression, all things considered.

"Is it? I told her that the best way to ease her conscience was to tell the truth, and later she said the lie no longer troubled her, so perhaps she did so."

And perhaps she had merely stopped worrying about it.

"Do you suppose I might talk to Daisy? If you have no objection?"

"I shall ask my aunt."

Within moments she was back, Daisy was sent for, and they talked for some time of the tower and all she had seen there. After Michael had exhausted that subject, he took the opportunity to ask about mules, and whether she had noticed any in the field beside the tower.

"I did not notice particularly, no. I am not sure I could identify a mule unless it— Oh, look! Daisy is running down the drive!"

Michael was out of his chair instantly, tearing out of the house in pursuit. Daisy was a little too plump for speed, and was besides hampered by her skirts, so Michael caught her just at the end of the drive and grabbed an arm.

"Stop right there, Daisy!"

To his astonishment, she dropped to her knees at his feet, tears cascading down her face. "Oh, please, sir! Please don't have me transported! Me ma would be that upset. Or lock me up, neither. Them gaols are foul places where people die, and the colonies are hot and nasty. Please don't send me there!"

Michael dropped to one knee beside her. "Daisy, I promise you no one intends to have you transported, but I do need to talk to you, and you must tell me the truth, do you understand? *All* the truth, nothing left out. If you can do that, you will not be transported or put in gaol or punished in any way. Is that clear?"

Mutely, she nodded. It took some little time to gently urge her back into the house, and then to persuade the hovering Mrs Cathcart, much inclined to scold, from the room. Then a glass of something and several more minutes of reassurance before Michael could begin his questions. But the first one got right to the point.

"Daisy, when I talked to you before, you told me that you were with Mr Eustace Atherton on that night in June when Mr Nicholson was murdered. Was that the truth?"

A long silence. Then she whispered, "You won't send me to the colonies?"

"Not if you tell the truth, but this is a question of murder, and lying about anything at all when asked is a very serious matter. People have been gaoled and even transported for that. But if you tell me the truth—"

"I weren't there!"

Michael sighed. "Mr Eustace paid you to say so, I suppose."

She nodded. "Twenty pounds! I never had so much money in my life before, and he said it weren't a real lie because I'd stayed the night there before, and he did have someone staying that night, but she were a real lady, and he didn't want it to get about that she stayed the night with him. She'd be ruined, he said, and he didn't want her name brought into it, but everyone knows I've obliged him from time to time, don't they? But then me pa found out about the money and wanted to know what I'd done to get so much, and he was that angry with me and told me I'd be transported if it came out. So he sent me to me uncle in Birchall and I were that upset to be away from home, sir, and nothing much to do, but Miss Katherine's been so kind to me and I really don't want to lose my place here, sir, truly I don't."

"And is this the complete truth, Daisy?" Michael said gently. "Mr Eustace told you there was a lady with him that night?"

"He did, sir, a proper lady, but he didn't want her ruined. Ladies can be ruined, can't they, sir? Then they can't never get married. Not like me! I'm just a farmer's daughter, and Jack Benson says he'll wed me as soon as he's got his own place and he don't mind me obliging anyone 'til then, cos it's good money for us, ain't it? But a proper lady can't oblige a gentleman without being ruined."

"That is so," Michael said gravely. He pressed Daisy a little harder, but although she prattled on at great length now that her fear of transportation had receded, she had nothing new to say, and Michael let her go. He made sure that Mrs Cathcart knew that the girl had been helpful to him, and could only hope she would not suffer too severe a scolding for trying to run away.

And then he sent for his horse, and rode as fast as his mount could manage to Welwood-on-the-Hill. It was just as well that a groom emerged at once to attend to the horse, for Michael was not minded to wait. He strapped on his sword and stormed up to the front door.

He had left Birchall mildly cross that he had been lied to by Daisy Marler, but the greater lie had gradually risen up in his mind and brought him to a boiling rage. Daisy was not the transgressor here. That crime lay at Eustace Atherton's door, who had bribed the poor girl to say she had been with him when she had not.

So he strode into the hall as soon as the manservant opened the door. "Where is he?"

"I am not sure if the master is at home, sir."

"He had better be, because if he skulks in a hole to avoid me, I am liable to tear this place apart brick by brick to find him."

"Perhaps you should make an appointment, sir," the manservant said frostily.

"And perhaps you should be thrown off the roof for insolence. *Where is he?* Oh, never mind."

He stomped across the hall and began opening doors, yelling, "Atherton!" at each. The third door brought results, for there was Mr Eustace Atherton sprawled at his ease in a chair beside the fire, a wine glass in his hand, with a man in the attire of a bailiff or gamekeeper sitting opposite him.

"Edgerton?" Atherton drawled, not moving. "What is the meaning of this unseemly row? As you see, I am engaged at present."

Michael crossed the floor in a few strides, and hauled Atherton bodily out of his chair, spilling wine everywhere. "You *lied* to me, you snivelling little snake! You lied to me and bribed that poor girl to lie, too."

"Really, Edgerton, what a fuss!"

"*What a fuss?* A fuss, is that all this is to you? Your own uncle by marriage was slaughtered in his bed, and you lied to me about your actions that night. Give me one good reason — just one — why I should not have you arrested for murder right now and thrown into York Gaol to rot."

"You cannot arrest me."

"Do you want to put it to the test?" Michael hissed, drawing his sword and levelling the point at Atherton's throat. "Do not *dare* to defy me, Eustace Atherton. You paid Daisy Marler to say that you were here all that night, she has confessed that she lied and now you have no one to vouch for you."

Silence fell. The bailiff, or whatever he might be, was edging out of the door, while the manservant stood motionless, his eyes flicking from one man to the other.

"Oh, put away your sword, Edgerton," Atherton said tiredly. "Your posturing does not impress me. You," he said to the manservant. "Get out and shut the door."

The room fell into silence again. Atherton produced a handkerchief and dabbed at the wine stains on his waistcoat.

"Look at this!" he said, gesturing at the stain. "A good waistcoat ruined. Do you have to be so damnably melodramatic?"

"You lied to me, when I am investigating a murder in your own family. What interpretation am I meant to put upon that?"

"The obvious one," Atherton spat. "You purport to be a gentleman, Edgerton. Surely you can think of an honourable reason why I might have asked Daisy Marler to say she had spent the night here — which she has done many times, in fact."

"I am not minded for guessing games."

Atherton sighed. "Are you going to sheathe your sword, Captain? I am not going to run away."

Michael reluctantly acceded, for it was obvious that Eustace Atherton was not intimidated.

"There was someone with me that night, but she is a lady and I did not want her name bandied about by the likes of you. Everything that Daisy told you happened was true, except that it was not Daisy but someone else."

"Her name?"

"Did you not hear me? I do not want her talked about as if she were nobody."

"She is gentry, then? Or nobility?"

"Not noble, but a very respectable family. Her father would be appalled to know that she spent a night with me."

"That I understand, but I can be perfectly discreet, when I choose to be. I must have a name and direction, Mr Atherton. Under the circumstances, you cannot expect me simply to take your word for it."

Atherton walked across to the window, and stood there gazing out at the neat gardens. Welwood was a modest estate, but he kept it in good order.

Eventually, he turned. "I am not sure I can tell you. I promised her that no one would ever know."

Michael moved to the side table where the wine decanters stood and poured two glasses of Madeira. "Mr Atherton, I do not seriously imagine that you crept out in the middle of the night, rode the twelve miles to Corland, murdered your uncle, and calmly rode home again with no one any the wiser. For one thing, your grooms all assure me that no horse or saddle was removed overnight, and I believe them. I also know perfectly well that you had *someone* in your bed that night, because your cook showed me her records of the dinner that evening, and breakfast the next day. So I am not here to trip you up. But you lied to me, and nothing less than perfect honesty will satisfy me now. I must have the name and direction of the lady."

Atherton chewed his lip, but then took a deep breath. "Her name is Rosamunde Wilkes. Her father's estate is beyond Newcastle, but she often stays with her aunt in Scarborough. That is how I met her. The aunt is... helpful, shall we say in the matter of overnight visits."

"Is Miss Wilkes at Scarborough just now? I shall need her direction, so that I can talk to her."

"No! You must not!"

"I shall avoid her father, naturally, but you must see that I have to talk to her. You can bring her here, if you prefer."

Atherton was breathing heavily, but after a moment he nodded, curtly. "Very well."

"And soon," Michael said. "York Gaol is still an option, Mr Atherton. You have one week to produce the lady."

22: Unexpected Visitors

Katherine had received sad news from Branton, for Mr Vance had finally succumbed to the many ailments that afflicted him. Katherine wrote her letters of condolence to Mrs Vance and her five daughters, and put on black gloves for a while. She had not known Mr Vance well, for he had been bedridden for many years, but Mrs Vance and her daughters were all good friends and Katherine knew they would feel the loss keenly.

. The other sad news was the departure of Mr Kent Atherton. She had the first word of this from Emily, who came to Cathcart House straight away to report that he had called at Westwick Heights to make his farewell, and was leaving that very day.

"I know you are not such good friends as you were, but you will be sorry to hear it, I am sure," Emily said.

"Yes," whispered Katherine, almost too distraught to speak. She had known he planned to go, but to discover that he was in fact leaving that very day, and with no chance of saying goodbye, was distressing indeed.

"He sent his regards to you," Emily said. "He mentioned you most particularly. *'All my good friends at Cathcart House, and especially Miss Parish.'* That is what he said. *'Tell her I shall miss our rides very much.'* Is that not something to be pleased about? And he will be back before long, I am sure. He said it would only be for a few weeks, he thought."

A few weeks! A few long, dreary weeks, but then he would be back. And he would miss their rides. Yes, that was something, at least.

"But where has he gone to?" Katherine said.

"No one knows! He was very secretive about it. He said he planned to look up some old friends, and after that he could not say. But I have some absolutely splendid news — at least, I think it is. Mama is to invite you to stay with us for a week or two. Is that not wonderful? It is because Julia and Penelope have gone off to stay with the Websters, to plan Julia's wedding in the spring, and Mama is busy getting the Dower House ready for Bertram's wedding next month, so she thought you would be company for me. We shall have so much fun!"

Since her aunt and uncle made no objection to this pleasant scheme, it was arranged that Katherine would move to Westwick Heights the very next day. That evening, Aunt Cathcart came to see Katherine before bed.

"I am sure I need not tell you what an excellent opportunity this is, Katherine dear," she trilled happily. "Mr George Atherton is not only Lord Rennington's brother, but he is the heir presumptive to the title at present. That may change, of course, but still, you will mingle with a most superior family, and with much association with the Corland Castle family. It will be very good for you, and you must be sure to make every effort to join in the conversation at dinner. And although perhaps your affections have been leaning in a certain direction, if Mr Lucas Atherton, say, should take an interest in you, I am sure you would not be so foolish as to spurn him.

But you need not attempt any of Aveline's clever little devices with him, for your natural ways seem to be quite effective. So just be yourself, dear."

Katherine had not the least notion how to be anything else, so she smiled and nodded and said nothing.

She found that the George Atherton family was not unlike the Cathcart family. The same abundance of children and servants brought the same bustle and noise, the same affectionate teasing amongst the children and even, occasionally, from Mr George Atherton, too, and the same gentle mothering from Mrs Atherton. Katherine found that so long as she carried a shawl everywhere, and was prepared to swathe herself in it if Mrs Atherton detected the least draught, all would be well.

But there were some differences. Westwick Heights had fewer rooms than Cathcart House, but it was built on a grander scale, with an imposing entrance hall fronted by a pillared portico, and large rooms with high, ornately plastered ceilings and elegant mirrors everywhere. It felt like the home of a nobleman, not a mere gentleman. Meals were different, too. Mrs Atherton had a dreadful fear of rich food and overindulgence, so she provided an array of plain dishes and simple roasted joints of meat, which Katherine enjoyed very much. And grace was said at every meal, so that she felt she had arrived at a proper Christian family.

The greatest difference was that Katherine shared a room with Emily. She discovered the joy of whispered confidences each night, and if she woke during the hours of darkness, it was surprisingly reassuring to hear Emily's soft breathing beside her.

So the days passed in pleasurable company, and even though the weather had settled into dreary autumnal rain, precluding any outings, there was enough enjoyment indoors that Katherine could not repine. There was still a deep ache in her heart where her grief for the loss of Kent

Atherton smouldered, but she was kept too well occupied by Emily to fall into a melancholy. Every day there was some new activity to entertain them, and still plenty of time for her music. There was an excellent collection of pieces at Westwick Heights, many of them new for her to try, so she happily played for hours while Emily worked on her tapestry or leafed through a journal.

It was inevitable that the two girls would be drawn into the plans for the imminent marriage of the eldest son, Bertram, to Miss Bea Franklyn, step-daughter of the fearsome Lady Esther Franklyn. The couple would live in the Westwick Heights Dower House after their marriage, and the place was alive with painters, carpenters and plasterers, with deliveries of furniture arriving on an almost daily basis.

This activity drew Miss Bea Franklyn there just as frequently. She was as unlike Emily and Katherine as it was possible for a girl to be, bouncing from one room to another with irrepressible glee, and filling the Dower House with her vocal enthusiasm. Only when she spoke of her betrothed did her voice soften, and her eyes shone as she enumerated his many perfections, and as often as not, broke into Latin to express herself adequately.

The Dower House was an exciting project, and whenever difficult decisions were to be made regarding the installation of a dado, or whether a floral style of wallpaper was to be preferred to the more fashionable chinoiserie, or whether celestial blue was a more restful colour than pomona green, as many opinions were needed as there were ladies in the house. This was especially so when Lady Esther Franklyn was present, for she invariably disagreed with Mrs Atherton, and neither lady being willing to concede defeat even in the matter of a wallpaper, Emily and Katherine were sure to be appealed to. Since Emily always sided with her mother, and Katherine was terrified of Lady Esther — a duke's daughter! — she dreamt up a desperate escape.

"Miss Franklyn, which do you suppose Mr Bertram would prefer?"

"Oh, the pomona green, definitely," Bea would say happily, and thus the matter was settled, for the wishes of the master of their modest household could not be gainsaid. No doubt Miss Franklyn would apprise him privately of his preferences later.

Into this placid routine came a most unexpected visit. Uncle Cathcart arrived one morning and asked to speak to Katherine alone.

"You may have the library," Bertram said at once, emerging to greet the visitor. "The fire is lit, so it is comfortably warm." He was a man of some learning, so he spent most of his days in the library with his books.

"If that will not inconvenience you too greatly..."

"Not at all. Let me show you the way."

He pointed out the comfortable chairs beside the fire and the tray of decanters and glasses, before gracefully withdrawing.

"A pleasant young man," Uncle Cathcart said, tugging ineffectually at the cuffs of his shirt and adjusting his cravat minutely. "He will make an excellent earl, when his time comes, if it should come to that. Of course, such matters are most uncertain. Lord Rennington may yet take another wife..."

"Is that what you wished to talk to me about, uncle?" Katherine said, puzzled.

"No. Not that, no. Something unexpected has occurred. We have a caller at Cathcart House, a young man by the name of Tiller."

"Mr Geoffrey Tiller? From Branton?"

"The very one."

"Whatever does he want? Oh, I hope it is not more bad news... another death, perhaps."

"No, no. Nothing like that. He wishes... he wishes to pay his addresses to you."

"Mr Tiller?" she said in some astonishment.

"He claims to have long held an attachment to you."

"Oh, yes... well, no, not to me particularly. To my dowry, rather. When Papa was alive and... and we were comfortably situated, it was well known that I would have a good dowry and would eventually inherit everything. Mr Tiller paid me some attention then, indeed, he offered for me twice. But unless his circumstances have changed, he cannot afford to marry me now."

"He tells me he is likely in time to become a partner to the attorney by whom he is employed," Uncle Cathcart said.

"Oh yes, but Mr Gray has not yet done it, and may never do it. Mr Tiller is thirty already, you know, and I do not think he is a very good attorney, for he gets in a muddle sometimes and Mr Gray has to look over everything he does."

"That does not sound very promising. But perhaps there is more to his prospects than the distant hope of a partnership, and if your feelings have undergone a change..."

"But they have not."

"Then shall I send him away disappointed? If you do not wish to see him...?"

"I do not mind seeing him. Any friend from Branton is welcome, for he will bring me news of my other friends."

"Then I shall send him up here to talk to you."

Mr Geoffrey Tiller was a personable young man, rather fashionably dressed for an attorney, but then he had always aimed high, and from the moment he qualified as an attorney, had pursued every heiress who crossed his path with relentless amiability and undisguised avarice. He had been part of Katherine's court for a number of years, only drifting away now and again when a more promising prospect hove into view.

He sat for some time with the Athertons making civil conversation before requesting a private interview with Katherine, and that business being speedily concluded with a gently worded but decided refusal, he settled down again, quite unabashed, to delicately flirt with Emily instead. Mrs Atherton, seeing only the agreeable young man and not knowing of his fortune-hunting ways, invited him to dinner, where he spent the evening bestowing every possible attention on Emily, quite undeterred by the fact that she was reduced to blushing incoherence in his company.

Even Mrs Atherton had tired of him by the time he bowed himself out of the door at midnight to walk down the hill to the White Horse, and forbore to ask him to call again. Katherine thought he was quite capable of calling anyway, if he thought it worth his while, but having found out from Emily that her portion would not be above five thousand, and not even that if a man could be persuaded to take her for less, she was sure he would not appear again, and so it proved. The servants brought word the next day that his hired post chaise had set off back to Lancashire shortly after breakfast.

Katherine was pleased to be rid of him. She could not at all understand why he had come, for the thousand pounds from her uncle was hardly an inducement to a man of Mr Tiller's ilk, and he did not even bring much news with him. He said very little of poor Mr Vance, and nothing at all of anyone else. He had been travelling about a bit, he said, and had spent the last six months at Mr Gray's office in Lancaster, so he knew nothing of Branton.

She was exceedingly disappointed in him. His only function, it seemed, was to provide gossip for the spinsters of the parish who gathered in Mrs Dewar's parlour to sew, and spent an inordinate amount of time teasing Katherine gently about what they described as her lovelorn swain. She was relieved to return after these outings to the less trying atmosphere of Westwick Heights, where the topic of the day had now progressed to the quantity of bookcases required for the Dower House library.

Katherine had no opinion on bookcases, and therefore was permitted to retreat to the pianoforte and play to her heart's content, mostly easy pieces that allowed her mind to wander freely over any number of subjects, such as where Kent might be, and what he was doing, and whether he would revert to his smuggling activities when he returned. Most of all, she wondered whether he thought of her as much as she thought of him, or whether she had already faded in his mind, like the paper on a sunny wall, becoming greyer and more indistinct with every day that passed.

***

Kent noticed the chimneys first. The town would look just like any other town were it not for the chimneys, monstrous great fingers pointing at the sky, clouds of smoke pouring from them. He could see warehouses, too, towering over the houses and shops below them. And everywhere he looked, he smiled as he thought of Katherine walking these streets, Katherine seeing the chimneys, Katherine gazing into shop windows. When he passed a gaggle of women chatting together outside a milliner's shop, he imagined her as one of them, laughingly discussing the bonnets displayed, wondering which was the most becoming. And although there was pain in remembering her, he was happy to think he was encountering her spirit on every street corner.

Branton! Her town... her home, the place that had shaped her. The one place where she had felt at ease in society, where she had not blushed and stammered and been rendered inarticulate. She had surely never been inarticulate amongst her friends here. She would have talked freely, just as she had with Mrs Vance, and given him that unexpected glimpse of the friendly girl beneath the terrified mask.

The postilions took him to a respectable-looking inn, where the innkeeper instantly recognised him as a person of importance. How did they do that? His manner of speaking, perhaps, or the quality of his clothes. He had never thought much about it, but it always happened that way. Was it the way he walked, with an air of assurance? Or perhaps he simply expected to be treated with respect, and thus it came about.

However it was, he was given a large bedroom and a pleasant parlour with a good fire already blazing, and a tray of refreshments followed him up the stairs.

"This is our best parlour, sir," the innkeeper said. "We've mutton and beef on the spit for your dinner, and the wife can do a chicken if you've a mind for it."

"Any fish?"

"I'll ask, sir. We've a cosy room for your manservant, too. I'll have hot water sent up to you right away."

"Not yet. I should like to pay a call on an acquaintance first... Mrs Vance. Do you know her?"

"Ah, the poor lady! Such a sad loss."

"She is dead?" Kent said, startled.

"No, no! 'Tis Mr Vance, sir. Went to the Good Lord's arms just three days ago, poor man. Buryin' him this afternoon, they are."

Thus, Kent spent his first day in Branton attending the funeral of a man he had never met. He could not now call upon Mrs Vance, but he had sent a note of condolence from the inn, and the innkeeper had directed him to the church where the funeral service was to be held. Kent sat at the back of the packed church, and then followed the mourners out to the graveyard, although standing a little apart, for he wanted to be able to give Katherine a full report. He wished he knew the names of those present.

After the interment, as the crowd began to drift away, a small group of young men came over to him at his vantage point beside a listing stone cross.

"Good day to you, sir," one of them said. "You are welcome here, naturally, but... were you a friend of my father-in-law?"

"Mr Vance? No, I never met him. I briefly met Mrs Vance, however, so as I happened to be in Branton, I thought I would pay my respects here, since I cannot call upon such a recently widowed lady."

"She would be delighted to see you, I am sure. Will you not come back to the house for refreshments?"

"No, indeed! I would not dream of intruding upon a grieving family."

"Then at least give us your name, sir, so that we may tell her of your presence."

"I am Kent Atherton, a friend of—"

They all cried out in delight. "Mr Atherton! We have heard so much about you! Indeed, you must come to the house with us, or Mrs Vance will never forgive us."

And so he went, and Mrs Vance greeted him with the same pleasure, brushing aside his apologies. "I'd have been mortified if you'd gone away

23: Branton

Katherine could scarcely believe it. Her brother Harold, thought to be dead ten years ago, was alive and well, and had come to find her.

"But... but where have you been all this time? Ten years, Harold! Ten years since we thought you died in the Battle of Cape St Vincent! What happened to you?"

His face clouded. "Oh... I am not entirely sure. A small coastal village somewhere hot... France, somewhere in France... that's all I can tell you. Must have had a bang on the head, for I had not the least idea who I was or where I was or anything, but one day a naval vessel anchored offshore and a party came ashore and someone recognised me. Brought me back to England, helped me remember bits and pieces, and as soon as I began to remember things, I remembered you, sister dear, and so here I am."

"Have you been to Branton?"

"No, I came straight here."

"Do you know that Mama and Papa are both dead? Mama seven years ago, and Papa just last year, before Christmas."

"I heard, yes. You're all alone in the world now, Katherine. Well, apart from me, that is. You and me against the world, eh? Just like it always was."

For an hour they talked, or at least Harold talked, while the Athertons plied him with questions. Katherine herself was too bemused to formulate any rational thoughts in her head. Harold alive! It was extraordinary! How was it possible? And yet, his explanation, sparse as it was, made sense.

He had now left His Majesty's navy, he told them, being unfit for the work any more, but he had received his full amount of back pay and even a modest bounty, so he was, in his own words, comfortably situated. He hoped to set up home with Katherine, perhaps in York.

That provoked a response from her. "Not in Branton?"

"I should find it confusing when I remember so little of my time there — mere flashes of memory, that is all."

"It might help your memory to return fully to be in the familiar places again," she said.

"But imagine how humiliating it would be to meet people who re-member me well, and be unable to name them or respond sensibly. No, better to start afresh, I feel, where I am not at all known, and can make new memories."

After an hour, Mrs Atherton deemed that Katherine needed to rest, to recover from the shock of meeting Harold again, and at once he rose.

"A thousand apologies, madam. I have been thoughtless in staying so long."

Uncle Cathcart offered Harold a room at Cathcart House, and Mrs Atherton invited him to dine at Westwick Heights that evening, after which he gracefully withdrew, taking Uncle Cathcart with him. Katherine had a few hours to contemplate Harold's reappearance. The matter was too exciting for a return to normal activities, so the books were abandoned, and the family gathered in the parlour to discuss it.

"When did you last see him?" was the first question.

"Let me see... I was six, so fourteen years ago. It was a very brief leave before he had to rejoin his ship. The last time he lived at home, I was only four."

"That is why you do not recognise him," Bertram said, "but Katherine, can you be sure he truly is your brother? Anyone could just appear and say he is Harold Parish. One hears such tales all too often, of unscrupulous men who prey on unprotected women."

"But I am not unprotected," Katherine said. "My uncle and aunt will look into it. I dare say one might write to the Admiralty to ask for more information. Besides, who would prey on me? I am not an heiress, likely to attract a fortune hunter. No, he must be genuine."

"Does he look like your brother?" Bertram said.

"He does. The fair hair, the blue eyes... that is certainly how I remember him. And he is the right height, I think. He is more weather-beaten than I remembered, but that is not unexpected after he has been living in a fishing village for so many years."

"And what about the accent?" Bertram said. "He does not talk in as refined a manner as you do."

Katherine frowned. "I cannot remember how he used to talk. My father had an accent, too, but my mother insisted I talk properly, as she called it."

"Bertram," his father said, "you spend so much time reading about the Romans, it is possible that the devious ploys of the Caesars have altered your vision of the world. Sometimes a young man seemingly returned from the dead is just what he appears to be. He may have an accent, but it is mild, and he dresses well, he mentioned a valet and he arrived in a hired post-chaise and four. He is not, I believe, intending to prey on Miss Parish."

"That is all very true," Bertram said with a rueful grimace. "I am too suspicious, perhaps. It is difficult to believe, but sometimes miracles do occur."

"Indeed. So let us be thankful for this particular miracle and not put distrustful thoughts into Miss Parish's head."

For several days, Katherine and Harold got to know each other again. She moved back to Cathcart House, where she found Aveline already employing her charms on him. Katherine was pleased to see that he appeared impervious. The rest of the family accepted him unreservedly, with none of Bertram's suspicions.

Katherine herself wondered about him. He had few memories of childhood, although if she reminded him of an incident, he would sometimes say, "I think I remember that." Nor did he recall much of his time at sea. His time as a virtual prisoner in a French fishing village he refused to talk about, saying only that it was a bad time and he disliked to be reminded of it.

There were two incidents, however, which convinced her that he was indeed her brother. Once she had spent an hour or so attempting to prod his memory of Branton, but without success. Giving it up, they had turned instead to the newspaper, reading over a piece about the Navy which she felt would interest him, when he cried out, "A balloon! One of those great contraptions that fills with air — I remember that!"

"A balloon? Oh yes, I did not see it. I was too little, but Papa took you to see it filled."

"It rose a few feet off the ground, that was all. But it was such an impressive sight to a small boy. I must have been six or seven at the time."

A day or so later, at dinner, he turned to Katherine with a puzzled expression. "Was there a fire? I have a vague memory of a fire in a large building."

"The mill, yes! Papa's first cotton mill, which burnt to the ground. You were a hero, Harold, for you saw the smoke and raised the alarm. Not that much could be done, for a building full of cotton burns all too well, but at least no one was hurt, except old Sam, the night watchman, who fell down the stairs and broke an arm in his haste to escape."

After that, all Katherine's doubts were swept away, and if his memories of Branton were sparse, at least they were real.

On any other subject, he was articulate. He spoke of his time in London, being physicked by naval doctors until they decided he was beyond any further aid and discharged him. Several friends there had known him before his disappearance, and they had told him of his parents' deaths, and that Katherine had gone to their uncle and aunt. He had stayed there until he felt well enough to tackle the journey north.

When he spoke of their future together, he became quite eloquent. A small house in York, he thought, with three or four servants. A town would provide competent physicians to monitor his continuing recovery, as well as amusements for both of them.

"We can go to the assembly room, sister dear, and find a husband worthy of you," he said merrily.

He was keen to leave almost immediately, but Katherine hesitated. At the back of her mind was the thought that if she went to York now, she would never see Kent again, and so she resisted. But her aunt soon made it clear that she expected her to go.

"Your uncle and I accepted responsibility for you in the spring because we thought you had no one else, dear," she said to Katherine, coming to her room at the end of the evening to talk to her privately. "We were glad to do it, and I always hoped that we would succeed in getting you satisfactorily settled. We made no distinction between you and our own girls in that regard. But now that your brother is here to take care of you... well, we must step aside, naturally. Your brother is the proper guardian for you. Little as we like to see you go, it is for Harold to make a home for you and make provision for your future. The world would look very much askance at us if we were to come between the two of you."

"I understand, aunt," Katherine said sadly.

"You are a good girl, and deserve better than all this jumping about from place to place. I am so sorry to lose you again, I cannot tell you! However, you are such an amiable soul, you will make new friends very quickly, just as you did here and at Helmsley. And at York, you know... well, in the much wider society there, and with your brother's wealth, you will be bound to make an excellent match. We would have taken you there ourselves in the spring with Aveline. Now we shall be able to visit you in your new home."

So Katherine made no protest. To York, it seemed, she was to go.

***

Kent found himself effortlessly drawn into Branton's society. Mrs Vance knew everyone of importance in the town and designated her five sons-in-law to take care of Kent and ensure he was kept well entertained. Thus he found his days filled with visits to mills and manufactories and warehouses, and he never once dined at the inn. All that was required of him in return was that he mention from time to time his father the earl, or his cousin the duke, or his two brothers-in-law, both viscounts. Brantonians were not unduly deferential, but they had an insatiable curiosity about the nobles in their castles, who helped the King to rule their land. They never expected to meet any of them, but Kent was an excellent substitute and they were determined to make the most of him.

He rapidly developed an admiration for these sturdy men of industry and commerce, who might never have ventured beyond the bounds of Lancashire, but they read the newspapers, and talked in their offices and parlours and clubs of everything that happened, and they were not afraid to give their opinions with spirit. Kent had deeper discussions in Branton dining rooms than he had ever encountered at Corland, for his family was not politically active. If Kent had ever had a full season in town, it might have been different, but he felt he had found a society in Branton that was alive in a way that he had never seen before.

It helped, of course, that he could talk to these men about machinery, and their eyes did not glaze over as his father's would have done, or his brothers'. For them, it was all horses or guns or the possibilities for the harvest. It was a joy to Kent to talk instead about coal and valves and canals and the price of wool or cotton. At least, the Brantonians talked, and he listened and asked endless questions and learnt vast amounts, while realising just how ignorant he was.

His greatest delight was in finally seeing the beam engines that had fired his imagination for so long. Mr Ridwell, the new owner of the Parish mill at Longfarley, showed him around personally, and then handed him over to the engineer who explained the workings of the engine. And Kent stood, mesmerised, watching it at work, the beam far above his head rising and falling, the massive wheels spinning, the valves opening and closing, and all accompanied by whirrings and clangings and whooshes of steam, so loud that he could barely hear himself think. Beneath his feet, the very ground shook, and he could feel the vibrations deep in his chest, as if its power was so great that it infiltrated everything within range.

For an hour or more he stood, awestruck, and felt that he had come home. This, this place of wonder and energy and majesty, was where his destiny lay.

"Have you any work suitable for a useless ignoramus like me at Long-farley?" he asked Ridwell, when he could finally be torn away from the great engine. "My paltry skills with broken fountains and clocks are inadequate to equip me to tend the noble beast that powers your mill, but perhaps you have some other work I might do? At least then I would be near to the engine."

Ridwell regarded him thoughtfully. "An earl's son can always be found a position, Mr Atherton. I could use a general manager. John Wilson is getting on, and he would be happy to retire in two or three years. You would be ready to take over by then. If you stay so long, of course. A hundred pounds a year while you're learning, if you find your own accommodation."

"That would suit me very well," Kent said. "I shall have to talk to my father."

"Will he refuse to let you do this?"

"I am of age, so he has no power to prevent me. No, I need to find out if he will continue my allowance. If so, I can afford a modest house. If not, I shall live in two rooms above a bakery or some such."

Ridwell laughed. "Very well. Let me know when you will be free to start."

Fired with enthusiasm, Kent went straight off to talk to an attorney about somewhere to live. He remembered Mr Gray from the funeral, who had also appeared at some of the dinners to which Kent had been invited, so he started there.

Gray's offices were rather imposing, situated between a bank and a large bookseller. Kent was ushered politely into a room gleaming with mahogany furniture, the desk adorned with a silver standish.

"Ridwell, eh? Why him?" Gray said, when he heard about the scheme.

"Is there any reason I should not work for him?" Kent said.

"No, no. Ridwell's perfectly sound, but... well, he keeps to himself as a rule. Has one of the fancy new houses on the hill and has ambitions for that daughter of his. Plans to take her to London and see if he can't get a lord for her. Mind you, she's a beauty, no doubt about it, and whoever marries her will get Cragforth mill. Might be worth your while..."

"I will bear that in mind," Kent said diplomatically. "I wondered if you know of any property I might rent."

"Furnished or unfurnished?"

"Either would suit me. Nothing too large, but suitable for a family... if I should marry in the future."

"Ah," Gray said knowingly. "If you don't mind unfurnished, I have just the thing on the Lancaster road. Very convenient for church and the better shops, and the market is only a short walk away. In excellent condition, a good size for a family and most elegantly appointed. Mrs Parish always had exquisite taste. The owner died last Christmas... oh, but you know Katy Parish, of course?"

Kent's throat was unexpectedly tight. "I... do, yes." He could live in Katherine's — *Katy's* — own house! And if he should marry her— But he did not dare to contemplate such a glorious future.

Mr Gray showed him over the house himself, and although the rooms were empty and sad, he could imagine Katy and her father living there. He identified the bedroom that assuredly had been hers, in his mind he filled a corner of the drawing room with her pianoforte and music cabinet, and he imagined her sitting in the dining room eating the plain dishes that she preferred.

"The bank owns it, but they won't consider taking less than sixty guineas a year for it, given the size and position of it, and in excellent condition, too, although for such a distinguished gentleman as yourself, I might persuade them down to fifty," Gray said. "It's a good family house, as you can see. The Parishes never had but the two children, but there's room for plenty more."

That gave Kent the delightful vision of Katy with her children gathered around her. She would be a wonderful mother, he decided. But such thoughts were too enticing. More likely was a future where she never spoke to him again, and she would be entirely justified. He was a despicable worm, not fit to crawl on the ground at her feet. But perhaps, if he applied himself to a career in Branton, he might one day aspire to be a good, honest man, and leave his history as a smuggler behind.

That night at dinner with several of his new friends, he mentioned the possibility that he might rent the Parish house, and that brought forth an outpouring of memories of the family. Mr Parish, a down-to-earth, good-hearted man, who took excellent care of his workers. Mrs Parish, from a grand family to the north, with refined ways but never high in the instep. Harold, the son, a bouncy, fair-haired child with a wonderful singing voice. And Katy, the quiet daughter, with her talent for music, who had stepped into the breach so ably after her mother died.

Such a charming family, but tragedy had gradually overtaken them. Harold first, lost in the Battle of Cape St Vincent off Portugal, although his body had never been recovered. Then Mrs Parish had died, and only the previous year Mr Parish had been lost, and his entire fortune swallowed up by the debts to the bank. The worthies of Branton shook their heads over it, and lamented the loss, but took it as an awful warning to anyone minded to take out a loan.

Kent knew most of it already, but he never minded hearing about Katherine — *Katy!* So much more apt a name, he thought, and she was rapidly becoming fixed in his mind as Katy now. So he listened, and although there was pain in the constant reminders, it was far outweighed by the pleasure of hearing how well-regarded she had been.

Kent wrote to his father to tell him of his plans and to ask for clarification of his financial position. He made it clear that he would stay in Branton regardless of the outcome, for he had three thousand pounds of his own money to support him until he was properly established, but he yearned to live in Katy's house, and that could not be done without his allowance from his father.

Before he had a reply from Corland, however, came news of a very different sort. First, a letter from Olivia.

'*My dear brother, Such an exciting development! Miss Parish's brother, so long missing after a naval battle that all hope was extinguished, has returned alive and well! After ten years! Is that not astonishing? He is very handsome and charming, and has made his fortune, so they are to set up house together in York. Is that not a pleasing outcome for her? The Cathcarts are well pleased to be rid of her, I dare say, for her elegant manners quite cast a shadow over the not quite so elegantly mannered Miss Cathcart, not to mention her divine performance on the pianoforte. We are all thrilled for her, that she will have a proper home at last where she will be valued as she ought to be, and no doubt you will be very willing to run any little errands that may be required in York in the days to come. We are all looking forward to Bertram's wedding. There is to be a grand ball here two days before, so you must be sure to return in time for that. Your loving sister, Olivia.*'

Kent had barely had time to digest that when Mr Gray returned from a visit to his Lancaster office in great distress, bearing a copy of a Lancaster newspaper.

"Look! Look at this!" he cried to the guests gathered for dinner at the home of Reggie Cruikshank, one of the Vance sons-in-law.

"Read it aloud, Gray," Cruikshank said.

"Very well, very well. *Tragic orphan revealed as great heiress'.* That is the headline. Can you guess who is meant by that? Listen, listen. *'Miss Katherine Parish...'* Katy, you see! They are talking about our very own Katy. *'Miss Katherine Parish, a young lady of only twenty years, has suffered more tragedy than most in so young a life. After losing her only brother and her mother some years ago, she lost her surviving parent, Mr William Parish, a mill owner of Branton, to a fever last year. The unfortunate lady was thought to be destitute and thrown on the mercy of kind-hearted relations. But fortune has smiled upon her at last, for she is now known to be the inheritor of a substantial fortune. Not only is there a trust fund left to her by her mother, the former Miss Elizabeth Hawley of Shillingburn, but she was also bequeathed the sum of ten thousand pounds in the will of the late Mr Harvey Vance, the much lamented former mayor of Branton, who recently passed away. We congratulate Miss Parish on her recent reversal of fortune, there being no more worthy recipient of such benevolence, given the sorrowful history of her family.'* And then they relate the whole of it — all about her childhood, her brother's loss at sea, her mother's death and then every detail of the loans being called in. It is despicable, quite despicable!"

"But this is good news, is it not?" someone said. "If Katy has come into a little money, I for one am very pleased for her."

"And so are we all, naturally," Gray said, "but no one was supposed to know about it. The will... a will is made public, so I suppose there was no avoiding that, but the trust fund! Parish went to so much trouble to ensure that no one knew of that. Even Katy does not know how much it is worth."

"How much *is* it worth?" Cruikshank said.

Gray heaved a sigh. "I cannot tell you. Indeed, that is the absolute truth, for I do not know myself. Mr Humber at the bank is the only person who knows. Parish always said it was not very much, but he made us all swear never to speak of it, which leads me to suspect that it may be substantial. Parish was doing very well for a while, so he could have laid aside quite a decent pile for Katy. Now here it is all over the newspapers and the poor child will be besieged by fortune hunters. Indeed, Tiller has already— Tiller! That must have been how all this got into the newspapers. He is my clerk, for my sins, and a very poor one he is too, but he has access to the files, and must have seen that there was a trust fund in existence. Well, he will not be my clerk for much longer! Revealing confidential information is the greatest sin an attorney can commit. But beyond that, I do not think there is much we can do about it, except to warn Katy's uncle to be on the watch for fortune hunters."

"I fear it may already be too late for that," Kent said, and told them of the contents of Olivia's letter. "He has been gone so long, and Miss Parish was so young when he left that she would not remember him. This man could well be an impostor."

"He sounds like a wealthy man," Gray said. "Some of these naval men have done very well from prize money and so forth."

"That may be so," Kent said, "but the newspaper gives full details of the Parish family, including descriptions. It would not be hard for a man to make a pretence."

"A suitor would be a concern," Cruikshank said, "but a brother, even an impostor, cannot hurt her."

"He could claim his share of the trust fund," Gray said gloomily. "The terms of the marriage settlement intended Mrs Parish's money to be divided amongst all the children. Besides, as her only male relative, he could take control of the entire amount, her share as well as his."

Kent nodded. "This man may be just as he appears to be, but I believe I shall not be satisfied until I have talked to Cathcart about this and met the man for myself."

24: Deception

Michael waited until Eustace Atherton had departed from Welwood in his carriage before examining the tower again. There was no particular reason for that, only that Eustace was the sort of person who would want to know just what he was doing there, and Michael was not minded to explain himself. He took Sandy and James Neate with him, because the more eyes, the better when a place was being searched. Michael no longer took his own infallibility for granted in his investigations. He had had a dismal record lately, and if Sandy or Neate could find something useful, he would be very pleased.

They found the key under the stone, exactly where it had been left. Michael rolled his eyes at the continuing lack of security, but it was certainly convenient for his own purposes. Everything downstairs was much as it had been on his previous visit, except that the cellar was now full of barrels. That was not surprising, and not of interest, so Michael locked up the cellar again and the three of them went upstairs. Sandy looked into every empty room on the way up, but Michael was tolerably sure he would find nothing, and so it proved.

In the top room, Michael said, "Tell me everything you see, anything you notice."

"There's a wonderful view of Welwood," Sandy said at once. "Ye can see most of the drive, the front door, and that must be the stables on the far side. Ye'd see everyone coming and going, and someone's been watching, look." He gestured to the telescope, still pointing directly at the house. "Why would anyone want to know who's been visiting Mr Eustace?"

"To do with the smuggling, presumably," Neate said. "Michael, what are we looking for, precisely?"

"Anything that might suggest that Miss Peach was ever here."

"But you are not convinced? Because of the green leather bag?"

"Which is not the bag that was found near the body, and it stretches credibility to suppose that she had two different bags."

"Really, Michael," Neate said in severe tones. "You used to be more suspicious than that. The bags are easy to explain. Kent Atherton discovered signs that someone was here when he visited with Katherine Parish. His brother being away, he took it upon himself to return the next day, where he encountered Miss Peach. Finding that she suspected him, he strangled her, took her body to Tonkins Farm, arranging the barn to look as if she had been living there. He knew that Miss Parish would confirm the green bag, so he put the contents into a different bag and disposed of the green leather one, to ensure there was no connection with this tower."

"That is—" Michael began, then frowned. "Actually, that is very logical. And that dilapidated old cloth bag is not the sort of thing Miss Peach would use. But... *Kent Atherton?* Do you truly think he murdered Nicholson?"

"Well, he *could* have done," Neate said with a shrug. "A great many people could have done."

"Yes, but *why?*" Michael said. "Give me a single sensible reason and I will arrest him today."

Neate sighed. "No idea."

They both laughed.

Sandy, meanwhile, had been prowling round the room, moving furniture, looking behind and under things, even raking through the ashes in the brazier. Now he rattled the door to the outside. "Is there a key to this door?"

"No. Atherton said it is missing," Michael said.

"Ye've two unexplained keys from Miss Peach's pocket," Sandy said.

"Oh, but that is—" Michael stopped. Impossible, surely, but it would not hurt to try them, would it?

The second key opened the door.

"There ye are," Sandy said smugly. "Now ye've the proof that Miss Peach was here."

"So we do," Michael said wonderingly.

He stepped out onto the balcony. It was only narrow, with a low wall on the outer side, and steps leading up to a covered viewpoint on the very top of the tower.

"A fine view," Sandy said, following him nimbly up the steps.

"A bit blowy up here," Michael said.

"Aye, and nothing left for us to find," Sandy said, looking around at the dusty, leaf-blown floor. "No green bag, for instance."

"Yet she must have come up here," Michael said thoughtfully. "She had the key in her pocket. Why else would she keep it except to use this vantage point?"

"When was the door locked and when was it unlocked?" Sandy said.

Michael frowned, considering. "It was locked when I was here before. It was *unlocked* when Kent Atherton was here with Miss Parish, but it was locked on his previous visit, and the key was missing the whole time."

"Ah!" Sandy said. "And what do you make of that?"

"If we assume that Miss Peach had the key the whole time... on one occasion she forgot to lock that door."

"And what was different about that one time? The time when Miss Parish was here?"

"Nothing... except that there were signs of someone living there. The bed, disordered... as if someone had just risen from it!" he cried excitedly. "They *surprised* her. She was sleeping, perhaps, woke in a panic hearing people coming up the stairs and rushed out onto the balcony to hide, but she forgot, or perhaps did not have time, to lock the door behind her. It was her hiding place, Sandy! At those times when the door was locked, she was out there, keeping out of sight. Probably she would have taken her bag with her, when she had sufficient notice of an arrival. And since she still had the key with her, that means she intended to return here."

A cry from below sent them running down the steps again and into the top room, where James Neate was waving something triumphantly. "Her notebook, Michael! It was stitched into the mattress. Neatly done, but that is an old trick."

"But what does it say? What was she up to? Why was she here?"

"Ah. It is all in code, sadly, but I shall work on it. It cannot be too complicated. I just need the book she used. There were some in her room, so I shall see what I can work out. It should not take long to decipher."

"Excellent," Michael said. "This has been a good day's work, gentlemen. At least we know now that Miss Peach was here, although for what purpose we cannot tell."

"She may have discovered some link between the smuggling and Nicholson," Neate said.

"Possibly. Or she may simply have become distracted by the smuggling and assumed it had some relevance when in fact it did not. Whatever the case, we cannot know until the notebook is understood. There is nothing more we can do here. Let us leave everything as we found it."

"And the key?" Neate said.

"I believe I shall keep it for now. Returning it will raise questions which I am not sure I wish to answer yet."

"Ye could simply leave it in the lock," Sandy said.

Michael laughed. "That will confuse everybody! Very well, but whenever this business is settled, if it ever *is* settled, I shall be obliged to confess."

"Confession is good for the soul," Sandy said with a grin.

"Ah, if only our murderer understood that," Michael murmured. "Confession — a *real* confession, that is — would make my life so much easier."

***

Kent left Branton within the hour, driven by a burning fear that Katy would be taken advantage of by a fraudster. Gray came to the inn with him, gave him the newspaper cutting to show the Cathcarts and talked to him while he packed. That is to say, Mitcham packed while Kent paced restlessly back and forth.

"It might not be as bad as you fear," Gray said. "Whether this man is indeed Katy's brother or not, he cannot seize control of her fortune by main force. He must go through the law, and you know how the law operates, Mr Atherton. There will be all manner of documents required, and he will have to prove that he is who he says he is. Lawyers are very reluctant to hand over money to unknown persons. Mr Humber at the bank has full control of every penny of Katy's fortune, and he will not give it away until he and all her trustees are satisfied with this man's claim."

"But he is to take her away from her aunt and uncle," Kent said despairingly. "She will then be completely in his power."

"Then we must hope that you arrive in time to prevent her from leaving. I wish you God speed, Mr Atherton."

Kent spent two slow, dreary, fretful days on the road, veering between hope that he would arrive before Katy had left and terror that he would be too late. And if this man was truly Harold Parish, and everyone laughed at him for his anxiety, what did that matter when set against Katy's safety? He had to be sure!

It was dark when he arrived in Birchall, but he could not wait another second to know how matters stood, so he drove straight to Cathcart House, startling the butler by striding past him into the hall, his mud-stained boots leaving a trail of footprints on the tiles. The ladies had already gone up to change for dinner, but Cathcart was still in his study, and emerged to greet him.

"Mr Atherton?"

"Is she here? Miss Parish? Is she still here? It is imperative I see her at once."

"Good heavens, whatever has happened, to bring you here with such urgency?"

"I must know that she is safe."

"She is perfectly safe. A miracle has occurred, Mr Atherton, for her brother is returned from the dead. Her own brother! No one is better suited to take care of her."

"But is she here? I must see her!"

"She has gone to York with Mr Harold Parish, where they will set up home together."

"Then I am too late!" Kent cried in despair.

It took some time to explain his fears to the Cathcarts, who were filled with incredulity.

"Such a pleasant young man," Mrs Cathcart said repeatedly. "So amiable and well-mannered. I am sure he must be exactly who he says he is, Mr Atherton."

But James Cathcart frowned as he read the newspaper cutting. "Here is mention of the balloon ascension he recalled seeing as a boy... and the fire at Mr Parish's mill, too! Everything he told us could have been obtained from the newspaper, for the entire history of Harold Parish is laid out here for anyone to read. It even mentions that Cousin Kate's new home is in Birchall, and your names, too. This man came straight here, did he not? He never went to Branton, where any number of people might have said at once whether he was truly Harold Parish."

By this time it was almost the dinner hour, and Kent's postilions were still outside and growing restless. The Cathcarts offered Kent a room for the night, he gratefully accepted and after unloading the luggage, the carriage was sent on to the White Horse for the night.

Nothing else was talked of at the dinner table but Katherine and her supposed brother.

"He was so open in his manner, I was certain we could not be deceived in him," Mrs Cathcart said distressfully. "Such a pleasant man! How could we have been so taken in? Surely he must be just what he claims to be!"

Kent said nothing, allowing Mrs Cathcart and her daughters to describe the many perfections of the supposed Mr Harold Parish, and how plausible he had been, and how no one could have guessed there was anything amiss. When the ladies had withdrawn, and Kent was alone with Mr Alan Cathcart and his three sons, he could speak more forthrightly.

"It may be that this man is just what he appears to be, and that all is well with Miss Parish, but I cannot be easy in my mind until I have seen them both. I intend, therefore, to go to York and find them, if they are indeed to be found there. If they are not, then I shall have to look further afield."

Cathcart raised his eyebrows. "I am by no means convinced that this man is a fraud, but I am decidedly of the opinion that if there is to be any intervention, it should come from her relations."

"You think I take too much upon myself, is that it?" Kent said hotly, too irate to be diplomatic. "I should simply stand aside and do nothing, because *you*, sir, have decided that there is nothing to worry about?"

"I say only that it is for her relations to protect her, if protection is needed."

Before Kent could answer, James Cathcart said, "But you have done nothing to protect her, Father. You have made no checks on this man. You simply accepted his own assertion that he is Harold Parish."

Cathcart reddened. "As Katherine herself did, if you recall. What, then, would you have had me do, James?"

"If nothing else, you could have asked him for his naval discharge papers, or information about his pension. You could have written to the Admiralty to enquire about him. Perhaps you could have insisted he go to

Branton to be formally identified. Instead, you have allowed Cousin Kate to go off alone with this man, who is a complete stranger, not just to us but to her, too. Atherton is right, *someone* needs to look into this man, and it should be for us to undertake the task."

His father sighed. "You think me neglectful, James, but some of this I have already done. I did not think of discharge papers, but I enquired as to his pension and other income, and his answers were satisfactory. I have written to the Admiralty, but have not yet had a reply. As for sending him to Branton, that might have been sensible but since Katherine was happy to accept him as her brother I did not wish to offend her by disbelieving him. I told her in the strongest terms to write to us as soon as she arrives in York. Perhaps I have been remiss, but I am not entirely heedless of her welfare and if it will satisfy you I shall certainly go chasing around the countryside to find her at the earliest opportunity."

"It does not satisfy me, no," James said. "You may wait here for any letters that arrive. I shall go to York myself. As Kate's cousin, I have the right, I believe. May I have the carriage?"

"Well... your mother needs it tomorrow, but perhaps the day after—"

"Never mind. I shall ride, then."

"You may join me in my carriage," Kent said. "It is hardly riding weather, and I have room for both you and your man."

"You still mean to go to York?" James said sharply.

"Certainly I do. Did I not say so?"

"Father is right. It is for her relations to protect Kate."

Kent's anxiety was such that he had no intention of ceding the point. He would go to York to find Katy with or without her relations' approval. But he had no wish to antagonise them, so he said mildly, "One does not need to be a relation to feel concern for a young lady taken to a strange town by an unknown man. Any gentleman would do as much. With two of us, we shall be able to discover them more quickly."

"If they are in York at all," James said.

"Wherever they have gone, I intend to discover them," Kent said grimly.

***

Before anything could be done about Miss Peach's notebook, Michael received a brief note from Eustace Atherton.

'Miss Rosamunde Wilkes, my future wife, is presently staying at Corland Castle. You may speak to her whenever convenient. E. Atherton'

"Future wife?" Sandy said. "Aye, he'd better wed the lassie, since he's already bedded her."

"And she will no doubt confirm everything he says," Michael said gloomily. "If only we could find one discrepancy in all these stories!"

"He's not likely to have murdered Nicholson, though, is he?" Sandy said. "Not when his entire household swears he never stirred from his bed, so it hardly matters."

"It always matters when people lie to us," Michael said tersely. "Perhaps the whole lot of them are lying. He *could* have murdered Nicholson, and that is what we must always bear in mind, but until we have a reason, we cannot narrow down our list of the scores of people who *could* have done it to the one who actually wielded that axe."

When Michael arrived at Corland, the butler told him that Mr Eustace wished to speak to him in the gallery. Fearing some stratagem, Michael could not help laughing when he reached the gallery, for there was Mr Eustace, stripped to his shirtsleeves, testing out a very elegant sabre.

"Ah, there you are, Edgerton," he called out cheerfully. "A new acquisition. What do you think?"

"Beautiful," Michael said, in genuine appreciation. "Prussian?"

"I would say so. Lovely falchion blade. Try it. I have a Spanish broadsword for you to look at, too."

Naturally, Michael could not resist, for although he was a connoisseur of weaponry, he had never had the leisure to become a collector, as Eustace was, and he never refused the chance to try out an interesting new sword. There was a peculiar satisfaction in the weight of it in his hand, the swordsmith's art exerted to make a blade which is both light to wield and yet strong enough to do battle. To hold such a superbly crafted piece of art, to slash and thrust against an imaginary opponent, to imagine himself in the intensity of battle once more brought him the utmost satisfaction. He had never regretted leaving the East India Company Army, and he sincerely hoped he would never be called upon to endure the torments of war again, but oh, the joy of a sword in his hand!

He was in a mellow mood by the time he made his way upstairs to join Sandy, Neate and Pettigrew Willerton-Forbes for the interview with Miss Wilkes. It was strange to be back in the old schoolroom at Corland Castle after so many weeks when they had been focused on Pickering. All the notes were still there, the axe on a sideboard, and the plan of the castle drawn up by Winnie Strong, marked with the occupants of every bedroom. He smiled as he saw her neat handwriting and the correction she had made. She had initially placed Walter Atherton, the earl's eldest son, in his usual bedroom, but as it was undergoing one of Lady Rennington's redecoration crusades, he had actually slept in a guest bedroom. A young lady with a commendable devotion to accuracy.

To one side was the blackboard, still showing the last list of suspects. *'Tess Nicholson, Tom Shapman, John Whyte'* it read, even though Michael was now convinced by the innocence of all three. Angrily, he scrubbed the board clean.

Miss Rosamunde Wilkes was an attractive young lady, elegantly dressed, her light brown hair piled high on her head, with just a few tendrils framing her face. She was accompanied both by Eustace Atherton, and by a severely featured lady's maid. Michael made no protest. Miss Wilkes would certainly have been told precisely what story to offer, and was not likely to fumble the telling, so there was no point in insisting on seeing her alone.

"Your card, Miss Wilkes?" Michael said, after ushering her to a seat.

She produced a silver card case and extracted her card. *'Miss Rosamunde Wilkes, Warriston Hall, Northumberland'*, he read.

"That is your father's estate? His name?"

"Sir Reginald Wilkes. Baronet." Her voice was pleasant and well-modulated, with a refined accent.

"Your mother's maiden name?"

"Winfell. Maria Winfell."

"Ah. Then she must be related to the Duke of Dunmorton."

"A distant cousin. My mother has been dead these ten years, Captain." Her voice wavered, as if she might cry, so Michael hurried on.

"Miss Wilkes, I must ask you some questions about a specific night in June... where you were, with whom, and what happened that night. Mr Atherton has taken steps to shield you from this, but I am investigating a murder and it is vital that everyone I talk to tells me the truth. I am not here to judge you and have no interest in the morality of your actions. I would also assure you that nothing you say will be repeated outside this room. It will not get back to your father through me, I give you my word on that. But you must tell me the absolute truth, do you understand? If I find out later that you have lied, I will certainly arrest you, and that cannot be concealed from your father."

"I understand," she said in a low voice.

She then told him exactly the same story that Daisy had told, although with a few more details. She remembered very well the dishes that had been served at dinner, unlike Daisy, who had guessed at mutton. She too said that she had slept late, only waking at around ten, to find Eustace still sleeping beside her.

There was only one odd point. "Miss Wilkes, Mr Atherton's servants told me that his companion that night had black, curly hair, which is an appropriate description of Daisy Marler's hair, but not of yours."

"I always wear a wig when I visit Eustace, to avoid being recognised," she said.

"Is there anyone at Welwood who might recognise you?"

"Not at Welwood," she said, smiling slightly. "The servants do not know who I am, and they were never told my name. Eustace is very discreet. When I visit him, I come from my aunt's house in Scarborough, where I am well known. I should not like anyone to recognise me in his carriage."

There was not a single point at which Michael could quibble. Despite the uncomfortable feeling that Eustace Atherton was running rings around him, he could not find any flaws in Miss Wilkes' tale. He spent a day at Welwood talking again to all the servants, who were relieved that the truth was now known. Eustace had told them the same story as Daisy, that he wanted to protect the lady's reputation, and it was merely the substitution of one lady for another.

"It seemed reasonable to us," Wallace, the head groom, said. "We knew he had someone in his bed, and it didn't seem to matter which lady he brought forward to vouch for him. We never said it were Daisy, sir. We agreed we wouldn't lie for him, no matter what, so we all agreed to say only what was true — that the lady was here for dinner and never left until late the next morning. And we know he couldn't have gone off to Corland that night, not without one of us knowing. We'll all swear on the Holy Book that no horse left the stable that night."

"There are horses in the field across the road."

"Which need a saddle," Wallace said at once. "There are only four saddles at Welwood, they were all locked away, and the key was in my pocket. No one left Welwood that night, Captain Edgerton."

"I believe you," Michael said. "In fact, I never doubted it, but Mr Eustace lied to me and I had to address that problem."

"Aye, you've a murderer to catch," Wallace said, "that's fair enough, but it weren't Mr Eustace, sir."

But if it could not have been Eustace, there was still the possibility that it was Kent Atherton. But how to prove it? And most of all — *why?*

25: Certainty

It took a full day of travel to reach York, and a tedious day it was too. Apart from the usual travails of any journey in the autumn, consisting largely of unremitting rain and a vast amount of mud, Kent had the dubious pleasure of the company of James Cathcart, as well as the two valets. Cathcart was usually good company, but he was not his usual ebullient self, and Kent himself could not summon his habitual cheerfulness. He was too distressed about Katy, wondering whether she was in York at all.

Just north of Easingwold, they were delayed for some time by a coach off the road some way ahead. Having discovered the hapless occupants had plenty of willing helpers from a nearby farm and two other carriages passing by, there was nothing to do but return to their own carriage and wait for the road to be clear again. Kent had thought to provide himself with a flask of brandy, which warmed their insides even if their fingers and toes remained frozen, and the atmosphere mellowed somewhat.

"I cannot but think we are worrying unnecessarily," Cathcart said. "Even if this man is not Cousin Kate's brother, he cannot mean her any harm, surely? It would be her money he wants, not her person."

"But he can obtain her money more surely by marrying her," Kent said.

"Yet he has not approached her as a suitor."

"That would take a long time to gain the trust of Miss Parish herself and also her uncle and aunt. But if he claims to be her brother, he can whisk her away from their protection and then... who knows what he might do? Gretna, perhaps."

"Dear Lord! Then she might be in the gravest danger!"

"Precisely."

Cathcart fell silent. When they moved off again, he said hesitantly, "Look, Atherton, I hope I did not offend you yesterday... suggesting you had no right to take care of Kate. I believe in this case you mean her well."

"When have I ever *not* meant her well?" Kent said sharply, as the two valets studiously gazed out of the window and pretended to be invisible.

"That is between the two of you," Cathcart said, not looking him in the eye, "but I know you made her unhappy. Whatever happened, it made her read her Bible a great deal, even more than usual, and she often looked as if she had been crying. Perhaps you did not mean to, but you hurt her badly, and if you want my honest opinion, I think she is better off without you. But I can see that you truly care about her, so it is right that you should help to rescue her... if she needs rescuing."

Kent felt anew all the pain of their disagreement. He had hurt her... made her cry... and it was the very last thing he had ever wanted to do. "Perhaps she is better off without me," he said in a low voice. "I am trying to be a better man, but... it is hard to change ways that have become ingrained over the years." A dreadful thought occurred to him. "Are you... do you... I mean, is there... something between the two of you? I would not for the world interfere if—"

Cathcart gave a wry smile. "I like her very well. I would even say that I admire her. I thought her too timid and mouse-like at first, but that night at Corland when you danced the reel with her, I saw then that she could be brought out of her shell. And she is beautiful! That gown she wore — so simple, and yet elegant. But my mother rang such a peal over me! I am the eldest, you see, so I am supposed to marry money and prop up Father's meagre finances, since he failed to do so. I am not supposed to fall in love with an impoverished cousin."

"And have you?"

"No. I could do so, believe me, if she had thirty thousand to her name, but not for a mere fifteen."

"Fifteen? How do you know that?"

"Ten thousand from this Branton fellow, remember? And her mother would have had the same dowry as my mother, since they were sisters. Five thousand in that trust fund of hers, that is all. Not enough for me and not enough for you, either, I wager. But perhaps your father will fund you."

Oddly, this conversation cheered Kent enormously. Fifteen thousand would bring in... perhaps seven hundred or so a year, and another hundred from Ridwell. That was enough to live on, with care. A manservant, a cook and a couple of maids. Perhaps a gig, although in town they might not need it. Even without his allowance from his father, he and Katy could—

Such foolishness! He would never be able to marry her, for she would never forgive him.

***

K atherine could not say at what point she began to suspect that all was not as it should be about her brother. There was no single moment of revelation, merely an unease that began as soon as she knew she was to leave the safety of her uncle's house to go to York with him, and slowly grew with every hour that passed. She remembered clearly the words of Bertram Atherton — *'Can you be sure he truly is your brother? Anyone could just appear and say he was Harold Parish.'* And yet, how would anyone know there was any such man, unless he truly was that man? And why would he appear now, so long after he was believed dead? He remembered details of their childhood that she herself had forgotten — like the balloon ascension! She had not seen it herself, but he had described it excitedly to her afterwards, and talked about it so many times. No, he must be her brother.

Still, she could not be easy about it. His loss of memory was very convenient, for it absolved him from remembering anything personal of their shared childhood, their home, or parents. There was not one detail he volunteered that she could point to and think, *'There! That proves it, for no one else could have known that.'* And there were oddities, too. He had been lost overboard during the Battle of Cape St Vincent, off the southern tip of Portugal, yet he claimed to have ended up in a French fishing village. He had been there for ten years, although he had acquired not a word of French. It was all very unsettling.

Yet he seemed to have plenty of money, and they were staying in a very luxurious hotel in York. Each morning, they viewed houses available to rent, and each evening discussed the advantages and deficiencies of each one. There was no rush, Harold said. They could take their time to find just the perfect house. She did not much care for Harold's valet, a dour-faced man who said little, and those few words in an impenetrable accent, but she had Daisy with her, whose excitement at being in York was infectious.

In the afternoons, Harold went off alone to deal with what he described as *'business matters'*, which Katherine took to be banks and attorneys, and establishing himself in the town. She passed the time by shopping with Daisy, or else stayed in their comfortable parlour beside the fire, reading.

On the third day in York, the rain pattering persistently on the windowpanes, the maid came in to tell her that a man wished to see her. The card she handed Katherine was for a Mr John Nesbitt, attorney-at-law.

"It will be about one of the houses we viewed," Katherine said. "Show him up, Molly."

Mr Nesbitt was a neatly dressed man of around forty, who greeted Katherine politely, accepted a glass of sherry and took the opposite chair beside the fire.

"I am glad to find you on your own, Miss Parish, because I wanted to ask you a question without your brother's presence. I understand he has recently returned after many years' absence, and has no papers to prove his identity."

"Surely he has his discharge papers from the navy," Katherine said, in some surprise.

"No. He was unable to furnish me with any such documents. But as his sister, you will be able to vouch for him, I am sure. You will be able to assure me that this man is indeed your long-lost brother."

Katherine hesitated. "Why do you need my assurance? I am sure his money is sufficient assurance to rent a house."

"Renting a house? No, that was not his business with me, Miss Parish. Now that he has returned, he wishes to claim his share of the inheritance.

There is a large trust fund, I understand? Naturally, I cannot undertake such work unless I am confident that the gentleman is who he says he is. I advised him to go to his home town — Branton, is it not? — and find someone there who recognises him. That is the sensible thing to do, but he seemed reluctant. So you are the only one who can vouch for him."

"I? But I have not seen him since I was six years old, and that only briefly. I was but four when he left home to join the navy. I cannot confirm his identity, not beyond all doubt. He must go to Branton."

"Ah! That is as I thought. Then I beg your pardon for intruding, Miss Parish, and wish you and your brother a happy residence in this wonderful town of ours."

Katherine sank back into her chair in some perplexity. Why would Harold think her trust fund was a large one? Would he even be entitled to a share of it? It would depend on the terms under which it was drawn up, she supposed. And why did he have no discharge papers from the navy? The Admiralty would have ensured he had some documents, and perhaps a pension, too. When he was thought to be lost, there had been any number of official letters from Vice-Admiral this and Commodore that.

And none of it reassured her that he was, in fact, her brother. If only her uncle and aunt had not been so quick to send her away! But they had been happy to pass the responsibility to her brother. Perhaps, despite all the kind words, they were glad to be rid of her, the unwanted poor relation, taken in out of kindness but sent off with a sigh of relief as soon as another relation turned up. And even he did not want her, only her trust fund, meagre as it was.

At that moment, she felt small and abandoned and very unhappy, and she knew precisely what she needed to raise her spirits — Kent would cheer her up, with his perpetual smile, his sunny outlook on life, his gentle kisses.

The man she had betrayed and rejected. She would never see him again, now, and she could not imagine a drearier prospect than a lifetime without him.

Thunderous steps on the stairs, voices outside the room, the door thrust open... and by some miracle, he was there! It was as if she had conjured him out of her own imagination. She needed him and there he was, wearing the widest smile she had ever seen.

"Kent! Oh, Kent!"

She tore across the room and hurled herself into his arms, wrapping her own arms around his neck and pulling his head down to hers. His lips... oh glory, his lips were on hers, he was kissing her frenziedly, pulling her tight against him so that she was almost rocked off her feet. But she was safe in his embrace. Nothing could worry her now, for Kent would look after her. She leaned into him, and let that wonderful kiss linger on and on...

No! Whatever was she doing? Shocked, she pushed herself away from him and backed across the room, her hands covering her still tingling lips.

"I beg your pardon," she whispered. "So sorry... never meant... so very sorry."

"No, no," he said gently, smiling at her. "You must not apologise for so lovely a welcome. Indeed, I am tempted to go out and come in again, just to have you kiss me like that once more. Will you, Katy? Will you kiss me again? Please?"

As he spoke, he was inching across the room towards her. Now he was so close she could feel his warm breath on her cheek. He cupped her face in his hands.

"Kiss me, *please*, Katy."

How could she possibly refuse him? She laid her hands on his chest, the wool of his greatcoat damp from the rain, and lifted her face to his. This time, his kiss was gentle and tender, as it had been at the tower. His fingers entwined with her hair and his other hand was around her waist, holding her snugly against him. It felt utterly right.

After a while, she sighed and laid her head on his shoulder.

"Is all well with you, Katy?" he murmured into the top of her head.

"All is very well with me now."

"This man... he did not... alarm you? Hurt you?"

"No. But I think he is not my brother. He has been talking to an attorney about getting a share of my trust fund." She lifted her head to look him in the eye. "How do you come to be here? You went away somewhere, and out of nowhere, just when I needed you, there you were. How did that happen?"

"I went to Branton and met all your friends and saw your wonderful beam engines and even got myself a job."

"As an engineer?"

"I am not qualified for that. I am to be general manager for Mr Ridwell at Longfarley Mill. And... Katy, your house is still unoccupied. I might even rent it. I have to live somewhere, and it would be wonderful to be in the same house where you grew up."

"Oh! I should like to think of you living there."

"You could live there, too. If... if we were married."

Her insides turned over in the most alarming way. "Kent, are you... I mean... is this... a proposal?" He nodded, a strange look on his face, almost as if he were afraid of her answer. "Then you have forgiven me?"

He looked startled. "Forgiven you? For what?"

"For betraying you to Sir Hubert. That was so foolish of me, and—"

"No, no! You were quite right. It was drastic, perhaps, but it needed that to make me see that I could not go on as I had done. So I went to

Branton. Katy— Do you mind me calling you Katy? Everyone at Branton called you that, so—"

"No, I love it."

He gave her a little squeeze, bestowing one of his widest smiles on her that warmed her to the tips of her slippers. "Katy, it is I who must beg your forgiveness. I have been—"

For answer, she placed one finger on his lips. "Hush. That is all forgotten, all in the past. Did you mean it? Talking about marriage, I mean."

"Of course I meant it. Will you marry me, Katy? I have not much to offer you, but—"

"Hush," she said again. "I will marry you, but I have not much to offer you, either. We shall have to budget carefully."

The door opened again, to admit another familiar face.

"James! You here too?"

"There you are, Cousin Kate, and... well, you are in safe hands, I see. Yes, yes, do not glare at me, Atherton, but we need to be ready when this impostor returns. Has Atherton told you, Kate? About the newspaper cutting?"

Katherine blushed, and it was Kent who chuckled and said, "We have been too pleasurably engaged to discuss that. Cathcart, will you see that Katy's maid sets about packing, and ensure there are carriages enough ready for us in... shall we say, two hours? Then we shall await this fellow's return."

"I shall arrange everything." And so saying, James disappeared, leaving Katherine alone with Kent once more.

She sighed. "Kent, will you marry me soon? I am tired of bouncing around from one house to another. All I want now is a home of my own, with you. I want you never to leave me."

Her voice wobbled alarmingly, but he pulled her close, and kissed her forehead so softly she barely felt the touch of his lips. "It would be the greatest privilege of my life to take care of you always, Katy, my love. My wonderful Katy, who is turning me into an honest, upright citizen. One day, I may even be worthy of you, my dearest."

"I love you so much it hurts," she whispered.

"I know what you mean," he whispered back. "It is just the same for me, too. But we are together now. We will always be together, my darling love."

***

Kent had arranged the little parlour carefully. Katy and Daisy sat on either side of the fire, Kent was at the table pretending to read a newspaper, while James prowled restlessly around the room. But eventually there were footsteps outside, the door opened and there he was. The man pretending to be Harold Parish.

He was rather a handsome fellow, that was Kent's first thought. The right age, the fair colouring, the blue eyes, just as described in the newspaper. Kent had shown the cutting to Katy, and she had exclaimed in horror at the amount of detail it revealed about her family.

"No wonder we were all taken in," she murmured.

Now she watched him calmly, having accepted that he was a complete stranger who had tried to help himself to her money. And if that had failed, perhaps he would have tried something worse. Kent had wished to spare her the most sordid of the possibilities, but she guessed much of it. A hasty marriage would have given him full access to her fortune.

The impostor was smiling as he entered, but seeing James Cathcart and Kent there, the smile slipped a little. "Visitors? I wasn't aware you had any acquaintance in York, sister dear."

"Allow me to introduce them to you. This is my future husband, Mr Kent Atherton, son of the Earl of Rennington, and my cousin, Mr James Cathcart. I am afraid I cannot introduce you in return, for I have not the least idea who you are."

The smile was entirely gone now, replaced with a nervous wariness. "Why, sister, how can you say so? Gentlemen, I'm Harold Parish."

"I think not," Kent said, smiling. He produced the newspaper cutting and laid it on the table. "I believe you read this and decided to take advantage of an innocent young lady by relieving her of her money."

"Nonsense! We're going to set up house and—"

"So why are you asking attorneys to help you claim my trust fund?" Katy said sweetly.

"I'm your brother! I'm entitled to it... half of it, anyway."

"If you were truly Miss Parish's brother," Kent said, "you would go to Branton and find someone who remembers you and can vouch for you. But you have avoided Branton, have you not? Very smart of you, because your little scheme would be uncovered instantly. I think you—"

With shocking suddenness, the man bolted for the door, where he found the solid form of James Cathcart blocking his way.

"What shall we do with him?" Cathcart said, holding the struggling man easily. "Break his legs?"

The man squeaked, and the carefully modulated accent vanished. "It weren't my idea, honest! It were me cousin made me do it."

"The fellow masquerading as your valet?" Cathcart said. "He is already locked up in the cellar. Cousin Kate, you may decide this miscreant's future. Broken legs or the magistrate?"

"Not the broken legs," she said. "Violence should be a last resort, James."

"Pity," he said. "The magistrate, then. He will be transported, at least, I should think."

The man squeaked again. "Please... I never meant no harm, just trying to make a living. Bin using my own money to fund everything, so I'm well out of pocket."

"That is a good point," Katy said gravely. "I have had a pleasant visit to York, which I have never seen before, so I am not minded to be harsh. But you must never do anything like this again... what is your name, anyway?"

"Jim Baring," he whispered.

"Where are you from?"

"Lancaster."

"Where the newspaper article was printed," Kent said. "Well, Jim Baring, if you will write a confession detailing who you are, how you and your cousin came by the idea and admitting that it was all a take-in, we shall let you both go."

He nodded eagerly. Kent produced the paper, pen and ink laid out ready for this eventuality, and Baring laboriously wrote his confession, while Kent leaned over him, watching every word and suggesting additions. When he was satisfied, he nodded.

"Very well. Off you go, and get your cousin out of the cellar. You will want to get back to Lancaster as soon as may be, I dare say, but remember to pay your shot before you leave the hotel."

With a quick nod, he scuttled away.

"An excellent day's work," Kent said in satisfaction. "No blood spilt, not a penny piece lost to the fraud, Katy unharmed, and a confession extracted from the villain of his own free will. Captain Edgerton would be proud of us."

26: Good News And Bad News

M ichael was full of energy all of a sudden. For the first time in weeks, he had a potential murderer to investigate. On the blackboard in the old schoolroom, he wrote *'Kent Atherton'* in flourishing script, then meticulously added *'Esq'* after it.

"It is all circumstance, Michael," Pettigrew Willerton-Forbes said, with a rueful shake of his head.

"Yes, but so many circumstances. He was here at the castle before the murder, with plenty of opportunity to hide the axe in the urn. He was here on the night of the murder itself. He slept alone, so there was no one to notice if he crept from his room. He was one of the first on the scene, and he told us he saw a man running away down the main stairs, which no one else noticed. That in itself is not particularly suspicious. But now we find out he is running a smuggling ring, he found signs of an intruder at the tower, most likely Miss Peach, and he could easily have returned the next day, discovered her, strangled her and carried her body away to Tonkins Farm, to throw us completely off the scent. He would have disposed of the green bag, of course, and substituted that dilapidated old woollen bag, which Miss Peach would never have used, in the hay barn, which she never entered in her life, I would swear. If we can find this mule that Miss Peach was riding in the field next to the tower, we shall know she was killed there, and then it will be all but certain. Sandy is taking the mule's owner there today."

"But *why*, Michael?" Pettigrew said firmly. "Why would Kent Atherton murder Nicholson?"

"Because of the smuggling," Michael said triumphantly. "You know how Nicholson got his sticky fingers into every shady venture, so why not this one, too? He threatened Atherton with exposure, and not gentlemanly Sir Hubert Strong, who will happily turn a blind eye, but His Majesty's Customs and Excise, who certainly will not. Perhaps Atherton was paying him off, but Nicholson got greedy, and Atherton decided to get rid of him once and for all. Miss Peach knew what was going on, so she had to be got rid of, too. It all makes sense, Pettigrew."

"You do realise that any half-decent barrister could tear a story like that apart in five minutes? Son of an earl, blameless life, only used the tower for star gazing — he loves that telescope. And, as I keep pointing out to you, it is all coincidence. Yes, he could have murdered Nicholson, but so could anyone. Walter Atherton was the first to arrive at Nicholson's murder, so why not him? And Eustace Atherton could have found Miss Peach at the tower and strangled her."

"Walter had no quarrel with the chaplain, so why would he? And Eustace *still* has an alibi," Michael said. "If you want him to be Nicholson's murderer, he had to have crept out of his house, ridden to Corland and then back again afterwards, and got himself back into the house with no one any the wiser. It defies credibility, Pettigrew. I am more and more convinced that the murderer came from *within* the castle, and that means Kent."

"Without evidence that there was blackmail or something of the sort, it will never stand up in court."

"If my half-decent barrister were to speak for the prosecution, he could convince a jury in five minutes."

Pettigrew chuckled. "If you mean me, probably I could, but you will have to convince *me* first, my friend. Did you check Miss Wilkes' story?"

Michael frowned. "I did. The baronetage confirms that there is a Sir Reginald Wilkes at Warriston Hall, that he married a Miss Maria Winfell, having issue two sons and three daughters. Rosamunde is the middle daughter, aged twenty-two."

"So that all tallies."

"Yes, and yet it is very convenient, do you not think?"

"Do you want me to go to Northumberland? Or I can write to the Duchess of Dunmorton. She will know the family, I imagine. A description of the girl, and confirmation of the existence of the aunt in Scarborough, would do it."

"Scarborough..." Michael muttered. "Yes, write, if you would, Pettigrew. It seems legitimate, but I am still cross with Mr Eustace Atherton for lying to me, so by all means, let us check every last little detail of his story. And when Sandy is finished mule-hunting, I might send him to Scarborough to find the aunt."

"What do you want me to do, Michael?" James Neate said.

"Decode Miss Peach's notebook, if you can. You will need to go to Pickering to examine the books in her room. One of them will give you the code, I am sure. I doubt it will be anything complicated."

"I can leave today if—"

The door burst open to reveal an excited Sandy Saxby. "Yer a genius, Michael! Mrs Markley picked out her mule in an instant."

"In the field next to the tower?" Michael said.

"Aye, looking as if he belonged there, too. No sign of a saddle, but we can search properly later."

"And for the green bag," Michael said, adding grimly, "There you are, Pettigrew! Miss Peach was murdered at the tower, that is now certain, and Kent Atherton was the only person who knew that. Now we have him! Finally, I can make an arrest."

Pettigrew sighed and shook his head.

***

K ent found the return journey from York far more pleasurable. He had Katy beside him, both her arms wrapped around one of his, as if he might fly away and she was keeping him safely tethered to her side. Her bonnet precluded any kissing, and often prevented him from seeing her face, but they were together and their future was settled. All his doubts and uncertainties had evaporated in that moment when he had entered the parlour at York and she had flown into his arms. That was precisely where she belonged and would always remain.

James Cathcart nobly took the forward seat and politely pretended to sleep, and the two valets and Daisy Marler were in a separate post chaise, so the betrothed couple had a semblance of privacy. Kent did not feel the need for it. Last night, he and Katy had talked all evening without cessation. Today, they were silent. They had their whole lives to talk and to kiss and to plan their future of perfect happiness. For now, all that mattered was that they were no longer separated.

Once again, the Cathcarts received Katherine with some surprise but expressed their pleasure to have her home again, and even more pleasure to hear that there was to be a wedding. Kent spent a little time talking to Mr Cathcart, as he was expected to, but he knew it would be up to Katy's trustees to reveal how much money she would have. Then he left them to their celebrations, for he had to tell his father his news before word reached him from some other source.

He found him in his bedroom, with luggage everywhere, his valet looking distracted.

"Going away, Father?" Kent said in some surprise. "Not before Cousin Bertram's wedding, I trust. We are all required to attend this grand ball to celebrate. You are the host, so you cannot avoid it."

"No, no, but Olivia is making plans to get me away from here. The trouble is, it is so long since I went anywhere that I hardly know what to pack. How do you manage when you go away?"

"That is what you have a valet for, Father. You tell him what you will need — shooting gear, full dress for evenings, whatever you think — and he packs the appropriate clothes."

"But your mother always used to take care of the details for me. She always knew what I would need."

"Then ask Olivia, since this is her trip. She will know. Father, I have news for you. Will you come downstairs and talk to me?"

Grumbling slightly, the earl led the way down to his study, and poured two glasses of brandy.

"Now then, my boy, tell me what is on your mind."

"Father, I have asked Katherine Parish to marry me and she has accepted. We plan to live in Branton. I have taken employment there."

It was probably not the wisest way to inform his father of his new circumstances, but Kent wanted to present it as a *fait accompli* and not have to endure a long argument about it.

"What sort of employment?" his father said, eyes narrowing.

"I am to be a manager at a cotton mill. An assistant at first, while I learn, but eventually I shall run the mill myself." His father sighed, but Kent straightened his spine. "I know it is not what you hoped for me, father, but I must make my own way in the world. You have taken good care of me — of all of us — but as a younger son, it is my duty to earn my living as best I can. I cannot respect myself if I live on your charity indefinitely, and after you it would be Uncle George and Cousin Bertram, upon whom I have no right to depend. It would make me the worst kind of scrounging leech. I am unsuited to the church, the law, the army or politics, but mills and engines are something I find fascinating. They are the future, Father, and I mean to play my part in it. In time, I hope I will be a mill owner and not just a manager, and Katy will help me do that. She knows everything there is to know about cotton mills, which is why she is the perfect wife for me. I hope you will give us your blessing."

His father rubbed his eyes tiredly. "Well, well, you are determined to have your own way, I can see. Olivia will marry and go away too, even Eustace will marry, and I shall be left all alone in this great barn of a place. It used to be full of noise and liveliness, you know, when your mother was here. Always something taking place, and guests coming and going, and now it is nothing but echoes."

Kent crept away as soon as he decently could, feeling sad for his father but determined not to change his plans. When he went down for dinner, he was pleased to see Eustace there.

"You will be here for this party for Bertram and Bea Franklyn tomorrow, so that will be two nights in succession we have had the benefit of your company, brother."

"I am staying here at the moment with my betrothed, Miss Wilkes."

"Oh! I had no idea that was in the wind, but then you always hold your cards close to your chest. My felicitations, brother. You may congratulate me, as well. I am to marry Miss Parish."

Briefly, Kent explained his plans. He knew Eustace would not be pleased that he was to give up his part in the smuggling, but he was unprepared for the coldness with which Eustace turned on him.

"I might have expected as much, little brother. You always were the weak link in this particular adventure. I wish you joy of your mill."

And he spun on his heel and whisked away, leaving Kent bemused and curiously disappointed. If his own family could not be happy for him, who would be?

***

"I have both good news and bad news to report," Neate said as they sat in the old schoolroom.

"Bad news first," Michael said. "Let us get the worst over with."

"Miss Peach's room above the chandlery at Pickering was broken into last week. The room was thoroughly searched, but the only things that appear to have been taken are the books."

Michael groaned. "So we cannot decode the notebook."

"Now let me tell you the good news," Neate said smugly. "The only book remaining was the prayer book, which was still inside her pocket that you brought from Tonkins Farm, and that was not searched, seemingly. She had marked the page, and I have decoded the entire notebook."

Michael grinned. "James, you are a genius! But does it say anything interesting?"

"Well... nothing definitive. Nothing that says *'The murderer is...'*. That would be far too convenient. There was nothing new from her observations in Pickering. She saw Mr Eustace's carriage collecting the ladybird from the brothel, but we knew about that. That was what led her to the tower. She seems to have been suspicious of Mr Eustace because of that. She was very pleased with herself for the mule idea, although she was concerned that the droppings would give her away, but then she found there was a field full of old ponies and donkeys next to the tower. She obviously knew about the smuggling and recorded everyone coming and going from Welwood as well as the tower. Very detailed notes, but I am not sure it helps us, except that the Pickering ladybird was a regular visitor at Welwood. Quite a rake, Mr Eustace. I wonder if his betrothed knows what he gets up to."

"Does she mention the laudanum?" Michael said.

"Oh, the laudanum! She was experimenting with it, but it was her own sleeping she was concerned about. The laudanum made her sleep late, and she was nearly caught out by Mr Kent and Miss Parish. She had to run outside and up to the viewpoint on the top of the tower, with no time to lock the door behind her or hide her bag. She stopped using laudanum after that."

"And the brazier? Why did she not light it when it must have been perishing at night?"

"She dared not, in case the glow could be seen. She used to light the kitchen fire once a day for hot water, and then she would heat a brick in the embers to warm her feet at night. But Michael, listen to this. *I am almost certain of the murderer's identity now. I only need to find the saddle, and then I shall have the proof. I will look properly in the obvious place tomorrow.'* And that is the last entry."

"But she does not name him?"

"No."

"But we know who it is — Kent Atherton."

Pettigrew was sitting watching this exchange, his hands folded over his stomach. "Are you certain of that, Michael?"

"Yes! You have heard my arguments, so you know how much evidence there is against him, and he was in charge of the smuggling operation. He had the most to lose if Nicholson threatened to report him to the Excise men."

"And he presumably stole the books from Miss Peach's room to prevent us from decoding the notebook?"

"Of course! Who else?"

"Almost anyone else *except* Kent Atherton. You told everyone at dinner here about the notebook and how you needed to decode it. I am not sure why you did that—"

"To see if anyone looked alarmed at the prospect, that is why. I should have thought you would have worked that out, Pettigrew. But sadly, no one did."

"Well, someone noted it, and stole the books to prevent us from decoding the notebook, but whoever it was, it could not have been Kent Atherton. Not only was he not here at that dinner, he was two days' travel away in Branton when the books were stolen."

Michael deflated instantly. "Then it is hopeless! We still have nothing."

***

K atherine could scarcely believe the state of grace in which she now existed. All her worries were swept away, and she no longer had to tell herself sternly not to harbour any hopes of Kent, that he was just being kind to a poor orphan. He *loved* her, truly loved her, and all her most extravagant dreams were coming true.

The Cathcart family shared her happiness, albeit slightly bemused that the inarticulate, unprepossessing mill-owner's daughter should have caught such a prize. Even Aveline was polite to her, perhaps seeing the advantage of the family connection to the Athertons. If she could not marry into that family herself, then having a cousin to boast of was almost as good.

Uncle Cathcart smiled benignly at Katherine, and murmured "All's well that ends well", as if he himself had effected her rescue, and had not sent her away with a stranger and retreated with a sigh of relief to his study. As for Aunt Cathcart, she was delirious with joy at the prospect of a wedding to the noble Atherton family, and was already planning the entertainments to celebrate the event. She carried a notebook everywhere with her, to write any little hints gleaned from the preparations for the forthcoming wedding of Mr Bertram Atherton and Miss Bea Franklyn. There was to be a grand ball at Corland Castle two days before the wedding, and she fully expected one at least as grand for the marriage of her dear niece to Mr Kent Atherton.

The night before this auspicious event, Katherine was just dropping off to sleep when she became aware of noises in the house, strange noises that she could not quite identify. Intruders in the house! Thoroughly awake now, she threw on a robe and crept to her door. Opening it a crack, she peered out. The landing was in darkness, apart from a crack of light from beneath the door of Alex and Neil's bedroom.

The noises were much louder now, strange moans and gasps, as if someone were in pain, and it emanated from the boys' room. Odd high-pitched squeaks were mixed in with the moans now. She was just about to rush across to see if one of the twins was ill, or under attack in some way, when Uncle Cathcart, resplendent in an embroidered nightcap, came marching up the stairs with a candelabrum. Behind him, still fully dressed, was James.

Uncle Cathcart threw open the boys' bedroom door. Instantly, silence fell.

"Father?" came a wavering voice.

"Get out!" Uncle Cathcart said, in tones sterner than Katherine had ever heard him use before.

To her astonishment, Daisy, her hair tumbled all down her back and wearing only a nightgown, scuttled out. Even more astonishingly, James burst into laughter. Then he noticed Katherine, frozen with shock at her bedroom door.

"Better go back to bed, cousin," he said. "You should not see this."

Uncle Cathcart turned and started at the sight of Katherine. "No, indeed! Into your room at once, lock your door and stay there. Nothing to alarm you, niece."

Obediently, Katherine did as she was bidden, but for some time afterwards there was a murmur of voices, and footsteps coming and going on the stairs. Eventually, all was quiet again. Then, a timid knock on her door, and Aunt Cathcart's voice.

"Are you awake, dear? May I come in for a moment?"

Katherine let her in, rather amused by the embarrassment written on her aunt's face. "It is quite all right, ma'am. You do not need to explain to me. Daisy will have to leave, I know that."

Her aunt gave a half smile. "You know what was going on, then? I am so shocked! And ashamed to think that my own sons—!"

"My father said it was natural for young men to... experiment. That was how he put it. One of our neighbours had a son who... experimented with the housemaid."

Aunt Cathcart patted her hand. "You were always a sensible child. I should have known you would not fall into hysterics."

"What is the point of that?" Katherine said. "I am excessively disappointed in Daisy, though. She appeared to be such a respectable girl. I found her weeping at the altar over a lie she once told, and now I find she does something far worse. I would never have introduced her into a Christian household if I had known she was so shockingly lax in her ways."

"She has an odd sense of morality. I have given her a severe talking to, as you may imagine, but she considers this... tonight's behaviour as something perfectly natural and acceptable. Well, it might be where she comes from, but not in my house. She will leave first thing in the morning."

Breakfast the next morning was the most peculiar Katherine had ever experienced. Alex and Neil were an odd mixture of chastened and triumphant, James was amused, their father was forbiddingly stern and their mother brightly pretending nothing was amiss. Aveline, Susan and Lucinda, having heard the disruption but not understanding the cause, asked sly questions which were ruthlessly suppressed by Aunt Cathcart.

Katherine said nothing. She could find nothing amusing in the situation, and it was an inconvenience to lose Daisy and have to engage another maid. Perhaps she could write to Mrs Vance, and ask her to find someone from Branton? Since the Cathcart sisters were engaged in torturing the pianoforte under Miss Harkness's watchful eye, Katherine retreated to the quiet of her room.

Having written her letter to Mrs Vance, she thought of her jewellery box. She was to be married soon, so she would need to let her trustees know of it, so that her trust fund could be made over to Kent. Lifting out the inner compartments, she retrieved the bundle of documents and briskly untied the string. Then she spread the papers out on the little table by the window, most of them in her father's distinctive hand that gave her a pang of grief.

But one was in a different hand, the name at the bottom *'Arbuthnot Humber, Humber Bank, Branton'*. At the top, it read, *'Summary of trust fund at commencement'*. The date was two years earlier, when Papa had first taken out the loan for the new mill, and had created the trust fund to protect her dowry. And there, in a neat list, were all the monies in the fund. Five thousand pounds as marriage settlement for Miss Elizabeth Hawley. The accumulated interest therefrom. A bequest from Miss Agatha Hawley, plus accumulated interest. A further bequest from Mr Thomas Hawley, being a half share in Whitmoor Mill, and a quarter share in a coal mine in Nottinghamshire, these to be made over to Katherine on her coming of age. And at the bottom, the total value, underlined twice, of seventeen thousand four hundred and sixty pounds.

And Papa had said it was only a modest amount! Great heavens! There was also the ten thousand pounds from Mr Vance, she remembered. *Twenty-seven thousand pounds!* She and Kent were rich, or at least rich enough to live comfortably while he established himself. She knew to the penny how much it cost to run that house in Branton, and although they would need furniture, they need not furnish the entire house straight away, just the principal rooms. Then they could open up additional rooms as they could afford it.

Whitmoor Mill... that was a small place, still water-powered, but ripe for expansion and a beam engine. Yes, that could be made a great deal more profitable. And coal was always a sound investment. With steam-driven mills opening up all over the north, there would be increasing demand for coal. And perhaps some of the profits could be invested in further coal mines.

Oh, this would be so much fun! This was what she understood, what she had been raised to do. She could abandon the ladylike embroidery and watercolours and get back to the real world of industry. She could not wait to discuss it with Kent that evening.

Humming with excitement, she began to make a list of what needed to be done.

27: A Grand Ball

Kent was caught up in the last-minute preparations for the ball being held to celebrate the marriage of his cousin Bertram to Bea Franklyn. Bertram had sensibly retired to his library until forced to become the centre of attention, but Bea and her stepmother, Lady Esther Franklyn, spent the day at Corland Castle, Lady Esther to issue a stream of wildly ambitious instructions to the servants, and Bea mostly to get in the way, or so it seemed to Kent.

"This is so much fun!" she cried, having just decreed to the long-suffering footmen that the flower arrangements in the great hall be moved for the third time.

"But a great deal of work for you," Kent said. "You will be glad when all the excitement is over and you and Bertram are safely married so that you can have a rest. Are you planning a wedding tour?"

"Oh, no, we have the Dower House to finish first. Perhaps in the spring. Do you think the purple and orange flowers look better by themselves or all mixed up?"

"I think they look perfect as they are. No one will notice them, anyway. They will all be looking at you."

Bea was not a person who blushed, but even she looked slightly conscious at this flattery. "Oh no, they will look at Bertram just as much, for he is always so elegant in his evening attire, do you not think? He has that quiet style that is never showy but always refined. Not like me! I wish I could be refined, but I never shall. I only hope I shall not shame him this evening by tripping over my own feet."

"You will be everything that is admirable," Kent said, "but do get some rest before this evening."

"Oh, but I want everything to be perfect!" she cried. "I so want Bertram to have a wonderful time, for it is almost his last day of freedom. He will be tied to me for the rest of his life, poor man, so he might as well enjoy himself while he still can. Oh! The salmon patties! I promised I would try them out to make sure they are good enough to serve. I shall see you tonight, Kent."

So saying, she dashed away to the kitchen, and Kent was left to surreptitiously shuffle the flowers into a more felicitous arrangement.

Late in the afternoon, he snatched an hour away from the castle to call on Katy, for heaven forbid that a whole day should pass without a meeting. He found Cathcart House almost empty. Katy was alone in the music room, her finger running lightly over the keys as she played a gentle air.

Her face lit up when she saw Kent. "I did not think I would see you before tonight," she cried, running into his arms and hugging him tight. "Oh, I am so glad to see you! I am always glad to see you, but today has been especially trying. There is such pandemonium upstairs, for Susan is to attend the ball too, although only until supper."

"Is she having trouble deciding on a gown for the occasion?"

"No, for she only has one ball gown, but as to hair and decorations and bracelets and gloves and... well, you can imagine. Shall we sit in the window seat, and you can tell me all that you have been doing?"

"I have been plying my father with brandy and extolling your virtues and convincing him that life in Branton with you as my wife will be the making of me. I also remarked that Mr Vance, a kind and generous man, had liked you well enough to leave you ten thousand pounds in his will. As a result, Father has mellowed sufficiently to agree to make over the sum of ten thousand pounds to me instead of an allowance. So we shall not be entirely destitute."

"And not dependent on your father, either," she said. "That is important. I have news of that type, too. I looked at the papers relating to my trust fund, and two years ago, when it was set up, it was worth seventeen thousand pounds."

"What! Then we are rich!"

"Not quite, but we will be, for my trust fund includes a half share in a water-driven mill, and if we install a beam engine—"

Kent gave a great shout of delight. "What an amazing girl you are, Katy Parish. Our own mill!"

"If we can buy out the other owner, or convince him regarding the improvements, yes. I have a share in a coal mine, too, and you know how profitable that can be, if it is the right sort of coal."

"I did not know," he admitted, "although coal was much spoken of at Branton. I have so much to learn about this business, and I cannot wait to get started. When can we be married, my love? Soon, I hope."

"In another month, it will be a year since Papa died. That would be an appropriate time, do you not think? We can talk to Mr Dewar on Sunday about the banns, if you wish."

"I do wish," he whispered, gently stroking her cheek. "I wish it very much, my sweet Katy. Our marriage cannot come too soon for me so that we can begin our new life in Branton."

He bent his head to kiss her and the music room fell silent.

***

M ichael gazed at his reflection in the mirror with a frown. "I cannot get this neckcloth straight tonight. Something about it is askew, and nothing I do seems to improve matters."

"Would you like me to try?" Luce said.

"How humiliating, to have to depend on one's wife to dress one with the proper symmetry," he muttered. "Now, if James Neate were here…"

"He is better employed where he is," she said sharply, her deft fingers pulling the linen at his neck into some sort of order. "He is not really a valet, however convincingly he portrays one."

"I know, I know. We must hear some news of poor Miss Peach's murderer soon. She cannot have been at that tower for weeks without someone seeing her, or noticing something amiss. And yet… no one did. It is no more than half a mile from Welwood village, yet no one saw her. Where did she buy food? Was she stealing it?"

"Michael, you have gone over all this a hundred times already. You will not find any different answers now. Let James do his job. He is very good at sitting unnoticed in corners of taprooms and listening in to conversations. Whatever she was up to, if it can be found out, he is the man to do it."

"But it makes no sense," he said, tugging at the neckcloth again.

"Michael, hush," she said, pushing his fingers away from the neckcloth and setting it straight once more. "Stop fretting over all this. It is not like you to take this so to heart."

"Miss Peach was my responsibility. We brought her here to give her a pleasant holiday, and now she is dead and it is all my fault. If I had caught the murderer, she would be alive today. She would be here tonight, watching everyone in their silks and jewels, and gathering stories to take back to her sister in Harrogate."

"Michael!" she said sharply, grabbing hold of his lapels to force his attention. "It is *not* your fault. No one could have done more to uncover this murderer than you have, and Peachy chose to go off by herself and not tell anyone what she was up to. You cannot protect someone who does not want to be protected. She had a wonderful time chasing round after the murderer or the smugglers or whatever it was she was doing, and she would certainly not have wanted to stay safely at home and miss all the fun. Now, tonight we are going to help Mr Bertram Atherton and Miss Beatrice Franklyn celebrate their forthcoming marriage, and you are going to dance with me at least once, and take me in to supper, and you are going to enjoy yourself, do you hear me?"

He grinned suddenly. "Yes, wife. It shall be just as you say. After all, with a splendid dinner followed by a ball, how could I not enjoy myself? If you are not already engaged, madam, might I secure your hand for the supper dance?"

"I am not already engaged, sir, and I should be delighted to keep the supper dance for you."

"Then, Mrs Edgerton, shall we go down and await the arrival of the principal guests?"

He bowed and held out his arm to her, and with a little curtsy, she rested her hand on his arm. Lord, he was a lucky man! He wished sometimes... often, in fact... that he could come out with the glib words he heard on other men's lips. *You look lovely tonight... you are an amazing woman... I am the luckiest man alive... you are the sun that lights up my life and I adore you.* But somehow the words would never come. He could only hope that she saw the adoration in his eyes that he could never express in words.

Slowly, they made their way down the stairs, following a little stream of others, passing the display of armoury on the half-landing, flanked by the two Chinese urns. Michael glowered at them as he passed by.

"The axe in the urn," he muttered under his breath. Those urns had caused him so much trouble, and as for the armoury—!

"Stop it, Michael," Luce hissed, but she smiled affectionately at him, and the little knot of anger inside him melted slightly.

"Sorry," he murmured.

The dinner guests were assembling in the great hall. The earl was smiling, moving from group to group, with Lady Olivia, practically bouncing with excitement, at his side. Mr Alfred Strong had Lady Alice on his arm, guiding her through the throng and explaining who was there. Sir Hubert and Lady Strong were keeping a watchful eye on Julia, Emily and Penelope Atherton, whose parents were to arrive later. The Cathcarts were standing a little aside, Kent Atherton and Miss Parish close together and talking excitedly. There was no sign of Tess Nicholson, but Michael hardly expected her. There was never any knowing what that girl would get up to next.

Mr Eustace Atherton was the first to approach them, the elegantly dressed Miss Wilkes on his arm.

"Mrs Edgerton. Captain." He made a graceful bow. "Delighted to see you both here, and that your investigations can spare you to us for one evening at least. Or is this just another part of your work? Are you watching us all for signs of guilt?"

He laughed heartily at his own joke.

"It would make my life easier if a murderer always looked shifty, but sadly, it is rarely the case," Michael said thoughtfully. "But I never entirely leave behind the investigation, either. Tonight I am here because of one of those little details that may or may not be connected."

"Michael," Luce murmured warningly.

"And so that my wife may dress in her finery, of course," he said smoothly. "One likes to see the ladies in their best gowns. Miss Wilkes looks charming tonight."

He bowed courteously to the lady, who acknowledged the compliment with an inclination of her head.

"Oh... thank you," Atherton said, smiling at her. "But then, my dear Rosamunde always looks charming. But what is this possibly unconnected detail, Captain?"

"I have not forgotten that Miss Franklyn was being watched by someone from the woods not far from here. You will remember it, too, sir, for you came upon her on one such occasion and were able to escort her safely home."

"Indeed, I do, and very glad I was to be of service. It was most fortunate that I happened to be passing. But I supposed the fellow was merely a stranger skulking in the woods for reasons of his own. Have there been other sightings since then?"

"Not that I have heard, but I shall be glad to have it confirmed by the lady herself this evening. Miss Franklyn has always been accompanied on her rides since that time, for Mr Bertram Atherton takes good care of his future wife, but I shall be happy to see her safely married the day after tomorrow."

"Amen to that," he said. "By the way, I have received word of a couple of interesting guns, a blunderbuss and a rifle, that may soon be in my hands. If I am successful, you must come out to Welwood to try them out." Then, with a bow, he moved away with Miss Wilkes.

"He is trying to butter you up," Luce said in her severest tones. "And he managed to wheedle information from you, too."

Michael threw a quizzical glance at Luce. "Well, I had to answer him when he persevered. It would not have been polite to refuse."

"I know, and he has always taken a great interest in your investigations."

"For which I am very thankful, for without his diligence we might never have found poor Peachy's body."

"You have forgiven him for deceiving you over Miss Wilkes, then?"

"His motives were honourable, to protect a lady."

"If indeed she is a lady."

He looked at her askance. "What does that mean?"

"Oh, she plays the part convincingly, but there is something... off about her. Nervousness, perhaps. A certain reticence, which is unusual in one of her rank. And frankly, Michael, no *lady* would spend the night with a man in that way."

"That is true. And there is the black wig, as well. One might want to conceal one's true appearance in a public setting, but at your lover's house? That seems strange. Oh! A wig! I wonder if Miss Peach had a wig? Perhaps that is why no one remembers seeing her."

Luce sighed. "There, I have set you off again. I really should know better by now. Look, we are moving forward. The bridal party must be arriving."

They followed the crowd through the passage to the entrance hall, where most of the guests lingered in a chattering, excited group, but several of the younger members of the party went outside onto the bridge to welcome the arrivals.

Michael, his insatiable curiosity unable to resist, went outside onto the bridge across the moat, too. A large cluster of grooms and gardeners and housemaids loitered a respectful distance away, at the top of the steps leading down into the moat. Two carriages lumbered slowly up the drive and drew to a halt at the far side of the bridge.

The two butlers stepped forward to open the doors and let down the steps. From the first carriage, the parents emerged, Mr and Mrs George Atherton, and Mr and Lady Esther Franklyn. From the second came Mr Bertram Atherton, who handed down his betrothed, Miss Bea Franklyn. They smiled, Miss Franklyn waved cheerily to the servants, they moved towards the bridge—

The bang echoed shockingly off the walls. Everyone froze, looking around, bewildered, for the cause of the explosion.

Bertram Atherton uttered a strange sound and then toppled backwards to the ground.

Someone screamed, shouts were heard and running feet, but Michael was already in motion. Bushes... the bushes just to one side of the bridge... that was where the gunshot had come from. Frantically he scrabbled from one bush to the next, pushing, pulling... surely the assassin could not have escaped? There was a low wall behind the bushes, but if he had jumped over that, he would have fallen clear to the basement level. He leaned over, saw nothing.

Where the devil could he have gone?

"Anything?" It was Lucas Atherton, his face ashen.

Michael shook his head. "Is he—?"

"Dead? No. Your wife has taken charge. Seems to know what she is about. For the love of God, Edgerton, what is happening here? Why would anyone shoot *Bertram?*"

But Michael could not answer him. The murder investigation had just become vastly more complicated.

THE END

The final book in the series is *Ambition*, wherein Olivia aims to become a duchess, her father settles on a wife and Captain Michael Edgerton finally works out who killed the chaplain, and why. You can read a sneak preview after the acknowledgements. For more information, go to https://maryk ingswood.co.uk.

Thanks for reading!

If you have enjoyed reading this book, please consider writing a short review on Amazon. You can find out the latest news and sign up for the mailing list at my website at https://marykingswood.co.uk.

A note on historical accuracy: I have endeavoured to stay true to the spirit of Regency times, and have avoided taking too many liberties or imposing modern sensibilities on my characters. The book is not one of historical record, but I've tried to make it reasonably accurate. However, I'm not perfect! If you spot a historical error, I'd very much appreciate knowing about it so that I can correct it and learn from it. Thank you!

Isn't that what's-his-name? Occasionally characters from an earlier series pop up, or are mentioned. Mr Ridwell and Mr Moreton, mill owners from Branton, appeared in *Woodside*. Note that this book is set four years earlier, so Mr Ridwell's beautiful daughter Ellen is not yet out.

About the series:

Book 0: The Chaplain: a man adrift, dreaming of a home (a novella, free to mailing list subscribers).

Book 1: Disinheritance: a man freed, looking for a new purpose in life

Book 2: Determination: a man pursued, forced to outwit his adversary

Book 3: Anger: a woman alone, trying to choose a different path in life

Book 4: Secrecy: a woman neglected, scheming to secure her own happiness

Book 5: Loyalty: a man of dreams, torn between the past and the future

Book 6: Ambition: a woman thwarted, unswervingly set on making a brilliant debut in society

Any questions about the series? Email me at mary@marykingswood .co.uk - I'd love to hear from you!

About the author

I write traditional Regency romances under the pen name Mary Kingswood, and epic fantasy as Pauline M Ross. I live in the beautiful Highlands of Scotland with my husband. I like chocolate, whisky, my Kindle, massed pipe bands, long leisurely lunches, chocolate, going places in my campervan, eating pizza in Italy, summer nights that never get dark, wood fires in winter, chocolate, the view from the study window looking out over the Moray Firth and the Black Isle to the mountains beyond. And chocolate. I dislike driving on motorways, cooking, shopping, hospitals.

Acknowledgements

Thanks go to:

Allison Lane, whose course on English Architecture inspired me.

Shayne Rutherford of Darkmoon Graphics for the cover design.

My beta readers: Charles Crouter, Kelly Darpinian, Sharon Flaherty, Melissa Forsythe, Donna Sue Holly, Leanne McKinley, Tina Miles, Pat Oen, Kristen Pinto-Coelho, Rosemary Paton, Melanie Savage, Wendy Stubbs, Carol Sturtz, Jeanne Thomas, Andrea Usami

Last, but definitely not least, my first reader: Amy Ross.

Sneak preview: Book 6 of The Chaplain's Legacy: Ambition

CORLAND CASTLE, NORTH RIDING: SEPTEMBER

Miss Olivia Atherton sat at the elegant escritoire in her bedroom and read the newspaper report avidly. It was the fourth time she had read it, and she still enjoyed the same little thrill as the first time, as if her very blood were fizzing with excitement. Every such report was glorious, of course, but this one was unusually long and detailed.

'An event of the greatest interest to students of the Latin language recently took place in the magnificent medieval setting of Landerby Manor in the county of Lincolnshire.'

Then a great deal about the house and its owners, the Duke and Duchess of Wedhampton, which was of little interest to Olivia. She jumped ahead to the important part.

'*Among the many distinguished guests, most notable of them was the Most Honourable, the Marquess of Embleton, heir to His Grace, the Duke of Bridgeworth. Lord Embleton graciously attended the entire event, and delighted all present by his contribution to the scholarly recitals, being a number of poems in classical Latin form, written by his lordship's own hand and agreed by all to be of the highest calibre, and comparable to the works of the great poets of the Roman era themselves. Lord Embleton being too modest to read his own works to the assembled company, this pleasant task was undertaken by Mr Bertram Atherton, nephew to the Right Honourable the Earl of Rennington. Mr Atherton performed this office with the greatest eloquence, ensuring that the true beauty of the verses could be fully appreciated by the rapt audience.*'

Too modest! He suffered from a stammer, that much she knew, so naturally public recitals would be a great trial to him. Well done, Cousin Bertram, for stepping forward to help his friend. Then there was a great deal more about the other guests and the Latin readings, which she cared nothing about. There was a brief mention of the Franklyns, and Lady Esther's father, the Duke of Camberley, was mentioned. How the newspapers loved the nobility! But how frustrating that Bea Franklyn should be there and actually meeting all these illustrious people, when it was Olivia who had studied them obsessively for so many years and knew all about them. And especially one of them in particular.

He had another mention later, for the gentlemen had held a fencing contest one day, which Mr Franklyn, astonishingly, had won, but the marquess had done almost as well.

'The match between Lord Embleton and Lord Grayling was of especial note for the skill exhibited by both gentlemen, Lord Embleton's performance being much admired for his graceful movements and Lord Grayling's for his strength and determination. The match was long and evenly balanced, but in the end Lord Grayling prevailed.'

Lord Grayling! That a mere baron should defeat a marquess and future duke was not how the world should be run, according to Olivia. And that a nobody like Mr Franklyn should defeat all the assembled nobles seemed unconscionable. Not that she had anything against Mr Franklyn, who was an amiable gentleman, and allowed Lady Esther to hold the most magnificent entertainments at Highwood Place, and he had not himself defeated her marquess, so she could not object to him on that score.

Not that he was her marquess, or ever likely to be, for she had never met him. Ever since she was thirteen and her older sister Izzy had come back from her first London season glowing with success, with a viscount on her arm and eleven other offers to boast about, Olivia had been determined to outdo her. A duke — nothing would do for her but a duke, and so she had assiduously studied the peerage to make her selection.

It was a depressing business. Twenty-seven dukes, that was all there were in the entire kingdom, and who wanted to live in Scotland or Ireland? A warmer, flatter southern county would be ideal, and preferably close to London. That narrowed her options, and a distressing number of those remaining were married already or too old or too young. Gradually, she had come to realise that there was just one man who encompassed all her requirements. The Marquess of Embleton. Ralph, for that was his Christian name, was heir to a dukedom in Buckinghamshire, of suitable age and unmarried.

She had watched for the reports of his activities in the newspapers, carefully cutting out each one, the important points to be transcribed into a book she kept for the purpose. For three years now she had tracked every ball he attended, every country house where he was a guest, every shooting party in which he participated, every horse race he watched. Three years, ever since she was fifteen, and he was now thirty and still unmarried. If she had gone up to town for her first season last spring, she would have met him there, and could have dazzled him with her knowledge of racehorses, and the Latin verses she had memorised.

But Grandmama had been so very ill that the season had been postponed and thus Olivia had not met the man who was to make her a duchess. Nor was it ever likely to happen, not now, not when everything in her life had gone so horribly wrong. Six months ago, she could have gone up to town as the Lady Olivia Atherton, legitimate daughter of an earl, and a catch worthy even of a future duke.

But in June their chaplain — her uncle by marriage! — had been murdered, which was dreadful enough, but the worst part was that he had never been ordained as a clergyman, and therefore her parents' marriage, at which he had officiated, was not legal. Her mother was no longer the Countess of Rennington, her eldest brother was no longer Viscount Birtwell and heir to the earldom, and all six of the earl's children were rendered illegitimate.

Now she was merely Miss Olivia Atherton, still an earl's daughter, still with the same dowry, but cast out of all good society, for surely no one would want to know her. It was depressing, but despite her reduced prospects, she still kept up her careful watch on Lord Embleton.

A knock on the door heralded the maid. "Beg pardon, milady, but Lady Alice says to tell you there's a caller."

Company! Olivia jumped up excitedly. As usual, she forbore to re-mind the maid that she was no longer Lady Olivia. The servants all kept to the same form of address and although it was incorrect, it soothed her a little to still be 'milady'.

"Who is it, Patsy?"

"Lady Esther, milady."

Now that was interesting. Olivia had not seen her since her return from Landerby Manor, so she could ask about that and perhaps have the felicity of hearing a mention of Lord Embleton. Ralph.

"Tell Aunt Alice that I shall be down soon."

A quick look in the mirror reassured her that there was nothing amiss with her appearance, but since it was Lady Esther, the daughter of a duke, she added a necklace to her attire — the amber cross elegantly combined demure piety and wealth.

Olivia skipped down the stairs, past Eustace's ridiculous display of armoury on the half-landing, flanked by the Chinese urns, which she rather liked, and into the great hall, the upper walls lined with a vast array of weapons. Corland Castle was not an ancient building, the scene of many battles, but the earl liked to pretend it was.

Her slippers making no sound on the tiled floor, she moved down the great hall into the passage beside the stairs and thence to the drawing room. She arrived just behind another group of callers.

"Lady Strong, Miss Strong, Miss Lily Strong, my lady," intoned Simp-son. Then, seeing Olivia coming up behind them, he added, "The Lady Olivia, my lady."

At Corland, even the family had to be announced, so that Aunt Alice, who had been blind since a childhood illness, might know precisely who was in the room. Her own daughter, Olivia's cousin, Tess Nicholson, was inclined to creep into a room unnoticed and take her mother by surprise when she spoke, but Olivia was not so ill-mannered.

Crossing the room quickly, she gave Aunt Alice a hasty kiss, then moved aside for the Strongs to make their greetings. Lady Esther, who had been sitting beside Aunt Alice, now rose and moved across to the earl, who was looking a little bemused.

"Ah, Olivia!" he called out. "Come and sit beside your papa, and tell me all that you have been doing."

She was happy to comply. Poor Papa! He looked so lost these days, for Mama had gone away now that she was not his wife any more, telling him to marry someone younger who would be able to give him legitimate sons. He was dutifully searching for a new wife, but he missed her dreadfully. Olivia would not have minded running away, too, but how could she leave poor Papa with no one to see to his comfort? Her brothers were useless and her older sisters were married. As for Aunt Alice, she was so sunk in grief for her murdered husband that she barely knew what day it was, and had only emerged from seclusion now that a man had confessed to killing poor Uncle Nicholson.

So Olivia sat on one side of the earl, and Lady Esther the other, although it was mostly Olivia who kept the conversation going, for Lady Esther seemed sunk in gloom.

Olivia could not wait to get to the important point, however, so as soon as the earl was drawn away to talk to the Strongs, she said, "How did you enjoy your stay at Landerby Manor, Lady Esther?"

"It was very pleasant. The Duke and Duchess of Wedhampton were most gracious. I felt quite at home there."

"And Mr Franklyn was a great success in the fencing tournament, I understand."

Lady Esther made a little moue of distaste. "Well... he enjoys the sport. For myself, I find it deeply unpleasant to watch men fighting, but it is more respectable than some hobbies, so I make no objection."

"And how did Miss Franklyn enjoy her stay? I am sure she was a great success amongst the gentlemen."

Olivia had heard certain rumours about Miss Franklyn's enjoyment, for Bea was not noted for shyness or even for good manners, if truth were told, but she expected a bland response from Lady Franklyn. After all, although she was not Bea's mother, as her stepmother, she had always put a good face on Bea's little transgressions.

Much to Olivia's surprise, Lady Esther's face hardened. "Oh, do not talk to me of Beatrice! I can barely speak her name. I intended to bring her with me today, and we set out just as planned, but then Mr Bertram Atherton came galloping after us, jumping hedges and I know not what to catch up with us, and behaving in the most appalling fashion to me."

"Bertram?" Olivia said, astonished. "Jumping hedges? He never jumps!"

"Well, he did today, forcing the coach to stop. Then he shouted at me, positively shouted, in the most uncouth fashion, dragged Beatrice out forcibly, and now he has ridden off with her. Such intemperance!"

"Bertram?" Olivia said again, trying to reconcile this passionate young man with her studious, bespectacled cousin, who never lifted his head from his ancient books and was unfailingly polite to everyone. The same Bertram who had sworn never to marry Bea Franklyn and had now apparently ridden off with her.

"You might well look astonished, Miss Atherton," Lady Esther said.

Oh. How lowering. She was Miss Atherton to her ladyship, of course. A duke's daughter would never get that wrong, or be kind enough to forget that she was no longer Lady Olivia.

"You will be even more astonished to hear that Beatrice turned down the possibility of being a duchess in order to ally herself with a man who might, or more likely might not, be an earl one day."

"Turn down a duke? Ohhh..." Olivia breathed. "I should never do that. I should love to marry a duke. I want to be a duchess above all things."

Lady Esther's face softened, and she turned fully to face Olivia. "A worthy ambition indeed. Every woman should aim as high as she can when looking for a husband. Beatrice's offer was not from a duke, but from the heir to a dukedom, which to my mind is even better. So many of the unmarried dukes are in their dotage."

"The Duke of Argyll is only thirty-nine."

"A Scottish peerage!" she said with a grimace. "Inveraray Castle is so far to the north, and think of the weather!"

"Oh, I know. I thought Buckinghamshire would be better situated for weather, and nearer to town, as well."

"Buckinghamshire? Then... you have a particular duke in mind? The Buckingham line is extinct, so you refer, I collect, to the Duke of Bridgeworth, or his heir, the Marquess of Embleton."

"The Marquess. He is thirty years of age and single."

"I was not aware that you were acquainted with Lord Embleton."

Olivia should, perhaps, have been more discreet in her disclosures, for not everyone would approve of her ambition, but Lady Esther was one person who surely would. "I have never met him, but I should very much like to. What is he like?"

"Not a distinguished man in appearance. Rather the opposite, but gentlemanly in his manner and style of dress. Very quiet."

"He stammers."

"Ah. You know about that."

"Izzy told me. I also know that he is a keen sportsman. He fences, rides to hounds, shoots, and keeps race horses."

"You are very well informed."

"I keep all the newspaper cuttings that mention him. I have been following him for several years now."

Lady Esther smiled. This was such a rare event that Olivia barely recognised her. She looked almost approachable. "Ah, if only you were my daughter! But I suppose with your mother away and your aunt confined to the castle by her unfortunate condition, there would be no objection if I were to… take you under my wing, so to speak. After all, Beatrice seems to have settled her own future, so now I am at a loose end. Should you like that? I believe I can help you achieve your ambition, Miss Atherton."

"Even though I am not legitimate?"

"You are still the daughter of an earl with a respectable dowry, no doubt, and Olivia — may I call you by your name? — Olivia, you are as pretty as paint, you know. You have all your sister Isabel's beauty and lively spirit, without her wayward turns, and you have a much, much better figure."

"I am very fond of cake," Olivia murmured, lowering her eyes.

Lady Esther laughed, an event so rare that Olivia wondered momentarily if she were about to have an apoplexy. But no, it was merely laughter. Leaning forward a little, she whispered into Olivia's ear, "Gentlemen are attracted to a lady who is fond of cake." Then, in a more normal voice, she went on, "Of course, it would not do to become positively fat, but you are very far from that state. Yes, you have a much better figure. There is a drawing on the wall over there that I should like to examine more closely, if you will be so good as to accompany me."

Surprised but willing, Olivia crossed the room in Lady Esther's wake.

"There! Now we cannot be overheard," she murmured, her voice so low that Olivia had to strain to hear it. "I shall tell you something in the strictest confidence, Olivia. The ducal heir that Beatrice turned down was none other than Lord Embleton."

"Then it is no use!" Olivia cried, before remembering to whisper. "If he is in love with Bea, he will not so much as look at me."

"No, it is very much to the point, for a man who is already thinking of matrimony is ripe to fall into willing hands. He is not so very much in love with Beatrice, I fancy, but he believed her to be in love with him, that was what drove him to offer for her, and I know precisely what gave him the idea — she kissed him."

"Oh! How very—"

"Forward of her? Yes, but that is Beatrice for you, and even though it was inadvertent in this case, it did the trick, for it brought him straight to the point. So that is what you must do when you meet him."

"But how am I ever to meet him?" Olivia said in crushed tones. "He is about to begin his autumn round of visits to relations for the sporting season, and I am confined to the castle."

Lady Esther smiled again. "Then we shall just have to bring him here, shall we not? I happen to know that he is staying with his sister, Lady Harraby, at Harraby Hall, which is three miles this side of Thirsk. If I pen a brief note, just to express my regret that matters with Beatrice did not work out as we had hoped, I could perhaps mention that Lord Rennington is in low spirits just now after his recent difficulties and would undoubtedly be cheered by a visit from a fellow peer... that should do the trick."

"But if he calls to see Papa, he will spend half an hour in Papa's study and then go away again."

"Now, now, where is your ingenuity? Naturally, you will ensure that your butler apprises you of such a distinguished visitor, and you can find an excuse to join them. Then you invite him to dinner. He will be too polite to refuse."

"He could come to our big party on Friday."

Lady Esther winced. "With the entire neighbourhood ogling him? And Beatrice will be there, who has just refused to marry him. No, a quiet family dinner, that is what is needed so you have his full attention, and you will have an entire evening to get to know him."

"And to kiss him?" Olivia said doubtfully.

"If the opportunity should arise," Lady Esther said firmly. "A kiss is so definitive, is it not? A man cannot mistake one's intent if one kisses him. It is better if the will to kiss should come from him, but one cannot wait for a man to realise what is needed or one might never get a husband. A lady must go out and seize her destiny in her own hands, Olivia, and I shall help you do precisely that."

Seize her destiny! How glorious that sounded! And perhaps, with Lady Esther's guidance, Olivia would one day be a duchess.

END OF SAMPLE CHAPTER

For more information or to buy, go to my website at https://marykingsw ood.co.uk.